Sherlock Holmes: After the East Wind Blows

Part III: When the Storm Has Cleared
(1921-1928)

Sherlock Holmes: After the East Wind Blows

Part III: When the Storm Has Cleared (1921-1928)

Edited by
David Marcum

Belanger Books
2021

CONTENTS

Forewords

Adventures

When the Storm Has Cleared

(Continued on the next page . . . .)

Additional adventures are contained in . . .

Part I: The East Wind Blows (1914-1918)

. . . and . . .

Part II: Aftermath (1919-1920)

COPYRIGHT INFORMATION

The following contributors appear in this volume:
After the East Wind Blows
Part III: When the Storm Has Cleared (1921-1928)

*The following contributors appear
in the companion volumes:*

Part I: The East Wind Blows (1914-1918)
Part II: Aftermath (1919-1920)

Editor's Foreword:
Holmes Retired? Not So!
by David Marcum

So Moses stretched out his staff over Egypt, and the Lord made an east wind blow across the land all that day and all that night.

– Exodus 10:13

"There's an east wind coming, Watson."
"I think not, Holmes. It is very warm."
"Good old Watson! You are the one fixed point in a changing age. There's an east wind coming all the same, such a wind as never blew on England yet. It will be cold and bitter, Watson, and a good many of us may wither before its blast. But it's God's own wind none the less, and a cleaner, better, stronger land will lie in the sunshine when the storm has cleared. Start her up, Watson, for it's time that we were on our way. I have a check for five hundred pounds which should be cashed early, for the drawer is quite capable of stopping it if he can."

– Sherlock Holmes and Dr. Watson
"His Last Bow"

"There's an east wind coming," said Sherlock Holmes to Dr. John H. Watson on the second of August, 1914 – *"the most terrible August in the history of the world"* – as they looked out over the moonlit sea off the Essex coast, (then called the German Ocean, and soon to be renamed the North Sea). This conversation is chronologically the last Canonical appearance of Holmes and Watson, at the conclusion of "His Last Bow". Britain would declare war against Germany just a couple of days later. The events of this particular story cover only a few minutes, giving hints at Holmes's activities as "Altamont" in the previous two years leading up to that night, and implications of what Watson might be doing in the days

1

soon to follow, but it can't be considered in vacuum. Holmes and Watson's war service started over a decade before the events of that adventurous August night . . . .

In the fall of 1903, Sherlock Holmes retired. Since the mid-1870's (except for a three-year stint when he'd faked his own death to go undercover, alternately tracking and fleeing from the agents of his enemy Professor Moriarty, and carrying out tasks for his brother Mycroft,) he'd been working as a Consulting Detective – the first to do so – in London, initially living in No. 24 Montague Street alongside the British Museum, and then, after 1881, at 221 Baker Street. In 1903, Sherlock Holmes was forty-nine years old – rather young to retire, especially for someone with his energy and unique gifts.

The Sherlockian Chronologicists among us can determine that Holmes retired in 1903 because that was when Watson was finally allowed to publishe "The Empty House", relating just how Holmes had managed to survive his encounter with Professor Moriarty at the Reichenbach Falls on May 4th, 1891 – "*Reichenbach Day*" – over a decade earlier. Not long after that, a grieving Watson, with the assistance of his literary agent, had begun publishing narratives of Holmes's adventures in a newly created magazine, *The Strand*. Although two of Watson's tales had previously appeared in print, *A Study in Scarlet* in late1887 and *The Sign of the Four* in early 1890, they hadn't generated the excitement that *The Strand* stories did. Between June 1891 and December 1894, there were two-dozen of Holmes's cases recounted in the magazine, before the public – those who didn't already know of Holmes's death back when it happened in May '91 – was shocked to learn that he had supposedly died over two years earlier.

The three years when Holmes was missing are called *The Great Hiatus*, stretching from his encounter with Moriarty on 4 May, 1891 to 5 April, 1894, when he suddenly reappeared in London, with the time now right to clean up a last bit of business with the Professor's right-hand man, a killer named Moran. One can imagine Holmes's reaction upon seeing those copies of *The Strand* with his cases written up as only Watson could – but not as scientific treatises that he would have preferred. It's almost certain that this is when Holmes forbid Watson to write any more of them.

For it was in the opening paragraph of "The Empty House", published in *The Strand* in October 1903 (and September 1903 in

Collier's) that Watson wrote an explanation why it took him so long to relate that Holmes was still alive, and *how* he was still alive:

> *Let me say to that public, which has shown some interest*
> *in those glimpses which I have occasionally given them*
> *of the thoughts and actions of a very remarkable man,*
> *that they are not to blame me if I have not shared my*
> *knowledge with them, for I should have considered it my*
> *first duty to do so, had I not been barred by a positive*
> *prohibition from his own lips, which was only*
> *withdrawn upon the third of last month.*

Holmes had "*barred*" Waston from sharing his knowledge with readers with a "*positive prohibition*", but it hadn't been entirely enforced. Holmes had allowed Watson (along with the first Literary Agent) to publish *The Hound of the Baskervilles* in *The Strand* from August 1901 to April 1902, but that was an adventure set in the late 1880's, *before* Holmes's supposed death, and it would have done nothing to inform those many people who hadn't had personal interactions with Holmes since his return from The Great Hiatus know that he was actually still alive. No, it was only with the publication of "The Empty House" in late 1903 that the world in general knew that Holmes still lived – and that some unexplained event had finally prompted him to remove his "*positive prohibition*" granting the publication of this knowledge – and also most certainly that of his retirement.

But why would it be important that this retirement be revealed? Knowing what we do of Sherlock Holmes, it was intentional, and it was certainly a distraction – something flashy happening in one hand while the other hand, unnoticed, performed the actual trick. In fact, Holmes wasn't retiring at all. True, he left London and settled into a "*villa . . . situated upon the southern slope of the downs, commanding a great view of the Channel*", but he didn't become a recluse, washing his hands of his former life, as some might picture. Rather, his life and work transitioned into something else entirely. He was too young to retire, and there was too much that needed to be done. He had other business to carry out, and it was important that people think he was no longer a relevant factor.

For decades, those who could see the signs – people like the Holmes brothers, Sherlock and Mycroft – perceived that war was coming, a terrible and entangling monster that would eventually drag in the whole world, country after country after country. Germany, for centuries a series of small bickering kingdom-states, had unified in 1871, and its leaders had a hunger for respect that became more and more reckless.

Italy had unified in the same way a few decades earlier. For decades, various smaller wars across Europe served to shift borders and loyalties, while ratcheting up inescapable tension. Germany and Italy, and other Continental players such as France and Belgium, the always-turbulent Balkans, and Russia to the East, were all rubbing up against each other in a small space. Each was growing more and more nationalistic, and to feed their ambitions they needed raw materials – lots of them, to be plundered by way of a race for colonies around the world, regardless of the cost to the native inhabitants of these lands. Obtaining and keeping these colonies meant a lot of stepping on one another's toes – and ever-growing strain. Of course England, with its mastery of the sea, was thickly involved in all of this as much as their Continental neighbors.

The leaders of a great number of these countries ended up having interrelated ruling classes, with many connected by close blood ties to Queen Victoria, the multi-generational British monarch. In spite of their ambitions and jealousies, these countries began to rope themselves together – both openly and in secret – with ever-tightening treaties and counter-treaties and secret agreements. It was an increasingly dangerous and flammable situation, and someone was bound to light a match. Sherlock and Mycroft Holmes knew this, and John Watson as well, and they worked together to prevent it – or at least to delay it as long as possible.

Almost one-fourth of the Canonical narratives regarding Holmes and Watson's activities occur after the start of the Twentieth Century . . .

<u>1900</u>
- June 8-10   "The Six Napoleons"
- Oct 4-5   "The Problem of Thor Bridge

<u>1901</u>
- May 16-18   "The Priory School"

<u>1902</u>
- May 6-7   "Shoscombe Old Place"
- June 26-27   "The Three Garridebs"

- July   "The Disappearance of Lady Frances Carfax (Various Dates)
- Sept 3-13   "The Illustrious Client"
- Sept 24-25   "The Red Circle"

1903

- Jan 7; 12   "The Blanched Soldier"
- May 26-27   "The Three Gables"
- Early Aug   "The Mazarin Stone"
- Sept 6; 9; 15-16   "The Creeping Man"

1907

- July 23; 30-31   "The Lion's Mane"

1914

- Aug 2   "His Last Bow"

. . . but only two ("The Lion's Mane" and "His Last Bow") occur post-retirement. The former, narrated by Holmes himself, gives us guarded details of where he lived, and the impression that he didn't do much more than keep bees, walk along the cliffs, occasionally converse with his neighbors, sometimes swim in the ocean at the base of the nearby high chalk cliffs, and devote himself to his studies. *"At this period of my life,"* Holmes wrote, *"the good Watson had passed almost beyond my ken. An occasional week-end visit was the most that I ever saw of him."*

This carefully constructed vision of Holmes as hermit is corroborated by Watson's "Preface" to the book *His Last Bow*:

The friends of Mr. Sherlock Holmes will be glad to learn that he is still alive and well, though somewhat crippled by occasional attacks of rheumatism. He has, for many years, lived in a small farm upon the Downs five miles from Eastbourne, where his time is divided between philosophy and agriculture. During this period of rest he has refused the most princely offers to take up various cases, having determined that his retirement was a permanent one. The approach of the German war caused him, however, to lay his remarkable

5

combination of intellectual and practical activity at the disposal of the Government, with historical results which are recounted in His Last Bow. *Several previous experiences which have lain long in my portfolio have been added to His Last Bow so as to complete the volume.*

John H. Watson, M.D.

This to also gives one the impression that Holmes didn't do much at all during those years between late 1903, when he "retired", and 1912, when he agreed to take on the role of Altamont, a two-year task leading up to the events of 2nd August, 1914, as he worked his way into the existing German spy network that was trying to gain advantages for their side, damage the British, and influence events leading up to the beginning of the inevitable war.

But Holmes was not a man to simply retire at age forty-nine. Clearly he had more to do with his life, and there were certainly many more adventures than the two published post-retirement Canonical tales that have been left to us. The Canon is the fundamental structure upon which to study the lives of Sherlock Holmes and Doctor Watson, but the overall sixty stories from which it's comprised are truly just the tiniest fraction of what Holmes and Watson did, and fortunately, a number of other later Literary Agents have followed in the steps of the first one, bringing literally thousands of additional adventures to light that reveal what else happened.

I've referred in the past to this vast interconnected network of further narratives as *The Great Holmes Tapestry*, with the sixty Canonical adventures serving as the main ropes, while all of the other tales serve to fill in the background threads. Since discovering Holmes in the mid-1970's, I've been collecting and reading and chronologicizing as many of these other adventures as I could, and by this point I believe that I own and have read almost every traditional pastiche in existence, except for some truly obscure pieces that I may never find – no life is long enough, nor are resources plentiful enough, to get all of them.

By way of acquiring and studying so many post-Canonical adventures, I've been able step back and see the Big Picture, with stories running from 1840, concerning Holmes's father and how he saved the life of Queen Victoria, all the way through to the morning of 6th January, 1957, when Holmes passed away while sitting on the cliff-tops above his Sussex home. Being able to study the overall gestalt of the *entire* lives of Holmes and Watson – and not just the pitifully few sixty Canonical stories – is truly a blessing.

By way of the chronology that I've constructed based on the Canon and these additional adventures, it can be seen that there are literally hundreds of cases that occur in the years between Holmes's supposed 1903 retirement and the beginning of the war in August 1914. Likewise, there are many adventures set during the war itself, and also quite a few during the 1920's which follow.

There are a few who chronicle these years that incorrectly give an impression that Holmes and Watson lost touch with one another during that time – that Holmes did indeed became the reclusive apiarist hermit character that he wished people to believe, completely withdrawn from his former life, wandering among the beehives and slowly curling in on himself, suffering with increasing rheumatism, or even dementia, and then an early death. Watson isn't given a much better fate by some of these later chroniclers. These visions of Our Heroes could not be further from the truth.

The purpose of this collection, *After the East Wind*, is to provide additional accounts of Holmes and Watson's wartime adventures, and also what happened during the post-war peace – what actually occurred, and not the idea that they simply drifted away into obscurity. The contents of these books don't pretend to offer a definitive and complete *A*-to-*Z* account of what happened during those years – for how could they, when there are so many other stories which also add threads to this particular part of The Great Holmes Tapestry?

There are some other notable adventures that took place during the war that should be located if possible: *Hellbirds* (1976, later re-titled *Sherlock Holmes and the Hellbirds*) by Nick Utechin (who generously provided a Foreword for this anthology) and the late Austin Mitchelson. I was particularly pleased when I first discovered this volume years ago, as it includes a most memorable encounter between Holmes and Watson, in disguise behind enemy lines and in the German trenches, and a shabby fellow there named Schicklgruber, whom Watson unfortunately allowed to live.

Besides countless short stories, other longer wartime adventures include *Sherlock Holmes and the Lusitania* (by Lorraine Daly, 1998), *Son of Holmes* and *Rasputin's Revenge* (1986 and 1987 respectively, by John Lescroart, serving as valuable links between Holmes and Nero Wolfe), *The Case of the Reluctant Agent* (2001,

Tracy Cooper-Posey), and *Sherlock Holmes on the Western Front* (2000, Val Andrews).

One war story that deserves particular mention is "The Case of the Last Battle" by L.B. Greenwood (1997, included in *The Mammoth Book of New Sherlock Holmes Stories*). It's a wonderful tale of the very end of the war, and how Holmes and Watson brought that about.

After the war, London tried to get back to normal, although it took a while. Fortunately, Scotland Yard had learned the lessons that Holmes had so valiantly tried to teach them, and other consulting detectives had stepped forward to fill the void, including Solar Pons, Hercule Poirot, Lord Peter Wimsey, and Albert Campion – all of whom have some small connections to this anthology.

Poirot, living at 14 Farraway Street, had a number of interesting cases before he too retired, traveling for a while and then settling back in London in Whitehaven Mansions while continuing to consult on a much more limited basis. Lord Peter, at 110A Piccadilly, and Albert Campion (at nearby Number 17A Bottle Street, Piccadilly), were more dilettantish about their investigations, but they were nevertheless quite effective. Certainly the best and most consistent of them during that time was Solar Pons of 7B Praed Street. If the reader hasn't yet met Mr. Pons, please do so at the earliest opportunity.

As I edited this set of stories, I was also concurrently working on the most recent set of the MX Holmes anthologies, *The MX Book of New Sherlock Holmes Stories*, Parts XXV, XXVI, and XXVII, and also *The Meeting of the Minds: The Cases of Sherlock Holmes and Solar Pons*. There were stories in the former's Part XXVII, and many in the latter set, which very much overlapped those contained in this anthology, and I highly recommend also seeking out those other books for additional narratives that help to fill in and around the Canonical ropes in The Great Holmes Tapestry.

There are many other amazing post-war and post-Canonical tales besides those contained in these volumes, but I must point out that after looking through my Chronology, a great deal of what's shown through the 1920's turns out to be *Prologues, Forewords, Postscripts,* and *Addendums* related to earlier adventures. Watson spent much of these post-war years writing up his notes before adding the manuscripts to his Tin Dispatch Box, or sending them to those who might be interested, such as individuals who had been involved in the original investigations. Thus, it's through Watson's monumental efforts during this decade, leading up to his death on

24th July, 1929, that we now have so many of these additional tales to augment the original sixty Canonical accounts.

For too many people, there is a belief that Holmes and Watson simply ended on 2 August, 1914. This is absolutely not true. There are so many other adventures that followed "His Last Bow", and the stories in this new collection will fill in some of those gaps, and also hopefully encourage Mr. Holmes's admirers to seek out the others. After 1914, Holmes didn't vanish, for *After 1914, he's still ours!* – the traditional Canonical hero that is just as important today as he was then.

*   *   *   *   *

"Of course, I could only stammer out my thanks."
– The unhappy John Hector McFarlane
"The Norwood Builder"

As always when one of these Holmes anthologies is finished, I want to first thank with all my heart my incredibly wonderful wife of nearly thirty-three years, Rebecca, and our amazing son and my friend, Dan. I love you both, and you are everything to me!

Also, I simply cannot find words to express the gratitude I have to all of the contributors who have used their time to create this project. I'm so glad to have gotten to know all of you. It's an undeniable fact that Sherlock Holmes authors are the *best* people!

Additionally, I'd also like to especially thank:

- Nick Utechin – Nick and I began exchanging emails in early 2014, when our mutual friend Roger Johnson forwarded a fan letter from me to Nick. We quickly determined that we are both Rathbones – each of our mothers was originally a Rathbone. Nick has traced a fairly close connection directly to Basil Rathbone, while I've yet to firmly establish the path from "Cousin Basil", as my sister and I always called him, to the American Rathbones.

  In 2015, I was in England for my Holmes Pilgrimage No. 2 and staying for a few days at the home of Roger Johnson and his wife Jean Upton. I mentioned that the next day I was going to Oxford, and Jean called Nick on the telephone and asked if he'd be my tour guide. He met me at the station the following morning and graciously set aside a huge part of his day. He is a resident of Oxford and alum of one of the colleges, and as such, he was able to take me into many colleges, buildings, dining halls, libraries, chapels, and gardens where I would have otherwise never been able to visit. (If I had gone by myself, I would have likely traveled a few of the main streets, thinking that I'd "seen" Oxford, and then caught the next train back to London.)

Additionally, Nick took me that day to several J.R.R. Tolkien spots, including The Eagle and Child Pub – where a shelf above Tolkien and C.S. Lewis's regular table wonderfully had a copy of *The Hound of the Baskervilles*, and also out to one of Tolkien's houses. (This side-trip satisfied my curiosity, and also was for my wife's sake – for she is a Tolkien fan at the nearly same level that I admire Holmes. In fact, she made her own Pilgrimage to England and Oxford, focusing on a Tolkien agenda, several years before I met her.)

It was while Nick and I were eating lunch that day that he expressed an interest in contributing to a future edition of *The MX Book of New Sherlock Holmes Stories*, and he ended up sending me several very fine stories over the next year or so, including one based on an Oxford statue (and the backstory related to it) that he and I had seen during his tour.

Since then we've stayed in touch, and I was fortunate to see him again in person most recently when he was at the amazing *From Gillette to Brett* conference in Bloomington, Indiana in 2018. I hope to run into him again in the future, either in the United States or in England, and I'm very thankful that he contributed the Foreword to this volume – which is especially fitting, since his 1976 pastiche *Hellbirds* was set in this period, and I'd enjoyed it long before I ever knew that I'd get to meet him.

• Derrick and Brian Belanger – I first "met" Derrick when he graciously reviewed one of my early books. Then he interviewed me several times, and when I had the idea for the first MX Holmes anthology in 2015, he quickly joined the party and contributed a fine pastiche. From there he's written a number of others, and then he formed Belanger Books with his brother, Brian. It's turned into a Sherlockian powerhouse, and I'm very grateful to have this and other opportunities to contribute to The Great Holmes Tapestry by editing and writing stories for their different anthologies. Derrick continues to write, but he also stays quite busy as a noted teacher, as well as running Belanger Books with Brian.

Over the last few years, my amazement at Brian Belanger's talent has only grown. I initially became acquainted with him when he took over the duties of creating the covers for MX Books following the untimely death of their previous graphic artist. I found Brian to be great to collaborate with, very easy-going and stress-free in his approach and willingness to work with authors, and wonderfully creative. His skills became most apparent to me when he created the cover for my 2017 book, *The Papers of Solar Pons*, which was one of the most striking covers that I've ever seen. Later, when the Belangers and I began reissuing the original Pons books in new editions, and then new Pons anthologies, Brian's similarly themed covers continued to astound me. He truly deserves an award for these. In the meantime, he has become busier and busier, continuing to provide covers for MX Books, and now for Belanger Books as well, along with editing and occasionally writing. (*Brian: I'm still waiting for you to write a pastiche for something that I edit!!!*) (*Note the three explanation points at the end of that statement – for I am not kidding.*)

I finally met both Brian and Derrick in early 2020 at the annual Sherlock Holmes Birthday Celebration in New York City, and they're just as great in person as they were by way of email. Keep up the good work, both of you, and thanks very much for all that you do!

Finally, last but certainly *not* least, **Sir Arthur Conan Doyle**: Author, doctor, adventurer, and the Founder of the Sherlockian Feast. Present in spirit, and honored by all of us here.

As always, this collection, like those before it, has been a labor of love by both the participants and myself. As I've explained before, once again everyone did their sincerest best to produce an anthology that truly represents why Holmes and Watson have been so popular for so long. These are just more tiny threads woven into the ongoing Great Holmes Tapestry, continuing to grow and grow, for there can *never* be enough stories about the man whom Watson described as "*the best and wisest . . . whom I have ever known.*"

David Marcum
May 4th, 2021
The 130th Anniversary of
Reichenbach Day
(When Sherlockians celebrate
"The Detective Who Lived")

*Questions, comments, and story submissions
may be addressed to David Marcum at*
thepapersofsherlockholmes@gmail.com

Foreword
by Nicholas Utechin

The period from August 1914 onwards in the Sherlockian Canon is especially fascinating. But there is nothing in the Sherlockian Canon covering that period. Therein, of course, lies the fascination.

The Valley of Fear and no fewer than thirteen of the short stories were published after the vital events of "His Last Bow" took place (including, naturally, "His Last Bow" itself); but all were actually dated (specifically or by scholars) previous to those events. "Shoscombe Old Place" was the very last tale to be published in *The Strand Magazine*, in April 1927, but its Canonical dating was actually – oh dear, here we go (damn those chronologists): 1882, 1883, 1894, 1897, or 1902! Sherlock Holmes was, we take it, only sixty in 1914 and Dr. Watson not much older. There was surely more to come in their lives.

In my own contributions to "The Grand Game", I have ventured only twice in this direction. In 1997, I much enjoyed discovering that from 25 April to 20 June 1913, the position in the British Government of Solicitor-General for Ireland was held by a certain J. Moriarty – which provided for added depths in researching Holmes's activities in the lead-up to the case of LAST. [1] As is the way in such matters, I chose to ignore the fact that the minister involved was John Francis Moriarty and – this *is* interesting – was one of the two Moriarty brothers who attended Stoneyhurst College at the same time as Arthur Conan Doyle: Wheels within wheels where worlds collide, indeed!

Twenty years later, I had an opportunity [2] to range far more straightforwardly over one specific area of work carried out by Holmes and Watson in the years following the First World War: How they collated the various notes of old cases (see above) for publication – and why. Somehow, I was led to what in the end seemed an inevitable conclusion: That Sherlock Holmes died in 1927, an outcome that had certainly not been on the cards when I first accepted the remit to write the paper.

That fine scholar, D. Martin Dakin, decided that Dr. Watson had passed away before then [3]. Having decided that "The Blanched Soldier" and "The Lion's Mane" were not only not written by Holmes, but perhaps even fictitious, he goes on: "*Why did not*

Watson instantly denounce these amazing forgeries? That he did not do so points, I fear, to the inescapable conclusion that the good doctor was by then deceased. Since the last undoubted publication by him was the introduction to His Last Bow *at the end of 1917, and the series in question started in October 1921, we may safely assume that his death took place between those two dates . . . ."*

Most scholars have tended to go no further than T. S. Blakeney – and usually along much the same lines [4]: *"No student of Sherlock Holmes can doubt that the years 1914-18 found him hard at work in the nation's interests – doubtless the perspicacity of the genial but anonymous head of the Secret Service secured the willing assistance of one who stood head and shoulders above the common order of men."* June Thomson – in the biography [5] she wrote which is often overlooked by those who only know her for her pastiches – is similarly inclined: *" . . . [G]iven his specialized knowledge of espionage and the activities of the Irish Republican movement, it is possible that (Holmes) remained in London, acting as a Government adviser, or travelled to and from Sussex to attend ministerial meetings."*

In terms of pastiche, no one has realistically taken matters further down the Sherlockian time-line than Mitch Cullin, whose 2005 novel *A Slight Trick of the Mind* placed Holmes in the year 1947 [6].

On a personal note, however, I find it recorded that it was in the year 1976 that I co-authored the second of two pastiches which appeared in the United States courtesy of a soon-to-be-defunct publisher [7]. It was probably not as a direct result of our post-*Seven-Per-Cent Solution* outpourings that it went bust, but they will not have helped. The events covered in *Hellbirds* opened in Baker Street on 18 December, 1914 and proceeded via The Tower of London, Dover, and the Western Front, to come to a resounding close in the Royal Albert Hall. Forty-five years after I wrote them, I see the final words read: *"Outside, the first snow of 1915 began to fall."* En route – on page 144 of the book, to be precise – my co-author and I committed one of the most ludicrous examples of "Look how clever we (think we) are" in Sherlockian pastiche history. I fear it was my idea.

But memories of inadequate pastiches should not be allowed in this volume. David Marcum, in his quest to squeeze the very last droplet of new story material from the quivering wrecks of writers old and new, has succeeded once again. The breadth of invention and intriguing plot-lines is impressive: Among them, we have more

Irish skulduggery, a pleasing re-appearance of former Irregular Wiggins as a middle-aged civil service mandarin, and a tale with strong *Titanic* links.

The East Wind blew strongly indeed, but so does the quality of present-day pasticheurs.

Nicholas Utechin
Oxford, U.K., 2021

NOTES

1. "Holmes's War Service: The True Story", contribution to *An East Wind – The East Coast Expedition of The Sherlock Holmes Society of London, 4-6 July 1997*. Sherlock Holmes Society of London,1997
2. "Aftermath – Holmes and Watson after 11 November", contribution to *Trenches – The War Service of Sherlock Holmes*, The B.S.I. MS series (LAST). The Baker Street Irregulars 2017
3. *A Sherlock Holmes Commentary*, David & Charles 1972 – This book is a completely essential contribution to the scholarship.
4. *Sherlock Holmes: Fact or Fiction?* John Murray 1932 – As is this, for historical reasons.
5. *Holmes and Watson*, Constable 1995
6. The novel was of course turned into the film *Mr. Holmes* (2015), starring Ian McKellen.
7. *Hellbirds*, with Austin Mitchelson. Belmont Tower Books 1976. (The first, also published that year, was *The Earthquake Machine*.)

Sherlock Holmes: After the East Wind Blows

Part III: When the Storm Has Cleared
(1921-1928)

The Adventure of the Silver Screen
by Gordon Linzner

Some months had passed since I'd last visited my friend Sherlock Holmes at his Sussex cottage, and my timing could hardly have been better. For an English winter, that January was unusually warm and dry. In fact, the entire year of 1921 would prove one of the driest on record. Moreover, despite his reluctance on other recent occasions, I was able to persuade Holmes to accompany me to London the following day and touch on a problem I was convinced that he would dismiss out of hand.

Not surprisingly, we sat up until considerably past midnight the evening before, reminiscing on old times and catching up on new ones. Holmes happily indulged himself with the cigarettes I'd brought from his favorite tobacconist, and even took out his violin to play a tune he claimed to have composed over the Christmas holidays. Our conversation ranged from the necessity of ensuring his bees were fed over the winter to discussing a variety of recent though not particularly baffling crimes, including the obvious murder of Irene Munro.

By the following morning, we had temporarily exhausted nearly every topic of interest and, given that in retirement Holmes had even less contact with people than before, my friend had little to say at breakfast. During the two hours it took for our train to travel from Sussex to London, he grew even more taciturn, not out of hostility, but due to his usual absorption in introspective observation, an attitude often mistaken by strangers as unsociability. By the time I hailed a motorized cab outside Victoria Station, he seemed barely able to communicate beyond an occasional grunt.

Persuading Holmes to leave the comforts of his rural life and revisit London, even for a day, had of late become increasingly difficult. At this point in his life, he was eager to avoid as much publicity as possible. Regrettably, I must take some responsibility for that, since I published so many of his most interesting adventures, albeit with his full permission. In no way could I have known these stories would continue to be read for decades, let alone provide so much fodder for the newly created medium of film.

19

"I miss the broader line of sight provided by the old hansoms," Holmes remarked, breaking his silence as he settled in the back seat, walking stick resting between his knees.

Pleased to hear my friend ready to engage in conversation again, I paused in my directions to our driver. Given Holmes's obsession with taking in as much detail as possible from his surroundings, I had to agree. Wider views, coupled with the greater maneuverability of two wheeled vehicles over those with four, whether drawn by horse or motor, were desirable. "A few hansoms still operate, if you wish to change."

"No need for that. I find progress, on the whole, a good thing. By no means do I miss the former filthy condition of London's streets. Remember the Manure Crisis of 1894!"

The fact that we were heading for the Stoll Film Studio in Cricklewood was not what convinced him to join me this day. Although he appreciated a good concert, Holmes was no enthusiast of this new media. He particularly disliked performances based upon my own narratives. A quarter-century earlier, he'd barely been able to sit through the first act of William Gillette's stage play. He claimed, between that production and the Manure Crisis, he'd almost wished he hadn't come back from the dead. If he was aware of the later filmed version of that same play, he never mentioned it.

"I presume it was by your request the driver took us past Baker Street," Holmes observed as we turned a corner halfway through our trip, "given that this is hardly the most direct route."

"It's only slightly out of our way. I thought you might appreciate the sight. It has been some time."

"Ever the sentimentalist! I find that one of your most maddening qualities, my dear Doctor. It is also one of your most admirable and endearing."

"Don't pretend you didn't feel a twinge of nostalgia, old man. I saw the glint in your eye."

"I'll admit, the old residence holds a fond memory or three. It will also serve as an appropriate prelude to today's main event."

As much as Holmes detested seeing his reputation abused in inaccurate portrayals of his life, he did not begrudge the additional film royalties that permitted me to retire from my medical practice. He also refused to accept any portion of that income, no matter how many times I offered.

I'd visited the Stoll Studios twice, by invitation, since November, when they began filming a series of short subjects based on my narratives. Those occasions gave me opportunity to befriend the lead actor, a gentleman named Eille Norwood, Mr. Hubert Willis, who took on the thankless task of portraying myself, and a few other cast and crew members. That relationship, also, would not in itself have sparked Holmes's interest.

We debarked outside the gates of the former aeroplane factory site which now housed Stoll Studios. Filming for the day should be ending more or less concurrent with our arrival, as I had confirmed by telephone that morning.

We were headed toward the security booth at the entrance when Holmes spotted a crook-backed man staggering toward us. His stained coat hung loose about his shoulders, and his walking stick struck the pavement with a sharp crackle. He lurched directly into our path. Holmes locked eyes briefly. The man then addressed him in a thick, slurred voice, his words whistling through a wide gap in his front teeth.

"Excuse me, guvs. Might one of you spare a few pence for a hungry old man?"

I covered my mouth, forcing a cough to conceal my reaction, at the same time striving to avoid Holmes's attention.

My friend pulled a crumbled pound note from his coat pocket and held it out. Instead of reaching for the proffered banknote, however, the beggar stood staring at the cotton currency with a brooding eye.

"Is that real, guv?"

"Quite real."

The beggar scratched the back of his neck with his free hand. "Well, I don't know. Someone like me, showing up at a shop, holding that much money, I could get in a lot of trouble. Many's the shop owner might think I'm trying to pass a counterfeit. How do I know you're not playing some trick on a poor old man? Wouldn't be the first time!"

Holmes leaned forward on his own walking stick, extending the banknote further. "I assure you . . . ."

"Now, if you were willing to accompany me to the shop, and pay the clerk on my behalf – "

"I'm afraid I haven't the time," Holmes replied. He tried to push the note into the man's pocket.

With a challenging clack, as if crossing swords, the old man struck at Holmes's walking stick with his own.

Holmes glared at the inexplicable assault, gave the man one of his quick, comprehensive glances, then burst into a silent, hearty laugh.

"Very good! Excellent!" He glanced at me as I struggled to conceal my own laughter. When he turned back to the beggar, the latter had straightened his posture to stand a full six inches taller. "You must be the actor Watson brought me here to meet!"

The other bowed as he removed the false front teeth. "Eille Norwood, at your service." The slurred speech and awkward whistling completely disappeared.

"I should have caught on immediately, if only because of Watson's uncharacteristically cavalier attitude. Another downside of my getting older. Your drunken movements, even though I detected no scent of alcohol. The fraying of your pants cuffs – "

"I see no fraying," I pointed out.

"Precisely, Watson. The moment Mr. Norwood stood fully erect, his cuffs no longer dragged along the ground. Had he actually been so short, that material would have worn thin long ago. You, of course, already knew whom we were facing without those clues."

"Mr. Norwood, like yourself, is a genius at camouflage. He was almost tossed off the lot one day while disguised as a cab driver, waiting for his next scene."

"It's perhaps the most enjoyable part of my job," Norwood admitted. "My director, Maurice Elvey, once even accused a visitor to the set of being me, even though I stood just a few feet away in my own costume. Shall we retire to my dressing room? We can talk in private while I remove this makeup."

"I should be delighted!" Holmes replied, to my satisfaction.

Norwood handwaved the security guard. "These gentlemen are with me, Harry!" he called.

Harry acknowledged Norwood's gesture with an eyeroll, undoubtedly used to the man's pranks.

Holmes and I occupied a couch in Norwood's dressing room while the actor settled himself before his makeup table and mirror. "This won't take long," he promised.

Holmes nodded, being himself used to quick changes. "I must congratulate you, Mr. Norwood, on distracting me, if but briefly. You invested as deeply into the part as I would have."

Norwood inclined his head in acknowledgment. "I do my modest best, Mr. Holmes, to follow your example. I've studied every one of Doctor Watson's narratives, even periodically wander about Marylebone, your old Baker Street neighborhood, copying your mannerisms, feeling what it might have been like for you, to add depth to my representation. Last week – "

"You've taken pains to learn the violin as well, I observe," Holmes interrupted. "The fresh callouses on your fingertips confirm this is a recently acquired skill."

"Again, I thank you, Mr. Holmes, and again, I'm certain I'm nowhere near your level."

By this time most of his beggar disguise was gone, but portions of the makeup layer beneath, which transformed Norwood into the world's greatest detective, remained.

"See, Holmes!" I could not resist pointing at the actor's reflection. "Look at his face now! You might as well be looking into a mirror!"

Holmes stood to lean over Norwood's shoulder, comparing their features side-by-side. "I am looking into a mirror, Watson. You overstate the case. My features are puffier, more drawn with age, not so well-defined. You might also take note of the difference in our hair – "

"Retaining the look of this hair takes some work," Norwood interrupted. "Nor is it comfortable, especially after a full day of filming. But allow the doctor to have his fun, Mr. Holmes. I find the comparison immensely flattering. I modeled my appearance after the illustrations in *The Strand*."

"Which are also not entirely accurate, but I take your point. On the other hand, Watson, your appearance is more refined than that photograph of your cinematic avatar."

"Mr. Willis' role is rather less demanding than that of his lead. Not unlike my own."

"As usual, you underestimate yourself," Holmes assured me. "Well. This chat is much more pleasant and enlightening than I expected, Mr. Norwood, but now to business. Watson gave me some of the details last night, but I prefer to hear your version, in your own words. I understand it may involve a matter of mistaken identity?"

"Indeed, Mr. Holmes. As mentioned, I like to stroll through Marylebone every week or so. Soaking up the atmosphere in your mindset."

"So you've said," Holmes replied. "I do much the same, when necessary."

"Afterwards I usually stop at a pub called The Globe for a pint, before heading home."

"Your wife is comfortable with your odd schedule?"

"Ruth is also in the acting trade. She knows how it is. Didn't Doctor Watson tell you about her?"

"It didn't come up in our talk, but her existence wasn't hard to deduce. I can go into detail later. Continue."

"I was standing at the bar, waiting for my pint, when a voice behind me whispered, 'I know what you did.'"

"In the same raspy tone you just used?"

"Yes. I started turning to see who was speaking. Something hard, metal, poked me in the back. 'Don't turn around.'

"For safety's sake, I presumed what I'd felt was a gun. Unlike yourself, Mr. Holmes, I do not wander about with a pistol like the one I see bulging in your right coat pocket. Nor have I anywhere near your proficiency in boxing and martial arts. I chose to do as instructed. 'What exactly have I done?'

"'You know. Letting murderers flee to Africa or otherwise walk free. Allowing slack to certain acts of thievery – particularly those committed by members of the upper classes. All justified in your own mind, I'm sure.'"

Holmes nodded. "Again, that distinctive rasp. That is exactly how the man sounded?"

"As best I can manage. The interview was rather short."

"I am impressed by the range of your mimicry, Norwood. It may prove useful in tracking down this man. These crimes he accuses you of – are they something you were involved in?"

"Nothing I recall."

"I ask because they could apply to some of my own cases."

"My thoughts exactly. I'm convinced this stranger mistook myself for you. Some of those cases he described, according to Doctor Watson's narratives, took place during the long period I was forced to recuse myself from the stage due to poor health. Others occurred earlier, in the three years I was touring Australia." Norwood's wide grin did indeed make him appear a different person. "But the good doctor told you all this, or you wouldn't have agreed to come here today!"

"With the omission or one or two key details," Holmes agreed. "You are not without some talents in my arena."

"I may mimic your style and gestures, Mr. Holmes, but the result is pure illusion. I don't possess anywhere near your level of insight."

"I suggest otherwise. You know your audience, just as my good friend Watson knows his readers. It is you who flatters me. One reason for my retirement has been, as I mentioned, a diminishing acuity over the past few years."

"I find that hard to believe, Mr. Holmes."

24

"Let us see how much further your observational skills take us. Did this stranger mention his reasons for making such accusations?"

"Nothing in the man's tone clarified the situation. He refused to say anything more in the loud and crowded pub, insisting instead we meet a few blocks away, outside the Baker Street tube station. Since I am not a fool, I begged off, claiming urgent business elsewhere that evening.

"'Working on a case?' he surmised.

"I nodded. 'Several.' Which is technically true, as the studio is in the middle of filming fifteen short movies based on your cases.

"He then proposed we meet the following week, again at the station rather than a pub, at a similar time, nine in the evening. 'You may bring a friend, if you like.' I assume he meant you, Doctor Watson."

Holmes nodded again. "In one of my cases, a client was told she could bring two friends to meet a mysterious stranger. That client later married Doctor Watson. Pardon the digression. Another artifact of aging."

"You keep mentioning your supposed decline, yet you're not much older than myself."

"In any case," Holmes replied, changing the subject, even though he kept bringing it up, "blackmail seems an obvious motive, but unlikely. It's hard to envision someone like Charles Milverton rescheduling his demands because his victim had a busy day ahead. Did you get a look at the man as he left?"

Norwood shook his head. "Regrettably, by the time I realized I was once more alone, he'd disappeared into the crowd. While we were speaking, I did try to focus on his reflection in the mirror behind the bar. The lighting was too dim to see clearly. His hair was dark and disheveled, coat collar turned up, an applejack cap slightly askew. His left hand, on the side that dug into my back, was buried deep in his coat pocket. I glimpsed a hint of thin, dark beard, but that could have been a shadow, or he simply might not have shaved that day."

"He never addressed you by name?"

"He acted as if that were unnecessary. As if my identity was obvious."

"Then we don't know for certain if he was addressing Sherlock Holmes the private consultant, or Holmes the actor."

"The former seems more likely. None of my Holmes films have been released yet."

"Agreed."

25

"Then I should go ahead with the meeting? You'll join me this evening?"

"That was already a certainty. I should not be here otherwise."

Norwood's beaming smile was definitely not Holmesian, a fact underscored by his having fully removed every smidgen of greasepaint. "Have you gentlemen dined yet?"

"We had some passable chips in Sussex before boarding the train," I replied.

"Then, since we have time, might I suggest we repair to The Crown? It's only a ten minute walk. I would greatly value the opportunity to gain more insight into your methods, Mr. Holmes."

Holmes mulled over the offer. He was naturally suspicious of, but not entirely immune to, flattery.

"Dinner at my expense, of course," Norwood added. "Or, rather, Sir Oswald Stoll's expense, since this meeting is ultimately to his studio's benefit."

"Then I fail to see how we can refuse." With those words, Holmes reached for his walking stick.

A gust of wind swooped down Baker Street as we huddled alongside the entrance to the Underground station. Or, rather, Eille Norwood and I huddled there. Holmes had gone his separate way after dinner but assured us he would be at the meeting place, on time, and so I was certain he was nearby. For the fourth time, I checked my pocket watch, a keepsake of my late brother, marred as it was with dints and scratches and the markings of more than one pawnbroker's ticket numbers.

"Another five minutes have passed." I peered down the near-empty street again. "It's twenty-past-nine."

"I don't know if the gentleman had a timepiece," Norwood replied. "He didn't check when he suggested a time. I'd allow him the benefit of the doubt. He may have missed a train."

"Or he could be setting a trap. It's been thirty years since Moriarty's death, but some of his old crew may still hold a grudge."

Norwood chuckled. "You don't believe that."

"No. It would make a rousing good narrative, though. I'm more concerned this affair may resolve as little more than an elaborate prank. I should never hear the end of it from Holmes."

"I believe your hopes have been answered." Norwood nodded toward a figure shambling cautiously towards us. "I recognize that applejack cap."

The stranger approached slowly, his gaze fixed on my companion. He kept his face partly obscured by the upturned collar, and his left hand thrust deep into his bulging pocket. Aside from the couple further down the street, too preoccupied with each other to notice us, we were the only three in sight.

The newcomer paused a few feet before us and turned to me.

"You must be Doctor Watson." I couldn't help but notice Norwood had copied that raspy voice perfectly.

"I am. May I ask whom we are addressing?"

Norwood waited, silent and patient, beside me. The expression on his face, or rather lack of expression, seemed to satisfy our inquisitor.

"No harm, I suppose." He lowered his collar, revealing faint stubble. The man looked to be in his mid-twenties at most, though with a hardness to his features I recognized from my own wartime experience. "I aimed for an air of mystery, though there's no point trying to fool you two. My name is Brett Miller. Thank you for agreeing to this encounter."

"It is my pleasure to meet you, as well, Mr. Miller." I recognized the voice behind the young man even before Holmes stepped out of the station and into the glare of the streetlamp. "I've heard a great deal about you. Be so good as to remain still."

Startled, Miller could not avoid looking behind him. After all, my friend had seemingly materialized out of thin air, a Webley Bulldog revolver in his right hand, walking stick tucked under his left arm. He'd been waiting out of our own line of sight as well, to preclude any risk of Norwood or me subconsciously betraying his presence.

"I see your left knee slightly bent, as if preparing for flight, Mr. Miller. I should strongly advise against that. My shooting skills may not be what they were, but I can hardly miss at this range. None of us wish to spend the evening chasing down darkened streets after a gentleman less than half our age."

Miller gave an exasperated gasp, then turned again to glare at Norwood. "I said *one* friend!" There was more than the expected accusatory bitterness in his tone, not so much anger or a threat as disappointment. His right shoulder slumped.

Norwood pointed past the young man's shoulder. "Any complaints in that department should be addressed directly to Mr. Holmes."

Holmes cautiously moved to stand beside us, so all three of us faced the young man.

"That can't be Sherlock Holmes!" Miller snapped, pouting. "He doesn't look anything like his pictures in *The Strand*!"

Holmes offered a slight, apologetic smile. "I've said as much for years, but I'm not the magazine's editor. Now, Mr. Miller, allow me to introduce the gentleman beside me, the man you approached in The Globe last week. He is actually a stage and film actor named Eille Norwood. He can also be Sherlock Holmes, but only when he's in front of a camera."

Or pranking his director, I thought, but kept silent. This was neither time nor place for such banal witticisms.

Miller raised his right hand dismissively. "Pull the other one! It's got bells on it! He doesn't look anything like that phony movie Holmes – you know, the actor with the razor-blade name."

"A few other actors have also taken on the role, though they are lesser known," Norwood corrected. "And you haven't seen me on screen yet. Stoll won't release my films until April."

Miller turned back to me, eyes narrowing. "I suppose you're Sherlock Holmes, as well?"

I shook my head. "Doctor John Watson, as stated."

"Can we expect more Watsons, then?"

Holmes stepped closer to our subject, casually lowering his Webley. "Just one Watson, Mr. Miller. The original. Let us rather discuss your reason for requesting this meeting. Your comments to Mr. Norwood last week don't quite hold water. You should know that my biographer here has been known to take certain liberties with his narratives, adding drama to a story that might ordinarily seem as exciting as completing a crossword in *The Times*."

"A few slight embellishments, Holmes," I protested. "I've always informed you of my changes."

Holmes seemed not to hear. "More often, however, he has altered certain events at my request, where discretion was called for. If the ostentatious flouting of the law you accused Mr. Norwood, or rather myself, of performing had taken place, and was as serious as claimed – well, such offenses have been public knowledge for years. Surely I'd have been charged for such interference long ago, no matter how useful I made myself to the constabulary in other cases."

Miller appeared unconvinced. "At least one of you is a distraction. I didn't need any distractions. Call me selfish, but how often does one get a chance to meet one's heroes? I was thinking, 'Never'." He indicated Holmes's revolver. "You can put that away. I'm not going to run, and I don't have a gun."

28

"I expected not. That's why mine isn't loaded." Holmes pocketed his weapon.

"Holmes!" I ejaculated. "If this man is unarmed, what is he concealing in his left pocket?"

Holmes looked at the young man expectantly.

"Very well." Miller unveiled his left hand, or, rather, the hook-shaped prothesis where a hand and lower arm should have been. "I lost my limb two-and-a-half years ago, in the Great War. Suffered some throat damage as well."

I turned to my friend. "How did you know, Holmes? Or should I even ask?"

"I'd be glad to hear," Norwood put in.

"A simple deduction, Norwood. That anyone would risk revealing a gun in a crowded pub was unlikely. Mr. Miller would have waited to follow you outside had he meant any harm. Yet you said you felt a heavy metal object pressing against your back, and I saw no reason to disbelieve you. As an actor you're familiar with the feel of all types of props."

Norwood offered Miller a sympathetic look. "Then why not show me last week?"

"I'm a bit self-conscious," Miller admitted. "Especially with people I don't know. Also, the hook doesn't fit very well. Sometimes it comes loose. To have it clatter against the floor of The Globe, attracting attention, would be humiliating. I wanted to have a talk with you first, share my thoughts. The pub was too noisy, and full of people."

"Thus your suggestion we meet here, at a public site, but one that would not be too busy at this hour."

"Excellent, Norwood," Holmes commented. "You are indeed making the role your own."

"What exactly did you wish to tell me – or rather Mr. Holmes, since you mistook me for him? It's quiet here for the moment, and I assure you all three of us are discreet."

Miller took a deep, calming breath, then focused on Holmes. "When I was growing up, my mother would read me your adventures, Mr. Holmes. I even daydreamed about one day joining your Baker Street Irregulars. When I was conscripted in 1917, I carried a copy of one of Doctor Watson's collections with me to Germany. Reading it over and over while crouched in the trenches got me through the surrounding chaos and death. After my injury, while recovering in hospital, I was able to access the rest of his books and again read them over and over. When I spotted you that night, I felt compelled to thank you – " He glanced from Holmes to Norwood, and back again, as if trying to decide to whom he should address his remarks. " – for helping me retain my sanity in my darkest hours. And you, as well, Doctor Watson, for creating and preserving those adventures, and making them available to all."

Norwood stroked his chin in a very Holmesian gesture. "May I inquire what you do for a living, Mr. Miller?"

"Odd jobs. This and that. There aren't many opportunities for a man with one arm." He raised his left arm in display. I could see the hook starting to come loose. Miller noticed it as well, hurriedly clutching the sleeve with his right hand to tighten the connection.

Norwood took a card from his jacket pocket, scribbled a few words on the back, and handed it to the young man. "Come by the studios Monday morning. I'll tell the staff to expect you. A man of your status and experience could prove useful as a background player, if you don't mind exploiting your disability. And if you do, there's still plenty of crew work. Mr. Stoll is constantly expanding his business."

The gratitude in Miller's eyes was inspiring. I also felt compelled to step forward. "Have any adjustments been made to that prosthetic since your release?"

He shook his head. "Can't afford them. Too expensive."

"You are a veteran. There are ways to pay for such treatment. Or there should be. Given the chaos of war, and hasty post-war treatment, such things are often rushed, key elements overlooked. When I was treated for my shoulder wound during the Second Afghan War, the entire medical staff, even myself, missed the additional minor injury to my right leg. There may still be bullet fragments lodged there, but they haven't bothered me for a few decades." I handed him my own card. "This is my London address, as well, not far from here. Give me a call and we can arrange for me to examine your injury. My practice is not what it was these days, but I can certainly provide some useful suggestions and referrals."

"That would be most kind, Doctor Watson."

And so, after more friendly chatter, we four parted ways.

The following morning I accompanied Holmes to Victoria Station, to see him off, as he was anxious to get back to the peaceful countryside. I was pleased to see my old friend more relaxed, almost cheerful, despite being called to London for a case that fizzled out almost immediately. It seemed a good moment to broach a subject I'd been putting off for years.

"You know, Holmes, I still have notes on some of our adventures that haven't yet seen print. All of them pre-War, of course. I know you asked that I not publish any more of your adventures, but Stoll Studios might be interested in those."

"Indeed," Holmes muttered, lighting his pipe.

"I'm thinking I might put together one more collection. A grand finale, so to speak. I would only do so with your explicit permission, of course."

The Great Detective took a few thoughtful puffs on his pipe before responding.

"Very well, Watson. For reasons that baffle even myself, I have accrued more unwanted publicity in retirement than when I was actively solving cases. If fresh material must come forth, I prefer the source to be my personal Boswell. You are the chronicler who best understands me."

"I appreciate your confidence."

"In fact, in response to your frequent urging over the years, I even penned a couple of narratives myself. You would be welcome to include them in your collection, if so inclined."

"I should be delighted!"

"But not this one, eh? This tale could come off as a bit self-referential. I doubt modern audiences are ready for that sort of thing."

"Agreed. I'm not even sure what I'd call it. *Too Many Holmeses*? *The Cricklewood Conundrum*? *The Adventure of the Silver Screen*?"

"It wasn't much of an adventure."

"Well, I'll dash off a few quick notes for my personal records when I get home, but most likely they'll end up buried in my dispatch box at Cox and Company."

"One more thing, Watson."

"Yes?"

"I gather you are in contact with Mr. Norwood?"

"We've chatted on the telephone a few times."

"I'd appreciate if you could advise me once his films have been released to the public."

"Are you saying that you would actually be interested – ?"

"Ah! I believe they're announcing my train now. Enjoy the rest of your weekend, Watson!"

The King of
Devil's Horn Prison
by Derrick Belanger

W arden Humphrey paced back and forth in his office, smoking like a fiend, pausing only on occasion to mutter aloud the thoughts drifting through his head. The warden hated when anything on the island was bent out of shape, and if it ever was, he gleefully straightened it out, often with the force of a hammer. But the current kink in his perfect little prison was yet to get beaten into proper shape.

"Where had that simpleton in Cell Block 3 disappeared to?" he muttered aloud, pausing in his pacing. He extinguished a cigarette butt in the ashtray which was overflowing to the point that a thin halo of ash now circled it upon the warden's desk. He lit another cigarette, inhaled the fumes deeply, and moved to the window. His eyes stared out at the calm seas and the craggy shore, nothing but sharp rocks and then miles and miles of cold and deadly waters. The island was inescapable! That's why the prison had been built in this godforsaken location. But now a prisoner was loose, a simpleton no less, who had managed to dig a hole through his cell wall and somehow make it outside the walls of the prison. If the politicians on the shore found out . . . .

But Humphrey couldn't think about that. It would only lead to worry and nerves, and if he became nervous he could slip up. He let the nicotine he inhaled relax his body. He had to stay focused and look at the situation rationally. Most likely the prisoner was already dead, lost in a cave, or possibly drowned at sea. While that gave the warden some comfort, he couldn't push away the suspicions he'd always harbored about the odd man known as Number Twenty-Three. Even when the prisoner had first arrived on the island, he had made the warden uneasy. The answer the man gave to his question that day left the man suspicious and unsettled. Why hadn't he done more to investigate and follow up on his concerns?

Humphrey shook his head, called himself a bloody fool, then took another long drag on his smoke. He thought back to that first day just over a month ago when the newest crop of prisoners arrived at Devil's Horn Prison. As usual, most of them looked pale. Fear was in their eyes, and their bodies trembled nervously. It was a larger group than normal, a full score of men, this time from British soil. Most of the prisoners at Devil's Horn came from Irish shores. When they came, they all looked lost, hopeless, and forlorn. The prison was on a small island in the middle of the sea, between Anglesey and Mann. There was nothing near it – nothing on it either, except guard houses and the impenetrable prison fortress. It was named the Devil's Horn due to its shape, similar to that of a mountain goat, and because of its harsh lifeless environment.

Jailer Ogg, tall and burly with a face as craggly as the island rocks, marched the new group into the yard, past the guards who glared and sneered at them. When the prisoners were forced into neat little rows, the guards roughed them up to get them in line, calling them "pigs" and "cows". It was good to smack them around a bit and call them animals. It dehumanized them, made them more malleable for the time ahead.

The performance of the warden and the jailer was as well-choreographed as a Mozart Opera. Ogg would play the role of the devil and Humphrey, as the head of the prison, would be the face of benevolence. He represented the beacon of hope for this lowly scum. They believed that if they followed the rules, they could make it through the horrors of living on Devil's Horn and might even find their way home. Most would, but Humphrey saw to it that a significant amount would not. Nothing maintains order better than a boot or a bullet to the head.

After he gave his routine speech of how the prisoners should see their time at the Devil's Horn as an opportunity to better themselves, he would walk among the men, leading to the climax of his performance.

"What's your number, son?" he'd asked the first prisoner in the lineup that day.

"Henry, er, I mean – " *Slam!* Ogg hit the man so hard that he smashed down into the mud.

"It's all right, Jailer," he reproached Ogg. "It takes some getting used to, losing one's name."

"How about you?" he said to the next prisoner, a grizzled-looking man who had the eyes of a child and the lined face of an elder. Humphrey guessed the eyes were closer to the man's true age. His troubled life had caused the face.

"Number 7615, sir," he answered in an odd drawl.

"American?" the warden asked, recognizing the speech pattern of the American West.

"That's correct. I was raised in Virginia, sir."

The warden nodded. He considered asking the man how he ended up in a British prison but thought better of it. He didn't much want to know. It really didn't matter. This one probably wasn't going to serve his full term. When Humphrey had this thought, he didn't mean that the man would be released early. Number 7615 would never see the outside of the walls again.

"Let me ask you, son," the warden tried to sound sympathetic when he asked this question, "what will you do when you get out of here?"

"Why, sir, I'll go home to my mum."

The warden nodded. He had expected him to say something about a girl, but family was a fine answer as well. "You do well here, and you'll see her again. Back in Virginia?"

"Yes, sir. Thank you, sir," the young man with the old face answered. There was something about his demeanor that disgusted the warden. What was the word that would describe him . . . Ah yes, the warden realized. *Pathetic.* The man was a pathetic worm and it would be his pleasure to relieve the Earth of the bother of enduring this man's existence upon the planet. However, it was not his time. Not yet.

The warden moved to the next man and the next. They had learned their lesson, gave their number, and gave an answer about seeing their wife or girl or family when they got free. One rather jolly man said he'd have a pint with his mates at the bar. He was the type that saw a joke in everything. Ogg broke his teeth and yelled at the man for laughing at the warden. He's a good man, that Ogg, thought Humphrey.

As he moved down the line, the warden hadn't quite found what he was looking for. These were British prisoners. Even being scum of the Earth they were better scum than those Irish. Then Humphrey came to an odd man, thin, with a horrid beak of a nose. He had a vacant look in his grey eyes.

"Number?" the warden asked with a raised brow. He was sizing up the scrawny man whose age he was having a hard time determining. Was this man older or younger than he looked? His face wasn't too lined, but there was much grey in his hair. Perhaps he greyed prematurely.

"Twenty-Three, sir."

"Twenty-Three?" the warden asked. Ogg was about to smack the man with the butt of his gun, but the warden held up his hand to stop him. "That's not your number."

34

"I like Twenty-Three," he answered with a distance in his voice. The man was a simpleton.

Ogg spit at the man's feet. "Better tell the warden yer real number or you'll get a taste of my fist!"

Humphrey thought for a moment about this scrawny new prisoner. He'd get one of these on occasion, those that were soft in the head. They'd be much better placed in Bedlam, but Humphrey didn't have the luxury of sending them back. If this man was assigned to him, so be it.

With this one not answering properly, the warden had a choice to make. Should he make an example of the man and have Ogg beat him to a pulp, or should he let it go to show a compassionate side? Humphrey thought it might be better to show kindness at the moment. Beating a simpleton would just anger the other prisoners. That could turn some of them to lions when all were currently lambs. Still, he hadn't found someone to make an example of quite yet, and this man hadn't spoken his correct number. Humphrey decided to ask another question to help make up his mind on how to proceed.

"What do you plan on doing when you get out of here, my friend?" The warden made sure to call this one friend. He was much too old to call him son.

The man looked up in the sky and his face twisted into a gleeful smile, like that of a child being handed a ball for play time. "I think I'll stay," the man answered.

"I mean," the warden clarified, "when you are released from prison. Where will you go?"

"I'll stay," the man gave a chuckle when he answered. "It's nice here. I'll stay."

The warden frowned deeply. This man was a muttering idiot. Still, he was harmless. No sense beating a man who was his ally. These simpletons could change as quickly as a coin flip. Why turn friend to foe?

"Very well," the warden answered with a sigh, then added, "Number Twenty-Three."

The warden left the man behind and continued down the line. He kept asking the same questions of the prisoners, and they all gave the same polite answers. Disappointing, the warden thought. Doesn't anyone here have some spirit?

Humphrey was considering having Ogg start some trouble, but then, he came to the kind of inmate he was hoping to encounter: A sniveling blonde haired man whose prison stripes dangled from his bony form.

"Hello," the warden said to the young man. "I'm Warden Humphreys."

The young man glared at Humphrey. His lip quivered, snots dripped from his nose. "Why the hell I should care?" he grunted, and wiped his nose with his sleeve.

"Why, you little runt!" Ogg snapped and kicked the lad in the gut.

The prisoner fell to the ground, but the boy pulled himself up, and to the delight of the warden, he spit right in Jailer Ogg's face.

Warden Humphrey shielded his mouth so that the prisoners nearby couldn't see that he was grinning. This one's got fire, he thought to himself. The blondes almost have as much fire as the gingers. It was Ogg's role to extinguish their flames. And extinguish it, he did.

"You filthy wretch!!" Ogg yelled at the inmate. "Here's how we treat your kind here!" he shouted. He removed his sidearm and gave two quick shots right into the blonde's meek body. The lad didn't have time to say a word. There was a look of utter bewilderment in his eyes just before he crumpled to the ground.

"Warden!" the prisoner next in line, a dark-skinned man, probably Italian, said to Humphrey. "He shot him! He shot him!" The prisoner went to grab the warden's arm to plead with him for help.

"Don't you touch me!" the warden growled. "That shot," he announced for all the prisoners to hear, "was in self-defense." Then he turned around in a circle, addressing all the prisoners. "Let that be a lesson to you! We don't put up with any insubordination here. You will follow the rules or you will pay the consequences!" he snarled.

It took a while to reach this mighty crescendo, and perhaps that was for the best. All the prisoners stood in line, quivering. Some had tears rolling down their cheeks. How marvelous, the warden thought. He had his grand opening. Order would be maintained.

Warden Humphrey looked over the documents on his desk about prisoner Number Twenty-Three. There had only been one issue of significance with the prisoner, a fight which had broken out in the mess hall. He had recently been involved in the skirmish, but Humphrey had always thought that was an accident, a case of him being at the wrong place at the wrong time. He spent most of his time seeing the priest and getting books from the library. That had always struck Humphrey as odd, that a simpleton would find the

36

time to read the Bible, Shakespeare, Chaucer, and Morley. Humphrey had assumed the man didn't actually comprehend what he was reading. How could a prisoner who had trouble lacing up his boots be able to understand the complexities of *King Lear*? Now, he wondered if he, himself, was the fool.

"'*I am a fool, thou art nothing*'," he whispered to himself. It was true. While Number Twenty-Three might truly be intelligent and could have possibly tricked him, he, Warden Humphrey, would get the last laugh. There were only so many places on the island for Twenty-Three to hide, the warden thought to himself.

He just needed to make sure this little problem was solved before any word of it got out. The last thing he needed were the politicians getting wind of it.

"Good group today. British stock. The lot of them will make it out of here alive," Ogg said to Humphrey. It was the evening after the new prisoners had arrived. They established a custom over the months to have a celebratory toast after they'd ensured the prisoners were properly greeted. Humphrey always had a glass of gin. Ogg's choice was vodka. "In fact," Ogg added with a chuckle, "I thought we might even make it to the end of them without much trouble, wot wot?"

"There's always one," Humphrey said grimly. He was in no joking mood.

"With the paddies there's a right lot more than one. It's like shooting bears in a zoo."

"You got your trophy for today," Humphrey said referring to the prisoner he had shot.

"Yes, sir, that's eighty-six for me. I've killed far more here than I did in the trenches." Then he put down his drink and leaned in towards the warden. He said with a snarl, "And every one of them bloody well deserved it, wot wot!"

Ogg clenched his glass, swigged the last bit of vodka, and slammed it down on the table. Humphrey would usually join him or give a "Here! Here!", lifting his glass in the air at each "Here!" This time he remained silent.

"Why so taciturn?" Ogg asked, changing his tone to be one of concern. "You're usually cheering along with me. Something the matter?"

"I . . . ." Humphrey moved his mouth as if chewing on his words, deciding which ones to spit out. "Something doesn't feel quite right. Call it intuition."

"What? You're an old woman now?" the jailer said in jest.

Humphrey ignored the joke. "I can't put my finger on it, but something about that new prisoner, Number Twenty-Three, leaves me feeling uneasy."

"Really? You mean the poof? I wouldn't worry about him. The prisoners will take care of him when they figure out what kind of man that one is."

"You think he's a homosexual?" Humphrey asked Ogg, trying to determine if that would explain his nervousness about the man.

"If he's not, there's not much in his head. Some of the gingers will rough him up. Just you wait. He's one less prisoner my men need to worry about setting straight. The other birds will do it for us."

The warden thought about his friend's words. He might be right. Perhaps he was overcautious. There was much that had happened in the last few years to make him that way. The Great War had ended, so there was no need for military prisoners. Now it looked as though there would finally be peace between Britain and the Irish. Once that treaty was signed, most of the island's prisoners would be released. He knew the exorbitant expense of the island prison, and if it was shut down or if the books were examined too closely, they would find that there was a significant amount of hidden costs which were going straight to Humphrey's bank account. He shivered for a moment at the thought of being caught and ending up as one of those numbers locked away in Devil's Island. Then he sobered up, shook his head, and thought of how difficult it would be to root out his monthly bonuses. He was being overly worried.

Humphrey bit his lower lip as he considered one other issue. "The new guards. That Walters seems a little green around the gills."

Ogg raised his brows and his eyes widened. "Is that what this is about? I told you, you don't need to worry about that. I took care of Jeffries. No one knows what happened to him. They suspect, which is a good thing. It keeps the men in line. I've already dropped my usual hints with Walters. Told him I might pay a visit to his family when I'm on leave if he didn't toe the line. He could read my insinuation."

The jailer did his best to form a smile, something the muscles on his face struggled with for lack of practice. "Cheer up, friend," said Ogg. "You are the king of this island and I'll make sure it stays that way."

There was just a slight glimmer of light when Humphrey heard a loud knock on his door. The sun hadn't come over the horizon, just that first glow, outlining the clouds in soft shades of red. Humphrey was already awake, having only a few restless hours of sleep. He had been staring out the window, looking at the changing sky, thinking of the missing prisoner, running a few instances in his mind over and over again when he heard the hammering on the door to his quarters.

The warden was still in his robe when he answered. The guard averted his eyes to the ground, quaking slightly, fearful that Humphrey would lash out at him for waking him at such an early hour. This was good. If the new recruits feared him, it meant they respected him. It was another sign that Ogg kept the men under control. There wouldn't be another incident, he told himself. There wouldn't be another Jeffries.

"Warden, we found signs of a fire in one of the caves, and we also found this." The young guard handed Humphrey a damp piece of paper with a crude drawing of stick figures below a cave entrance. Humphrey looked over the paper and had to contain his excitement. He remained stoic, thanked the guard, and sent him off to return to the search party.

This was excellent news, the best-case scenario. Number Twenty-Three was still on the island and would either be caught soon, or he was most certainly deceased. The warden thought back to the first time he'd seen those crude drawings in Number Twenty-Three's cell.

Contrary to Ogg's belief, Number Twenty-Three was not beaten by the other men. In fact, they seemed to have adopted the dullard. A number of them, both dark and ginger haired, kept an eye on him. The prisoners greeted him warmly when he entered the mess hall, and even the guards had a twinkle in their eyes and a grin on their faces when the fool was in their presence.

When Humphrey asked his men why they treated the prisoner so kindly, they all said the same things. "He's as harmless as a child," was one sentiment. "He's kind, that one. Gotta love a man who brings happiness everywhere he goes," was another. The clearest reason was given by Ogg, "He's a scrawny weakling, but he's a calming presence. There's never any trouble when he's around." That statement didn't last, though. He had been in a fight, but that was weeks later.

The warden regularly visited prisoner Twenty-Three in his cell in Block Three. That was one of the biggest surprises to Humphrey, that the prisoner was in the cell block reserved for the worst prisoners. He had no cellmate – deemed too dangerous. Yet, Twenty-Three appeared as gentle as a lamb. The scrawny simpleton supposedly had gutted an entire family who were boarding him.

The idiot was making one of his crude drawings when the warden first visited him. He was sitting on his bunk with *The Complete Works of William Shakespeare* on his lap, using it as a table to hold his paper. He was fervently drawing as if he were working on a masterpiece, but all he was producing was stick figures and thick lines representing mountain peaks.

Humphrey gave a loud "A-hem!" to get the prisoner's attention. The idiot didn't look up from his work, but just kept practically carving lines into the paper with his graphite. "Good day, Number Twenty-Three," Humphrey said gruffly. Gone was the kindness from his voice he applied when he greeted the man in the prison yard.

The simpleton paused from his scratchings to gaze vapidly up at the warden. "Hello, Warden. Do you like my picture?"

"Very nice," Humphrey answered. "Do you draw often?"

"Yes," the man answered distantly. "I like to make pictures."

"Well, you can draw all you'd like as long as you stay out of trouble." Humphrey eyed the graphite to make sure that there was no way that it could be sharpened into a weapon.

"Oh, I would never make trouble. Just pictures. I like to make pictures. I'm going to stay here, you know."

"And what are the pictures showing?" Humphrey asked, trying to figure out if the man was really an imbecile.

"These are my friends," Number Twenty-Three said, pointing to the crude stick figures. "I have lots of friends."

"Mm-hmm," the warden grunted, "and where do your friends live?" He was wondering about the hills.

"They live here. They live on the island."

Number Twenty-Three must have heard about the caves on the island. Perhaps he saw them on his way in. The warden said goodbye to Number Twenty-Three and then left the cell. Why, he asked himself, why did this prisoner make him feel uneasy? He'd had simpletons in the prison before. Why did this one feel so different? The warden thanked the guard for letting him in to view the prisoner. Humphrey turned to continue on his rounds when he saw a coin on the ground.

"Looks like you dropped a farthing there, Samson," he said to the guard. He reached over and picked it up. When he did, his eyes glanced over at Twenty-Three. He saw that the man, just for a moment, was peering over his drawing, gazing at the warden. Gone was the vacancy from those grey eyes. Instead, there was a clear intelligence, an intensity as though he were analyzing the warden like he was a specimen in a lab. The moment was fleeting for when the warden turned to look directly at the prisoner, the vacancy had returned.

The warden gave Samson the penny, and the guard thanked him for it.

"Tell me, Samson – Number Twenty-Three here. Does he ever visit with anyone?"

"Not really. He likes his art and his books. He's friendly enough with everyone. Gets books from the library cart. Goes to see the priest on Sunday."

"The priest? He sees Father Alvey?"

"No, sir," the guard corrected. "He sees Father Don."

"He's a Catholic." The warden was surprised by this fact. Adding a Catholic priest at the prison was done at the behest of one of the stuffed shirts in London. They thought it would help keep the bog-trotters in line. What drivel! All they needed was a swift kick to the head to maintain order. Forcing them to go to Anglican Church would civilize the lot of them. Humphrey mulled how he might make that happen, then discarded the idea as too much work. They were heathens, after all. They deserved their place in Hell in the afterlife.

The priest was only allowed to have a small parish on the island, much smaller than the one allotted to the Anglicans. The gingers went to mass at the small shed of a church on Sunday and often stayed for confession. Father Alvey was the Anglican priest on the island and his church was four times the size of Don's. Yet he had a smaller flock to tend due to the high number of Irish prisoners. Alvey had been on the island for ten years. The Catholics didn't last long, didn't have the stomach for it. Father Don was the third priest they'd had in fifteen months. He had only been stationed at the prison for five weeks. The warden didn't fraternize much with the clergy, but perhaps it was time to pay the priest a visit.

Father Don was a short and plump little man who was often seen walking the prison yards and speaking mostly with the ginger prisoners. Humphrey avoided the man for he found the priest repugnant. His physical shape, or lack thereof, made him the type of person the warden scorned. That, coupled with the fact that preaching his belief system went against the church established by King Henry, made him a man that the warden wanted nothing to do with. In his eyes, this flabby priest was as bad as some of these prisoners, a traitor to his country. He knew there was a special place in Hell reserved for one such as him.

The priest's small parish was located in a corner of the Yard in the shadow of Cell Block One. Father Don was standing out front of his parish doors, saying hello to some of the unsavory prisoners. The way he cavorted with them left the warden with a bitter taste in his mouth.

"Good day to you, Warden," the priest called out to him in greeting. Humphrey wondered if it was also a warning as the prisoners sauntered away at hearing Father Don call his name.

"Good day to you as well, Father," the warden politely responded. There was no reason to be discourteous even though the man disgusted him. Perhaps he would write to his Bishop and ask for the priest to be transferred. He would have to come up with some grounds for doing so, but he could create those grounds later.

"What brings you to see me on this fine day?" the priest asked. Humphrey wondered what was so fine about it. The sky was dark and overcast. Rain was surely on the horizon.

"I am inquiring about a prisoner who visits you with some regularity."

The priest looked serious. "I see. You will have to be more specific. There are many in my flock whom I see on a daily basis."

"I refer to Number Twenty-Three."

The priest squinted his eyes as if the prisoner were standing next to the warden, as though he was attempting to use his weak eyes to bring Twenty-Three into focus. "Let me see . . . let me see . . . ." the priest started. "The men use their Christian names with me. I sometimes have trouble remembering their numbers."

"I can be of assistance. He is thin, with a large beak of a nose, and his mind is a bit fuzzy."

At the last bit, the priest's eyes opened wide. "I know exactly to whom you are referring. British man. He likes to draw. Yes, I enjoy his visits very much."

"What do you discuss with him?" the warden asked.

"Not much. He prefers to draw. We spend most of the time drawing together. He draws his little stick figures. I draw along with him. I believe it gives him comfort."

"Has he said anything about his past with you?"

The priest looked offended. "Warden, you know I cannot divulge information confessed to me."

The warden gritted his teeth. He wanted to slug the man – give him a shiner for being so disrespectful, but he held back. The priest was fully in his rights. He'd be breaking his oath to the cloth. Humphrey decided to use a different tactic.

"I didn't mean it like that. He is here for murder. Since he's arrived, his behavior has been exemplary. I merely want to make sure it remains that way."

The priest looked relieved. "I can assure you, Warden, that the man has not expressed any thoughts of violence. As you said, his behavior has been exemplary in my presence. I don't believe he shall cause any physical harm to anyone while he is here. He appears to be simple. Simple-minded people often don't cause any trouble."

"Yes, well. Thank you, Father, and a good day to you."

"A good day to you, Warden."

The warden had seen the priest and Twenty-Three together on a few occasions after that talk. They were always drawing those crude pictures, never talking.

The priest was now gone. He'd left the island hours before Number Twenty-Three's escape was detected. For the first time, a sinister question entered the warden's mind: Could the priest have assisted in the prisoner's escape? It would go against all that the priest held dear to aid in a jail break. Perhaps, though, the priest was not aware of it. Perhaps he realized his mistake and took the opportunity to leave the island when it was presented to him, when that elderly doctor's heart gave out, or perhaps Number Twenty-Three did something to the priest. He did carve up a family. Perhaps the simpleton's violent side was shown to Father Don. Perhaps he threatened him in a way that scared off the buffoonish priest. This would need to be investigated.

Humphrey opened his filing cabinet and took out several of the drawings that the prisoner and clergyman had created together. There was something about the pictures that suddenly made the warden suspicious. He couldn't place his finger on it. They were just crude drawings. What more could there be? They didn't have anything to do with the break. Or did they?

The warden thought back to the incidents of the previous day. A supply ship had arrived that morning. There was nothing out of the ordinary about that. Supplies arrived from the mainland twice a week. This was what the warden called a quiet week. There were no scheduled prisoner transports and no guards or other workers were assigned leave.

The steamer sat in port for two hours while the supplies of water, food, and cigarettes were unloaded. There were no odd reports during this time. A skirmish occurred between two prisoners in the mess hall, but fights between the Brits and the micks were common. It was a small one anyway, just a few punches before the guards broke it up. Prisoner Twenty-Three was peripherally involved, doing some minor injury to his hand, but after a trip inside to visit the doctor, he returned to finish his hour of time outside before returning to his cell, where he worked on one of his sketches.

Shortly before the supply ship was scheduled to return to the mainland, one of the doctors suffered an attack. Dr. Murray was an older doctor who had returned to practice and taken a position on the island. Rumor had it the man suffered from a gambling problem, and he took the job to either pay off his debts or escape from his debtors. The cause of the attack was believed to be a weak heart, and without additional support he probably wouldn't survive the night. The warden was surprised to discover that the doctor was a Catholic and requested Father Don to accompany him should he need his last rites. The request was granted, and the ship with the two additional passengers returned to mainland shore.

The warden had confirmed from several guards that Number Twenty-Three was in his cell well after the ship departed from the island. The doctor's malady and the escape didn't seem to be linked at all. There was no record of the prisoner ever seeing the doctor. If the priest had something to do with the escape, he couldn't have known that the doctor was going to suffer an attack and request his last rites. No, it seemed that the priest was innocent of aiding and abetting the escapee.

Number Twenty-Three broke out in such a way that it was difficult to know if he had any assistance, and if he did, those who assisted him were most likely not aware of what he was doing. At ten o'clock the night of the escape, when the guard on duty on the ground floor of Cell Block Three walked the halls and flashed his torch in Twenty-Three's cell, he saw the simpleton sleeping in his bed. At the eleven o'clock check, Number Twenty-Three was gone. A search of the cell revealed a hole he had chiseled in the bottom of his cell using a rock and several discarded nails he must have discovered in the Yard and snuck back to his cell. There was a weak spot in the wall under his bed. The concrete was crumbling and the boards behind it were rotten.

He must have made the final break through the wall that night. There was a service corridor behind the cell which was only used

44

during the day. Twenty-Three must have chiseled through the last part of the wall that evening. The hole he climbed through was small, just about a foot in diameter, and it was only that big, the warden surmised, to account for the fellow's rather large head. The striped pants and shirt of his prison uniform were left pushed into the hole, indicating that he had other clothes to change into. The warden guessed that Twenty-Three had somehow gotten some clothes from someone in the prison laundry.

He still wasn't sure how the prisoner had tunneled through the wall undetected. What did he do with all of the waste? Even after getting through the wall, how did he get outside? He'd have to walk past guards at certain checkpoints. How did he dodge them?

Humphrey gave a grunt and shook his head. Most likely, it wouldn't matter. Either the prisoner would be captured and beaten until he explained everything, or he was already deceased, making the answers to the questions irrelevant. In either case, Number Twenty-Three was a dead man. The warden would make sure of it. The escape attempt officially never happened. No one outside of the guards knew of it, and Ogg would put the fear of God into his men to make sure that their lips remained sealed. Number Twenty-Three, like many of the other prisoners who caused the warden trouble, had merely suffered an untimely death.

The sound of commotion outside drew the warden's attention and focused his mind away from his speculation. A smile pursed Humphrey's lips. The noise could only mean one thing: That Twenty-Three had been captured. A corpse wouldn't cause that much of a ruckus, so he was still alive. Good. He decided that Ogg would not take part in the prisoner's interrogation. He, the warden himself, would question the prisoner. He thought of all the ways he could torture the man, leaving him in agony, begging to end his life, but the warden would hold back. He'd see to it that the man lasted days in horrific pain until he finally succumbed to his wounds.

A loud banging sounded on the door to the warden's quarters. He composed himself to make sure that he wasn't grinning when he answered the door. He had to keep a dour expression to keep the men in line. The warden threw open the door and saw a panicked guard, Walters was his name, looking wildly at his door.

"Well, what is it?" growled the warden.

"Sir, it's a whole platoon of constables. They've landed on the island and are rounding up all of the guards. They . . . they arrested Ogg, sir!"

"Arrested Ogg?" The warden was astounded. "Ridiculous! I'll bloody well get to the bottom of this!" He pushed past Walters and stormed out of his quarters, heading straight for the prison gate. As he walked up the path from the guards' housing to the prison walls, he heard shouts from inside. "You are under arrest – !" he heard called out, but shouts covered up the remainder of the sentence. Humphrey didn't know why the guards were being detained. Could it be because of Twenty-Three? He pondered. No, he decided. Even if word of the break reached the mainland, there would be no reason to arrest the guards. Then a chilling thought entered Humphrey's mind. What if the guards were running some illegal scheme on the island? It was a perfect spot for smuggling. But could that have happened without Humphrey's knowledge? Perhaps it could have if Ogg was behind it. The warden gave a nod of agreement to a decision he made based on a case he'd concocted in his head. If there was some kind of scheme going on, some gambling or arms running, then Ogg would take the blame. There always had to be someone who was held responsible. Once Humphrey knew more, he could determine how best to show himself in a positive light. Perhaps he could even find a way to be the hero.

In front of the prison gates, there was a group of about a half-dozen constables surrounding a man who was their commanding officer. Perfect, Humphrey thought. I'll show ignorance and they can explain everything to me. "What is the meaning of this . . . this . . . this outrage?" Humphrey called to the men.

"And who might you be?" the commanding officer asked in a thick cockney accent, stepping forward and eyeing the warden.

"I'll tell you who I am. I'm Warden Frederic J. Humphrey. And who might you be?"

"Warden Humphrey, eh? Why, we was just about to look for you. I am Sergeant Kingsley, but you'll remember me as the bloke that done arrested you."

"Arrested me?" Humphrey protested. "There must be some mistake." He held up his hands in protest and was surprised to feel the cold iron of manacles shackled around his wrists by a constable standing beside the sergeant.

"Take him away," the sergeant said, and two constables grabbed each arm of the warden and hauled him away past the sergeant and the other men.

"Unhand me! This is ridiculous! Absolutely ridiculous! Why, what are you charging me with? I have a right to know! I *demand* to

46

know!" the warden blustered as he was led away by two burly officers.

The two men practically lifted the bellowing warden off the ground as they led him inside the prison gates. As the warden was forced inside, another constable walked toward him, hedging in the opposite direction. Just before the constable passed by, he tapped his hat and called out to the man. "I told you I would stay." The warden looked in horror as he saw the beaming face of Number Twenty-Three.

The three inspectors burst out laughing. "Jolly good!" said the sallow-faced Inspector Lestrade. He leaned back in his chair as much as he could without putting too much strain on his lower back. Gregson wiped away tears from his eye from guffawing so loud, and the poor Inspector Bradstreet was left gasping for breath after hearing of Holmes's last words to the warden. "Just like that, eh Mr. Holmes? You were always one for theatrics. What did he say after that?" Lestrade asked the detective.

Watson, Holmes, and the others, were lounging about in the doctor's parlor, hearing a recount of the happenings at Devil's Horn Prison. The doctor and the group of retired inspectors got together once a month at the Watson residence. The group almost always included Lestrade, Gregson, and Bradstreet. Jones and MacDonald joined on occasion, as had Lanner before his untimely passing. Today it was just the core group who had, despite their differences when they were on the Force, become good friends in their retirement. Watson always hosted the group in the parlor of his home where they enjoyed bourbon and cigars while reminiscing about old times and complaining about politics, traffic, Germans, and the problems of age.

Holmes gave one of his odd silent laughs. "There wasn't much Humphrey could say. Just pointed and got his tongue tied up for a bit. When he finally found words, he was distant enough from me that whatever he was screaming about I'm sure sounded like nonsense to the men who were dragging him away." Everyone nodded and chuckled.

Sherlock Holmes was one of two guests of honor at this month's get-together. The detective joined his former comrades when he could find the time in his schedule. That usually meant he joined them no more than twice a year. The other guest was a first timer, and one that made the former inspectors watch their words a little more carefully. This guest was a Catholic priest. His name was Father Brown.

"Tell me Father, what made you bring this case to Mr. Holmes?" Inspector Lestrade asked. His back was hunched over a bit in his old age which only made him look more like a rodent. "You've solved a few mysteries yourself."

"Well, Inspector," the soft-spoken priest answered, "the case was brought to me by one of the prison guards, a young Londoner. His family have been members of my parish for a good many years, and he broke down in confession one day and told me that he had seen the head jailer shoot one of the guards in the back, a friend of his named Jeffries. He didn't know why the jailer shot the guard, but he did it when the man's back was turned, in cold blood. The guard was wise enough to not report what he saw, as he figured that if one superior was involved, others could be, too, and he didn't want to suffer the same fate as his friend.

"As the days went by, the other guards talked about the cruelties they saw at the prison. They told of the horrid treatment of the prisoners, how some were outright murdered on the warden's orders. Many of the guards had taken lashes from Jailer Ogg, and some had even been struck by Humphrey. They also pointed out how the warden had clothing and accessories that seemed too fine for a man of his station. My parishioner's conscience became more and more unsettled. He had to tell someone about the horrors at the prison which he was starting to see more and more with his own eyes, and so he told me.

"When I heard the story, I gained the lad's permission to involve Mr. Holmes. I knew he had connections in the government. Perhaps he could tell me if there was any noted corruption at Devil's Horn Prison. Perhaps we could make a case."

"As a matter-of-fact," Holmes said dryly, after taking a swig of his brandy, "the government was already suspicious of the goings on at the island prison. Devil's Horn had run far over its allotted budget during the Great War. With the end of the war and peace within reach in Ireland, there was discussion of shutting the prison down as a cost saving measure. There were also a high number of prisoner casualties on the island, mostly Irish. Our negotiators feared that the island could become a wedge in establishing peace between our countries."

"Typical Holmes," Bradstreet smiled. He wheezed a little when he spoke, and he had to pause to catch his breath. He and Father Brown were the only men not smoking that day. Bradstreet, while the youngest of the men, was suffering from a decline in his health. Sadly, Watson could tell from the signs that the former detective wouldn't be making their meetings by year's end. "Using one of your disguises to gather intelligence, eh," Bradstreet managed to finish his thought after he regained control of his breathing.

"Actually, I had the smallest role in this affair," Holmes confessed.

Watson was in the envious position of taking over the story from Holmes. "Holmes and Father Brown came to me and asked for my assistance. Holmes had worked his contacts in the government and Brown his contacts in the church. With both organizations sharing concern over the island, they agreed to work together. Brown was briefly transferred to serve as the priest at the island prison. He was the first to arrive. I was the second. Due to the isolation of the island, it was difficult to retain medical staff. I concocted a story that I was still working at my age due to being in debt. I told them I had a gambling problem."

"That's an easy story for you to use," Gregson chimed in. The others heartily agreed. Even Watson chortled a bit in agreement.

"That's true," Watson admitted. "It made my role easier to play. Anyway, I applied and, despite my age, was hired almost immediately. Even with me joining the medical team, the prison hospital was still understaffed.

"I arrived just over a week after Father Brown. We started obtaining information on the island. Being a doctor and a priest, we were in the perfect positions to see and hear the horrors that were occurring there."

"I see," said Lestrade. "But how did you get information on the warden's embezzlement? Is that where Mr. Holmes came in?"

"Actually, that was also the good doctor's doing," Father Brown explained. "When I get to know a criminal, I try to put myself in his position, to understand his mind, and figure out how he and his men would commit their particular crime. Although I didn't speak much to the warden, through others I learned how meticulous he was, how organized. I knew that a man like that would keep detailed records of all of his transactions. I also knew a man like that, not fearing any reprisal, would have his crime fully documented, locked away in an office file."

"That's where I got to use some of Holmes's methods," the doctor admitted. He gave his detective friend a beaming smile which was reciprocated. "I was able to arrange a break each day when I knew the warden was walking the halls of the prison cells. During

49

that time, I left the prison and went to the quarters outside the gate. Anyone who saw me would think that I was just returning to my home – which is what I did, for in my rooms were two things I needed: One was my lock picks. The other was a guard's uniform I had taken. Early on, I learned where the discarded uniforms went to the rubbish pile. I found one that was about my size and kept it in my closet.

"I would dress as a guard, pick the lock of the warden's door, and then go inside his office. I always made sure that no one saw me, and even if I was spotted, people would assume the warden sent me to his office to retrieve something. Within a week, I had discovered the file containing all the evidence of the warden's embezzlement. It took another week to use my vest-pocket Kodak to capture photographs of all the documents."

"Well, Mr. Holmes," said Lestrade. "It sounds like you weren't needed this time around." He chided the detective as he often did.

"I still had a role to play," Holmes confessed. "My imprisonment served two purposes. First, it distracted the warden in case he held any suspicions towards Watson. Second, if I escaped from the prison then it would show the island was not as mighty as one would imagine. What I didn't expect to find was the poor condition of the prison structure itself. With the warden siphoning funds away from maintenance funds, the prison had deteriorated quickly. That's what happens to buildings near the coast. The salt in the air eats away at the structures. Originally, I had planned to grab a guard uniform from the prison laundry just as Watson did, pick the lock to my door, and simply walk right out the front gates. While I did purloin a uniform, when I detected the condition of the prison structure, I decided to take a different approach for my escape. I wanted it to be quite clear that repairing the prison would cost upwards of a million pounds. It made the closing of the prison a certainty."

"So it was when you had tunneled your way through the wall that Watson and Father Brown returned to the mainland?" asked Bradstreet who then fell into a coughing fit.

Once Bradstreet regained his composure, Holmes explained that was precisely what happened. "When I knew it would be a matter of days before my escape, I took advantage of a fight that broke out in the dining hall. The timing was perfect, as I knew the warden was becoming suspicious of my time with Father Brown. I could tell he was starting to wonder if there was a code in the drawings that I shared with the priest."

Holmes paused and explained to the men on an aside, "You see, Inspectors, there were no dancing men this time. No secret code in the images. It was all gibberish. It served its purpose of making the warden suspect me and the Father. He had no suspicions of Watson.

"With the prison fight, I played the hapless victim who was accidentally injured. This allowed me to go to the hospital and have my injured hand bandaged. Watson wasn't the doctor who treated me, but when he saw me, he was able to pull me away for a few minutes. That's when I told him it was time to put the final part of the plan into action.

"The rest you know, gentlemen. Watson feigned a heart attack, and Father Brown joined him on the voyage back to the mainland. Once they arrived, they brought the evidence to the proper authorities, and a police boat was dispatched to Devil's Horn. The guards were rounded up, though most were innocent of any crimes and released. The warden and the jailer were arrested and imprisoned. They turned on one another in their confessions and instead of making themselves appear innocent, they both assured each other would be found guilty. Since one of the crimes is murder, I dare say neither man shall be long for this world."

"Remarkable, Mr. Holmes," Lestrade said with admiration. "But I do have a question for you and one for Father Brown."

"Go on," said Holmes.

"Why Number Twenty-Three?"

"Ah," Holmes smiled. "I was having a bit of fun with that. I used the number to test the warden and the jailer. I thought I might take a boot to the groin or a fist to the head when I spoke up, but it played out the way I'd hoped. The warden saw me as an imbecile, and held Ogg back from striking me. That was good. It meant my character was already established.

"As for the number, I thought back to my old dwellings with Watson, 221b, and simply added the number *two* to *twenty-one* to get at *twenty-three*."

The inspectors told Holmes that they admired his cleverness and congratulated the detective, the doctor, and the priest on the success of their mission.

"Just one thing, Mr. Lestrade," said Father Brown. "You said you had one more question for me."

"Why yes," the ferret-faced man recalled. "I'd almost forgotten. I wondered how you, a man of the cloth, could get away with being undercover? You had to commit the sin of lying. Did you have to get absolved?"

The priest looked gravely serious. "I did no such thing. Only truths left my lips. I really was a priest who was moved from London to the island's parish. During my interactions with the warden, the guards, and the prisoners, I chose my words carefully, making certain not to tell a falsehood."

"But you used an alias," Lestrade pressed.

"Ah, that. I said my name was Father *Donn*. Those on the island thought it was spelled *D-o-n*, but in actuality, it was spelled, *D-o-n-n*. For you see, *Donn*, in the Irish tongue, is *Brown*."

Lights! Camera! Murder!
by Sonia Fetherston

We had an engagement, Sherlock Holmes and I. The two of us were urgently summoned, not on an investigation as in the old days, but on an adventure of another sort. We were to meet what are called "stars" – actors who were engaged in making a photoplay. To my great enjoyment, the subject of this moving picture was our own selves!

My snug retirement home, where I've lived for nearly twenty years now, is located in Queen Anne Street, not far from our old digs in Baker Street. Holmes was my guest, up the evening before from his cottage in Sussex, having arrived at Victoria Station in time for our reunion supper. It had been a wet September night, and our cigars were taken in cosy companionship beside a hissing coal fire. This morning's sun, however, promised a bright day ahead.

After a hearty breakfast we descended to the street where my trusty Ford motor car waited. [1] One of my gloved hands concentrated on the steering, while the other intermittently touched the pocket of my overcoat to make sure the letter was still there. It was from a man called Bert Ridley, London publicity agent for Goldwyn Studios, the American "movie" company. He had invited us to pose for a publicity photograph with the leading actors, Mr. John Barrymore and Mr. Roland Young, our counterparts in the film. [2] Afterward, we might tour "the set" and watch as "exteriors" were being "shot".

Secretly, I was thrilled. I like to go to the cinema, and sometimes Mrs. Hudson joins me. Our former landlady lives nearby with a niece, and I'm often able to look in on her. So far as Mrs. Hudson and I are concerned, no one exceeds Mr. Douglas Fairbanks for action, and little Colleen Moore is our favourite comedienne. I could hardly wait to see how a moving picture is made – especially one about Holmes and me. This reverie was interrupted by one of Holmes's snorts.

"Really, Watson," said he, "try and contain yourself."

I feigned diffidence. "'Contain'? I'm simply minding my driving, Holmes."

"When I see the bloom upon your cheek and that certain sparkle in your eye . . . when an irrepressible smile unrolls across your face . . . when you repeatedly check to make certain the letter from the

53

publicity agent is still there – the letter, I might add, which you read twice at the breakfast table . . . when you rap your fingertips on the steering wheel in anticipation and exhale small sighs . . . when you lean forward impatiently in your seat . . . the sum of a man's features and actions express his frame of mind," Holmes concluded. "You have burst out of your frame, Doctor." Such are the perils of having a detective for one's friend and colleague.

After fewer than ten minutes we alighted in Torrington Square, not far from the British Museum. To our surprise there were nearly fifty persons milling about, men and women of all ages and descriptions. A half-dozen newspapermen advanced upon us as we stepped to the pavement. They were brandishing sharp pencils and small notebooks, and some of them also had cameras and tripods. A few called out questions: *What did we think about our lives being the subject of a photoplay? Was it true that we'd attend the movie's premier? Would we have small roles in the film?*

Not one to conceal his annoyance, Holmes swatted at these queries as if they were insects. A short, barrel-chested young man, florid of face, with dark, curling hair and a ready smile, came to our rescue. "Mr. Holmes! Dr. Watson! Welcome to the set," he cried. "I'm Ridley, your escort for the morning."

"How do you do?" I enquired politely. "Is it always this hectic in the moving picture business?"

"Very much so," Ridley assured me. "It's one of the things I like about it. I'm new to motion pictures, you know," he added, as we walked along. "I've had this job for only a week, since the Goldwyn lads arrived in London. Before that I was one of two sorry underlings charged with preparing obituaries at *The Saturday Herald*, each of us hoping for a better opportunity. There was an opening for an entertainment reporter, and we both applied for it, but the position went to my colleague. I won the prize, though – with this job I'm paid much more and I arrange things so the newspapers have a grand story to tell. I don't mind saying that having both of you on the set with the actors who play you is a feather in my cap, wouldn't you agree?"

He didn't wait for an answer, but clapped his hands. "Hello, Ted! Happy to see you, Pat!" he called, jovially. "Photos can be made in a quarter-hour. We'll be with you shortly, Bruce!" Then we were ushered through the throng. "These are the extras," Ridley explained.

"Extra whats?" Holmes inquired after his bored fashion. He stopped to take a cigarette from his pocket case.

54

"Extra performers," Ridley explained. "They earn three shillings a day, plus lunch, in exchange for which they appear in crowd scenes. Some are students, some were soldiers in the late war, and a few are real policemen on their day off. Look around and you'll even see some 'authentic types' – men we found living rough in the East End. They make the movie more realistic."

Our new friend led us into a Georgian townhouse that was leased by Goldwyn for the week, he said – it was equal parts office, lounge, canteen, and dressing room for the actors. Between the excitement of our visit and the presence of newsmen, Ridley explained to us that the Goldwyn Company secretaries, cooks, and wardrobe assistants were already outside, waiting for the "show" to begin. We stood expectantly on the polished floorboards in a bright, airy entrance hall. "Jack! Rollie!" Ridley called. "Mr. Holmes and Dr. Watson have arrived."

Along a short passage a door flew open and a human tornado spun into view. "You have been on the South Downs, I perceive," this new man laughed, pumping my friend's arm up and down. His accent was distinctly American, but with the rounded vowels of someone trained to the stage. "I've wanted to say that to you for years, Mr. Holmes. I grew up reading about you, you know. What a treat it is to play you – and to finally meet you!"

I recognized him then: John Barrymore, scion of the famed family of actors. Known as "Jack" to his intimates, he was smiling up at Holmes. Despite being twenty feet high on the silver screen, in real life Barrymore was of middling stature. I gazed in admiration at his splendid nose, an attribute which prompted fans to call him *The Great Profile*. The most remarkable thing, however, was the pale yellow powder that was carefully applied to his face. I knew from reading Mrs. Hudson's battered copies of *Photoplay Magazine* that motion picture film caused one's facial contours to appear flat. To counter that, actors smeared sticks of grease paint on their faces, then applied yellow powder on top to achieve a visual lift. The fact of it being yellow mattered not at all since the movie was filmed in black and white.

Barrymore bowed like a dandy and asked in a deep, affected voice, "How do you do, Mr. Sherlock Holmes?"

Before my companion could answer, the actor excitedly turned to me. "You'll be Dr. Watson," he exclaimed, as if I were some exotic discovery. "Rollie is really eager to meet you. He's playing you, you know."

The well-known stage actor Roland Young materialized beside us. If Barrymore was high energy and laughter, Young was calm, quiet, and understated – just the sort of person I'd have chosen to depict my own self. Holmes is on the record elsewhere stating that he likes to meet Americans, [3] such as Barrymore, but I was drawn to Roland Young's obvious English sensibility, yellow powder and all. His erect carriage, twitching moustache, and broad forehead were very much like my appearance in years gone by. We exchanged pleasant greetings.

"Very sorry I wasn't here to meet you as you came in," Young told us. "Gussie has been showing me his latest acquisition." He turned and looked up toward the landing, where another gentleman was just rounding the post and descending to join us. This was a tall, handsome old man with an aristocratic bearing. Unlike our screen counterparts, his face was bare. In his hands was a long wooden box with a silver clasp.

Young did the honours. "Allow me to present our esteemed colleague, Herr Gustav von Seyffertitz, who plays Professor Moriarty in the film."

"Why, I know your name!" I exclaimed. "I read an article about you in *Cinema Monthly*. You come from Vienna, have appeared on stage throughout the Continent, and your specialism is portraying 'bad guys', as they say."

"Yes, it is so, Dr. Watson," he replied. "A pleasure to meet you and Mr. Holmes." His English was quite good, though I could hear a faint Germanic gurgle at the back of his throat. "I've been showing Rollie a vintage Klingenthaler." He held up the box. Ridley whistled in appreciation.

"Ah!" Sherlock Holmes was on the scent. "An Alsatian sword? In my college days I was a keen foil and sabre man. Watson here knows you from his fascination with the cinema, but I am aware, Herr von Seyffertitz, of your unequaled empty fade."

"Really, Holmes!" I admonished, but immediately I could see that, as has long been my habit, I'd failed to grasp something of significance.

"Mr. Holmes is correct," von Seyffertitz nodded. "In my youth I was Austrian Imperial fencing champion. The 'empty fade' was my best move. Nowadays I leave swordplay to young men and instead I collect historic arms – like this one, sent round by a Bayswater shop." He popped open the box to reveal a finely-wrought silver sword, nearly three feet in length.

"Such as would be carried by an officer of the French light cavalry a hundred years ago, if I'm not mistaken," Holmes said. "You will observe, Watson, that, unlike our English swords of the era, this has a brass hilt, the better to resist pitting. From the old charcoal forge at Klingenthal, you say?" There was no end to the trivia my friend carried around inside his brain-attic.

Von Seyffertitz beamed. "You can see the manufacturer's mark on the *ricasso*," he said, pointing to a spot near the base of the blade. "It is dated 1822, ninety-nine years ago. The following decade the Alsatian forges were considered vulnerable to German aggression, and so they were moved – "

" – to Châtellerault, near Poitiers," Holmes finished smoothly. "It's a splendid example of post-Napoleonic workmanship. My congratulations."

"She's a real beauty," Ridley said. "Would you mind . . . ?" He held his hands out, and von Seyffertitz invited him to remove the sword from its case. Ridley held it aloft, then lowered it to the counter-cut position. "Very nicely weighted," he murmured. "Maybe I'll have one like it, someday."

"You've handled a sword before," von Seyffertitz observed.

"My grandfather collected them," Ridley told us. "Unfortunately, there were debts to pay and he had to sell them – nearly seventy, all told."

"His loss was somebody's gain," von Seyffertitz said. "I, for example, am very glad to add this beauty to my own collection."

Ridley watched with something between envy and wistfulness as the sword was put away, the case being deposited on top of a mahogany *demilune* table placed along one wall. He then came to himself with a start and engaged in a show of diplomatic throat-clearing and wristwatch-checking. "I'm sorry to interrupt you, gentlemen, but it's nearly time for our Holmeses and Watsons to pose for photographs in the Square. We must give the press a good story."

"And I must visit my cosmetic box," von Seyffertitz explained with a wry shake of his head. "I'm to be shot – that is, *filmed* – within the hour, so I must hurry. Enjoy yourselves, gentlemen!" He turned to climb back up the stairs just as a striking woman of middle years with a scandalously short hemline, quick step, and perfectly Marcelled hair entered from the street. Her face was carefully coated in the now-familiar yellow powder. She smiled up at the departing Austrian, waved, and bobbed a little curtsy. "Good day to you,

Fräulein Hopper," von Seyffertitz nodded pleasantly to her, and continued to ascend.

"Dearest!" Barrymore cooed fondly. "Come and meet the *real* Sherlock Holmes and Dr. Watson. Gentlemen, this ravishing woman is my old friend, Hedda Hopper."

"*Old*, Jack?" She joined us and playfully tickled Barrymore's chin. "You have a couple of years on me, dearie."

"And you both have a couple of years on me!" Roland Young said with a chuckle.

"Pooh! Men look wonderful on the silver screen, no matter their age," Miss Hopper said, depositing a small cosmetic case under the *demilune* table. "You, Rollie, and Gussie are proof positive!" She sighed deeply. "I've just been applying my makeup outside. The sunlight is so bright, I don't need electric lights to get myself camera-ready. But you know," she added with a wag of her finger, "the brighter it is, the more obvious every single wrinkle becomes. It won't be long before I have to find another line of work." She turned to Holmes and me. "I'd shake your hands, but I'm afraid mine are covered with greasepaint and yellow powder at the moment," she said cheerfully. "Still, it's a pleasure to meet you both."

"Have you been an actress for very long, Miss Hopper?" I asked.

"Longer than I care to recall," she replied. "I'm just about ready to try my hand at something new."

"What do you suppose your next career will be?" I wondered aloud.

"I've been thinking that I'll go into publicity. With my knowledge of movies, and the people who make them – why I could steal Mr. Ridley's job right out from under him. Think of it: I could be paid just for nattering about movie stars!" She winked at our young escort, and he winked back.

This was news. Wait until I told Mrs. Hudson that Hedda Hopper wanted to be a professional gossip. [4]

"Which part do you play in the film, Miss Hopper?" Holmes asked her.

"I'm Madge Larrabee, the bad girl from the play that William Gillette wrote about you, Mr. Holmes. This movie is based on his script."

"Ah, yes. Larrabee," Holmes reflected for a moment. "It was I who suggested that name to Gillette. It came from a case Watson really ought to chronicle: The Parasol Poisoner. We were quite busy that year – 1889 – with the Forged Chinese Scrolls, and the Baltic

Bludgeoner, but the Parasol Poisoner was singular. Larrabee was the name of his second-to-last victim, you know."

"My goodness, Mr. Holmes," she remarked, "if we tried to make photoplays of more of your cases – like Ellie Norwood is doing at this very moment – we'd just drop dead from sheer exhaustion! [5] I don't know how you managed in real life. Now, you gentlemen must excuse me . . . I need to go scrub my hands and sort through some of my costumes." With a "Toodle-loo!" she departed along the passage to the rear of the house.

By now Ridley was tut-tutting, so we accompanied him outside – Holmes and John Barrymore close behind, followed by Roland Young. I was last out the door. The press had gathered in the middle of the square, and it was there that we assembled before them. Holmes and I were presented with gifts from Goldwyn Pictures – a handsome briar for my friend, and a fine fountain pen for me. Rather than hold these presents as the official photos were made, Ridley collected them from us to run across to the townhouse for safekeeping. As the publicist stepped to the back of the crowd, Barrymore gamboled this way and that for the benefit of the cameras. All eyes were on him.

He was, I suppose, what one might call a "ham". He told an amusing story, warbled a couple of colourful lines from a music hall song, and, of all things, he managed a few kicks of a can-can dance! It was his practice to offer onlookers the left side of his face. "My only good angle," he jested. In our long association Holmes and I have met some memorable persons, but surely none as amusing as John Barrymore. I noted a possible source of his relentless good cheer. He discreetly took a nip from a palm-sized flask drawn from his pocket. [6]

At the behest of one of the reporters, our two Holmeses posed in the centre, bookended by their two Watsons. For a moment all was quiet save the sound of the shutter mechanisms of their cameras. When they were finished, Barrymore invited the press to ask a few questions. Hedges of *The Times* wanted to know if it was true that the opening scene would be shot from a bi-plane flying high over London. (It would.) Gibbs of *The Despatch* asked how true crimes differed from those projected onto a movie screen. (In real life the blood wasn't faked.) Gaines from *The Evening Review* enquired whether Holmes and I would accompany the movie's cast and crew back to America to wrap up "shooting". (Holmes allowed the only "shooting" he'd done recently was to add a "*G.R.*" in bullet holes to his library wall.) [7] Monahan of *The Herald* took a last informal photo as we stood chatting with the actors, his hand-held trough emitting a blinding flash. A metallic tang hung in the air for a moment, and then the gentlemen of the press began to pack up their equipment. Our part in this show was over. Even the "extras" started to wander off.

Suddenly, everything came to a stop.

A wild, unnatural scream rose from the open door of the film company's townhouse, until it seemed to hover in the air over our heads. I was dumbstruck with horror. As the shrieks continued, the stars, the "extra" crowd, and the newspapermen stood rooted in shock and confusion. Only Sherlock Holmes, a man approaching seventy years of age, was all action. He strode stiffly across the narrow lane and toward the door to the house. "Come, Watson!" he barked over his shoulder. It was the summons I'd heard many times in our years together. I eagerly trailed after him. As I did so I was vaguely conscious of Roland Young and John Barrymore following behind me in my wake.

We hurried into the house to find Holmes standing beside the motionless figure of a man. He lay pinned to the oak floor of the entryway like a specimen, the Klingenthal sword protruding from his chest! A small circle of blood darkened the front of his shirt where the sword had entered. Holmes smoothly extracted a magnifying lens from his coat and began to examine the sword's hilt and blade. Miss Hopper – who was the source of the terrible shrieks – stood screeching and sobbing at the rear of the entry hall.

"Oh, be still, Hedda!" Barrymore scolded. "Get hold of yourself."

If his admonishment was harsh, it was also effective. She muffled her screams with her hands. Above them her dark eyes began to roll up and I feared she would faint, but Roland Young dashed to her side to support her. She buried her face in his shoulder, smearing greasepaint and yellow powder onto his jacket. Just coming into sight on the staircase was Herr von Seyffertitz, a towel tucked into his collar and yellow powder half-applied to his greasy face. He stopped halfway down the stairs. A look of horror rippled across his countenance as he absorbed the scene below.

My gaze returned to the dead man, and I saw to my amazement that it was Bert Ridley, Goldwyn's publicity agent!

"Watson," Holmes said, with quiet urgency. "Kindly step out and ask that fellow Monahan to bring me his camera – it was a Graflex, if I'm not mistaken."

"Of course."

"And Watson . . . I saw Constable Lestrade in the street. Send him to me at once."

My friend was growing old, but until now I hadn't suspected that he was also becoming feeble-minded. "But Holmes," I began in a soothing tone, "*Inspector* Lestrade retired a dozen years ago . . . ."

Holmes viewed me over his shoulder, spurring me into action with one of the cold, commanding looks of which he was renowned. I stumbled to the door. Standing nearby, wearing the uniform of a London Bobby, was a young, ferret-faced man with a familiar look about him. "I say, you wouldn't happen to be Lestrade?" I enquired breathlessly.

"Yes," he replied. "Constable I. Lestrade, at your service."

"*I?*"

"My grandfather is Superintendent *G.* Lestrade, now retired," he explained. "My dad, *H.* Lestrade, works as a detective from at Scotland Yard. *G.* and *H.* for *Gerard* and *Harry.* My name is *Ivor,* but everyone calls me '*I*.' May I help?"

I hesitated. "Forgive my asking, but is that a movie costume, or are you a real policeman?"

"I'm real enough every evening, walking my patch in Finchley Precinct," he explained, pulling his shoulders back and standing smartly at attention. "My wife is going to have a baby any day now, so I'm earning spare money this morning working as a film extra."

"You're wanted immediately, by Mr. Sherlock Holmes," I told him and pointed to the open doorway. The reporter with the camera was easy enough to round up, though there was some jealous grumbling from his colleagues. It seems they smelled a story. Word of Ridley's demise was already sweeping through the Square.

Inside, Holmes had taken charge. Constable Lestrade was busy scouring the garden at the rear, searching for Ridley's killer. When he re-joined us, panting, he reported that the garden was surrounded by a high brick wall. There were no trees or ladders that could have helped the killer to go up and over. The back gate was securely chained in place, seemingly against film enthusiasts who might intrude on the actors.

Holmes next bade Lestrade to scurry upstairs, to see whether anyone was concealed in wardrobes or under chairs. A moment later the constable reported that, save for those of us in the entry area, the house was quiet, secure, and empty. Holmes nodded a distracted sort of thanks and stationed Lestrade at the foot of the staircase where Miss Hopper now sat on the bottom step, von Seyffertitz beside her. Monahan was told to remain at hand. Photographs would be needed

61

of the sword, the table with the still-open sword box, and other evidence. "So that there's an accurate record of the scene before the official force arrives and makes of it their usual muddle," my friend explained. "We'll send for the rest of the police shortly. Friend Ridley is in no hurry."

Then he turned to me. If his face was weathered, age had not touched Holmes's piercing gray eyes. "What's your opinion, Doctor?" he asked.

Like Holmes, I was older. Unlike him, I was somewhat flustered by the savage turn this day had taken. "It was not suicide," I pronounced solemnly. Only when I saw Holmes's disdainful look did I realize how foolish I must sound. "It also was not a mishap," I continued, gathering my dignity about me. "We saw the sword safely back into its box, so he did not trip and fall upon it."

"Very good, Watson," Holmes said, with a touch of asperity. "You have ruled out two completely useless lines of inquiry. How about you, Lestrade? Can you deduce anything useful?" But the lad merely stood gaping.

Holmes pointed with his magnifying glass. "The bloodstain isn't very large, which suggests that the sword-thrust was the cause of death. It killed him quickly – from all appearances it went straight to the heart. Had he lingered, the bloodstain would be bigger, and had it been inserted *post mortem*, the stain would be uninteresting."

Using his stick as a sturdy assistant, my friend lowered himself beside the body Holmes gently lifted Ridley's head, running his fingers through dead man's hair. He examined each of the publicist's hands with his lens, intently studying the palms and fingers. He looked at the soles and toes of Ridley's shoes, and then stood. Once upright, Holmes leaned in to sniff the hilt of the sword.

"There is no indication that he was hit over the head – no bump or fracture of the skull that I could feel," Holmes told us. "There is no telltale smear of blood, nor are his shoes scuffed, so he wasn't dragged here. This is the spot where he met his end. You will observe greasepaint and yellow powder on the hilt of the sword. Greasepaint has a distinctive, waxy odour." Here, Barrymore leaned over for a closer look, and to smell the handle of the sword, nodding in the affirmative. "There are traces of greasepaint and yellow powder on Ridley's hands, as well," my friend added.

We looked across at Barrymore and Young, with their yellowed visages, and then to the two yellow-faced players seated upon the staircase. A reluctant idea was forming in my brain: *One of the actors has done this dreadful thing!* I was not the only one who'd come to that conclusion. Miss Hopper twisted away and raised her expressive eyes to Gustav von Seyffertitz. "Gussie!" she exclaimed in a breathy voice. "You have greasepaint and yellow powder all over your hands. Did you kill Bert?"

"*Mein Gott*, never!" he exclaimed, bristling. "My hands are covered with the stuff because I was applying my make-up. Your screams interrupted me." He pointed at her hands. "Yours are stained with yellow cosmetics, too. Are you the killer?" At this Miss Hopper burst into noisy sobs once more.

"Hedda, your hands were greased and yellowed when you came into the house," Roland Young reminded us. "You went to wash them before handling your costumes. But your hands are still dirty."

"I *did* wash them!" she gasped, and stared at her hands. She cast a pleading look at each of us, and wailed, "I don't know how I got greasepaint and powder on them again!"

"Elementary," Holmes calmly told her. "When Mr. Barrymore rather forcefully directed you to 'Be still,' you clapped your hands over your made-up face. Touching your face got your hands dirty again."

"Then I'm in the clear?" she asked. I was compelled to suppress a smile – her use of faddish American gangster argot seemed oddly misplaced in the presence of a proper London murder.

"I didn't say that," Holmes replied smoothly. "There's the matter of your wanting to take Ridley's job away from him, to practice his line of work yourself," my friend continued. "The position is now open."

"I was *joking*," she insisted. "I wouldn't harm Bert, or anybody else."

"In any case, I question whether you, Miss Hopper, have the strength to thrust a sword through a body, and on into the floorboards." Holmes remarked. "That requires strength and skill." Holmes lifted one eyebrow and turned his gaze to Herr von Seyffertitz.

The Austrian was indignant. "I was upstairs with my cosmetics," he protested.

"Young Ridley was quite taken with your Klingenthal," Holmes commented. "He brought in Watson's pen and my pipe and placed them, as you see, on the table beside your sword case. The case is now open. I expect Ridley did that. Did he help himself to your sword and you surprised him?"

"I've no way to know what Herr Ridley did, or didn't, do," the Austrian actor exclaimed with offended tones. "I was upstairs from the moment I took leave of you, until Fräulein Hopper began to shriek."

All was quiet for a moment and then Holmes forcefully bounced his stick on the floor and caught it in mid-air. "You will both remain where you are in Constable Lestrade's care and keeping," he told them. "As for John Barrymore and Roland Young, you may be ruled out as suspects. After all, you have the perfect alibi, having been with Watson and me when Ridley came inside. However, Herr von Seyffertitz and Miss Hopper were in the house when his murder occurred. The handle of the murder weapon is smeared with greasepaint and yellow powder. Both of you have been in contact with greasepaint and yellow powder.

"Ridley's hands," he continued, "reveal traces of greasepaint and yellow powder, too, as though he attempted to fend off his killer." Having been at Holmes's side for many years, I heard the slight question in his voice. Did he doubt the substance on Ridley's hands was transferred there as the result of trying to defend himself? Had his killer overdone the evidence left at the location of the crime? I recalled another case, many years earlier, in which the culprit was identified because, as my friend observed at the time, "*he had not that supreme gift of the artist, the knowledge of when to stop.*" [8] Holmes waved to the photographer to step forward with his camera. "If you would be so kind, Mr. Monahan, I require a photo of Ridley's body."

The photographer quickly set up a tripod. He mounted the camera atop it, inserted the film holder, cocked the focal plane and focused. He pulled a small lever. The mechanism whirred and clicked sharply, and then he removed the plate. Holmes next directed him to make photos of the demilune table, along with the hands of Gustav von Seyffertitz and Hedda Hopper. "Thank you, that's enough," my friend announced. "Watson will telephone the police."

"You're turning the investigation over to them?" Roland Young asked.

"No, I'm turning my prisoner over to them."

"Holmes!" I ejaculated. "You've identified a suspect?"

"I've identified the murderer," he simply said, handing me my pen from Goldwyn Pictures, while slipping his new pipe into his pocket. "No sense leaving these behind, Watson – they're not evidence. Anyhow, they're rather nice."

"Who did it, Mr. Holmes?" John Barrymore wanted to know. "Who killed Bert Ridley?"

64

Holmes smiled tightly. "There was a Roman whose name escapes me now – forgetfulness being an unfortunate corollary to growing old. In any case, the Roman said that a guilty person often becomes his own hangman. [9] And it is true – the guilty *do* often hang themselves – by clumsy actions during and after the crime," my friend explained "Such is the case here. Lestrade, you will place your darbies on Mr. Monahan."

A gasp went around the entry hall as Lestrade hopped up to the photographer and secured the handcuffs on his wrists. "Monahan?" I said, incredulously. "But Holmes, he was with us, outside."

"Indeed he was," Holmes replied. "Monahan was with the other reporters and photographers when Ridley escorted us to the centre of the square. When Ridley left to take our gifts inside, we all were distracted by John Barrymore – he is very amusing and we enjoyed his jokes and songs. Monahan took advantage of Mr. Barrymore having diverted our attention. He was able to follow Ridley unnoticed."

Lestrade's mouth rearranged into a round *O*. "Blimey!" he exclaimed. "That's where I've seen him. He walked past me, in and then out of the house. I never – "

Holmes crossed his arms and shook his head impatiently. "No, you never. It's why I called you in here, Lestrade. You are witless, but nonetheless a witness. Your colleagues will need to take your statement. I expect when they dust for fingerprints they will find that Ridley, after he placed the pipe and pen on the table, reached for the sword case. By his own admission he was intrigued by the Klingenthaler. It is probable he lifted it out of its case. Perhaps he held it aloft again. And then you, Monahan, tip-toed up behind him. You knocked the publicist to the floor and thrust the Klingenthaler into him. You spotted Miss Hopper's cosmetic box there under the table. I venture to say there's a handkerchief in your box, Miss Hopper?"

She nodded vigourously.

"You likely used that, Mr. Monahan, to wipe your fingerprints from the sword. Then you smeared greasepaint and powder you found in her cosmetic box onto the hilt, and also onto Ridley's hands. Your purpose was to implicate one of the actors – never mind which one – to ensure that you would not be suspected yourself. As you went about planting evidence on his corpse, you didn't consider that Ridley was a short man – his arms weren't long enough to reach the hilt where his killer's yellow hands rested. It was impossible for him to have a defensive transfer of the cosmetics to his own hands.

65

Happily, as a result of your mistake I have discerned a fingerprint left in the grease on one of Ridley's palms. That would be *your* fingerprint, Mr. Monahan, would it not? After you killed him and left misleading evidence on his body, you thrust the makeup box back under the table and hurried out past Lestrade, to rejoin the other reporters.

"But now the telltale yellow makeup was on your own hands . . . how to dispose of that inconvenient evidence? If you'd wiped your hands on your trousers, for example, the yellow mixture would remain there for everyone to see. Just look at Roland Young's jacket. Hedda Hopper's cosmetics stained it when she placed her head against his shoulder. But you had a brainstorm. You plunged your hands into your camera bag, into the pouch of magnesium powder and potassium chlorate that photographers carry with them. Those are the gray particles used to create a brilliant flash of light for the benefit of a camera. Those gray particles served to obscure the yellow smears on your hands. In fact, your hands remain gray. When they examine you, the police will find greasepaint and yellow powder under the gray. For your part, you hurriedly sprinkled more of the chemicals into your powder trough and took the final photo of the morning – remember that blinding flash, Watson?"

"I do, indeed" I replied. "And on a morning so bright and sunny that Miss Hopper chose to apply her make up outside. None of the other photographers needed to use flash powder. The day is so bright that he didn't even use a flash to illuminate the photos that he just made, here in the entry hall."

"Quite so," Holmes agreed. "But creating that flash in the square was necessary to explain why his hands were suddenly caked with gray," Holmes continued. "It also served to cement his presence there, and not in the house where Ridley was killed.

"Ridley told us there was another junior employee of his former employer, *The Saturday Herald*, who applied for and got the position of entertainment reporter," Holmes continued, turning to Monahan once more. "You are the man named 'Pat' whom he greeted before we came inside to meet the actors. Ridley identified his future killer by waving at you and calling out your name – you knew each other because you'd worked together. You received the coveted position at the newspaper, but he won the bigger prize, coming to work here. Doing away with Ridley eliminated a more successful rival, but most importantly it assured assured you a spectacular story with which to begin your new career: A murder on the set while Sherlock Holmes was present. Well, Mr. Monahan, you'll find that in England we give

66

accused persons plenty of column inches in the newspapers. Then the courts pronounce their judgment."

"You miserable old man!" Monahan sputtered. "This was to be the story that marked me for greatness, a murder under the very noses of not one, but *two* Sherlock Holmes-es! And to see the last of Ridley – him with nothing but scrambled eggs betwixt his ears, and so full of himself for getting this high-paid job." He quieted only after Constable Lestrade thumped him on the side of his head.

Holmes leaned back against the wall. I thought he might be tired, but he drew on deep reserves of energy. "Ambition and jealousy, the twin roots of so many towering trees in the forest of crime." Holmes looked around at everyone. "He's freely admitted his guilt. This case draws to a close."

I telephoned Scotland Yard, and within moments, sirens whining, a couple of their automobiles pulled to the kerb outside. An inspector and several uniformed officers rushed in. "Hello there, Parker," Holmes greeted the inspector. "I'm afraid you are two minutes too late to make a pounce yourself. With all the cunning and sagacity of his illustrious forebears, Constable Lestrade has just taken your suspect into custody."

"Marvelous!" John Barrymore exclaimed, clapping his hands. "You have an actor's sense of timing, Mr. Holmes."

Monahan was taken away in the paddy wagon. [10] The police surgeon collected poor Ridley shortly after. We said our goodbyes, wishing John Barrymore, Roland Young, and the others a very successful production.

I have to confess that all that I could think of was telling Mrs. Hudson about this day's adventure! I turned to lead the way back to my motor car. To my surprise Sherlock Holmes stopped on the pavement and lifted the silver head of his cane to salute the driver of a cab just rounding Torrington Square – one of the few remaining hansoms in London. [11] It clip-clopped up to us and stopped. Holding the reins was a smart-looking fellow, considerably more respectable in appearance than the first time ever I clapped eyes on him at the beginning of our acquaintance. [12] He tipped his hat to Holmes and climbed down from his perch to help my friend settle into the leather seat beneath.

"Ah! Wiggins, you're just in time," my friend sighed. "This old detective wants only to sit and watch London go by at a draught-horse's pace. Be home in time for supper, eh Watson?"

Just after the New Year I was visiting Holmes at his cottage. Tully, of the Fulworth Post Office, left a package at the front door. Holmes tore off the wrapping to reveal none other than Gustav von Seyffertitz's Klingenthal sword! "Hmm!" he remarked thoughtfully. "There's a letter." He unfolded a sheet of paper and quickly scanned it. "It's from Lestrade," he told me.

Dear Mr. Holmes,

The court, having found Monahan guilty, has sentenced him to hang. It was just like your Roman friend predicted! We tried to return this evidence to Herr von Seyffertitz, but he declined. Instead, he suggested that the sword might find a good home with you. The movie people departed for America this morning to finish "interiors" in their New York studio.

Constable I. Lestrade

"I really must call on him when I return to town," I commented. "What do you say, Holmes, to my bringing him something for the new baby? I wonder if Mrs. Lestrade had a boy or a girl?"

"Didn't I tell you?" Holmes asked, lifting the sword. "It is a boy. They call him *J.* Lestrade."

"*G.*, *H.*, *I.* – and now *J.*?"

"Yes, they named the baby after you, Doctor. The little fellow's full name is 'John Sherlock Lestrade'," Holmes said, and we shared a great-grandfatherly sort of smile.

NOTES

1. Readers may remember Dr. Watson's Ford from the Canonical story, "His Last Bow", which took place in 1914 on the eve of World War I.

2. Goldwyn's silent film, *Sherlock Holmes*, was released in the spring of 1922.

3. Holmes expressed his "joy" at meeting Americans in the Canonical tale, "The Adventure of the Noble Bachelor".

4. Hedda Hopper left acting and became a famous Hollywood gossip columnist in the 1930's.

5. English actor Eille Norwood appeared in a total of forty-seven silent films based on the Sherlockian Canon.

6. John Barrymore eventually died from complications of chronic alcoholism.

7. In the short story, "The Musgrave Ritual", it's mentioned that Sherlock Holmes once famously shot a "*V.R.*" into the wall of his sitting room at 221b Baker Street, a tribute to "*Victoria Regina*", Queen of England. The "*G.R.*" here would be for "*George Rex*", or King George V, who ruled England when this story takes place.

8. Watson's reference is to Jonas Oldacre, in the tale called "The Adventure of the Norwood Builder".

9. Holmes is quoting the Roman statesman and dramatist, Seneca the Younger (4 B.C. – 65 A.D.), who observed that "*Every guilty person is his own hangman.*"

10. Paddy wagons were so named because many criminal suspects, including reporter Pat Monahan, happened to be of Irish ancestry.

11. Hansom cabs finally disappeared from service after World War II.

12. At the time of *A Study in Scarlet*, Wiggins cut a grimy and "insignificant" figure, though he was spokesman and leader of the little Baker Street Irregulars.

The Lonely Cavalier
by Tim Gambrell

Part I

Birling Gap, South Downs, Sussex
Monday, 10th April, 1922

My Dear Watson,

I have been endeavouring to write to you for some weeks now. The approach of the Easter weekend has spurred me, finally, to put pen to paper. Alas, my days are easily distracted in the spring, but I can advise you now as to the results of my recent investigations: The hives are all in good order and the colonies have, once again, weathered the winter months well. I look forward to a fine harvest this year, as does the Reverend Silsby, who sends salutations of goodwill to my door, almost weekly. His messages are laced with *essence of hope* that I will make provision, once again, of my wares for the church fête later in the year.

I can only conclude that the keeping of bees and the producing of honey are just as much an exacting science as the recognition of tobacco ash, the colour separation of inks and dyes and, as a whole, the solving of pernicious crimes. I seem to have excelled on all counts thus far. I have, on a number of occasions, apprised you of the fact that my honey is much sought after in the local area – so much so that there are times when I'm convinced that my quest for solitude was easier on the first floor of Baker Street than it is here, on my secluded farm. But before you chastise me for being churlish, I know, deep down, the nonsense of such imaginings, for the callers are few. And the background hustle and bustle of London is nowhere to be heard. Not even Eastbourne on market day makes an audible impression out here.

I continue to be charmed by all that nature has to offer, and the challenges she sends my way: Tending to my land, my crops in all weathers. Minding the bees and observing their ranked community. Their single-minded efficiency is simply breath-taking. If only human beings operated that way. So much could be achieved for the greater good of all men, instead of the selfish bickering and warmongering which has brought continual pain and suffering to people's lives. Perhaps, one day, some great political philosopher will take the lead from the bee, or the ant, and show us a better way. Perhaps. We shall see.

I ponder on such things, you see, Watson. And more besides. There has been much to ponder on in the world of late, I must say. Although I came here to retire from society, it is difficult not to keep half an eye on what is going on in the world. One of the village boys delivers me *The Times*, for a small weekly consideration. I have found myself much moved by the situation in Ireland and, alas, I do not believe that the way forward will be a smooth path. The same, I fear, for King Fuad and Egyptian independence, but we shall see. The world has changed considerably over the past ten years and will, no doubt, continue to do so for as long as we yet may live.

I suspect your attention has been focussed very much on the cost of the flu epidemic. We've been spared the worst of it in our distanced rural communities down here, but no doubt the situation in the London slums has been appalling, and more so in the crowded Northern manufacturing communities. I was going to write to you back in January and ask how you fared. I read at that time of Banting's treatment of diabetes in Canada. It certainly gives one hope of progress in other areas of medicine, I must say. I always think of you when I see such items of news reported.

Do tell me how life is for you in London, Watson. We must arrange a time when you can visit again. Come and clear your lungs on the South Downs! Do you still own that motor car?

With fondest wishes, as always,
Holmes

* * * * *

Birling Gap, South Downs, Sussex
Wednesday, 12th April, 1922

My Dear Watson,

Whilst I was naturally pleased to receive your swift reply and learn that you weathered the winter months without any ill effects, I'm a little frustrated at the need to remind you, yet again, that I do not wish to have a telephone re-installed. I'm well aware that it makes distant correspondence that much quicker and easier, but I retired here to the South Downs to escape from such intrusions. I see little point in seeking peace and solitude if the telephone can disturb me at all hours. I have never been one for small talk. What need have I for casual acquaintances? More likely I would receive further pleas from Scotland Yard for me to step out of retirement and provide them with assistance. You, my friend, are a different matter. Hence, with few exceptions, you are the only correspondent I maintain in my retirement.

And after several months of silence before this week, you may also wonder at me writing to you again immediately upon receipt of your reply. If you were a superstitious man, or possibly a betting man – it could be argued they are often one and the same – you may, perhaps, be alarmed by what I allude to in this brief missive. One thing is for sure: There's no denying the coincidence of us reengaging in regular correspondence only to find that a case – the death of a local resident, no less – comes knocking at my door to intrude upon us, and upon my retirement. I will feel something of my old assurance knowing that, although you are not at my side, I am at least keeping you abreast of developments – which I will do in due course. But for now, I can send only this and the promise that should your services be required in person, my message would arrive with you with all haste.

Holmes

* * * * *

Birling Gap, South Downs, Sussex.
Wednesday, 12th April, 1922

My Dear Watson,

I trust my brief earlier letter hasn't alarmed you. The hour is now much later, but the day is the same, and if I'm not unfortunate, this should follow hot on the former's footsteps and ease you of any concern.

I will start at the beginning, in the way that you always preferred to tell our tales. One of the village boys, Tom Markham – the same, in fact who brings me my *Times* – arrived at my door just as I was finishing a light lunch today, with which I accompanied reading your reply. Young Tom informed me, much to my surprise, that there was "summat up with old Miss Gladwish". Constable

Anderson had sent him off to seek my assistance. I'm imagining the smile which will be curling your lips as you read this. And well you might smile, for I have never managed to fully escape the minor celebrity status that your publishing of certain of my cases has brought to my name. Constable Anderson is the local policeman for East Dean and Friston, and is a perfectly capable chap for the sort of challenges rustic village life usually presents. For him to request my assistance, therefore, I was certain he had to be somewhat out of his depth.

I hastened along with the lad. Florence Gladwish was a local spinster. She lived in one of the more well-to-do cottages in East Dean, having been the daughter of a gentleman of some repute in the area. I found the front door ajar and the constable waiting in the hallway. As he beckoned me inside, I sent Tom on his way, with a shilling for his expediency.

The cottage was stuffy and poorly lit, crammed with knick-knacks and bric-a-brac in the old cluttered Victorian style. No doubt every item will have held fond memories for the lady. She was in the sitting room, slumped forward in an equally Victorian over-stuffed armchair. The village doctor, Brownlow, was in attendance, undertaking some no-doubt cursory checks on the deceased. The constable cleared his throat and looked at me apologetically. He informed me that my journey had probably been a wasted one. He liked to get a second opinion in matters of death, and between sending Tom off to summon me and our arriving, Doctor Brownlow had appeared, having been alerted by the Reverend Silsby. It was the good reverend, it seems, who first discovered the lady. Normally, the reverend would be the constable's second opinion, but the shock of finding Miss Gladwish had been too much for him and he'd had to return home.

I stemmed the flow of words as quickly as I could, for fear the constable would continue until I knew the situation of everyone whom he had encountered that day. You will, perhaps, accuse me of being my own worst enemy in such circumstances, but I will admit to being curious and wishing, at least, to examine the scene of death while I was there. There is no harm in testing out one's former skills during retirement.

Heart failure was the doctor's prognosis. She'd died only that morning. Brownlow looked up from rummaging in his bag as I entered the sitting room. His expression suggested I was a novelty guest who merely required humouring. What I wouldn't have given, at that moment, for it to have been Sherlock Holmes and Doctor

Watson, rather than Sherlock Holmes and Doctor Brownlow. The deceased was seated as if she'd been comfortably reading. There was a rather bulky typed document in her lap, and this caught my attention first. It was bound together by string. The top sheet was yellowed through age and bore the legend *The Lonely Cavalier*, a novel, by Florence Gladwish. The latter had been added by hand. Clearly this was a manuscript of sorts. Neither the constable nor the doctor had paid it any heed. Neither were they aware of the deceased harbouring any literary aspirations.

Miss Gladwish was clutching the document oddly. I took the opposing end in my own hands for comparison. The doctor confirmed that Miss Gladwish did not suffer from any joint disorder or arthritic condition, but it was clear that the document did not sit comfortably in the lady's hands. Alas, this was not considered a matter of importance to either of my companions. whereas I felt it was very telling. I suspected that the document had been placed in the deceased's grasp *after* she had died – in which case, if she had died of natural causes, she had been interfered with. And if she hadn't died of natural causes . . . I knew at this point that the death of this poor lady was not going to be a circumstance from which I could walk away. My bees would have to wait.

Brownlow seemed to take exception to me focussing on accessory details, rather than the lady herself. He pushed her back from her slumped position so we could all see her face. She appeared to be around fifty years old, even allowing for her blue-tinged lips and anguished, staring eyes. I had seen similar death masks often enough. The constable commented that she looked like she'd seen a ghost. It seems that was what had discomfited the reverend so much when he'd discovered her. I didn't linger on such thoughts, but merely lowered her eyelids.

There was a faint aroma of menthol in the room. Some judicious sniffing on my part revealed it to emanate from the deceased's face – specifically the mouth and nose. Brownlow advised me that Miss Gladwish had used mentholated ointment at night, to try to ease perpetually blocked sinuses. I asked if it was applied directly to the upper lip and nostril region, and he stated it was recommended for a few drops to be applied to the underside of the pillow before bedtime, so that it could evaporate and be inhaled during the hours of sleep, but he couldn't say for sure if Miss Gladwish chose a different method of application. I held my counsel on this for the time being, but I was certain the aroma would have been much stronger if the deceased had habitually applied the ointment directly to her face, even if the application had been several hours earlier.

Brownlow huffed a little and checked his fob watch. It was clear this was taking longer than he'd anticipated and, indeed, he advised that he was overdue for an appointment elsewhere. I told him I was not yet convinced that this was death by natural causes, and I would consult him further once I had completed my investigations. He seemed to believe I was being rather fanciful and left the constable and me to it. I immediately checked the front and back doors and found no signs of forced entry. Assuming that Miss Gladwish had been murdered, it must have been someone whom she knew, or at least had willingly permitted entry to, since she was seated in her comfortable chair when the death eventually happened.

Next, the constable and I ventured upstairs and examined Miss Gladwish's bedchamber. The bed looked tidy and well-made. The cottage may have been full of clutter, but Miss Gladwish was a lady of neat and precise habits – so much so that when I noticed that the edge of the counterpane had been left folded back by less than half-an-inch at the head end, I instinctively knew this would not have been how she'd left it. The underside of the comfy top pillow, and the top of the thinner, firmer lower pillow, showed clearly where the drops of oil had been applied each night. The fragrance was very strong. Even regular laundering of the pillowcases couldn't fully remove the residue or prevent the scent from infusing the down stuffing over the months or even years of use.

I was now certain that Miss Gladwish had been murdered, downstairs where she still sat. She had been suffocated using the top pillow from her bed, which had then been replaced and everything left, seemingly, as found. Her unpublished manuscript had been placed in her hands on the way out, as a kind of touching afterthought. I took the constable through my reasoning, watching his face turn paler with each logical step. I could see that he'd never had to deal with anything like this before.

It was clear that we couldn't leave the deceased as she was indefinitely. We needed to get her interred. But we also needed to be sure we'd captured all the available evidence, first. Before we could agree on the next steps to take, we were alerted by a hollering from downstairs. Young Tom Markham was back. He'd been sent to find the constable because a lady from Friston had apparently gone over to Beachy Head on a bicycle. I flicked the lad another shilling and told him to send word that the constable and I would be along in due course. Then I escorted the poor, blanched policeman to the Tiger Inn and plied him with some Dutch courage.

I am sitting in the Tiger Inn now, quickly scribbling this rambling reply to you, in the hope that I can catch the last post. I will update you further as soon as I can. I fear great wickedness is afoot in sleepy Sussex, and if these two deaths are not connected in some way then I am not your ever-faithful friend,

Sherlock Holmes

P.S. Maundy Thursday, April 13th

I missed the last post yesterday. By the time we arrived at Beachy Head a most foul storm had hit us, and the tide was almost full with it. It was deemed too dangerous for us to investigate. The lady's name was Prudence Duley and she had not been seen since early that morning. I have pondered much on the matter overnight, and Constable Anderson and I are returning to the scene this morning. The sky is clear and the weather clement. I only hope the actions of the high tides haven't deprived us of our evidence.

* * * * *

Birling Gap, South Downs, Sussex
Good Friday, 14th April, 1922

My Dear Watson,

You won't now receive this until after Easter, there being no form of postal service here on Good Friday, but I needed to put pen to paper while everything remained fresh in my mind. Last night, I was too fatigued. Two days of the sort of activity to which I have been unaccustomed for several years now took their full toll on me. Instead, I have set aside this morning to write to you. Tomorrow, my world returns to solitude and bees, and I shall no doubt wipe much of this mournful case from my memory.

I had just left the house yesterday morning, Thursday, to meet up with Constable Anderson via the village post office – I still had to send you my amended letter from the previous day. Beachy Head Road in front of my cottage had not benefitted from the previous evening's heavy storms. At the lowest point, by the gate – you know the place I mean – I was surprised to find a police car blocking the way. As I approached, the reason became more clear – it was mired just inside the gate. Constable Anderson was attempting to push the vehicle back onto the lane while the driver did his best inside. The wheels simply span in the mud, defeating them both and caking the poor constable.

I offered to lend a hand, since they were in my way. With the three of us pushing and no one turning the engine, we quickly succeeded. Once back on the road, the driver introduced himself as Sergeant Butchers, from Eastbourne. It seemed the constable had reported matters up the line the previous evening. The station at Eastbourne had felt it best to provide some additional manpower to assist our efforts – as well as a motorboat to transport us to the base of Beachy Head. This was by far an easier route than any the constable and I could have managed ourselves on foot.

Having been delayed by the mud, the sergeant was eager for us to make all haste and catch the low tide. I had to prevail upon him to first take me the short distance to the village so I could at least post my letter to you first. This also allowed the constable to return home for his spare uniform trousers. Thereafter, it should have been a short drive back to Birling Gap, where we were to meet the boat, but the road was cluttered with sheep, which added to the sergeant's frustrations. It was clear, too, that poor Constable Anderson preferred his bicycle, or a sedate horse and cart to a motor car journey. His nausea was very evident when we arrived at the launch. Unfortunately for him, he was no better a sailor than a motor car passenger, and spent most of the short trip around the cliffs with his head over the side, much to the amusement of Butchers and his two constables, who were waiting for us with the small six-man boat.

Prudence Duley was the deceased lady's name – recently widowed wife of Archibald and a resident of our sister village of Friston. Archibald had died suddenly of heart failure two weeks previous. Prudence had last been seen alive, as far as anyone knew, by the Reverend Silsby at about ten o'clock, on the morning of the previous day, Wednesday, as she rode her bicycle from Friston, through East Dean and towards Birling Gap. The parish church and the vicarage are both on the road which connects the two small villages.

As we came ashore, I was relieved to find that the sea had left Mrs. Duley and her bicycle largely untouched. There was a patch of discoloured sand beneath the body where the high tides and storm hadn't managed to wash all the blood away. A few fronds of seaweed had caught on the back wheel and spokes of the bicycle, as a marker of how near the sea had reached.

It was impossible to tell for certain, but I was convinced that the fall had killed the lady and we weren't dealing with a cover-up for a murder. The body and the bicycle were a twisted, mangled mess, but her hands remained firmly gripped around the handlebars. Prudence Duley had been determined in her endeavours. I informed the sergeant that she had taken her own life. My reasoning was that if she had been pushed or tumbled over the edge by some accident or other, it seemed logical to me that she would have thrown her hands up in alarm. Not so, here. Even the impact and instantaneous death hadn't made her release the handlebars and now *rigor mortis* saw them permanently wedded. (*Rigor mortis* often sets in hours after death, but as you will recall, in certain cases of traumatic death it can be immediate.) I was reminded of Miss Gladwish the previous day, and the unnatural way she had been clasping at her manuscript. It was enough to make me take a second look here, but no – the curve of the fingers and the placement of the knuckles were beyond suspicion.

Having examined the scene as thoroughly as I could, I allowed the constables to separate the corpse from the bicycle. Constable Anderson obtained some justice here. His constitution was firmer when dealing with dead bodies than the Eastbourne constables. Either that or, having already emptied his guts, he was better able to cope than they. With Mrs. Duley's remains removed, I checked for any obvious signs of the bicycle having been tampered with – snipped brake cables, sheered bolts, and suchlike. As with the remains of Mrs. Duley herself, I was never going to be absolutely certain, but I was reasonably confident that there was nothing essentially wrong with the bicycle that couldn't simply be attributed to it having plummeted down such a high cliff.

Sergeant Butchers asked if I suspected foul play, and I found myself surprised at how willing these policemen were to trust to the word and theories of a retired consulting detective. I took the sergeant to one side as the others collected up all the parts of the bicycle and loaded them into the boat. I explained to him my thinking. Mrs. Duley was, after all, recently widowed. Could she, perhaps, have found herself in that unenviable position of being unable to cope with the loss, with the loneliness and solitude after however many years of marriage and constant companionship?

I had written in my previous letter that I would be surprised if these two deaths were not somehow connected. At this point I was doubting that assertion, and seeing instead merely an unfortunate coincidence.

Constable Anderson remained with Sergeant Butchers and me while the others returned the deceased and the remains of the bicycle to the station at Eastbourne. There wasn't room for us all on the same boat, which would return for us once it had unloaded. I noticed the constable waving and followed his line of sight to the top of the cliff. A small crowd had gathered there, peering over the edge at us. I cursed my lack of forethought in not having secured the cliff edge from tampering before we I left my cottage earlier. Should there be any indication of foul-play, despite my theories to the contrary, any evidence was likely now being muddied and trampled by gruesome onlookers.

Indeed, this proved to be the case when the sergeant and I walked to the cliff top a while later. The locals were moved on unceremoniously by the Eastbourne constables – all except young Tom Markham, from whom I was eager to obtain any further insight. The bright lad had been there the previous day. He knew the tyre marks that showed where Prudence had gone over the edge – for who else would be foolish enough to otherwise ride a bicycle at the top of the tallest cliff in Britain, if not planning mayhem? The tracks remained, although the storm had done more to erase them than the onlookers had. It wasn't a straight plummet – the wind had taken the lady off to one side. But the grassy land betrayed no signs of a struggle or of anyone attempting to wrestle with an out-of-control bicycle.

Leaving a constable to patrol the cliff-top this time and dissuade any further onlookers, we drove the short distance to East Dean. The police were in need of some lunchtime refreshment, so I found myself patronising the Tiger Inn for the second time in so many days. The landlord was even so good as to send some refreshment to the constable who'd remained at Beachy Head.

Fortified, Sergeant Butchers, Constable Anderson, and I continued on to Friston to search Prudence Duley's cottage. We found the Reverend Silsby there. Sombre – not to say wretched – he seemed confused. When challenged as to what he was doing there, the best we could get from him was that he simply felt he ought to be there, that's all. His visage was greyer, and more drawn since I'd last chanced across him only a few days prior.

Butchers attempted to move the reverend on. The older man pulled himself together somewhat at this. He told me he felt very deeply the loss of not only two of his parishioners, but two of his oldest friends in Florence and Prudence. Three, if he counted Archibald, who had only been buried a week or so earlier. He had endeavoured with all his might to help dear Prudence to overcome the loss of her husband, but, alas, it seemed to no avail.

A telling declaration, indeed. Clearly the reverend was also of the mind that Prudence took her own life. I didn't respond to his assertion, but I still needed to speak to him regarding the state in which he'd found poor Miss Gladwish the previous day, so I arranged to call on him later at the vicarage and he left us to our business.

If Florence Gladwish was a neat and tidy person, the same could not be said of Prudence Duley. The cottage was smaller than Florence's and generally less well-kept. Some areas were, however, far worse than others, with pictures, documents and writings strewn about. It seemed likely that Prudence had been sorting through her late husband's affairs. It was with these strewn papers, then, that I felt it would be best to start.

It didn't take long to find what I was looking for. Archibald's bureau had been left open, drawers and pigeonholes stripped of their contents. Some papers had been torn up, and others scrunched and creased, but sufficient remained either intact or merely legible and it was clear what they were: Love letters. Piles of them, going back years and years. All of them from "*Your Flossy*" to "*My Lonely Cavalier*". I was immediately reminded of the name of the manuscript in Florence Gladwish's dead hands and there it was, the link for which I had been waiting.

I assumed that, had Archibald not died suddenly, he would have taken the time to deal with all such romantic keepsakes both to save his name and prevent his widow from succumbing to needless, additional grief. I needed more proof that this infidelity was his, though, to be certain. Between us, Sergeant Butchers, Constable Anderson and I turned the whole cottage over. Nowhere could we find anything that linked Archibald Duley with the name or role of "The Lonely Cavalier".

A return to Florence Gladwish's cottage in East Dean seemed the next best course of action. Butchers had left his other constable in East Dean after we had luncheoned at the Tiger Inn, to stand guard over Miss Gladwish's cottage and assist with the removal of the deceased to the local mortuary. No doubt she now lay there alongside Prudence Duley. Anderson informed me that Miss Gladwish had a private income and had lived in the cottage owned by her father before her. The constable's father had often said she'd

80

been considered a prize amongst the eligible young ladies in the area, back in her youth, but it seemed she had spurned all advances and chosen the life of a spinster.

I thanked Anderson for his candour and set about trying to find any love letters from Archibald that might show that she was his "Flossy" and he was her "Lonely Cavalier". The words had no sooner left my lips but I reached for the manuscript, discarded on the poor lady's now-vacant chair. I began to flick through it. The narrative opened with a description of the actions that led to the English Civil War, how the Cavalier, whose given name was Nathanial, had gone against his Roundhead family and followed his loyalty to the Crown onto the battlefield. Injured, and on the losing side, he then returned home to make peace with his family in what was now Cromwell's new Commonwealth. There, he met a sweetheart who also shared his Royalist sympathies and they began an amorous correspondence.

I was about to discard the manuscript as historical romantic drivel when I found my original hunch was well-founded. The remainder of the novel, such as it was, was epistolary. The correspondence was, in essence, that between *"Flossy"* and *"The Lonely Cavalier"*. I had brought some of the letters with me from the Duley cottage and quickly found the relevant pages in the manuscript to compare them. With some minor tweaking to add a period feel, the letters I held were repeated word-for-word in the manuscript, and the responses – from the Lonely Cavalier to his *"Sweet Flossy, forever mine"* filled the return gaps between those letters. I had seen Archibald's birth certificate amongst his papers. The name Nathanial had not appeared. I wondered, then, if Archibald was the Lonely Cavalier in the book, and from where had the name *"Nathanial"* come?

It was clear from the paper and the various typewriter inks used that the manuscript – or typescript, if you will – had been compiled over a long period of time and likely only recently been finished. In the final section, the Lonely Cavalier had died and his ever-loving Flossy, heartbroken, had written a final, touching epistle to her deceased lover, promising to see him soon in Heaven. But that final word had been struck through and the handwritten word *"Hell!"* added instead.

Several thoughts now possessed me, Watson. Taken at face value, that final entry to close the novel could be considered a suicide note from Florence. Even the handwritten word change could have been her acceptance of the sin she was about to commit in the eyes of God. But unless it was found that there was some poison in her bloodstream, I didn't see how Florence could have taken her own life in the way we found her. But perhaps she'd sought assistance in so doing. There was, after all, the tell-tale evidence of the mentholated ointment and the aroma around her mouth and nose. Could she have asked someone else to take her life – holding the pillow over her and then replacing it on the bed? Could that person have then amended the end of the novel because of what they'd been implored to do?

My own inclination still leant towards Prudence Duley finding the letters, knowing somehow that Archibald was the Lonely Cavalier. She then came here and took Florence's life by smothering her with her pillow, before then taking her own. That would also tally with the scribbling of "*Hell*" at the end of the manuscript, which was then placed into Florence's hands.

I was still due to call on the Reverend Silsby, of course. It was nearing the time for dinner and the policemen were starting to bemoan their long hours on duty. Mealtimes have always held less importance to me, as you know, and I wanted to get to the bottom of this matter that day, if at all possible. The Easter weekend was almost upon us and I wished to return to my state of retirement. I was sure that we could achieve a solution of sorts if we kept going. I convinced them to stay by promising the sergeant and his men a fine supper at the Tiger Inn afterwards. Thus enthused, we headed back towards Friston, to the vicarage.

The Reverend Silsby was reading from his Bible when the housekeeper showed us into the sitting room. On the wall behind him was a rather grand family portrait. I recognised the man on it as the reverend in younger days, standing proudly with what I could only assume was his wife and their two sons. Before I could seek confirmation, he told me that his wife had passed away some years back, and his sons had both fallen in the Great War. No wonder the loss of two friends in so many days had hit the man hard.

Unless . . . Yes, Watson, I know what you'll be thinking as you read this. There was still an outside possibility that this gentleman of the cloth, loved and respected by his parishioners, was also a murderer – or at least guilty of assisting a suicide. And should that be the case, I had no doubt that it would lay more heavily on his conscience than anything else.

I sent the sergeant back out to the car. I felt that his presence would only inhibit the reverend. When we were alone and seated, I told him that I had made some discoveries about the deaths of the two ladies, and that I feared they were connected. He nodded in response, as if he already knew. I offered him a laurel leaf at that point. I asked him to unburden himself to me, to tell me everything about the matter. I've done my best to record his narrative as accurately as I could in what follows.

The reverend told me he had known Florence, Prudence, and Archibald all his life. He was just a little older than the three, but they had all grown up together, as happens in small rural communities. The reverend's father had been the parish minister before him. The Silsby line went back many generations at East Dean and Friston but, thanks to the war, it would soon end. He had no blood relative to take over.

Florence and Archibald had been madly in love almost from childhood. This was no secret from anyone and, naturally, when the time came, they wished to marry. But Florence's father wouldn't hear of it. Mr. Gladwish considered himself a gentleman, of sorts. He certainly never laboured in his life. Archibald was from Friston. Gladwish looked down on folk from Friston. Florence had considered running away with Archibald. The reverend, who hadn't long taken over the parish from his father at that point, recalled conversations with her about the situation. His advice always came back to the Fifth Commandment: *"Honour thy father and thy mother"*. And Florence did. So she didn't run away, and she didn't marry Archibald. She didn't marry anyone.

Archibald, however, found himself another wife from the local girls in Friston. Prudence Baker. The reverend recalled talking at length with them both about the wedding and looking for the light of love in their eyes. It shone in Prudence's, but in Archibald's eyes he could only see that something was missing. Only a few years after Archibald and Prudence married, old Mr. Gladwish died, leaving Florence a woman of independent means.

The Duleys' marriage remained childless, and gossips would occasionally murmur about Florence adopting spinsterhood. Sometimes the reverend found himself duty-bound to speak to both Archibald and Florence, separately, and ask them how they were getting along as friends within the parish community. Florence, in particular, threw much of her energy into church life. Always the subject would be brushed aside by them both. They were perfectly comfortable as friends, they would say.

But Florence couldn't forget her true love and it seems Archibald couldn't let the flame die either. The fire was there in their eyes: It didn't escape the reverend's notice when he saw the two of them together. They kept up their love affair in secret, for years. Florence remained a spinster, spurning all comers, and Archibald was trapped in a loveless marriage for appearances only. Many people turned blind eyes over the years, including the reverend. He never knew if Prudence was aware of the situation in any way, although he suspected she was not, from the revenge that had since been enacted.

The reverend finished his story by stating he'd feared from the moment he found Florence dead that it had something to do with their secret lives. I asked him if this was based on hard evidence, or just a hunch. He reached into the fly leaf of his Bible and brought out a postcard-sized photograph. Florence and Archibald, not yet twenty years of age. Possibly the only known picture of just the two of them. Taken at a church summer fête, winners of the fancy dress competition. She was a Georgian lady, he a Civil War Cavalier. This was what Florence had been holding when he'd found her. On the reverse was written the word *"Forever"*, and the imprint of a kiss. The handwriting matched that of the letters I'd brought with me.

Worried that the photograph would automatically lead people to point the finger at Prudence, the reverend removed the photograph from Florence's grasp and replaced it with the manuscript of the novel. He'd known Florence had been working on that for some years and that it was special to her. He broke down at this point and begged my forgiveness. He'd also lied about seeing Prudence riding her bicycle. He *had* seen her, but she'd been cycling *away* from the Gladwish cottage and she hadn't seen him approach. When he found Florence still warm, yet unresponsive, he'd known immediately what had happened. And he knew where Prudence would be heading. All he could do was pray for her.

There was no reason to assume, as far as the reverend knew, that Prudence was aware of what had gone on between Archibald and Florence until she'd found the letters, although she'd have known from their youth that the two had been in love. He was grieving for her, and possibly for himself for his years of inaction and his years of ignoring a situation in which no one appeared to be happy. What a terrible truth for anyone, after they've devoted the best years of their life to someone, to learn that they were simply a screen to hide the other person's shame. The heartache, the humiliation of finding that nothing that she'd ever done or given had ever mattered, or could ever matter. It had been too much for poor Prudence.

I couldn't doubt the reverend's sincerity, Watson, regardless of my earlier worries. The situation was as I originally envisaged it had been: Murder and suicide.

Sergeant Butchers was in full agreement with my summation as we sat in the Tiger Inn later, enjoying an ale and a bowl of stew, although he queried why Mrs. Duley would have bothered to cover her steps so carefully after killing Miss Gladwish if she'd already decided to take her own life afterwards. This was a fair point and I congratulated him on his perspicacity. My only theory was that it might go easier on their memories, and on the parish community as a whole, if it seemed that one was death by natural causes and the other was a terrible accident. The actions were that of a vengeful, grieving – and wronged – woman. There was certainly no evidence to suggest Prudence wished to drag the two villages through the mire with her. The sergeant was, again, happy to take my word on this and even suggested that they should record the deaths as being by natural causes and misadventure, under the circumstances.

I stayed for one drink, then made my excuses and left them to it, on the promise of footing the bill for another round of drinks on my way out. That sort of evening has never held any great appeal to me, regardless of the company or the establishment. A brisk walk home to my farm in the fresh Easter air was all the restorative I required.

And so there you have it, my dear Watson. Another case for the retired Sherlock Holmes, and one that carried with it such an air of tragedy that I'm duty-bound to cast it from my memory with all haste and return to the glorious positivity of beekeeping – although doubtless it will live on in the stories of village gossip for years to come.

I'm certain that you will have already replied to me after my letter of Maundy Thursday, and that letter will no doubt crossing this one as they wend their merry ways to their recipients. I look forward to that, and your final thoughts on this matter once you have considered the whole, now that I've laid it all out before you.

Until then, I remain, as always, your true friend,
Holmes

Part II

I had been corresponding with increased frequency with my good friend, Sherlock Holmes, during the middle part of 1922. The commencement of the run of letters coincided with him being approached by the local constabulary in Eastbourne to assist them regarding the deaths of two residents within his rural community. Holmes detailed much of his investigation into the matter over the course of several letters to me in the week leading up to Easter – which had fallen, that year, in mid-April.

By June, this frequent correspondence had reduced to a more sedate single letter a week between us. Now, into July, the frequency had reduced further still. Having not heard from Holmes in two weeks, then, imagine my surprise that particular morning when a knock at my door revealed my good friend to be standing there, on my very doorstep!

I hastily welcomed him inside and, since I lacked company that day, I asked if he cared to join me for lunch. He gratefully accepted.

"Dash it all, though, Holmes," I said with good humour. "The least you could have done was written to tell me you'd be in London."

"My dear fellow!" he replied. "If I had done that, you'd have known all my news and then we'd have nothing to talk about over the next few days."

My eyes widened. "Days? You've come to stay?"

He puffed on his pipe before answering. "I've had my fill of London for now. I was hoping I might tempt you down to East Dean, perhaps until after the weekend. You do still have your motor car, don't you?"

I laughed heartedly at this. Apart from anything else, he had come by for a lift home. Holmes informed me he had been summoned to London urgently a few days previously, by Buckingham Palace – a request he would never decline as long as blood coursed through his veins. He'd been assisting in a matter involving the Prince of Wales. He told me no more, and neither did I enquire any further. Doubtless he had already revealed more than he ought and, as there had been nothing involving the Prince in the papers of late, this was certainly due to the success of Holmes's services.

As it happened, I had no pressing engagements for the remainder of the week, merely a few appointments that I could easily reschedule, and the prospect of a few days away near the coast definitely held appeal. After we had eaten, I quickly attended to my necessary affairs. My housekeeper packed me a suitcase – no formal attire, just anything suitable for the country. Before long, Holmes and I were comfortably ensconced in my four-seater Austin 12 tourer, bound for the Sussex Downs.

I freely admitted to Holmes how much I enjoyed driving, and how liberating I found owning a motor car. I needed no persuasion to make this journey, although the experience was much improved by the fine July weather. Once we'd left the heavy traffic of the city environs behind, it was just us, the panoramic countryside, delightful colours, and rustic scenery. Such joy. And oh, the freshness of the air.

We arrived in Birling Gap rather closer to evening than afternoon. Holmes's farm was several miles west of Eastbourne – understandably enough, since he'd retired there to adopt a life of beekeeping isolation as much as possible. As I drove carefully through the large gate at the roadside entrance to his land, he pointed out to me the rucked-up ground where Sergeant Butchers' car had become mired after the storm, back in April. The muddy ground had dried now, of course, but the indentations left by the spinning wheels remained. Holmes had no desire to lay a proper track there. Such a gesture would be seen to encourage visitors.

The house was secure, as he'd left it – and just as I'd seen it on my previous visits. But someone had been there in the meantime. Outside the front door, under the canopy, there sat a large ancient wooden chest. There was a note tacked to the lid. It read, *Found this in Miss Gladwish's loft when we cleared out the cottage. Contents may be of interest to you.* It was signed *Constable Anderson.*

Holmes looked at me, his eyes gleaming. "How interesting, Watson, although I think, perhaps, this can wait until later. I find myself in need of refreshment, but I must admit that I maintain rather a bare cupboard these days, as a rule. What say you to a jaunt to the Tiger Inn?"

I told him I thought that a very fine suggestion after a long drive, and the exercise would do me good. It had been a while since I'd visited the village. We carried the trunk inside. It was so large it needed the both of us. It was surprisingly heavy, and its contents clanked and clattered, but we held our curiosity in check and set off for our evening jaunt.

The landlord of the Tiger Inn greeted Holmes like a regular, much to my amusement, although Holmes appeared indifferent. There followed any number of greetings and felicitations from fellow patrons as we headed for a vacant table in the corner. I was pleased to see him embraced in that way. I knew it wasn't why he'd retired to the area, but after so many years living there, I would be

87

troubled if he hadn't built up some familiarity in such a small and contained community – regardless of his celebrity status.

The ale was fruity and refreshing. Holmes satisfied himself with a simple bread and cheese, but I was in the mood for something more substantial. The only hot food available was a mutton broth – not the likeliest of dishes for the summer, but very homely and satisfying, and served with a generous crust of fresh bread. I extended my compliments to the landlord's wife for the dish.

"Thank you, Doctor Watson," said the landlord as he removed my empty bowl.

We spent a pleasant hour or so at the inn before heading off for a bracing evening's walk. Holmes led me up to Beachy Head, directly across from his farm, where poor Prudence Duley had taken her own life. I found myself yet again enchanted by the view and humbled by the sea. I was beginning to feel a little unsteady on my legs and so I stayed well away from the edge. I was glad for my stick, but I found the walk back down the hill to Holmes's farm to be an increasing struggle.

Walking used to be one of my singular pleasures and my exercise of choice, but alas, these days I was feeling my age – now about to enter my eighth decade – more than ever. While Holmes bounded over the terrain with much of his old zest, fascinated by this and enchanted by that, I can honestly say I felt like an aged relative by comparison. It was then with enormous relief that we reached the farm. I took a little something medicinal from my bag to ease the throbbing in my legs and washed it down with a brandy. Ensconced in a comfortable seat, I informed my host that I would not be moving again until the drive home.

I awoke the following morning feeling largely refreshed, but very stiff about the legs. Holmes had already been up and about for some hours, he informed me, tending to his bees before breakfast. He had baked a fresh loaf and it was undoubtedly the aroma of this, as much as the insistent cock in the yard, which urged me from my slumbers. I once again took a little something for the pain from yesterday's walk before we breakfasted. Holmes's housekeeper being away meant that we had to do for ourselves. We had a boiled egg or two, freshly collected from the hens, followed by the bread with some of last year's honey. Beautiful.

How idyllic it was, to be able to gaze out through the kitchen window at an expanse of greenery and blue sky, with no sounds save for the therapeutic clucking of the hens as they scratched away at the dry yard immediately outside. But if the previous evening had taught me anything, it was that I was too much in need of the conveniences of modern city life. This would be a pleasant break, I was sure, but I could never live the life that Holmes had chosen here.

A loud scraping interrupted my musings and I turned to find Holmes dragging the large chest – in fact it was more like a trunk – into the centre of the sitting room. Somehow, I had forgotten about this mystery prize which had been left for my friend. It was about five feet long by three feet wide, and of a wooden construction, held together with iron bands. It was sealed at the front and rear with leather straps which had grown musty and worn with age. If there had been leather handles on the sides, they had long since decayed. I helped Holmes lift the trunk onto the hearth rug. In endeavouring to carefully release the straps, they broke. We removed the lid and set it to one side.

The trunk appeared to contain pieces of armour, along with ancient scraps of clothing and some handwritten papers. These latter were tied together and contained within a decaying leather pouch. Holmes glanced at me and I shrugged. There was a look about him that usually told me wordlessly that I had missed something important and that he was waiting for me to take the lead so he could reveal it. I was too old for games, so I immediately reached in and grabbed the nearest item: A helmet. I slowly raised it, examining it as I did so.

Holmes spoke. "I believe, my dear Watson, that what you are holding is the helmet of a Civil War soldier. A Royalist, or Cavalier if you will. But that is not the most interesting aspect of these contents."

I nodded. "The pouch of papers – of course."

By way of answer, Holmes asked me to run him an errand.

By the time I arrived back at the farm, Holmes had cleared all the sitting room furniture to one side and emptied the trunk. He had neatly laid out the pieces of armour and threadbare remains of clothing, such as they were, on the floor. There were actually only two proper pieces of armour – the helmet and a breastplate, plus a rapier. The breastplate was badly damaged down one side. I wondered, in passing, why the trunk had been so heavy – the contents didn't appear to amount to that much when laid out thus – although the trunk itself was obviously of a certain weight.

My errand had taken me off in the motor car to call upon the Reverend Silsby. I returned with the photograph of Archibald Duley and Florence Gladwish, which Holmes had reported in his correspondence a few months back. The reverend was a short, pleasant man, a little older than Holmes and me. A life lived exposed on the Sussex Downs had given him a permanently bewildered look, although this was by no means the case when one spoke to him. After reading the brief note I'd carried from Holmes, he shook me warmly by the hand, nodded, and removed the postcard-sized photograph from a locked drawer in his bureau. I felt duty bound to join him in a cup of tea, which his housekeeper was just then serving, before I could make my way back.

Holmes gave a sly grin when I reported the detail. "That bureau previously belonged to Archibald Duley, you know."

I advised my friend that the reverend had enquired at some length about my life in London, and particularly the years Holmes and I had lived and worked together.

"I trust you were discreet?"

"As much as I could be. It is easy, these days, to blame a failing memory on one's advancing years."

"Good. That was slightly underhanded of him. Not that I would imagine the reverend to have any ulterior motive, but I do prefer to keep myself to myself here and rarely, if ever, discuss my former life."

I handed him the photograph and he set it down next to the helmet on the floor.

"The same," he said with a nod. And, again, for the rapier. Indeed, there were signs that the rapier had been misused. The blade was kinked under the hilt. Probably where it had been worn under a heavy belt as part of the dressing-up games, as shown on the photograph. There was no reason to assume it hadn't been used and worn for similar amusements on other occasions.

I looked again at the photograph. I was surprised that the breastplate hadn't been used in play, too, but it was rusted through on the right-hand side of the chest. Perhaps it been that way for many years.

"So," I said, "this adds a little more clarity to the Lonely Cavalier mystery, I presume?"

"In some ways, yes," Holmes replied, enigmatically. "But I fear, Watson, that you are still missing one vital – and, frankly, obvious – fact."

"The papers – of course. Are they legible?"

He shook his head. "I believe I know, roughly, what they will tell us. But no. This is a question of *volume*. Look again at the trunk."

I did, and I thought again on how heavy it had been when we'd moved it. I looked inside. Holmes had emptied the trunk, but for good measure I tried lifting it. It was still very heavy. I examined the exterior. And then I perceived what my friend had undoubtedly spotted immediately when he'd opened it. I placed my hand inside and rapped on the wood at the lowest point, while kneeling beside it. My knuckle-rap was roughly three quarters of the way down. I rapped on the inside of the base. It wasn't *that* thick. There had to be a hidden compartment within. That would account for the extra weight. Holmes joined me in an instant.

"You've no idea how much it pleases my old heart that you figured that out, Watson," he said with glee.

There was no obvious way into the concealed compartment from the inside, and Holmes was loath to damage the trunk if we could avoid it. We tipped it over and examined the underside instead. There was a shallow ridge around the base on three sides. Knowing what we were looking for, it became clear that the underside of the trunk was supposed to slide out. The edge of the groove was visible, along which the base should run. However, try as we might, we couldn't move it. Age had swelled the wood, although not enough to crack the running groove. But alas, the trunk wouldn't reveal its hidden secrets without intervention.

To that end, Holmes returned shortly with his tools, and in very little time at all he'd chiselled off one of the long edges. We then pried the base up until the remaining edges gave way. I'm not sure what I was expecting the hidden compartment to contain – we hadn't really paused to think – but nothing prepared me for what was revealed: Human remains.

I baulked at the stench – well-concealed within the tightly sealed compartment after who knew how many years, but now released. This was an old corpse – very old. Wrapped in a linen shroud (reduced, by the years, to threads) and now little more than bones with strips of grey, desiccated flesh remaining. There was some hair about the skull, which rolled away onto the floor. It bore a goodly number of teeth, too, and not too worn, suggesting that the deceased had still been young at the time of death – not a child, yet not too far into adulthood.

As I stood and coughed into my handkerchief, I noticed a mildly triumphant expression on Holmes's face, and it struck me what I'd heard him cry as we'd opened the compartment: "As I thought!"

He spoke again. "If I am not mistaken, Watson, I believe we have stumbled across the entire remains of our mysterious Lonely Cavalier."

It was late into the afternoon before we finished laying out the macabre remains next to the pieces of armour and clothing. My back was playing merry hell by the end. Long gone were the days when I was happy to be grubbing around on all fours on the floor for hours on end. I felt I'd earned a more sedate life by now, and as much as the thrill of an impromptu mystery with Holmes had fired my imagination at first, I had to admit that, physically, I was now far less able than willing.

But we had succeeded, at least. We had the complete skeleton of a man. Holmes was determined to confirm that all the necessary bones were there, and that any omissions could be accounted for. Everything was as it should be, but there were three noteworthy areas: The right-hand side of the ribcage showed signs of outside influence. Perhaps the Cavalier had been burned on the battlefield, or struck heavily and the wound had turned septic. That may very well have been what killed him, in fact. The left shoulder blade had a scrape, as from a bladed weapon piercing the skin, and the right femur showed signs of having been blasted with lead shot and never having fully healed.

The skeleton was of a size to fit the armour and clothes, suggesting – if we ever doubted it for a second – that the one belonged to the other. The curious damage to the ribcage was replicated by the damage to the breast plate which I'd noted earlier, and also on the remains of what was presumably a white linen shirt. Whatever had happened to the soldier, the breastplate hadn't provided him with any protection.

While I finished work on the body, Holmes prepared us a dinner, along with perusing the papers from the trunk's main compartment. We dined in the yard at the back, with the chickens pecking and clucking around our feet. The interior of the farmhouse needed to be aired to remove the fustiness of the corpse. I asked if the papers had helped reveal anything about the Cavalier.

"They have revealed the deceased's name, which answers one outstanding mystery from April. He was one Nathanial Moore. So, that's where Florence got the name of her hero. Moreover, the papers have revealed a plain case of plagiarism! If I had Florence Gladwish's manuscript to hand, I would prove it to you in a trice, Watson, but I recognised the contents of the papers as having been transferred almost word for word into the opening chapters of Miss Gladwish's epistolary novel."

"Then the trunk was hers?"

"Possibly – although there remains an outside chance it was Archibald Duley's and he left it with Florence either as a keepsake or as something to do with their romantic roleplaying."

"Really, Holmes! I find that possibility utterly tasteless."

"I'm not suggesting for a second that they knew of the dead body concealed underneath. I don't believe that anyone has known of it since those who concealed it there passed on. I suspect the trunk was kept as a box of remembrance, as a gesture by the family, and contained all Nathanial's worldly possessions. It may even have remained that way until some of those items became mere toys and playthings for childish amusement. And as to which family it belonged, the name will no doubt prove the case, either way. I'm sure I've seen a number of Moore family gravestones in the churchyard. I suspect that there will be one there for our Cavalier Nathanial, only if we were to dig it up, we would find it empty."

He lit a pipe before continuing. I'd barely yet touched my dinner.

"As for the papers, there is a letter from Nathanial to his mother, dated 16th June, 1645, asking her to plead clemency with his father and the rest of the family on his behalf. Nathanial had been wounded at the Battle of Naseby, as Florence recorded in her novel, and wanted to return home from Northamptonshire, in light of the King's defeat. This area of Sussex was largely Roundhead in Civil War times. Clearly the Moore family was, too, and Nathanial being a Royalist caused a divide. Once he died, Nathanial would still have been allocated a grave in the family plot, but what if his bones were left here in this trunk, with his Cavalier effects, as a perpetual punishment for going against the rest of the family?"

"Nearly three-hundred years ago, now, Holmes," I said with a hearty chuckle, as I finished the crust of my pie. "Who knows how or why he ended up in there. But I'd lay money on it being his battle wounds that saw him off. Chalk another one up for Cromwell."

My friend puffed on his pipe and relaxed into the summer evening. "We shall see," he said.

I slept fitfully that night, no doubt due to my discomfiture at the mouldering remains lying on the sitting room floor below. I was glad when dawn broke through the curtains and I could rise. Holmes was, of course, up and tending to his morning duties around the farm. I prepared us some coffee and took a look through the papers from the trunk. They were very fragile, stained with age, and torn through folding and handling. The ink had faded almost completely in places and I found the handwriting very difficult to decipher at first. I noted, however, that in his letter Nathanial stated he'd received injuries to the shoulder and leg, so it would take him some time to make the journey home.

Further to Nathanial's letter to his mother, which was written in hiding and marked Northampton, there was one other document. This was a single sheet laid out like a bill or receipt, more faded and damaged than the other. At first all I could distinguish was the date: 20th July, 1645. But as I slowly began to make sense of the odd word here and there, I realised it was in fact a record of poor Nathanial's death – presumably from a physician. It accounted the death to Nathanial's injuries received "*in the line of duty to his King*" (not "the *King*", I wryly observed). It listed the injuries as a rapier wound to the shoulder, a shot to the leg, and an unspecified wound to the chest. I noted with some degree of sadness that it wouldn't have been long after Nathanial made it home to Sussex from Northampton when he died.

I informed Holmes of as much when he returned from his work and we broke our fast. He peered at me from under his furrowed brow as he wiped the toast crumbs from around his mouth.

"Doesn't that strike you as being rather convenient, though?" he asked.

I shrugged. "Sometimes life can be *convenient*, as you put it, in that way. It's quite a trek to the Sussex Downs from Northampton, particularly if one is having to move stealthily and by foot. Add to that the injuries sustained on the battlefield, and the journey must have been a terrible strain for the poor lad."

"By injuries, do I take it that you refer to his shoulder, chest, and leg wounds?"

I told him I did. He led me through into the sitting room.

"Rapier blade to the shoulder," he stated. "Would you agree?"

"It's what the report states, and I think that's a fair assumption, yes."

He pointed to the right femur. "Right upper leg. Judging by the fractures, a gunshot wound. Shot later removed, but untidily – probably on the field."

"Yes," I concurred. "There's little evidence that the bone started to heal again."

"How, then, would you account for the damage to the breastplate, shirt, and ribs?"

"I'm not entirely *au fait* with civil war period armaments and battle techniques, Holmes, and the death report states, '*unspecified chest wound*'."

"Of which I am instantly suspicious."

I held out my hands in mild exasperation. "Maybe our Cavalier was struck a glancing blow by a cannonball, enough to damage the breastplate which has since rusted over time. Even a glancing blow would cause injuries, but he may not have even realised that he was wounded at first, if the damage was mainly internal. The wound perhaps turned septic and left evidence on the shirt and skeletal remains as the flesh decomposed. Blood poisoning would certainly have led quickly to death. But as I said yesterday evening, we're talking about something that happened nearly three-hundred years ago. What urges you to dispute what the preserved record is telling us?"

There was a glint in Holmes's eye as he grabbed the breastplate from the floor and tossed it around in his grasp.

"Because of this. Examine, if you please, both the inside and the outside of the breastplate."

I did. And then I looked again at the desiccated ribcage which I'd laid out adjacent to it. A shudder swept over me.

"Murder?" I said in hushed tones.

"That is what I believe, Watson. Yes."

The breastplate had corroded, as I recorded when we first examined it. I took it to have been eaten away by rust. But what I could now see was that the inside of the breastplate – that which pressed against the shirt and the body – was stained and corroded to a greater degree than the exterior. Not by much, but enough to be noticeable – including odd spots or splashes beyond the main area of corrosion. Whatever the substance was, it had been applied to the inside of the breastplate. At the edges of the area affected, and the splash points, the concentration had been weaker, and its effect lessened. At those places, it had marked the inside but not eaten through to the outside. And what the damaged ribs on the corpse were telling me was that as the corrosive substance had eaten through to the outside, so it had also eaten inside into poor Nathanial Moore. This was no accident, no battlefield injury. It was premeditated, done deliberately to kill him in the most heinous and painful way.

Holmes continued, confirming much of what I had speculated. "I think an acidic potion will have been applied to the inside, just before Nathanial wore it. He will have died from the wounds, unfortunately in great pain and probably not very quickly, either. Therefore, I don't believe it happened to him at or just after the Battle of Naseby. Nor do I think it was done to him as he travelled south to his family home. I think we can trust that he arrived home alive, at least."

"Murdered here, in his home village, after all that."

"Local allegiance was Roundhead, not Cavalier, as I've already stated."

"But what reason would he have for putting on his armour again, here?"

"Assuming that he did so. We know Nathanial was concerned about his family accepting him again. And we know, from records, the shame some families felt at their divided loyalties."

I didn't like where Holmes was going with this logical progression.

"He would have been met by his staunchly Parliamentarian family, doubtless demanding that he recant. If he remained fiercely loyal to the King, their views would have been irreconcilable." Holmes gazed at the floor, grimly. "I believe this happened at his home. The already weakened and exhausted Nathanial Moore, outnumbered, was forced back into his Royalist armour, a corrosive agent having been applied to the inside of the breastplate, and then he was trapped, as its effect took hold and he doubtless continued to refuse to renounce the King. Afterwards, they built this special trunk in which to conceal his body and his worldly goods. And a false funeral would have been held for an alleged repentant son who had returned to the fold only to die from his wounds in his loving mother's arms. It was deliberate and pre-meditated. And ever since it's been forgotten."

I took a long breath. "I shudder to think that any parent could accept that being done to their offspring, let alone do it themselves, However, what you say has the distinct ring of truth about it. It's fanciful, it's heart-breaking, and most importantly it's nearly three-hundred years too late for us to do anything about it."

Holmes steepled his fingers and smiled. "Possibly, but we can at least try to leave things a little tidier, don't you think? I'm not sure the remains of poor Nathanial should be returned to that trunk, for a start. It's time he was laid to rest properly."

A sudden thought gripped me. "Hang on. The local constable brought that trunk to you, didn't he? I wonder what he knows . . . ?"

Constable Anderson didn't know anything, as it turned out, and it was clear from the moment we entered his cottage that he was thankful he hadn't discovered the hidden compartment and the skeletal remains himself. Anderson advised us that the whole affair was an act of pure chance on the part of Sergeant Butchers, who had found the trunk and recalled that Holmes was interested in trying to find out more about Miss Gladwish's Lonely Cavalier character. Three constables had nearly done themselves a mischief trying to get it down from the loft in the first place. Butchers told Anderson to send it Holmes's way, in the hope that the armour was Civil War period and that the papers may offer some clues.

Holmes gave a brash bark of a laugh and shook Anderson firmly by the hand. The trunk had revealed more than anyone could have hoped, after all. At further mention of the skeleton, the constable had uttered a mild curse under his breath and seated himself, coming over quite pale and nauseous.

"My good man," burst Holmes, "whatever is the matter? You were fine when dealing with Prudence Duley's remains below Beachy Head back in April. You managed to spend hours in the same room as the corpse of Florence Gladwish. Yet here you are, floundering like a maiden aunt at the mere mention of a skeleton!"

"I know, Mr. Holmes," he said between ragged breaths and apologies. "It's just that I'm all right with the recently deceased – all in the line of duty and all that. Skeletons, though, and decayed corpses – they don't half give me the willies!"

At a nod from Holmes, I sorted the constable with a brandy. I was barely able to pour straight, such was my mirth.

Before we left, having made sure the constable was quite himself again, Holmes informed the policeman that he'd be asking the Reverend Silsby for an exhumation of the original grave, with official permission, and suggested Anderson ask Butchers to call around at Holmes's farm, with the coroner, at his soonest opportunity.

I teased Holmes as we walked up the road. "I get the feeling you have a bit of time for your local bobbies. Better not let the Met find out."

Holmes's mouth made a moue. "Perhaps I'm going soft in my old age," he said, as his lips curled into a smile. "Although I have to wonder if there's ever a day when Constable Anderson isn't overcome at something. The poor man seems to have the constitution of a wilting lettuce leaf!"

It was another fine afternoon, and we were now headed for the vicarage, on the road towards Friston.

Reverend Silsby studied the borrowed photograph fondly as I returned it to him, before slipping it inside the embossed Bible he carried. We were in an annex off the church, where the parish records were stored.

"Was there something in particular that you were looking for, Mr. Holmes?" the reverend enquired.

Holmes was seated at the desk and didn't look up. He'd immediately run his fingers along the spines of the large leather-bound volumes on the shelves above. He selected one and began to immerse himself in the information. I smiled apologetically at the reverend.

"Note this, Watson," Holmes called, as if the reverend wasn't with us. "Archibald Duley's maternal grandmother was born a Moore."

"So, the trunk was his, then, after all."

"Trunk?" enquired the reverend. "Ah," he burst. "You found the old dressing-up trunk – hence the photograph, of course! Where was it? My, that takes me back. I haven't seen that for years, now. Were the helmet and rapier still there?"

"It was found amongst Florence Gladwish's possessions," said Holmes. "But it belonged to the Moore family."

"A popular name around these parts. Archibald's grandmother was Eliza Eastman, neé Moore. The only child of her family to reach adulthood – thus that particular line of Moores ended with her. Now, of course, any trace of the bloodline has gone, since Archibald died without issue." The reverend looked sadly at his Bible, before perking up again. "I can show you Eliza's grave in the churchyard outside, if you'd like?"

Holmes brushed the offer aside. "Actually, Reverend, we're looking to trace one Nathanial Moore, late of this parish, who died in July 1645. Perhaps an ancestor of Eliza's?"

"I see," the reverend replied, turning and running his index finger along the spines on the shelf above. He extracted another thick, leather-bound ledger. Holmes replaced the volume he'd removed and very soon we had Nathanial Moore's entry in the parish records laid out before us.

"We are fortunate," the reverend commented. "My forefathers were the most fastidious of men, capturing much detail and local colour which is sadly lacking in latter days."

His self-criticism was evident, but the Great War and all the turbulent international social upheaval had cut a deep chasm across many of us. There had been times when I had questioned the significance of my own existence.

"Here he is," the reverend continued. "Nathanial Henry Moore, third son of Ruth and Samuel Moore. Born March 23rd, 1621. Died July 20th, 1645. It says here he died of his wounds, having only just arrived home to his loving mother and father following a misguided stand for the King at Naseby. It lists his injuries as having been shot in the leg, cut on the shoulder, and stabbed through the eye. Buried in the churchyard, it says, alongside the rest of his family, several of whom had also fallen, but in the service of Parliament's victorious army."

I noted the mention of an eye injury. I'd studied the skeleton closely as I'd cleaned it up and laid it out, piece by piece. That's how I'd spotted the nick to the shoulder blade. I'd seen nothing around the eye sockets to suggest an impact. A direct hit from an arrow or dagger thrown on the battlefield may not have scored the bone. But it would certainly have killed him instantly, passing through the soft eye tissue and into the brain. There was no eye shield or visor on Nathanial Moore's helmet. My stomach churned as I found myself speculating whether this was another example of the unloving familial welcome he'd received upon arriving back home. Brutal times.

"What do you think, Mr. Holmes?" asked the reverend.

Holmes closed the ledger and stood. "I think, Reverend, that we'll need to exhume Nathanial Moore's grave. Watson and I have reason to believe that the casket will be empty."

"Empty?" The reverend looked at Holmes and I as if expecting it to be some kind of tasteless ruse.

"We've found Nathanial Moore's remains concealed in the bottom of that trunk you and your friends used for dressing up, years ago."

The reverend fell back into a chair. "Goodness me!" he said. "Whatever next?"

As I drove back to London, I reflected on what had been a pleasant but eventful several days. *So much for a holiday*, I thought, with a wry chuckle. As Holmes predicted, exhuming Nathanial

Moore's grave revealed a rotting casket containing what looked to have been two sacks filled with shingle, but certainly no evidence of a body. That was then addressed after a lengthy discussion with the local coroner, who recorded a verdict of death through injuries sustained in battle, not wishing to go against the established historical record.

"This far down the line, gentlemen," the coroner wheezed, "I don't think we should be looking to create sensation. It's not like anyone alive today would be affected by it, either way."

This was true. However, it didn't stop Holmes from talking Sergeant Butchers through our reasoning, step by step, over a drink or two at the Tiger Inn. Holmes was right, Butchers was a good sort. Intelligent, quick-witted, and not too proud of his position. He'd go far, I was sure. Butchers jovially congratulated Holmes on solving a three-hundred-year-old mystery that no one had known about, along with the less important mystery as to how the Lonely Cavalier had come into being.

The re-burial of Nathanial Moore had taken place the morning before I left East Dean. There were four of us mourners. Holmes, Butchers, Constable Anderson, and me, with a short sermon from the Reverend Silsby. This time Nathanial's remains were laid properly to rest in peace, along with his armour and clothing. The reverend kept the pouch of papers, claiming them for the Parish archives. If Florence Gladwish's novel ever became published, Nathanial Moore would live on through those pages.

Over the generations, the trunk had been handed down through the Moore family, until recent generations where marriages had seen it come under the Duley family. Archibald had obviously found the chest and used some of the contents for dressing up games with Florence, then at some point Florence had taken possession of it – totally unaware of the truth of its contents. When Florence and Archibald found their love forbidden, they fell back on the character of Nathanial, as a mask to hide behind, enflamed by Florence's romantic notions.

"Florence Gladwish made him into a troubled, romantic hero," said Holmes, as we'd walked back to his farm after the funeral. "In actuality, Nathanial Moore was a tragic victim of a familial – nay a national – division."

Later, as the words played through my mind, I found myself nodding. I glanced over at the passenger seat next to me, and the two jars of honey nestled there. *No*, I thought, *retirement hasn't changed*

Sherlock Holmes that much. And it won't be too long until I see my friend again, I'm sure.

The West Egg Affair
by Joseph S. Walker

It is surely obvious from even a casual perusal of my reports of the exploits of my friend, Sherlock Holmes, that the cause of order has known no greater or more successful champion. It would be difficult indeed to come to a full accounting of the scoundrels and villains who would today walk the world freely, sowing unknown terror and suffering, if not for his genius and determination. For all his extraordinary abilities, however, Holmes is, in the end, not infallible, though it galls him to be brought to the point of acknowledging this. On those rare occasions when he is prevented from bringing his quarry to ground, he would prefer to think that justice has only been deferred, not denied.

In today's newspaper, I find evidence that such an optimistic view may well be justified, and I am reminded of a journey I took with Holmes not many years ago. At the time, it appeared that he had been thoroughly frustrated, and that the deaths of three unfortunate souls, struck down by a fatal combination of lust and vengeance, would go unpunished. As Holmes has demonstrated to me many times, however, appearances must never be assumed to be identical with reality. Recognizing that today's events signal his designs may be reaching their desired end, I take up my pen again to record, for the first time, his role in certain tragic events that unfolded among the estates of America's wealthy, in the early part of this decade, on Long Island. I do so despite realizing that circumstances may well demand that this particular exploit of the great detective remain unknown.

In the summer of 1922, His Majesty's Government requested that Holmes and I travel to the United States. Certain of our activities during the Great War, too sensitive to be committed to writing even today, were of urgent interest to the American government and, as Sherlock's brother Mycroft made clear to both of us, the continuation and deepening of a strong mutual alliance between our two nations was considered essential to maintaining the fragile new order that had been established in Europe. Although I had found a degree of satisfaction in simple domestic comforts as old age crept upon me, and although Holmes had become devoted to his quiet life tending bees in Sussex, we were both willingly convinced to undertake the journey in service to our nation.

Speed being considered of the essence, we were given berths on *HMS Marlborough*, a battleship which had seen honorable service during the recent conflict. It was during our crossing of the Atlantic, completed at a furious clip, that I began to become fully aware for the first time of how my advancing years, coupled with the various injuries I had suffered in Afghanistan and afterwards – to say nothing of the fearsome demands upon my energy exacted during the war – were beginning to tell on me. My companion, rapidly approaching his eighth decade, had if anything seemingly grown ever more resilient and energetic over the years. Holmes retained the lean, efficient frame and keen eye of a greyhound, and though he did employ a cane as he strolled about the deck, this was in part, I think, out of a sensitive desire to spare me from feeling the full measure of my own decline. I myself was confined to my tiny cabin for the bulk of the voyage, and I found that even accommodations intended for a senior officer ill-suited me. My mattress seemed no thicker or more comfortable than the felt stretched over a billiard table, and while I had previously endured many water voyages without complaint, I found now that my stomach was disinclined to tolerate the rough, continual rocking occasioned by the speed of our passage. By the time we were mercifully permitted to disembark at the American naval base in Annapolis, Holmes was regarding me with real concern, and he insisted upon a full day of rest before we continued on to the American capital in Washington.

The delay restored me somewhat, although Washington soon proved itself to be another form of trial. Its many imposing structures, and all the bustling activity of a government enjoying prosperity and growth in the wake of the war, could not disguise the fact that the city had been built upon a swamp, and that while American ingenuity may have tamed the land, it had done nothing to reduce the oppressive heat and humidity. I was repeatedly reminded, as we engaged in meeting after meeting with a seemingly endless stream of American officials, of the brief visits to India which had played a role in the very adventures we reported on. The sun beat down upon us on the banks of the Potomac with no less force than it had on the thronged shores of the Ganges.

I could not, however, complain of our reception. Our visit was unofficial and, in some technical sense, even secret, but this didn't prevent a number of the city's most dignified citizens from requesting an audience, in addition to the military and intelligence officials we had originally been asked to meet. Of course, I understood from the start that it was primarily Holmes who inspired such interest, but we were both treated everywhere with the utmost respect and consideration. The deference we were shown culminated in our summons, late one night, to the White House, where President Harding, though regretting that the ceremony had to be performed in secrecy, was pleased to bestow upon both of us the Congressional Gold Medal.

If this marked the zenith of our sojourn, however, the next day was to prove the nadir. The heat of the city was more brutal than ever, and from the moment I arose that morning, I felt an internal conviction that I was approaching the limits of my fortitude. It was tested still further by the American official with whom we held that day's conference, a humorless, condescending young man named Hoover from the Bureau of Investigation. Far from regarding us, or at least Holmes, with any degree of esteem or respect, his unblinking eyes and the positively hostile bent of his rigidly upright bearing conveyed nothing more strongly than suspicion and distrust. He went over aspects of our narrative multiple times, probing repeatedly at encounters we had reported with agents of the Russian government and its allies. I saw the corner of Holmes's mouth twitch upwards at several points when Hoover, apparently believing himself subtle, tried in various clumsy ways to tie these agents to elements within the British government. As the interview dragged into its third hour, I found that I had reached my breaking point, and moreover that there was a welcome relief in owning the fact.

I stood up, causing Hoover to break off in the middle of a speech about, if memory serves, the inevitability of the downfall of the Soviet regime. "Holmes," I said, "you may stay if you wish, but I find that can no longer suffer this insult. When I think of the good you had already done in the world at the moment when this smug bounder was born, and of the fact that he has not so much as offered you a glass of water, the question of whether to continue subjecting myself to his misapprehensions and insinuations ceases to be a challenging one. I am returning to the hotel."

"By all means, Watson," Holmes said. "I have but one more call to manage today, and then I will join you."

I nodded at him, and much more briefly at Hoover, and left. We had been provided with a car and driver, and I was soon back at our accommodations, sending the man back to find Holmes and conduct him on his further errands. I took a light lunch and rested as best as

I was able, taking notes on the conversations of the preceding days and wondering how such an obvious, blustering fool as Hoover had achieved a position of authority at such a young age. I could only conclude that ill fortune had sent all the men who might have prevented his regrettable rise to die in the trenches of France.

It was some hours before Holmes rejoined me, and when he did finally stride into the room he cast his stick in the corner and seized my hand heartily. "My dear fellow," he said. "I really owe you the deepest of apologies. I have not been entirely insensitive to the toll this weary campaign of diplomacy has taken upon you, and yet I have failed to act to relieve you of any part of the burden. I can only say, Watson, that I have been for many years so reliant upon your endurance and strength that I failed to take a full accounting of your present state."

"Really, Holmes," I said. "I have no basis for complaint. It has been most gratifying to see you receive some small measure of the recognition you are due."

"Nonetheless," he said, pulling up a chair close to the couch where I rested, "I believe I am now in a position to give you welcome news. At the very least, I can tell you that you have not many more hours to spend in the disagreeable climate of this city."

"Good news indeed!" I said. "Do we return to the *Marlborough*, then?"

"I think we can do considerably better than that. Our errand here being done, we may return to England at our leisure and in comfort. I have engaged two of the finest cabins aboard the *Mauretania*, reputed to be the most luxurious liner currently in the Atlantic. I trust you will find its mattresses a considerable improvement upon those the *Marlborough* offered. We depart from New York in three weeks."

"I am most glad to hear it," I said. "And in the interim?"

"I have been in conference with Sir Geddes on that very question," Holmes said, referring to His Majesty's ambassador to the United States. "One of his chief secretaries has a nephew, currently taking a large estate on Long Island. We are to lodge with him. There are people in New York with whom I wish to confer before we leave these shores, and the estate is convenient to the city. It is also, however, rural and secluded, and I'm told that its situation upon the water is most pleasant and restful. If you think you can manage the train voyage, we can be there tonight."

I was already standing. "You have my warmest thanks. I can be packed in half-an-hour."

105

We were met at the train station in New York City by a tall, impeccably groomed man who radiated calm. He presented himself the moment we stepped down from the car, seeming to move through the most crowded part of the platform without actually coming into contact with anyone. "Mr. Holmes," he said. "Dr. Watson. I am Jeeves."

"Ah," said Holmes. "Watson, our host's butler."

"Valet, sir," Jeeves corrected, "though I do have the honor to manage his household this summer, so technically 'butler' is not incorrect. If you'll be good enough to follow me, gentlemen." He conducted us through the station to a magnificent black Rolls Royce where, by some alchemy, our luggage already awaited us. We were soon installed in the spacious back seat of the vehicle and, driving with steady precision and skill, Jeeves took us through the bustling heart of the city, which I regarded with great curiosity. I could see why it was being so often said that New York was displacing London as the center of the Western world. In every direction I looked there was a sense of unrestrained vitality, of ambition and enterprise at work. If there was also evidence of considerable poverty and some signs of desperation, these were easy enough to overlook in the ceaseless noise and movement, so unlike the order of our London thoroughfares.

We crossed an enormous bridge to Long Island and gained speed as the road before us, and much of the landscape, emptied out. In the gathering dusk I was at first concerned that we had been misled as to the quality of our new resting place. We passed through a long valley of ash heaps and gray desolation, the only sign of life a petrol station where a weathered man sat and watched as we raced by. The surrounding countryside soon became green again, however, and there was a sense of open water off to our left, the presence a great body of water imposes on one's soul long before it can actually be seen.

In due course we arrived at the estate. The moment I saw it, my fears were allayed. It was a solidly built edifice of three stories, with long wings thrown out to either side of a palatial central entry. The drive curled around through the exactingly manicured grounds to come to the front of the house, which was on a small bluff looking out over a placid bay. A tributary of the drive ran down to a bare wooden dock which extended well out into the water. It was almost dark now, and we could see, across the bay, the lights of many other homes, some seeming nearly as large as this one.

Holmes stretched as he stepped from the car. "A lovely evening," he said. "Fully twenty degrees cooler than when we left Washington, wouldn't you say, Watson? I believe I'll stroll down to the dock and enjoy the air before going inside. Will you join me?"

I willingly assented. We ambled down the slight rise and walked about halfway out onto the dock. After the suffocating air of Washington, and even our brief exposure to the clamor of New York, the cool silence of the gathering night was a balm, and I took the clean salt air deep into my lungs with satisfaction. "This place is doing me good already," I said. "I'm only surprised that our host hasn't yet appeared to welcome us."

"He is already out for the evening, I'm afraid," Jeeves said from immediately behind us. I started, not having realized he was there. "He has taken the yacht across the bay to Mr. Gatsby's house in West Egg. You can see it there, sir, the large establishment ablaze with light and activity."

"West Egg," I said. "What a singular name. Is this then East Egg?"

I had intended this as a joke, but Jeeves nodded gravely. "Yes, sir. Both communities are considered very fashionable, I believe, although East Egg has been longer established and has a larger number of sizable estates."

"It appears that this Mr. Gatsby greatly enjoys entertaining," Holmes observed. "I fancy I can almost hear the music even at this distance."

"Indeed, sir. His galas have generated great social enthusiasm throughout the summer."

"Things seem much quieter on this side of the water," Holmes said. He gestured at the estate adjoining the one where we stood. This house was slightly smaller, but it had an even longer and more substantial dock, culminating in a tall pole where a bright green light burned. "Who resides there, Jeeves?"

"That is the residence of Mr. Thomas Buchanan, a financier, and his wife Daisy, sir." I couldn't help but sense a frostiness in Jeeves's tone which had not been there before. "When you are ready, gentlemen, I have had refreshments prepared and your rooms are ready for you."

In the following days, the estate proved to be exactly the cure I had needed for my earlier exertions. The rooms we had been provided were spacious and comfortable, with invigorating views of the enchanting bay dividing West Egg from East Egg. Our meals were generous and delicious, and the weather continued clear but temperate. I spent many hours reading on a balcony overlooking the central courtyard, frequently falling into pleasantly prolonged slumbers in the sun. Holmes, on those occasions when he wasn't in conference with various visitors who made the pilgrimage to East Egg to see him, took long, rambling walks around the village.

For the most part I was satisfied to take what I felt to be a long-deserved rest, but I did join Holmes on some of his shorter walks. On our second day, ambling along the shore, we encountered Mr. Buchanan and his wife, going out to the trim little cruiser tied at their dock. They were accompanied by a young girl I took to be their daughter, an athletic woman with short dark hair, and a nondescript man who seemed to fade into the background even as one looked at him.

As the others went on to the boat, the Buchanans hung back and introduced themselves. They were young, extremely attractive, and very fit. They were also, I perceived immediately, among that class of Americans so consumed with their own status and wealth that any real interest in others is entirely eclipsed. Once he had established that neither Holmes nor I was wealthy, and that we had nothing to offer him in the way of business connections, Buchanan hastily disentangled himself from us and resumed his walk out to his boat. His lovely wife, who had barely said a word, followed obediently in his wake.

Holmes leaned on his cane and watched them, frowning. "Those two make me uneasy, Watson," he said. "The man especially. He has the air of one who knows and enjoys cruelty. I believe he will come to a bad end – or should."

The encounter was a rare unpleasant moment. Holmes and I were usually left to our own devices, as we saw very little of our host, who proved to be an extremely amiable, if rather vacuous, young man. It developed that he was in the habit of going out every night, either to parties, often at Gatsby's, or to clubs in the city. His usual pattern was to return home near dawn to fall into bed, and stay there until well into the afternoon. His conversation, in the hours between his rising and his inevitable departure for another night of bacchanal pleasures, was invariably little more than a ceaseless stream of gossip about the activities and dramas of his small social circle.

He regarded these as being of paramount importance to the operations of the world, and took it for granted that his listener joined him in this belief. It would have shocked him to the core, I think, to learn that there was such a thing as war in the world, and he was aware of poverty and hunger only because some of the parties he went to raised funds to combat them. He had no more hope of understanding their reality than I did of understanding the new physics being put forward by Professor Einstein. Holmes, to my amusement, found him completely fascinating.

"That man may be the first true and complete innocent I have ever encountered, Watson," he said one night after our host had donned the tuxedo which served as his uniform and ventured out once more. "He drifts in a veritable sea of his own perceptions, untouched by the real world, anchored only by one bedrock certainty: Jeeves will make everything right. If his type populated the world, I should never have had a moment's occupation, for any real crime would be unknown."

By this time, I was myself prepared to endorse the idea of a bottomless faith in the tireless Jeeves. He seemed to be everywhere at once and able to anticipate every mood and every idle desire on the part of his employer's guests. He was equally considerate and perceptive in his treatment of the many visitors Holmes and I entertained during our stay. Once it became generally known that we were in East Egg, a steady stream of these made their way from the city and beyond. Some were old colleagues and brothers-in-arms from my days in service who had since made their way, by various winding paths, to America. I was also visited by representatives of my American publishers, whose urgent interest in seeing more from my pen was gratifying. Always, however, the most part of the pilgrims were drawn by a desire to see and speak with Holmes, and in their variety they represented a fair cross section of the world, a testament to the universal interest in his adventures and his singular set of skills.

I can scarcely recall all those that Jeeves ushered into our presence in those weeks, though I will mention a few by way of example. One afternoon brought three of the most famous practitioners of law in America: Clarence Darrow, baseball commissioner and judge Kenesaw Mountain Landis, and Supreme Court Justice Oliver Wendell Holmes, who proclaimed himself a distant cousin to my companion. Had I taken comprehensive notes on the discussion the four of them had of American law, its distinctions from the British, and its likely development in the coming years, reading them would surely be sufficiently educational to prepare many men for the bench. The American boxing champion Jack Dempsey came for lunch one day, and Holmes earned his astonished respect by demonstrating a one-inch punch he had learned in the Orient. A rather eccentric scientist named Nikola Tesla had grandiose ideas about the role future machinery would play in the justice system. A group including Charlie Chaplin, Buster Keaton, and Will Rogers sought, fruitlessly but amusingly, to persuade Holmes to undertake a vaudeville tour of the nation. General "Black Jack" Pershing, who had been away from Washington during our stay there, came with his aide, Major Patton, to discuss the state of affairs in eastern Europe. Robert Lincoln, the son of President Abraham Lincoln, spent a very pleasant evening with Holmes and me reminiscing. We had met him when he was the American ambassador in London in the 1890's.

Of course, members of Holmes's profession were well represented among those who made their way to Long Island. As it happens, a conference on the proposed establishment of a new international police force had recently concluded in Philadelphia. Holmes had long ago declined an invitation to address the gathering, but many who had been present came to pay their respects and probe his methods and theories before leaving the region. Among these were a Honolulu detective of Asian extraction named Chan, a brusque Englishman named Drummond, a fussy little Belgian of our acquaintance named Poirot, and an abrasive operative of the Continental Detective Agency whose name has disappeared from my notes.

Holmes was generous in sharing his ideas and experiences with these disciples, though I believe he found some of them rather trying. "Really, Watson," he said after the Belgian's visit, with an exasperation that surprised me, since he was actually rather fond of the fellow and they had worked together a number of times. "This is the third recent occasion Poirot has found to impose upon me with his prattle about little gray cells. He is not without talent, but if he would shave that ridiculous mustache he would find it much easier to focus his attention on what is before him."

For the most part Holmes and I received all these callers together, but there were a few whose identities and purpose I was never completely sure of, and who spent time with Holmes alone. One was a striking Negro woman in her fifties, who gave only the name Callisto. She and Holmes spent several hours walking up and down the shore together, and he had nothing but praise for her when she had departed. On another afternoon, when Holmes and I were strolling about in the yard, we were abruptly approached by a rather stout man, about thirty, whom neither of us had seen in quite some time. He nodded at me, clasped Holmes urgently by the arm, and whispered in his ear. It was one of the few times in decades of acquaintance that I saw my friend genuinely surprised. He pulled back and looked the younger man in the face.

"Watson," he said, "will you excuse us?"

He and the stout man walked away, and were gone until long into the night. When I asked him about it at breakfast the following morning, Holmes looked out the window, dabbing at his lips with a napkin.

"It concerns Montenegro," he said, and he would say nothing more.

I left the estate only once during those weeks, when our host, about to cross the bay for another of Mr. Gatsby's parties, invited us to join him. To my surprise, Holmes indicated that he would be gratified to accept. When I looked at him with raised eyebrows, he returned my gaze with a cool smile. "I have become curious to see Mr. Jay Gatsby," he said. He took me by the elbow and turned me slightly away from our host. "I am given to understand by local gossip that the man is a bootlegger and a notorious gambler. In short, what the Americans call a gangster. No, Watson, I have no desire to rouse myself to his pursuit. You will allow me, though, the nostalgic bemusement of a former big game hunter who visits the zoo."

Roused to curiosity myself, I agreed to make a third member of the party. Since neither Holmes nor I seemed likely to wish to stay as late as our host, it was arranged that Jeeves would wait an hour, then drive the car around to bring us back.

Having not been on the water since the nerve-wracking crossing on the *Marlborough*, I was somewhat trepidatious about trusting our host's yacht, but the water was smooth and the evening quiet, and to my surprise our host proved a nimble and capable captain, something he attributed to his time on a rowing team in school. We made the journey quickly and without incident.

Once there, however, we were confronted by rather more incident than any narrative could comprehensively account for. There seemed to be hundreds of people milling about on the yard, inside the enormous house, and around, and in, the large swimming pool overlooking the bay. The party spilled down onto a private beach where people in swimming gear, and a few out of it, splashed about in the moonlight. A band was playing Dixieland music from a platform near the pool. The confusion of noise, music, laughter, and shouting voices was such as I have seldom heard in my lifetime.

111

"Our Mr. Gatsby is not a man of subtle pleasures," Holmes murmured.

Our host having vanished into the throng immediately, Holmes and I wandered the grounds, our age making us effectively invisible to most of the people there. Given the state of intoxication many of them had achieved so early in the evening, we likely would have been invisible to them in any case. I had, during our stay in America, long since realized that the prohibition upon alcohol was observed only in the most desultory fashion. Even in the very seat of government, we had been offered drinks on many occasions, and our host's estate was well stocked with many varieties of spirit. I have never in my life, however, seen liquor flowing as it did that night. Had Jay Gatsby's swimming pool suddenly been drained, he could have made a credible effort to refill it with the contents of the bottles ranged like battalions on the tables and passing freely from hand to hand.

As we walked, Holmes stopped a few people who seemed to still be at least somewhat in possession of their senses and asked them where Mr. Gatsby might be found. The first two people he asked did not know the name, having been brought to the house by others. Finally, the third man, a broad-shouldered gentleman who seemed ill-at-ease in the suit he was wearing, stuck his cigar in his mouth and turned in a broad circle, scanning the crowd. At last he took the cigar out of his mouth and used it to gesture at the broad porch overlooking the pool. "'At's him," he said. "Gatsby. Fellow in the white suit." He stuck the cigar in his mouth and wandered away.

"Most interesting, Watson," Holmes said. "Observe with whom the famous Mr. Gatsby is speaking."

Gatsby, when I picked him out from the crowd, was a blond man in his early thirties, attractive enough, though there was something rough and unshaped about him that was difficult to pin down. He was standing, apparently at ease, speaking with Thomas Buchanan and the nondescript man who had been with Buchanan the day we met. A short distance away, Daisy Buchanan and the athletic woman were leaning against a railing, listening to the band and drinking from glasses of champagne. As we watched, Buchanan turned fully to the nondescript man and gestured, pointing at something back in the general direction of his own home. The very instant Buchanan was turned away from him, Gatsby looked at Daisy Buchanan with a gaze of such intensity and focus that, even from thirty feet away, I had not the slightest doubt of its meaning.

"Good heavens, Holmes!" I said. "The man's in love with Buchanan's wife."

"Transparently so," Holmes said. "There will be trouble there, Watson. Buchanan is not the sort of man to tolerate such things."

"Should we intervene?"

Holmes shrugged. "I have prevented murders in my time, as you well know. I have prevented thefts and assaults and treason. It could be argued with some justification that I have prevented wars. If there is a way to prevent a man and a woman who are determined to come together from doing so, I have not discovered it. But come, let us see what else we can determine about this developing drama."

By the time we made our slow way through the crowd to the patio, the other members of the little group had vanished off somewhere and Gatsby was standing on his own, holding a drink and staring off toward the water with a certain element of despair in his eyes. Attempting to follow his gaze, I saw, distinct even at this distance, the green light that was burning on the Buchanan dock across the bay. I wondered if this meant that the little party from East Egg had already left to return there.

We came up behind Gatsby and Holmes tapped his shoulder. He turned to us and smiled, and for the first time I sensed that there might be something extraordinary about the man. There was nothing artificial or calculated about his smile. It conveyed, as clearly as if he'd said it out loud and with more conviction, that seeing us was the single thing he would have wished for in the world to make his happiness complete. There was not a trace of the melancholy I'd seen just a moment before. "Well, old sport!" he said. "So delighted you could make it. Can I get you anything?"

"Thank you, no, Mr. Gatsby," Holmes said. "We merely wished to introduce ourselves and express our gratitude for your hospitality. This is Dr. John Watson. I am Sherlock Holmes."

"No!" Gatsby said. "Are you really? *The* Sherlock Holmes?"

"I have that honor."

"I say, old sport, the honor is all mine," Gatsby said. He pumped Holmes's hand energetically, then mine. "I'd heard you were knocking about the neighborhood, you know, but I never thought you'd actually turn up here! Delighted, of course. I feel I ought to get an autograph or something."

"You flatter me," Holmes said. Only my decades of closely observing him enabled me to discern that he was preening.

"Not at all, old sport. Someone was saying just the other day that it's chaps like you who really make history, you know, while

113

the rest of us merely live through it. Who was that? It will come to me. I say, you know, you really must allow me to get you two drinks."

"I don't believe we'll be staying long, Mr. Gatsby," I said. "Being of advanced age, we lack the energy, I fear, to do justice to your celebration."

"Oh, that's too dashed bad. Let me – " At this point Gatsby broke off abruptly, looking over my right shoulder. Turning in that direction, I saw a flash of blue, matching the dress Daisy Buchanan had been wearing, at an upstairs window. "That is to say, please make yourselves at home here for as long as you wish," he continued. "I must excuse myself for a moment."

He rushed off toward the doorway into the house. A glance at Holmes was enough to show me that he, too, had seen Daisy. He shook his head. "There will be trouble, Watson," he repeated. "But not tonight, I judge, and not the kind of trouble in which you and I specialize. Come. This music is making me long for my quiet room and my violin. Let us seek Jeeves and the car."

We didn't see or hear of Gatsby or the Buchanans again for some time after this. In the hours when we weren't entertaining visitors, I continued my recuperation and Holmes continued his explorations of the area, having sought and obtained permission to use one of the estate cars in addition to his long walks.

One evening, with the date of our departure drawing near and the hour approaching ten, Holmes and I were sitting on the porch, smoking and chatting in a relaxed way about friends and foes who hadn't survived the war. I could tell from his rather grim choice of topic, as well the listless posture with which he sat, that my friend, after so many weeks of movement and engagement, was approaching one of his darker moods. I was reflecting that at least he no longer relied upon cocaine to get through these, and further that the enforced passivity of the impending voyage was well-timed, when Jeeves came out of the house.

"I beg your pardon, gentlemen," he said. "I fear I have received some unpleasant news. Given its nature, and your profession and history, I thought it something of which you would wish to have knowledge."

Holmes looked up, a gleam in his eye. "Pray tell us, Jeeves."

"I regret to say that a young woman named Myrtle Wilson has died, sir. She is, or rather was, the wife of the gentleman who owns the fueling station on the main road to the city. She was struck and killed by an automobile, which did not stop."

"Terrible," I said. "Surely nothing more than an accident, though."

Holmes was sitting upright now, his fingers steepled. "Perhaps," he said. "Was the car going toward or away from the city, Jeeves?"

"Away, sir. It is reported to have been a large yellow vehicle, the number of occupants undetermined. There is a witness, sir, who claims that Mrs. Wilson ran deliberately toward the car, as though trying to flag it down."

"Indeed," Holmes said. "A most intriguing detail. Thank you, Jeeves."

"Sir." Jeeves vanished back into the house.

"Enlighten me, Holmes," I said. "Clearly you think there more to this. What do you see that I do not?"

"As ever, Doctor, the answer is not what I see, but what I mark," Holmes replied. "For example. Did you notice when we last saw a car turn into the Buchanan drive?"

I laughed. "Of course not. I have no doubt you did."

"There have been two within the last hour," Holmes said. "The first came and left again almost immediately. The second is still there. Of course, with the hedge between the two drives we cannot see the cars themselves, only the lights as they go past." He stood. "I believe I will take a short amble along that hedge. Will you join me?"

I took up my cane willingly. "This Wilson woman," I said. "You didn't know her, surely?"

"I met her," Holmes said. "On three occasions, when I took drives and stopped for fuel. Her husband is a dull, lifeless sort, utterly resigned to being crushed by the world until it is done with him. It was a poor match. She was by no means an intelligent woman, but she had too much spirit for him."

As we strolled toward the dividing line between the properties, with Holmes restricting his pace to what I could manage, we heard another car. It didn't enter the Buchanan drive, but idled briefly at its end, then sped away.

"Taxi," Holmes said. "There's no mistaking an engine that has been used so roughly. And who is leaving, I wonder?"

We reached the line of bushes that formed the boundary with the Buchanan estate and began to walk along it, getting closer to the bay. We had gone perhaps twenty yards when Holmes held up his hand, bidding me to stop. He stood perfectly still for a moment.

"Good evening, Mr. Gatsby," he said.

There was a momentary pause, then the bushes beside us parted and Jay Gatsby stepped out, looking rather chagrined. "I was going to ask how you knew I was there," he said. "And then I remembered who you are. Good evening, Mr. Holmes. Dr. Watson."

"Mr. Gatsby," I said.

"It's a pleasant night for a walk," Holmes said. "But you seem to have wandered quite far, Mr. Gatsby."

"Oh, yes, rather," Gatsby said. He then glanced over his shoulder in the direction of the distant Buchanan house. "I was just – " He broke off, embarrassed.

Holmes nodded as though Gatsby had finished the statement. "Have you heard of the tragedy tonight, sir?"

Gatsby swallowed. "I suppose you mean the woman who was killed."

"Yes."

"Yes. I've heard. Terrible business." He glanced back at the house again. "I – I was afraid Daisy would hear, you see, and take the news badly. So I thought I should be here. In case she needs – " He gestured vaguely with his hands. "You know. Support."

I looked away, unable to bear the man's naked misery.

"Of course," Holmes said. "We have access to a car, Mr. Gatsby. May we offer you a ride home?"

"No," he said. "No, I think I'll stick here, for just a bit longer. Daisy is very sensitive, you know. This will be a terrible blow to her. Frightfully decent of you to offer." He turned, moving slowly as though he expected Holmes to stop him, and went back between the bushes.

Holmes sighed deeply and led me back toward the estate. "This is a bad business, Watson," he said as we drew near the house. "The storm is upon them now, and none of them are equipped to endure it."

"What can be done, Holmes?"

"Tonight? Nothing, I think. The die is cast. Tomorrow? Something, perhaps. I will think on it. Good night, Doctor."

I awoke the next morning eager to hear Holmes's conclusions, but when I went to breakfast, Jeeves informed me that he had already left, taking the car and asking that I remain at the estate to be summoned if needed. That proved to be a long, fruitless, empty day.

116

No telephone call ever came, and no matter how I paced, no matter how many times I jotted names and times and theories in my notebook, I could reach no conclusion as to what Holmes might be doing. I had no doubt that he wished to see Myrtle Wilson's killer brought to justice, but who that might be, and how he could achieve the goal, was more than I could determine.

It was past six in the evening, and I was half-dozing in a chair in the library, when the door opened and Holmes finally came in. I saw at a glance that his day hadn't taken the form he'd hoped for. He nodded in my direction, sank upon the couch, and ran his hands through his thinning hair, looking, for once, as though he felt every one of his years keenly.

"I grow old, Watson," he said. "I shall wear my trousers rolled."

"I'm afraid I don't understand your meaning, Holmes."

"I have failed, utterly and completely," he said. "I could indeed blame my age, but what would I have done differently ten years ago, or twenty? Perhaps it's only that I could have done it faster."

"Holmes, what on earth has happened?"

"Jay Gatsby is dead, Doctor. Dead by gunshot not three hours past, at the hand of George Wilson, who then turned the gun upon himself." Holmes closed his eyes and his head fell back upon the couch. "I had a choice to make at the start of the day, Watson. Attempt to trace Myrtle Wilson's killer, or prevent George Wilson from seeking an ill-considered revenge. I chose poorly. I judged that Wilson was too weak a man to take decisive action, and perhaps that would have been the case had he not been shaped into a weapon by another and pointed at Gatsby. By the time I realized the danger, it was too late. When I should have been pursuing Wilson, I was instead traveling to the city and back, tracking the movements of all those involved in the tragedy."

"It's ghastly, Holmes," I said. "Wilson must have been convinced that it was Gatsby who ran down his wife. But why would Gatsby have done so? And how did Wilson learn of it?"

"How indeed," Holmes said. "Wilson was, it appears, on foot, though he must have obtained rides at some points. Still, he was on the road, Watson, which means I must have driven past him. Two times today? Three? And yet he evaded me."

"You cannot blame yourself, Holmes. If Gatsby did kill her, then perhaps this is a form of justice, grim as it might be."

"Ah," said Holmes. "But I tell you he did not. Gatsby may have been guilty of many things, Doctor, but the blood of Myrtle Wilson stained other hands than his."

117

I felt myself smile very slightly. "Whatever your age, Holmes, you haven't tired of presenting me with riddles. Will you not tell me whose hands you refer to?"

"Not just yet, Watson," he said. He looked at his watch. "I have been in communication with the local police and shared my knowledge with them. I believe they will act upon it, and then we shall hear something, probably within the hour. I will share the full story with you then, once it has a conclusion."

I had long since learned that it was useless to seek to shake Holmes from such a determination once he has made it. Resigned to a wait, I rang for Jeeves and requested a whisky-and-soda.

The hour came and went, and a second on its heels. Holmes grew increasingly restive as the time advanced, pacing the room and frequently pausing to look out the window facing the Buchanan estate. Several times he moved as if to pick up the telephone, but restrained himself. It was almost nine when we heard a car pulling up outside. Holmes had been slouched on a chair, but at the sound he sprang to his feet. "At last," he said. "Now, Doctor, you shall hear some news."

Jeeves opened the library door. "Mr. J. Edgar Hoover," he intoned.

Holmes and I looked at each other in shock. Strolling into the room behind Jeeves was indeed the unpleasant young man we had seen weeks ago in Washington, the look on his face now even more insufferably self-satisfied than it had been then.

"Mr. Holmes," he said. "Dr. Watson. I am here to formally request that, as foreign nationals, you refrain from interfering in the criminal justice system of this nation. Should you continue to do so, you will be arrested for deportation or, at my discretion, trial on the charge of obstructing justice."

"Outrageous!" I said. "You overstep yourself, sir."

"It's you who oversteps," Hoover said. He turned to Holmes. "Or more specifically, *you*. I've heard all about your attempt to take control of the local police force this afternoon."

"This is absurd!" I said. "You came all the way from Washington because you heard that Holmes talked to the police?"

"No," Holmes said. "Observe the state of his trousers, Watson, the crispness of his cuffs. This is not, I think, a man who has just come from a train station. He was already in New York. I wonder why." He sat down, studying Hoover closely. "Have Tom and Daisy Buchanan been arrested?"

118

Hoover crossed his arms and scoffed. "Of course not. Arrested for what?"

Holmes smiled tightly. "Don't play the fool, Hoover. It was Jay Gatsby's car that struck Myrtle Wilson, but Daisy Buchanan was driving it. She and Gatsby were having an affair, just as Tom Buchanan was having one with Mrs. Wilson. I haven't been able to speak with Mrs. Buchanan, so I don't know if she knew that, or if the death of Mrs. Wilson was truly an accident. But I do know that Wilson was at the Buchanan estate today, and it is logical to believe that Buchanan convinced him that Gatsby was at fault." Holmes splayed his hands. "By my understanding of American law, that makes Daisy guilty of, at the least, manslaughter, and Thomas Buchanan of conspiracy to commit murder. You represent one of the main arms of American law enforcement. Will they be arrested?"

"No," Hoover said. "You can't prove any of that."

"We shall see."

"We certainly shall not. You have no jurisdiction on this side of the Atlantic, Mr. Holmes, and no police agency or other official body will give you any attention for your wild theories. At any rate, the Buchanans are no longer here." Hoover looked at his own watch. "I believe they are on a train to Montreal."

Holmes's eyes were hooded now. Hoover may have thought he was an old man falling asleep. I could have warned him that Holmes was now at his highest state of mental activity, but I kept my chair and my silence.

"He called you," Holmes said.

Hoover shifted his feet. "What?"

"Buchanan called you. Last night, when he learned what had happened. That's why you came to New York, last night or very early this morning." Holmes pointed at him. "You're protecting him. Which means either Buchanan is blackmailing you, or you have some use for him."

Hoover was turning red. "You don't know what you're talking about, Holmes."

Holmes cocked his head. "Buchanan is a financier. He socializes with the elite of American wealth and business. No doubt in the course of those associations he learns secrets, rumors, incriminating stories. You are using him, Hoover. You've made of him your tool. In all probability it's you who is blackmailing him. How many scalps has he brought you?"

"That's enough," Hoover snapped. He grasped the back of the chair in front of him and pointed a shaking finger at Holmes. "I have

119

had enough of your Limey accent and your smug face. The great Sherlock Holmes! Your time is almost up, and mine is just beginning. Your ship sails the day after tomorrow. You'll be on it, or you'll be arrested. I have a file on you. You too, Doctor. You do not want me opening those files in public. You talk about American law? There's only one thing you need to know about American law, Holmes: I'm it."

Hoover spun on his heel and left the room. A moment later we heard his engine start and his car race down the drive and away.

"What a vile little man," I said. "What will you do, Holmes?"

He was leaning back in his chair, his fingers steepled, his long legs stretched out before him. He shook his head almost imperceptibly. "I believe we're stymied, at least for the moment. It would be a difficult case to prove at any rate, and with the police of the continent arrayed against us it is hopeless. The Buchanans have slipped the net, at least for the moment."

"How galling. Three people dead, and they will be permitted to move on as though none of it happened."

"For the moment," Holmes said again. He sighed. "I fear for this nation, Watson. There is much that is good here, much to inspire all of humanity. And yet I fear the future of America is figured in J. Edgar Hoover. He is so assured of his own virtue that there is no vice he will not engage in, so invested in his need for strength that he must crush anything he finds weak, so convinced he is right that everything and everyone else must be wrong. It is said that the twentieth century will belong to America. Perhaps it is as well that we shall not live to see most of it."

I grunted. "I am certainly ready to see England again."

"As am I. Still, Watson, we're not entirely without cards to play. If we cannot stop Hoover, we can at least hope for the opportunity to blunt the tools he wishes to employ. Jeeves?"

"Sir."

Once again I started, having entirely forgotten that the man was there.

"Jeeves, you have heard what occurred here this evening. Are you convinced that Tom and Daisy Buchanan bear responsibility for the deaths that have occurred?"

"Indeed, sir," Jeeves said. "They have behaved most outrageously."

Holmes nodded. "I would find it fitting, Jeeves, if the Buchanans were never again able to employ a servant who remained unaware of that behavior."

120

"That is quite easily arranged, sir."

"I would also be very appreciative, Jeeves, to learn of it immediately should the Buchanans ever plan to come to England."

"I would be most pleased to inform you of it, sir."

"Satisfactory," Holmes said. He rose to his feet. "Watson, it would seem that we have only a limited time left to enjoy these most enjoyable grounds. Will you join me in a walk?"

That night three years ago was the last time I heard Holmes mention the name Buchanan, and yet I believe he adhered to his determination to someday exact a measure of retribution for the deaths of Gatsby and the Wilsons and, simultaneously, to deny Hoover whatever further use he had for the wealthy, selfish, careless couple. I am confirmed in this belief by the news, reported today, that a police search of the London residence of Thomas Buchanan, a visiting American businessman, turned up a cache of stolen bonds and jewels. Along with these goods were files of documents and photographs intended, to judge from the dark hints the press offers, as blackmail material against a number of prominent citizens of both England and America. Buchanan fiercely denies his guilt, and the American embassy has become involved. It seems likely that he ultimately will face no legal punishment other than expulsion from England. It seems even more likely, however, that in the wake of the scandal the Buchanans will never again be accepted in society, rendering them useless to Hoover's plans. For people of the Buchanans' class, such exile, and the subsequent loss of Hoover's protection, may well be a worse fate than prison.

I wonder if Mr. J. Edgar Hoover has yet realized the error he made in telling Sherlock Holmes that his time was at an end.

The Curious Case of President Harding
by John Lawrence

Part I – Things Come in Threes

"Have you ever noticed," I asked Sherlock Holmes as we sat overlooking the magnificent cliffs of Sussex, "that things come in threes?"

Holmes stifled a yawn. "Really?" he responded in a bored tone. "I was not aware." He looked up from *The Police Gazetteer*, which, even in retirement, consumed several minutes of every day at his home in Sussex. "Nor can I imagine that the aphorism has any basis in fact."

"Well, The Holy Trinity, for example," I offered, regretting immediately having offered a theological example would make little impression, given Holmes's skepticism of all things ecclesiastical in nature. He predictably sniffed his indifference. "The primary colors, then. The Brontë sisters!"

"Watson, you might just as well say 'Good things come in twelves' and cite the number of inches on a ruler – or the days in the Christmas song," he added. "Certainly there is no significance to such an observation if one is focused purely on facts, not sentimentality or coincidence."

After more than four decades of friendship and collaboration, I was well aware when my words were unlikely to influence Holmes, and I decided to abandon the discussion and focus instead on the brilliant white of the Dover seashore.

"Ah, this is magnificent," I said. "The sea, the blue of the Channel, the white cliffs. What a welcome change from the congestion and bustle of London. You have made a very wise choice in selecting the south for your retirement home."

"Yes, my bees keep me quite busy," he replied. "And yet, there are times when the lure of London – the challenge of a perplexing case, the intelligence of a conniving criminal – all exert a very strong nostalgia."

"Why, Holmes!" I cried. "You are a sentimentalist after all!"

"No, but there are aspects of the chase that even the intricacies of the apiary cannot replace," he admitted.

"Possibly you should think of a diversion," I suggested. "A trip? Perhaps a return visit to America. I would be pleased to accompany you on such a journey: New York, Boston, Washington. If we are to consider such an excursion, I say, we should get on with it." I tapped the cane I used for steadying myself. "We aren't getting any younger."

"No, America is too far a journey at this point," Holmes said, shaking his head. "Perhaps the Continent would be rejuvenating. But no, not across the Atlantic. I could not bear how stultifying such a trip there would inevitably be."

And yet just three weeks later, at the beginning of August 1923, Holmes and I could be found sunning ourselves on the deck of *HMS Olympic*, bound for New York, and enjoying a whisky-and-soda, as well as the brisk salt air. "A perfectly relaxing way to spend several days, don't you think?" I inquired. "We'd better have another one of these," I said, raising my nearly empty glass as a steward walked by. "We certainly won't be enjoying a good stiff drink in the States, what with this silly Prohibition they've implemented!"

We landed in New York on 5th August, but there was little of the gaiety one typically associates with ship arrivals to greet us. "Good Lord!" I cried, "Look there!" The sign displayed on the newspaper seller's kiosk proclaimed in bold, six-inch high letters, *"Harding Dead, Body Being Brought to Washington, Burial To Be In Ohio"*. All about us on the quay, peoples' heads were buried in the open newspapers as they read about the shocking development.

I hurried to buy one of the papers and together we scanned the story as we rode in a clattering automobile to our hotel. Harding, who had been elected in a landslide not even three years earlier, had been engaged in a cross-country trip that included a visit to the territory of Alaska. It had been reported that there had been some concerns about his health and state of mind of late. While in Alaska, he had referred to being in Nebraska, and had teetered while behind his podium. His physicians had ministered to him when he arrived in San Francisco, the last stop on his journey.

"Death, apparently balked by medical science, struck suddenly and with no warning, at 7:30," the newspaper account read. *"The President had been believed definitely on the road to recovery from ptomaine poisoning, acute indigestion, and a pneumonic affection which followed them."* Evidently Mrs. Harding had been reading to him by his bedside in the Palace Hotel. He had bade his wife to

123

continue when he suddenly threw his hand up over his head and convulsed. *"Then the President stiffened and as suddenly dropped back limply,"* the story continued. His wife, who had in an instant passed from being the nation's First Lady to that of a widow, was quoted as resolutely stating, *"I am not going to break down."*

"What do you make of it?" Holmes asked. "Does anything about this narrative strike you as unusual or suspicious?"

I thought for a moment. Despite some concerns about Harding's health following his bout with the flu, he hadn't appeared to be at risk of dying. Indeed, the scandal sheets had been filled with allegations of chronic promiscuity that, if true, would surely qualify Mr. Harding as America's most virile leader ever. And yet, here he was dead at the age of only fifty-seven, thousands of miles from home, in a hotel room.

"I cannot say without more facts," I responded. Holmes smiled at my utilization of one of his own axioms: Never form conclusions without facts. As a medical man myself, it did appear strange for an energetic man to be cut down so quickly, but then again, there were millions of people who had suffered just such unexpected deaths from the recent influenza pandemic.

We hired a Negro porter to gather up our bags and arrange for a taxicab to our hotel, the Ritz Carlton, where we were shown to our room, which afforded us a magnificent view of the city. We were in the midst of unpacking our trunks when there was a sharp knock on the door. I opened the door to find a serious-looking young man with two companions standing behind him.

"Thank you," I said before he could speak, "but we have just arrived and do not have time just yet for tea. If you don't mind, could you return in perhaps a half-hour?"

The young man coughed uncomfortably. "Excuse me, but are you Mr. Sherlock Holmes from England?" he asked.

"I am Dr. John Watson," I replied. "Mr. Holmes's friend."

"Ah, Dr. Watson," the young man said, brightening somewhat and extending his hand, which I shook. "Mr. Holmes's scribe! A real honor to meet you. I've read your adventures in *Lippincott's*. Most entertaining!" He paused. "However, I wonder if I might speak with Mr. Holmes."

"We have just arrived by steamer and are quite fatigued," I answered. "Mr. Holmes is on a private holiday, and – "

"On, forgive me," he said smiling. "I am not an acolyte! My card," he said, presenting a small white business card embellished with a small shield.

124

"'*Jonathan Radner*'," it read. "I'm a member of the United States Secret Service," he explained. Noting my confused look, he added, "Our organization has as its primary mission the safeguarding of the President."

"Ah, I see," I responded, looking at the card carefully. I looked up into Mr. Radner's face. "And what may I tell Mr. Holmes you would like to discuss with him?" I queried.

Suddenly, Holmes appeared at my side and the Secret Service man swallowed hard and bit his lower lip in awe.

"I think it is perfectly self-evident, Watson," Holmes responded. "These gentlemen want to talk with me about the possible assassination of the President of the United States."

Radner's expression was one of complete shock. "But . . . but how could you have guessed that, Mr. Holmes?" he sputtered.

"I never guess, Mr. Radner," Holmes archly responded, inviting him into the room. "I would have thought you would know as much from reading Watson's little essays." He motioned Radner to one of the chairs in the sitting area and sat in the other one himself while I perched on the edge of a bed. Radner's companions closed the door, remaining in the hallway. "Tell me how I may be of service."

Radner's face grew grim. "What I'm about to tell you, Mr. Holmes," he began, "requires the strictest of confidence. Disclosure of unproven suppositions could have the most calamitous implications for the United States government. May I have your assurance of complete confidentiality?"

"Mr. Radner, you are far from the first client of mine with connections to the highest levels of his government," Holmes assured. "I have counted kings and prime ministers amongst my clients. I ensure them the very same level of confidentiality I give a secretary whose fiancé has gone missing – that is, complete discretion."

"Very well," Radner answered. "And I do want to assure you that the government is prepared to pay you a handsome fee if you can shed light on this cataclysmic situation."

Holmes waved his hand. "My fees are fixed, except when I choose to forgo them altogether," he insisted. "Pray, how may I be of service?"

Radner studied Holmes carefully, as if attempting to assess the trustworthiness and intellect of the actual person rather than the larger-than-life subject of my accounts. Holmes was now considerably older than the incomparable sleuth recorded in *The Adventures, The Memoirs,* and other stories as illustrated by Mr.

Paget. What hair he retained was grayer but still combed backwards. His face, still thin, was more lined, but his aquiline nose remained just as prominent and his eyes burned with an intensity undimmed from those days in Baker Street.

"Our country has just suffered a great calamity," Radner began. "The President – " His voice caught, and he took a moment to calm himself. "Our President is dead. Dead! He was taken ill in San Francisco where he died."

"So we have read in the newspaper," Holmes noted, adding his condolences. "And what was his condition on this journey? Was he healthy? Vigorous?"

"To tell you the truth, Mr. Holmes, the President hadn't been well," Radner admitted. "He had a bad case of influenza earlier in the year and had remained quite fatigued and weakened."

"So we gathered from the press accounts. And his habits?" Holmes pressed.

"President Harding indulged in heavy drinking and heavy smoking," Radner admitted somewhat sheepishly.

"And in several other vices, I understand," Holmes added, making it clear he would abide no withholding of pertinent information.

"It is true," the officer agreed. "He stopped drinking, or so he said, but he wouldn't give up his tobacco."

"And what do the doctors say was the cause of death?" Holmes asked.

"Perhaps apoplexy, perhaps a heart attack," Radner answered. "Perhaps a combination of factors. There was some thought he might have eaten something that disagreed with him – possibly tainted seafood – and the doctors purged him to reduce the effects."

Holmes sat upright. "Then they haven't ruled out poisoning as a cause?" he asked.

Radner regarded Holmes closely. "I believe they are focused on natural causes, Mr. Holmes."

"And yet you have come to see me, Mr. Radner," said Holmes, "which tells me you have suspicions that you are cautious about sharing with the regular police."

"Sir," he said, adding a small cough and looking over his shoulder at me, "let me be honest with you. Some of us suspect that the President was murdered."

"Yes, so I concluded when you announced your employer," said Holmes. "If you accepted without question that the President had died of natural causes, surely you would have had no reason to

126

interrupt my holiday in New York, so you must harbor suspicions as to who might be behind this devilry."

Radner remained quiet for a long moment. "Mr. Holmes, I must admit I have no evidence of foul play. But it seems to me prudent to make inquiries surrounding his rapid decline, and those are questions I cannot pursue in my official position with the government." He paused and looked at Holmes. "Might I persuade you to take on this case? There is no promise of official recognition or even public acknowledgement of your efforts, and there might well be some resistance from the Harding family and those in his administration to a public discussion of this topic. But history must have answers, Mr. Holmes!"

Holmes looked hard at the young man. "Very well," he said, "let us see where this journey takes us."

'I think the first step must take us to Washington, D.C.," Radner suggested. "Most of the individuals you'll want to speak with are going to be there. We've already begun that process, and I can fill you in on the train. One is leaving in an hour-and-a-half."

Fortunately we had barely begun to unpack, and within a few moments, the three of us were on the way to Pennsylvania Station, the enormous *Beaux Arts* edifice in mid-town Manhattan. The ride through the streets of New York was fascinating – columns of stone, glass, and concrete soared overhead, leaving much of the street in shadow. Throngs of people, automobiles, buses, and an occasional horse-drawn wagon clogged the streets. The smells, costumes, and languages of dozens of cultures assaulted one's senses as we strode from our cab up the stairs and into the magnificent station.

Within a half-hour, we were nestled into our private compartment as the train pulled out of the station, traversed the Hudson River, and crossed into New Jersey and then southward. There was little time, however, to consider the countryside as it rushed past.

"This is Agent Withers and Agent McCloskey," Radner said, motioning to his two companions. "They've been in touch with the President's – I mean, the *late* President's – party in San Fran. Jack, whatcha have?"

The agent identified as Withers hunched forward to speak in a low voice, "Harding certainly wasn't well," he began. "He was complainin' to the agents up in Alaska. Then once he got to Washington – that's Washington State, not D.C. – " he clarified for Holmes and me, " – he was really gettin' bad. By time he got to Frisco on the 29th, he had a fever, so the doc gave him some

127

medicine, but it didn't seem to do no good." I saw Holmes wince at the American grammar, but he said nothing. "Well, yesterday, about 7:30 in the evening, his wife was reading to him and – Poof! – Out he went! Never knew what hit him."

"Doesn't it seem odd that he was strong enough to recover from a flu that killed millions of people in recent years, and yet succumbed so suddenly?" Holmes inquired.

"Oh, yes, Mr. Holmes," Withers agreed. "He had quite a time of it in January."

"I wonder," Holmes said aloud. After a few moments, he looked up at Radner and Withers. "Mr. Coolidge becomes President now, is that right?"

"He's already President," Radner responded. "Sworn in by his own father, a justice of the peace, up in Vermont."

"And who else is on the obvious list?" Holmes asked.

The agents looked at each other in confusion. "What 'list' would that be?" said Withers.

"Why, the list of who might benefit from the President's sudden and unanticipated demise," Holmes replied. The agents looked at him as though he had begun to speak in a foreign language.

"Benefit?" Withers asked incredulously.

"Whenever a crime occurs – and I consider an unanticipated death a potential crime – I invariably ask who stands to benefit," said Holmes. The agents looked skeptical. "Who had a motive? In this case, surely there are a great many people who stand to benefit immeasurably by the death of President Harding. Of course, I don't mean Mr. Coolidge necessarily, but colleagues, political rivals, or foreign despots."

The Secret Service agents stammered, pledging to assemble a list of possible beneficiaries of the President's death.

"And the autopsy results, once the *post mortem* is completed," Holmes continued. "I would like for Dr. Watson and me to examine them at the earliest opportunity," he explained, nodding in my direction.

Agent Withers coughed and said, "I'm afraid that won't be possible, Mr. Holmes. There was no autopsy. Mrs. Harding strictly forbade it. Our agents spoke with Dr. Ray Wilbur of Stanford who was with the President when he expired. He confirmed the First Lady wouldn't hear of a *post mortem* examination. In fact, the President's body was embalmed within an hour after he died."

I drew Holmes from the compartment, out of earshot of the agents. "Do you seriously suspect foul play?"

"Facts are more valued than suspicions," he said, "and in this very significant case, a great deal of effort appears to have been made to obliterate any evidence of the actual cause of death.

"It is curious, is it not – such a drastic turn in the President's health," Holmes said after we'd returned to the cluster of agents. "Not what one might expect in the case of a middle-aged man whose health is so carefully attended and guarded."

"Well, perhaps not as curious as you might think, Mr. Holmes," Radner said. "Our President's endure a great deal of stress, and it isn't unusual for their health to suffer. Why, President Harding's predecessor, Mr. Wilson, suffered a severe stroke just a few years ago that very nearly killed him, and he was just sixty-two! And he still was thinking of running again for a third term!"

"And T.R. had a stroke earlier that year, and he was just sixty!" added Withers. "That's Theodore Roosevelt. Teddy wasn't President any more of course, but he was sure thinking of running again in 1920."

"Things come in threes," Holmes turned to me and murmured, barely loud enough to be heard.

"What's that you say, Mr. Holmes?" asked Radner.

Holmes ignored his question and grew quiet. He turned in his seat and looked out the window as the rolling fields passed by. I waved off the agents, knowing that Holmes had entered his cerebral stage, analyzing information in ways that could not be replicated by the average brain. Several minutes later, he motioned for me to lean in.

"Watson, doesn't this strike you as curious?" he asked softly.

"That three men should suffer strokes?" I responded.

"That three men who all served as President – all of an age when they should have been physically robust – that all three should suffer the same deadly attack," he said. "Wilson survived, it's true, but he could barely function during his last year or so as President and has been an invalid ever since, if memory serves me correctly. The agents just told us that Roosevelt and Wilson both were planning to run in 1920, and Harding most certainly intended to seek another term in 1924, one must presume. All were stricken a year in advance of the coming election, ending their candidacies. Doesn't that strike you as, at a minimum, *coincidental*?" Holmes grew quiet again, and I dared say nothing while his mind considered his own observations.

After a few moments, I dared to offer an observation. "I will admit the coincidence seems striking," I said. "But are you

129

suggesting a plot against these three Presidents? And who would wish to harm three completely different men?"

"Someone who also wished to be President," he reasoned, "and who wished to eliminate the opposition." Holmes sat back in his seat and leaned towards me. "If I'm not mistaken, you are the one who recently noted that 'things happen in threes'."

"Yes, but Harding wasn't stricken in 1919 or 1920, but three years later, so if someone was plotting to affect the 1920 election, they would seem to have missed their mark," I suggested. "Harding didn't become a target until this year – 1923 – although he, too, had been running in 1920."

"True enough," Holmes acknowledged. "And yet . . . ."

The impact of Holmes's words rang in my ears. Could he possibly be serious? He was proposing a conspiracy so monstrous that it hardly seemed plausible – three Presidents, each the victim of a plot designed to clear a path to the White House, with two of them in office at the time of the attack? And how would such an outrageous scheme be carried out?

"What do you want to do?" I asked.

"*We*, Watson, *we*," he replied, "for I will certainly need medical skills beyond my own capability to uncover this plot, if there is such a plot at all. For the moment, however, we must share some information with Mr. Radner – but not *too* much, for if there is a conspiracy of some type, it may well be orchestrated out of the Secret Service itself!"

Holmes asked Radner to confer without the other agents, who soon stood outside and guarded the sliding doorway, which Radner had closed behind them. "Did you have a thought, Mr. Holmes?" he asked.

"If you have read Watson's little stories about my methods," he said, "you are aware that I cannot reach conclusions without facts. I will need more information. I want to find more about President Harding's medical condition, including any medications and procedures to which he was subjected over the past two weeks. I also require the names of all those who were in close contact with him over the past week including his staff, his family, hotel employees, and medical attendants."

Radner's eyes opened wide when he heard this last statement. "What's that? Those traveling with him? Why is that a matter of concern?" he asked with alarm. "No one goes near the President without the approval of the Secret Service!"

"Yes, precisely," Holmes responded. He sought to deflect Radner's sudden concern about the need for information. "I simply wish," he explained, "to investigate whether anyone who was close to the President might have observed changes in his health or demeanor in the days leading up to the tragic event, you understand."

Holmes's explanation seemed to reduce Radner's distress. "I can get you that information," he explained. "We will be in Washington soon, and I'll have a discussion with the White House physicians."

Radner made some notes in a little book he carried with him. We rode along in silence until we arrived at Washington's Union Station, a massive building just a few city blocks from the U.S. Capitol. When we arrived, Radner slipped away and made a quick telephone call.

As we emerged from the station, we could see the gleaming dome of the Capitol building, topped by a statue, towering over the bustling city. A black automobile was waiting for us and we were hustled into the rear seat. In just a few moments were on our way to the Treasury Building, where the Secret Service offices were located. Black bunting had quickly been hung in windows and over the entry ways of many of the buildings lining our route. Many of the passing vehicles had their headlights illuminated in honor of the late President.

"Will the materials concerning the President's health be available for my review at your office?" Holmes asked.

"To the extent that we have them, yes," he replied. "I've asked that they be brought over from the White House, which is just across the street from the Treasury."

"And I will need to examine the President's body when it arrives," Holmes informed him.

"Oh, I'm not sure that can be arranged," Radner said, furrowing his forehead.

"Please turn the car around," Holmes said, addressing the driver, who ignored the request. "Driver! Turn the car around!" Holmes commanded again although the driver showed no sign whatsoever of following the instruction.

"What are you doing?" asked Radner.

"I have no intention to commence an investigation with one hand tied behind my back," Holmes said. "I must insist that I have full access to the President's remains to conduct an examination."

131

Radner's face froze. "I . . . I don't think that will be possible, Mr. Holmes," he stuttered. "There will be so much security. And Mrs. Harding is being very protective of her husband," he added.

"I appreciate the deep shock that the passing of the President must have caused his widow and the nation, but my concern is quite apart from such considerations," said Holmes. "I have imposed these same conditions on Scotland Yard detectives and village constables: Either I conduct the inquiry as I choose, and without a scintilla of interference, or I shall return to my holiday. The choice, sir, is entirely up to you."

Radner considered Holmes's statement and gave a quick nod of consent.

The car deposited us at the rear entrance of the Treasury Department and we passed by a statue of Alexander Hamilton, the first Secretary, as we entered the building. Inside, we were met by a white haired gentleman of perhaps sixty wearing heavy glasses and a somber mien. Moran immediately took him aside and they conferred for a few moments before returning to us – Radner having no doubt explained Holmes's conditions.

"Mr. Holmes, this is Director William Moran of the Secret Service," Radner said. Moran shook Holmes's hand. "And Dr. Watson," Radner added as I also shook hands with the director. Moran looked closely at both of us. "Glad to meet you," he said. "Come on to my office and let's talk."

As Holmes and I settled into leather chairs in the director's office, Moran thanked Radner and the others who had escorted us from New York, closed the door, and settled behind his large desk. "Coffee?" he asked us, but we declined. He already had a steaming cup on his desk and he took a sip before speaking.

"Been here six years," he said, pointing to the array of autographed photographs on the wood-paneled walls. He pointed out one of an ascetic-looking man in spectacles. "He appointed me in 1917," he continued. "Woodrow Wilson. Hell of a guy." I was startled by his irreverent reference to the former President. "This guy – " he said, jerking his thumb to the autographed photo of the late President Harding. "A different kind of man."

"Yes. The Teapot Dome matter," Holmes added.

"I see you follow the news on this side of the Atlantic," he said appreciatively.

"We do have newspapers in England," Holmes responded with a smile, "and from time to time they will report events in our former

132

colonies, particularly scandals involving the President and his Cabinet. I must say that I'm curious as to how you knew of our presence in the States."

Moran looked carefully at my friend for a long moment, then slapped the desk with his large hand. "Okay, Mr. Holmes, let's put our cards on the table, what do you say?" he asked. 'We have our ways of knowing things."

"As do I, Mr. Moran," responded Holmes. "For example, I know of your familial connection to Colonel Sebastian Moran – I believe a great-uncle – whom I was compelled to send to the gallows some years ago for his collaboration with Professor Moriarty."

I recalled the air gun attempt on Holmes following his return from exile after disposing of Professor Moriarty at the Reichenbach Falls. "Are you truly related to that Colonel Moran?" I asked.

"I regret to say I am," Moran said, "although the two halves of the family had little to do with each other after my father left England. I learned of his criminal activities long after his encounter with you, Mr. Holmes. Anyhow, no hard feelings! I'm glad to meet you, and maybe you can be of assistance."

"I should like to believe that I might be," Holmes responded. "Why don't you tell me what you know, what you suspect, and what service I might provide to you and the Secret Service?"

"On its face, this would seem to be a cut-and-dried tragedy," Moran began. "The President wasn't well. He'd had the flu and other health problems. Drank a lot. Smoked a lot. Caroused a lot. Had been treated for neurasthenia for years."

Holmes looked to me. "A serious nervous condition," I explained.

"Yes. He was hospitalized a few times in the 1890's for depression," Moran continued, "although it wasn't widely discussed, of course. Part of the idea for his trip out to Alaska and California was to get him away from some of the stress – let him see some wide, open parts of the country, breathe some fresh air. But he wasn't feeling so good for most of the trip, and then he arrived in San Francisco, and – well, you know the rest."

"How unfortunate that there was no *post mortem* examination to clarify the cause of death," Holmes said.

"Yes, that is true," said Moran with a weary sigh. "The Duchess wouldn't hear of it."

"The Duchess?" I questioned.

"Mrs. Harding," Moran explained. "Very much in charge. Screened most of his mail and readings. Told him how to dress. Lots of people think she was the reason he got into politics instead of sticking with publishing a newspaper in Ohio. He never much liked it."

"The newspaper business?" I asked.

"No, politics," Moran replied. "Too many people with their hands out and in his pockets. Not really what he enjoyed. And the inquiries – perhaps you have heard of the scandal at the Veterans' Bureau? There is more to come on that front, I fear. Those oil leases out at Teapot Dome. And then," he hesitated, "there is the problem of Mrs. Carrie Phillips and Miss Nan Britton. " He took a deep breath. "Did you know Mrs. Phillips and her husband were blackmailing him during the 1920 election over his old letters? And she was a German agent during the war, involved with a senator! It was quite a great burden for any man, let alone one with a weak heart."

Holmes took in this full report with his hands on his chest and his index fingers peaked and touching his lips. "I am impressed that he found time to govern a nation," Holmes said. "You have described a complex and troubled man, but more importantly, a man who might have multiple people who would gain financially, politically, or emotionally from his death." He paused for a moment. "How utterly convenient that he died when he did – at least for someone."

"It is for that reason that I entreated you to come to Washington and look into the matter," Moran said. "It may well be there is nothing to the rumors that are beginning to circulate already – of a plot, or revenge, or an effort to silence Harding. Or," he paused, "there may well be something there. As you have noted, there was motive, and it seems likely with all this traveling and various people coming and going in the official party and at receptions and meals that someone may have taken the opportunity to accelerate the pace of the President's demise a bit quicker than nature might have intended."

"Was it thought he would stand for re-election next year?" Holmes asked.

"Oh, yes," Moran answered. "Not that he loved the job. In fact, he told the historian Nicholas Murray Butler, 'I am not fit for this office and should never have been here,' but that consideration alone discourages few men from seeking the presidency. Even if he preferred to retire, there is little doubt that his wife would have pressed him to run again. She quite enjoyed the power and prestige of being First Lady."

134

"And does she have as colorful a background as the President?" asked Holmes.

"Well, sir, not as recently, so far as we know. But before she married Mr. Harding – well, that was another matter," Moran admitted. "A marriage – we think – when she was little more than a girl, a drunkard for a husband (if he truly was her husband by law), a child, a divorce (if there had been a marriage), a fair amount of running around. Not the typical preparation for a First Lady! She became an active suffragette, concerned about the rights of Negroes, very devoted to her husband despite his . . . " Moran paused. ". . . *indiscretions.*"

"She sounds perfectly fascinating," Holmes said. "Let me ask how you are investigating the President's death."

"To tell you the truth, my hand are a bit tied," Moran admitted. "We have a Bureau of Investigation at Justice, run by William Burns. You've probably heard of his detective agency." Holmes nodded his familiarity with the firm. "They tend to think of such matters as their responsibility. Touchy about their jurisdiction."

"I see some things are similar on both sides of the Atlantic! Shall we speak with Mr. Burns?"

"We can try," Moran said, standing up to signal the end of the meeting. "Come around about ten tomorrow and we'll go see Burns together. Oh, the train with the President and First Lady aboard arrives tomorrow, so there will doubtless be some official activities which I'll need to attend during the day."

"Very well, but please keep in mind I still want to see the late President's remains," Holmes declared. "Even at this late stage, there may be suggestive clues if there was, in fact, any wrongdoing."

Holmes and I left the Treasury Department and strolled along Pennsylvania Avenue, enjoying an excellent view of the massive White House that serves as he President's official residence and working office. We took in some local sights before arriving at the Willard Hotel, one of the capital city's finest which had been refurbished after a fire the previous year. Our trunks had been sent on ahead while we met in Moran's office. After a brief rest, we took dinner up the street at the Old Ebbitt Grill, the oldest restaurant in the city.

"An odd situation, don't you think?" asked Holmes. "Why we were brought into it? There is no allegation of wrong-doing. There may be a shortage of clues, but there is certainly no shortage of people and agencies to investigate what meager ones exist. There are law enforcement officials not only in Washington and San

Francisco, but the Secret Service, and this Burns fellow as well. So why engage me?"

I thought about Holmes's question as we began our meal of grilled oysters and roast beef. "I can only imagine the coincidence of Sherlock Holmes being in America at so propitious a moment intrigued them," I said. "You are the disinterested party. You neither guard the President nor investigate crimes involving his administration. You have no particular stake in this issue or its outcome, whereas the reputations of Moran or Burns, and likely others, might well be affected by the outcome of the case should they attempt to close the matter too quickly."

"Exactly," he said. "I believe you have hit on it. I am the proverbial 'honest broker' – not because here are not sufficient American investigators, but because none of them trusts the other to conduct a fair and thorough inquiry. Well, if a dispassionate inquiry is what they want, that is what they shall have, and let the chips falls where they may!"

Part II – The Facts of the Case

In the morning, Holmes and I breakfasted at the Willard and waited for the car that would take us a few blocks to the Justice Department. The newspapers were filled with little but accounts of the tragedy that had occurred in San Francisco, the arrival of President Coolidge in the city, and the train bearing Harding's body, which was scheduled to arrive in the city that evening. There would be a short laying-in at the White House and then a brief funeral at the Capitol the following day. Harding's casket would then be placed on the train and taken to Marion, Ohio for another funeral and internment. As a result of this tight schedule, Holmes's opportunity for examining he body would be extremely limited if, which seemed unlikely, he was able to do so at all.

Moran and Radner arrived promptly at 9:30 and we were soon deposited at building that housed the Bureau of Investigation. Promptly at ten o'clock, we were shown into the director's office. Burns, a burly man with a great mustache, was about sixty years old. He came around from his desk to greet us. He extended his hand to Moran first, uttering a gruff, "Hello, Bill," while eyeing Holmes and me suspiciously. Moran reciprocated the terse greeting and turned to us.

"This is Sherlock Holmes and his associate, Dr. John Watson," he said by way of introduction. Burns nodded, continuing to look us up and down. "You surely know of his great reputation."

"I've read the penny stories," Burns said dismissively.

"And I have heard of *you* mentioned as the 'Sherlock Holmes of America'," Holmes offered, receiving no response.

"They're here to explore some matters related to the President's passing," Moran continued. There was a loud and derisive snort from Burns. "I have promised them that their presence here will remain strictly clandestine," Moran continued, ignoring Burns's reaction. "Neither they nor we have any benefit to be gained by knowing that a British detective has been summoned to assist in our investigations."

Burns walked back around to his desk, signaled us to be seated, and then sat down heavily into his chair with a grunt. A two-inch stub of a rancid-smelling cigar lazily burned in an ashtray, the thin line of blue smoke spiraling upwards and spreading out into the room. He picked up the cigar and took a long pull on it, the end brightening to a fierce orange glow. "I have no problem keeping your presence a secret, 'cause I don't know what you're doing here in the first place, Mr. Holmes. I think we have the situation well in hand," he added confidently.

"I have no reason to believe anything to the contrary," Holmes answered. "I might mention that I did not seek to intervene in this matter. We were on holiday . . . ."

Burns interrupted him brusquely. "Look, Holmes, Moran here provides security for the President and that's fine," he said with a dismissive tone. "You can check with the Garfield and McKinley families about how well the Secret Service carries out its duties." Moran shifted uncomfortably in his seat at the mention of two Presidents who had been assassinated since the Secret Service was formed in the aftermath of the assassination of Abraham Lincoln nearly sixty years earlier. "But I run a criminal investigation bureau here, not a babysitting service."

"Knock it off, Bill," Moran said sharply. "We don't need to air our rivalries in front of Mr. Holmes and Dr. Watson."

"There hasn't been a crime that anyone's alleged, Holmes, so my shop ain't involved," Burns continued, ignoring Moran's protest. "I suggest you and Dr. Watson head back to New York and enjoy your vacation, and let me worry about people breaking the law in this country. In the meantime," he said with determination, "if it's

137

all the same to you, I will have a few of my boys keeping an eye on you – just to be sure nothing happens to our guests from England."

Moran began to say something but Holmes was instantly on his feet. "I couldn't agree with you more, Director Burns," Holmes said. "If there has been no crime, there surely is no need for my involvement and, as you say, this is detracting from a rare holiday. Good day, Mr. Burns," he concluded, picking up his hat and turning to leave. I rose as well and was right behind him when he stopped and pivoted to look back at Burns.

"Ah, one last point," he said. "I understand the President died at 7:30 and was embalmed an hour later. The next morning, his body was on a train back to Washington."

"Yeah, that's true?"

"I have a question about the *post mortem* examination."

"There was no *post mortem* examination."

"Yes, that is my question."

We left Burns with a pinched mouth and exited the building. The heat was quite stifling outside and we decided to walk back toward the Treasury Department, stopping at a café on the way for something cool to drink. Choosing a table at some distance from the nearest patron, we discussed our next moves in hushed voices.

"The President's remains will arrive at the White House at about eleven on the seventh," Moran said. "I'll be able to arrange your entry to the White House and, with any luck, a short time for you to examine the body. I suspect it will be kept in the East Room, the large public room on the first floor. But we'll have to act very quickly because the plan is for a service at the Capitol, and then removal back to Ohio."

Holmes nodded his head in agreement. "Then I will meet you at our hotel at nine o'clock tomorrow evening," he said, "which should give us time to gain entry and devise a plan once inside the building. In the meantime, I have some additional research I would like to conduct."

"I can have you driven down to the Library of Congress, if you like," Moran offered as we left the café.

"No, my research must take place in *your* records," Holmes said.

"*My* records?" Moran replied aghast. "What might you be searching for that would be in the files of the Secret Service?"

"I would prefer not to say at this point, if you don't mind," he responded, "but I'm considering every possibility, and based on what I've learned so far, some matters definitely warrant additional

138

scrutiny. I presume that your records will reveal the identity of everyone who had access to the President at various times of the day and evening."

"Unquestionably. We monitor every person who comes into proximity of the President or his wife. That includes those who prepare meals, lay out clothing, or provide security services."

"And all of those records remain in your office, I presume? Good! I shall have a most productive afternoon."

We were just arriving at the Treasury Building and Moran agreeably took Holmes and me down to his records office. "This is the safest place to examine my records," he said. "I'll be sure that all of the wires and memos from the last few days are brought down to you. In the meanwhile, please feel free to use any one of these desks. I am sure Miss Miller will be pleased to provide you with any materials you may require." He introduced us to the young woman he'd mentioned who served as a clerk in the records office.

We settled into our seats at a large desk, once Moran had departed to return to his own office in order to prepare for the arrival of Coolidge. Within minutes, a sheaf of papers – the cables from those attending Harding in San Francisco – appeared on our desk, and Holmes began to thumb through them, reading quickly as his eyes flashed across page after page of the memos. He withdrew a pad of paper and pencil from his attaché case, looked up to the ceiling, and then turned to me.

"Suppose you wanted to poison someone already in somewhat compromised health," he asked. "It would have to look sufficiently natural so as not to raise alarms, especially if the victim were a powerful and prominent individual. What would be your candidates for such a crime?"

Holmes knew as much about poisons as I – likely far more given his criminal researches – but I was willing to play along with his game. "Well, I might think of *Cicuta maculate* or perhaps *Ricinus communis*," I speculated. "But see here! Do you seriously thinking Harding was poisoned?"

"Oh, I have little doubt about it," Holmes replied distractedly. "Yes, those are most certainly effective choices, but not in this case. *Cicuta maculate*, or hemlock, would surely cause symptoms uncharacteristic of what has been reported to have afflicted Mr. Harding."

"True. Convulsions and cramping, although he had complained of stomach pains," I offered.

"As to *Ricinus communis,* yes, castor is a deadly plant, but again, it would have induced very noticeable symptoms that the physicians haven't mentioned in these cables," he countered.

"Well, let me see. There is *Abrus precatorius,* the inappropriately named '*Rosary Pea*', extremely deadly in small doses and difficult to detect."

"Yes, a possible candidate, especially as it can cause organ failure, but it isn't especially fast acting."

"Well, what about *Atropa belladonna*?" I asked. "In the proper dosage, it can paralyze the organs of the body, including the heart, which could create the semblance of a coronary thrombosis or a stroke."

"Yes," Holmes said in a half-dreamy way, indicating the idea had occurred to him as well. "Belladonna. '*Deadly nightshade*', as it is more commonly known. Certainly a possibility, although one would have to have access to it." He became quiet as he pored over cable after cable, passing them along to me as well. They seemed to recapitulate the account we'd already heard: The President complaining of feeling poorly, a number of treatments administered by the physicians, and then a sudden worsening of the condition and death.

"Watson, I shall be consumed by some of this work for the rest of the day. I wonder if you might be willing to pay a visit to the National Botanic Garden, which is located near the Capitol, and then meet me back at the Willard for dinner by six."

"Are you sure that I cannot be of assistance to you here?" I inquired. "It seems a waste of my time to be looking at flowers."

"I will be fine and properly focused on these materials," he replied. "But I need you to examine their collection of plants carefully."

"What am I looking for?" I asked.

"Why, any of the poisonous plants that we've been discussing. Few grow in this climate, and unless acquired in a powdered form, which would easily be traceable from the chemist, a Botanic Garden might prove a ready source for all sorts of lethal flowers, roots, and berries."

I didn't like the idea of leaving Holmes alone, but as it seemed his desire, I gathered my things and walked out of the building, turning to the right to follow the broad expanse of Pennsylvania Avenue as it jogged around the Treasury and continued to the end of the boulevard, where the gleaming white Capitol building sat atop a low-rising Hill overlooking the city. It was a stroll of nearly a mile,

I should think, and I was fairly dripping with perspiration by the time I arrived at the base of the hill leading up to the Capitol. There I found the glass building that served as the Botanic Garden and went inside. The high degree of humidity maintained for the benefit of the tropical vegetation unfortunately made the interior of the building even more uncomfortable than the out-of-doors, but at least I was afforded some relief from the brutal sun.

I browsed amongst the orchids and palms and every variety of plant in between, it seemed, but I didn't see a section devoted to the dangerous varieties I was seeking. Soon, however, an official looking chap in a uniform passed me and I hailed him. He wore a small piece of black crepe pinned to his chest to signify, I presumed, his mourning for the late President.

"Good afternoon, sir. May I be of assistance?" he asked.

"Yes, my good man. I need some advice."

"Ah, a visitor from England, I take it? What can I do for you?"

"Yes, London," I replied. "I wonder if you might have any plants here that might fall into the category of 'dangerous'," I asked.

"A 'dangerous' plant?" he repeated, barely suppressing a smile. Then he became serious. "Ah, you mean something that's poisonous to eat, or that could hurt your skin? Something like that?"

"Yes, precisely. Do you have any examples of such plants?"

"I do, yes sir, I do," he responded. "Let's just go over here." He wound his way through the broad green leaves and bright flowers that engulfed the building and stopped in a section of low-lying plants. "Here you are, sir. One deadlier than the next! Don't be touching them please. I wouldn't be wanting something to happen to you like what happened to our Mr. Harding!"

"What on Earth do you mean by that?" I asked. "Was he poisoned?"

The guide blanched. "Oh, no! I only meant his sudden death. I surely don't think . . . Why, who would do such a thing?" he asked. He turned away and examined his plants for a moment.

"Have you by any chance an example of *Atropa belladonna*? I inquired.

"I certainly do," he responded, pointing to a plant with small, broad leave and purple flowers with five-petals. Many of the branches had small, purple berries on them as well.

I fairly flew out of the Botanical Garden and hailed a cab to take me back up to the Treasury Department where Holmes was working, but as we pulled up, I saw my friend emerging from the great stone building. "Holmes!" I cried. He glanced up with a look of satisfaction on his face.

"Hello. Did you have a productive visit to the garden?"

"Deadly nightshade!" I cried. "Here in the capitol!"

Holmes brought his hand up to his face and raised his index finger to his lips, signaling that my outburst had clearly piqued the interest of Miss Miller, who had also exited the building and started down the step in a different direction.

"Wait until we're in the hotel."

Departing Moran's office, the two trackers following us at a discrete distance, we crossed the street and hurried to the Willard and up to our room. Holmes peered down onto the street and then drew the curtains against the late afternoon sun. "Now, tell me what you learned," he entreated.

I related the events of my trip to the Botanic Garden, my discussion with the guide, and the discovery of the deadly nightshade bush. "I should think that it would have been child's play to secure a sample of the poisonous berries," I offered.

"Excellent!" Holmes said. "A bit of luck there, I should say. Now, let us have a nice quiet dinner." We went to the hotel restaurant and ate a delicious meal, strolling afterwards along the broad boulevards of the city. Washington was clearly a growing metropolis, and the new official buildings contrasted markedly with many rooming houses and shops that clearly dated from the turn-of-the-century. It was difficult to gauge the typical gaiety of Washingtonians, however, since a subdued atmosphere had descended upon the residents following the President's passing.

The next day was spent with Holmes again reviewing papers at the Secret Service office while I gathered information about the train carrying Harding's body, which was due to arrive at 10:30 pm. I met Holmes at a local restaurant for dinner at six and we enjoyed a hearty meal. By nine, we were waiting in the hotel lobby when Moran appeared alone. Lurking near the door, however, were the same two men we had noticed earlier, and Holmes discretely pointed them out to Moran.

"Yes, I recognized them when I came in," he said. "They're Bureau people. Come with me." He grabbed Holmes's arm and hustled us quickly back into the lobby, then through the restaurant and into the kitchen. Rushing down a corridor, we emerged into the sticky night air on the opposite side of the building from the entrance where the Bureau men had been lurking, and we were quickly swallowed up into the night.

There were hoards of people lining the route from the White House down towards Union Station, where Harding's train would soon be arriving. As we looked down the avenue, we could see that black bunting and crepe had been hung on many storefronts and decked the trolleys and carriages that ferried people down towards the station. We, however, moved in the opposite direction, towards the side entrance to the White House near the Treasury Building. Moran showed his credentials to the officer at the guardhouse, who snapped to attention when he read the name. "Yessir, Chief Moran," he barked, and then cast a sideways look at Holmes and me.

"These are the special security men I am bringing to prepare for Mr. Coolidge," he explained. "They haven't had time for their credentials to be prepared, but they are with me." The guard obediently nodded his approval and we passed onto the grounds of the looming white mansion. We walked quickly to the rear entrance where Moran repeated his masquerade, and within moments we were inside, passing by the library and several other well-appointed rooms, past portraits of former Presidents and first ladies. I couldn't help feeling a sense of awe at being in such an historic place, but Holmes gave no indication of curiosity or excitement.

Moran opened a door, above which was written "*Secret Service*", and we walked into a small office with a desk and several chairs. "This is my White House office," Moran explained. "We're going to park ourselves right here till I get a call that the train is in, and then we'll make our move." Within a half-hour, the telephone on his desk rang and he picked it up, spoke briefly, and replaced the receiver. "The train is here," he reported. "They'll be arriving at the White House in about five minutes. It's time to go."

We walked up a back stairway and found ourselves at the broad transept that connected the State Dining Room on the west side of the building to the East Room, where there was feverish activity. Crepe was prodigiously hung in the doorways and up the bannisters to the private residence on the second floor, and in the center of the East Room was a platform covered in black cloth.

"The Lincoln catafalque," Moran explained softly. The platform had been hastily constructed in 1865 to hold the remains of the assassinated sixteenth President, and since then had been used to hold the caskets of other Presidents and dignitaries.

We walked to the foyer of the mansion where a number of guards and dignitaries were awaiting the arrival of the President's remains. Within moments, the large black hearse arrived with a phalanx of other vehicles and the doors to the White House were swung open. A group of soldiers entered carrying the President's coffin, which was covered by an American flag, followed by Mrs. Harding who was dressed entirely in black. The group proceeded to the East Room and the coffin was placed on the catafalque. The military escorts quickly dispersed, leaving only a few men to watch over the scene. When most of the others had filed out, the widow, who appeared quite stolid, approached the coffin for a few moments of private reflection. When she stepped back, she was engulfed by a small group of well-wishers, some of whom also made their way to the flag-enshrouded coffin to pay their respects.

This scene continued for about a half-an-hour in near silence, and then the guests were escorted out of the East Room, as we remained by a little-used entry door at the top of the stairs we had ascended from Moran's basement office. I had barely noticed that Mrs. Harding had departed as well, leaving only four military guards standing at each end of the coffin. Suddenly, after the bustle of the preceding hour, the room seemed still and eerily quiet. The lights throughout the first floor were dimmed and the entire White House itself seemed in a state of quiet mourning.

Moran signaled to us that it was time to make our move. He stepped into the East Room, drawing the attention of the guards, two of whom turned towards us.

"Who are you, sir?" one asked.

Moran had his identification card with him, as well as a badge of some kind identifying him as the Chief of the Secret Service. "These are my mortuary assistants," he said, motioning to Holmes and myself. "We must confirm the President's body has been properly preserved. Until he is safety interred, under federal law, I am personally responsible for his safety and care."

"Well, I hardly think his safety is a major concern under the circumstances," said one of the guards suspiciously.

Moran leveled a disapproving eye at him. "Unless you would like me to report your insubordination to your commanding officer," he said with a firm voice, "you should hold your tongue, soldier, and let me do my job! Now, we are going to take a brief moment to evaluate President Harding, and then we'll get out of here." He spoke the words without a hint of conditionality, as though he was giving a direct order that the guards dare not countermand. Indeed, the lead guard looked around at his colleagues, and then gave a short nod to Moran.

The flag was removed and Moran, Holmes, and I went to the casket and raised the portion of the lid over the late President's head.

144

A chemical odor escaped from the coffin but quickly dissipated. Moran shone the light from his torch into the coffin and illuminated what was incontrovertibly the well-preserved face of the late President.

"Who goes there?" shouted Moran suddenly and he spun around towards the main doors that opened onto the transept. I had heard nothing, but like the guards, I reflexively turned. Two of the guards followed Moran to the door, but there was no one present. "Must've been one of those White House rats they're always complaining to me about," he said. He returned and asked if we were nearly finished.

"Yes, all done here," said Holmes in a most credible American accent. He reached up for the lid and brought it down with a gentle thump. "No doubt, Director Moran, that's him. And a first-class embalming, I might add. I guess we can head home now." We thanked the guards for their indulgence and made our way towards the empty foyer.

We were nearly to the door when Holmes stopped abruptly, his chin slightly elevated. "Do you smell it?" he asked anxiously.

"Smell what?" Moran asked. I admit that I detected no odor, but Holmes's sense of smell was remarkably acute.

"Something is burning. Upstairs," he said, casting an eye towards the staircase that rose from the first to the second level of the building where the First Family resided. "Most certainly."

"A fireplace?" I suggested.

"In August, and in this stifling heat?" Holmes responded. "I think that most curious." He thought for a moment. "Moran, Watson – you must both leave so that our departure is clearly noted by the guards. Hopefully they will overlook the absence of one of your number. But I am remaining. There is something foul afoot, I have no doubt, but you must leave it to me to determine what it is. I shall return to the Willard later tonight, assuming I am not apprehended here, and hopefully will be able to give you a full report at that time."

Moran looked quizzically at Holmes. "I don't know," he said. "That's not even close to being authorized. Leaving you alone in the White House?"

"Your mission is to protect the President," Holmes reminded him. "Well, the President is now Mr. Coolidge, and he isn't here, so you aren't violating your duties."

Moran looked dubious, but he shook his head. "Only because it's you, Mr. Holmes," he said. "But I sure would appreciate it if you could avoid being apprehended."

"That is my own fervent hope as well," Holmes said. "And by the way," he said handing Moran a thin stick with a swap of cotton on the end, "have your chemists analyze this sample I took from Harding's mouth when you so admirably distracted the guards, as I had requested. Please see if they can find any traces of chemicals on it."

Moran accepted the swab uncomfortably and, with a considerable amount of trepidation, I said goodbye to Holmes. Moran and I then returned to the basement and exited into the White House garden. It was a beautiful if muggy evening, and the flowers and trees were lush and the air filled with the scent of nature. It was a welcome contrast to the somber scene we had just left in the East Room, and as we departed the grounds, I couldn't help but cast my eyes backward towards the illuminated mansion and think of my friend still inside.

Part III – The Man with the Green Hat

Moran and I dropped the swab at his office with instructions for the laboratory assistants to analyze its contents as quickly as possible. Then we walked down F Street into the downtown, saying nothing of what we had just done or what Holmes might be engaged in doing at the moment. My thoughts were swirling – here we were in Washington, the President had died, and we had been summoned to ascertain whether the reports of a natural death were accurate or if something far more nefarious might be at work. My plan for a summer holiday to give Holmes the chance to inconspicuously visit the United States for a restful vacation couldn't possibly have gone more off track!

My agitation must have been evident. "Could you use something to calm your nerves?" Moran asked, raising an eyebrow.

"I certainly could," I replied, "except that you Yankees have gone and imposed Prohibition. If we were in London right now," I explained, "we would be having a pint or two at The Donkey and His Keeper."

"Well, we don't have pubs here, but we do have something that might help," said the agent. We walked into a narrow alley and up to the rear door of a shop that fronted on G Street. Moran knocked three times, then twice more, and the door opened a crack.

"I've come to see the man with the green hat," he said. There was a grunt of recognition from inside. The door opened slightly and

146

a middle-aged man peered out through the crack and looked us up and down.

"Ah, it's you," he said to Moran without mentioning his name. There was the sound of a chain being removed, and the man said, "Come right in and enjoy." We walked down a set of stairs and Moran pushed open another door and we found ourselves in a well-appointed pub, or bar, as the Americans say, with men and women drinking what certainly appeared to be prohibited beverages while a Negro woman sang gently to a small group of accompanists.

"But I thought – " I began.

"There are laws," Moran said, "and there are laws, Doctor."

"Who is this man in the green hat?" I asked, looking around for the colorful headwear.

Moran laughed. "Oh, a very highly regarded bootlegger who supplies the White House, Congress, and just about every other powerful figure here in Washington," he replied. He looked around. "I come here rather more frequently than I should, I suppose. That's why I was quickly admitted."

We sat down at a small table somewhat away from other patrons, and shortly I was enjoying the first welcome spirits I had tasted since the steamship.

"There's plenty of government folks here, including quite a number of congressmen and senators, who voted for Prohibition. Lawyers from the Justice Department. That man over there – " He subtly jutted his thumb toward a rotund gentleman. " – is one of the city commissioners."

He assumed a more somber demeanor. "Our late friend back there in the box – " He motioned over his shoulder towards the White House. " – he was known to indulge quite a bit when he was a senator, but then his wife got him elected President against his wishes, and he had to give up the speakeasys, though I think he had a pretty good stash up in his personal quarters for his card games. A least that was the rumor."

"An indulgent man," I noted.

Moran looked hard at me. "Booze wasn't all of it," he said. He lowered his voice. "Carrie Phillips. Nan Britton." He rolled his eyes.

"Yes, those names were mentioned earlier, but I admit to not recognizing them," I confessed.

"Well, let's just say Warren Harding had a roving eye," Moran said, "and there was quite a gleam in it when he spotted an attractive young woman."

"Was Mrs. Harding aware of his carrying on?" I asked.

147

"Ha!" Moran laughed, causing a few heads to turn in our direction. "She would've been the last person to know if she wasn't! But she had what she wanted – respectability – which wasn't bad for where she came from. Her husband as President. It's made a former piano teacher one of the most well-known and influential women in the world." He moved closer to me and put his face next to mine. "Tell me, – what's Mr. Holmes doing? Do you have any idea?"

"I presume," I responded, "finding out the source of that smoke. You know what they say, don't you. Where there's smoke – "

"There's fire" the slightly tipsy Moran finished the expression.

It was well after midnight when I heard the key opening the lock of our sitting room at the Willard Hotel and I started awake. I had intended to wait for Holmes, but the overstuffed chair had proven too comfortable and I must have drifted off to sleep. The overhead light clicked on and Holmes walked into the room, accompanied by two men I would have guessed were in their thirties.

"My apologies at disturbing you, Watson," he said, "but my escorts insisted upon returning me to these quarters." The two men we had spotted watching us over the past two days were on either side of Holmes with their arms holding each of his. They looked decidedly unfriendly and officious.

"Just be sure you remember, Mr. Holmes," one of them said. "The first train in the morning." He looked around the room and at me. "No calls. No leaving the room," he said. "No talking over the telephone," he added, leaning down and pulling the wire out from the wall. "On second thought, I'll take this with me." The two men looked around the room again, paying little attention to me. "I suggest you grab some sleep. It's been a long night."

With that, they turned and walked out, closing the door behind them. Holmes watched them go and then turned to me. "Well, I think we can consider ourselves very fortunate," he said as he took off his jacket.

"Why do you say that?" I inquired.

"Because we will spend the night in this very comfortable hotel, and we shall enjoy a hearty breakfast in the morning before our train to New York. And that is a decidedly better prospect than the alternative that presented itself only a short time ago."

"And what was that?" I asked.

"I believe the exact quote was, 'Twenty years in Leavenworth'."

"I was always convinced there was more to this case than was originally presented to us," Holmes began as he lit a cigarette and settled into a chair. It was after one in the morning, but neither of us felt tired now, and it was impossible to consider sleeping before I had the full account of Holmes's adventures after I'd left him in the White House. "Frankly, as my ideas coalesced this afternoon, I doubted my own reasoning, but the facts, Watson! The facts! They became incontrovertible. And they all led to one conclusion."

"Was Harding murdered?" I asked. "Was he the victim of an assassination conspiracy?"

Holmes leaned back in his chair and took a long pull on his cigarette, inhaling deeply and sending a blue stream towards the fan rotating in the centre of the room. "Yes," he responded wearily. "Yes, he was. But his murder is not the most consequential or even the most remarkable part of this story," he added. "Nor is it the only portion that must remain confidential. Yes, Watson, I must entreat you to refrain from committing what I am about to tell you to writing."

"For how long a time?" I asked.

"I am afraid I must ask that this never become an '*Adventure of Sherlock Holmes*'," he replied. He looked at me intently and tilted his head, as if to seek assent. I paused before responding.

"It is never my intent to violate a trust or disclose material related to national security," I said, hedging my promise.

A sharp laugh escaped from his lips as Holmes's face broke into a smile, the lines around his eyes crinkling into deep folds as his mouth formed a smile. "Washington must agree with you, Watson," he said. "You have been here but three days, and that evasive answer indicates that you are showing true signs of becoming a politician! That is not an answer, but let us trust your judgment. When you have heard this tale, I suspect you will understand the necessity of confidentiality.

"It was the smoke, Watson, the *smoke* in the White House that convinced me swift action was required," he began. "After you and Moran departed, I flew up the stairs and, as silently as I could, and began checking the rooms on the second floor for the source of the smoke. The third room I looked into contained a sight as startling as any I have seen over our forty-plus years of knowing one another.

"There was a roaring fire in the hearth, which was producing the only light in the room, as well as the odor I had detected as we

149

had left the East Room. Stacks of papers and notebooks were piled up in front of the fireplace. A woman dressed in black sat on the floor near the papers, briefly looked at each document for a moment before throwing it into the flames, where it quickly burst into brilliant orange and was consumed. Standing several feet away in the darkened room was a man who silently watched as the woman intently reviewed the materials. Neither heard me enter.

"'Are you going to burn it all, Mrs. Harding?' I asked.

"The former First Lady, whose husband lay in a casket one floor below, looked up and was about to scream, but she could see me holding up my hands. The man was also startled and quickly opened his jacket and withdrew a revolver, which he menacingly pointed at me. They regarded me for a moment, and then the woman stood erectly and smoothed her dress. She motioned to the man to lower his pistol, which he did. 'May I ask who you are, sir, and why are you trespassing in my house at this hour,' she asked, 'and why I should not immediately summon the police?'

"'I do not think calling for the police would be in either of our best interests, Mrs. Harding,' I replied, casting an eye towards the armed guard. 'And I presume you would be Mr. Clayton Graham of the Bureau of Investigation.' I walked closer towards her. 'My name is Sherlock Holmes. Perhaps you have heard of me?'

"She took several steps towards me and looked at me carefully, as if to confirm my identify. She is a woman in her mid-sixties, with graying hair piled on her head, wearing rimless eyeglasses and a serious mien. She is most commanding in appearance, but clearly didn't appreciate my presence."

"'Yes, I have heard of you, Mr. Holmes, and I heard that you had appeared in this city at the most unhappy of times for me and for our grieving nation.'

"'Also a most inconvenient time, I might add,' I responded. 'No doubt that report originated with Mr. Burns at the Bureau of Investigation, your ally – and your supervisor,' I added, looking to Graham. She nodded her assent after a moment, but Graham remained rigid.

"She took a deep breath and looked about the ornate room with rich furnishings and portraits on the wall. The fireplace was of elaborately carved marble and the rugs very fine Persian. She turned on several electric lights and I could see the richly furnished room, as well as the face of her young guard who had returned his firearm to his pocket. 'Clayton, why don't you wait for me outside?' she said. 'I have no doubt I'm quite safe here with Mr. Holmes.' The young man looked disapprovingly at me, but followed her instructions and left the room, closing the door behind him.

"'This is the Treaty Room, Mr. Holmes. Did you know that?' she asked. I shook my head negatively. 'Before Mr. Roosevelt built the new wing with the President's office, this was used by my husband's predecessors – Lincoln, Grant, McKinley,' she mused. 'Since then, it has been the President's private study – for Roosevelt, that uncontrollable child who stumbled into office. And Wilson, that insufferable, priggish racist!' She paused. 'I loathed him for his indifference to the plight of our Negro citizens.' She paused again. 'And Harding, my husband.' She turned to face the desk, from whose open drawers she evidently had removed the papers she had been busily feeding into the inferno. She stood and walked back to the pile of papers and threw more into the fireplace without looking at their contents, and then returned to her chair.

"'I understand this was also a favourite room of my late husband for his trysts with Nan Britton in recent years.' she added. She turned away from me and walked to a large sofa. 'Come, Mr. Holmes, why don't you sit down and tell me what you think you know of all this business, and I might as well fill in any of the blank spots.' She sat down and patted the sofa next to her. 'I promise not to bite you.'

"'It is not your bite nor your bark that worries me,' I replied. 'But there is more than good reason to be wary of you, isn't there? You see, I have spent the last two days looking at a great deal of material about you and your husband, the late President, and I spent much of the evening putting the pieces together. It is a complicated story and one that, I suspect, you would not want publicized.'

"'Suppose I tell you four names," I suggested, 'and one word, and then you can decide if I am on the right track." Her tired eyes searched my face in the darkened room as the fire burned down – a wisp of gray smoke escaped from the flue and spread through the room like a London fog. 'Clayton Graham, Roosevelt, Wilson, and Harding, and belladonna.'

"Her eyes opened wide and she sat forward in her chair. Her mouth moved slightly, as if she were uttering a silent exclamation. She licked her bottom lip and sat back in the chair.

"'All right, Mr. Holmes, I can see your reputation is well-earned,' she said. 'I can tell you the story, but I suppose you will tell me the ending. I would ask that the facts go no further than the two of us, but I doubt you would make such an agreement.' I shook my

151

head silently. 'Very well, very well.' She paused, and this is the tale
she told me . . . ."

Part V – Mrs. Harding's Story

"I married Mr. Harding in 1891," she said, "but it was not my
first marriage. Many people are not aware of my earlier marriage
when I was just nineteen, to a young man named Pete deWolfe. It
was an impetuous decision, but I was frantic to escape from my
father, an uncivil and even violent man. Although he had begun life
as a hardware salesman, my father had proven adept at business and
by the time I was a young woman, he had become quite prosperous.
Not surprisingly, he didn't approve of his daughter even socializing
with a common laborer. The thought of marriage was utterly out of
the question.

"When I found that I was to have a child, Peter and I agreed that
we didn't want the baby born out of wedlock, and so we eloped to
escape my father's disapproval. Eight months later, my son,
Marshall, was born – a strong and healthy baby – but my life was far
from an easy one. Within just two years, my husband had become a
drunk and abandoned us. After I divorced him, I couldn't support
Marshall. He went to live with my father, who refused to allow me
to live under his roof.

"A decade later, I married Mr. Harding, the publisher of *The
Marion Star*, in whom I saw great promise. He and I worked closely
together to make the newspaper a success, and he also began to
dabble in local politics as an ally of Governor Foraker and Senator
Hanna, which led to his election to the State Senate in 1899.
Although he was a reluctant politician, he proved quite adept at
speaking and greeting crowds, and he developed an admirable
following.

"We didn't have children of our own, and so we put all of our
energies into the paper and then into building Mr. Harding's political
career. He was doing quite well – he was elected lieutenant-governor
in 1904 – but then there was a bitter public disagreement with Mr.
Roosevelt, who had become President after our Ohio native, Mr.
McKinley, was murdered. That quarrel helped contribute to Mr.
Harding's defeat for governor in 1908, and many thought his
political career was over. But not I, Mr. Holmes. Not I!

"As you may know, Mr. Roosevelt soured on President Taft,
whom he had essentially appointed his successor, and in 1912, he
challenged Mr. Taft for the Republican nomination. Taft won, but

T.R. ran as an independent – he called himself a 'Bull Moose', and his antics cost Mr. Taft and the Republicans the presidency. That insufferable little southern schoolteacher Woodrow Wilson was elected." She gave an involuntary shudder.

"As fate would have it, Mr. Harding won election to the Senate just two years later, and embarked on a career that I had determined would eventually place him in the White House. After the death of my son soon after the election, I had no other distractions and no goal on Earth higher than for my husband to become President. I resolved I would let nothing stand in the way of achieving that ambition. Nothing! Did you know that Madame Marcia, the Washington astrologer, predicted that Warren would become President! Yes, she did, and that he would die suddenly, perhaps by poisoning!

"And yet two obstacles jeopardized our reaching that goal in 1920. One was that horrible Mr. Roosevelt, who had been traipsing all over South America doing who knows what since he had nearly destroyed the Republican Party. And the other was that bigot and liar Wilson, who had been re-elected in 1916. You know, he had campaigned on the slogan 'He Kept Us Out of War', but as soon as he was re-elected, he could not wait to send our boys to die in the trenches in France. And his new wife, Edith, wanted him to run for a *third* term – could you imagine such a thing?

"Those were the men who stood between my husband and the White House! Horrible men.

"That could not be allowed! One man had tried to derail Warren's political career and then nearly ruined the Republican Party. The other had caused tens of thousands of deaths by lying to the American people. I resolved I would do anything to ensure they never had the chance to run again and keep my Warren from his destiny.

"You mentioned Clayton Graham, Mr. Holmes, which tells me you have untangled much of the story. Your reputation is well-deserved.

"Yes, Mr. Graham was an Ohio native, an orphan, whom Mr. Harding and I came to love like a son during our early years in Washington, and we helped him find a job at the Bureau of Investigation and work his way up quickly. Mr. Harding was always happy to help him along with a favourable word to the right superior at the Justice Department, and I think it's fair to say that as much as we regarded Clayton as the son we had never had, he regarded us as substitute parents. Clayton had no less ambition for the senator than

I, and we often discussed – just the two of us – how to further Mr. Harding's fortunes.

"When Roosevelt began making comments about running in 1920, we were very concerned. Yes, he remained popular with some of the party faithful, but he was hated by others – like us, who blamed him for Taft's defeat. And he was a very sick man, from illnesses contracted during his adventures in South America. He had been hospitalized late in 1918 – did you know that? Why, he might not even survive a term as President! When Clayton was assigned to provide protection to him during January of 1919, we considered that it might be best for our party, and for the country, to ensure Teddy's candidacy went no further than his own ambition.

"I was the one whose ambition would not be denied! Madam Marcia had described me as 'a dominant, willful, tenacious person with a great desire to rule'. I remembered her prediction, and I became determined to see it through!"

> Holmes paused in relating Mrs. Harding's account. "Of course," he said to me, "by this point, it had occurred to me that the lady was quite mad."
> I nodded my head in agreement.

"That is when the idea came to me," she continued. "Surely there must be a substance available without going to a pharmacy that might help Mr. Roosevelt on his way to his greatest glory before he could make good his intention to run for President again. It did not require much research to discover the remarkable qualities of deadly nightshade or, as you called it just now, bellandonna. Of course, that plant isn't native to Washington, but it was a simple matter for Clayton to acquire a sample from the Botanic Garden and to take it to Oyster Bay during his assignment to guard Roosevelt. A bit of the berry crushed into his drink and Mr. Roosevelt was no more. They called it a stroke – a blood clot in his lung."

> The enormity of what Mrs. Harding had just admitted to Holmes took my breath away. I looked carefully into his eyes to see if he doubted what she had confessed, but Holmes's eyes were resolute and his face grim. He continued his account of her story.

"Mr. Wilson still remained a formidable foe in 1920, should he break with precedent and run for a third term. Having taken our first step with Roosevelt, executing a plan to ensure that Mr. Wilson ended his presidency in 1921 was, in my view, merely a 'next step' in our efforts to place Mr. Harding in the White House. What great fortune occurred in October of 1919 when the President journeyed westward to promote his ludicrous League of Nations and Clayton was assigned to aid in the security plans.

"Once again, Clayton made a visit to the Botanic Garden and acquired an additional sample of the nightshade which had proven so effective with Mr. Roosevelt. Wilson was exhausted and not in the best of health, so Clayton gave him perhaps a smaller dose than he should have when they were in a hotel in Pueblo, but the effect was quite stark. Like Roosevelt, he suffered a stroke, but Wilson survived, though terribly disabled. However, any discussion of his seeking a third term was ended and the route for my Warren to win election was that much clearer."

> *I couldn't believe my ears. The former First Lady of the United States, whose own husband had died of a stroke just a week before, had admitted to Holmes her role in eliminating two of her husband's most feared rivals in the 1920 election which had resulted in Harding's election. Suddenly, however, the awful conclusion of the story dawned on me.*
>
> *"No!" I cried. "You cannot be serious. It isn't possible that such devilry exists!"*
>
> *Holmes said nothing, but gazed out the window. Even at this late hour, there remained traffic and crowds on Pennsylvania Avenue as the capital prepared to mark the departure of the funeral train for Ohio in just a few hours. He reached for another cigarette and the flare of the match lit up his face. I don't believe I ever saw it so drained of energy, so filled with a sense of tragedy, as in that hotel room.*

Mrs. Harding continued her narrative. "Well, as you know, Senator Harding did win the election in 1920. In fact, he not only won it, but he won the biggest victory in history. In history! And do you know what was especially pleasing? He defeated the cousin of that Teddy Roosevelt – Franklin – who was the Democrats' vice-presidential candidate!

"But, Mr. Holmes, the presidency was not what he had expected. Not at all. He was unhappy with the demands of the job,

155

as he had told Nicholas Murray Butler, the president of Columbia University. Isn't that so sad? And then his supposed friends were creating such embarrassments, like Mr. Fall selling those oil leases on the federal land at Teapot Dome. It seemed that these scandals might even complicate his efforts to win a second term in 1924, assuming I could persuade the President to run (although I am quite sure I could have done so).

"But then, reports began to reach me that Warren's enemies were organizing against him. If Warren didn't step aside, he learned, the newspapers would run stories about my first marriage, my divorce, about Marshall dying from alcoholism, about whether I had even been married to Pete at all. His rivals began to circulate rumors about my husband and his relationships with those other women – even about producing a bastard daughter with that whore Nan Britton!"

At this disclosure, she dabbed at her eyes and took several moments to settle herself. She suddenly looked very old and very exhausted despite the alarming admissions she was making.

"And then there was the rumor that he really was a Negro, or at least that he had some Negro ancestors," she said. "You know, we have been very supportive of the Negroes – we really were, not like that horrible Mr. Wilson. But in this country, Mr. Holmes, there mere suggestion of having black blood would instantly disqualify any person from being elected President, and it will always be that way."

"So, three terrible rumors – about my marriage and divorce, about those trollops and a bastard child, and his alleged Negro ancestry."

Hmm, I thought, as we had discussed – things do come in threes!

"He was so miserable and depressed," she continued, "and his health began to fail. I could see it happening in January, when he got the flu, and I thought I would lose him then. The doctors advised us to take a trip out West, to California and Alaska, in hopes it might revive his weakened state of mind that had necessitated several hospitalizations when he was a publisher. Did you know that, Mr. Holmes? Another story we didn't want to see promoted!

156

"So we went on the trip – seven-thousand miles by train and ship – and yes, some of it was magnificent, but I could see the toll is was taking on him. Once we arrived in San Francisco, I knew the end was near, and I didn't want him to suffer. At my request, Clayton had brought with him a small amount of the nightshade in the event it might be needed. The doctors had just about worn him out with their purges and medicines. I felt I could help him go to his rest and avoid all the embarrassment and humiliation that would follow him back to Washington and through the next campaign.

"Don't you see, Mr. Holmes? It was better to end it this way, on *our* terms, free from the mortification his enemies would cause, tainting his legacy forever. And so, yes, I did give him a little nightshade in his milk as he was resting, and he went to sleep forever. Although that horrid Mrs. Johnson, the owner of the Palace, nearly ruined everything by insisting the police test the milk remaining in the glass! But I put a stop to that! I grabbed the glass and poured the residue down the drain!"

* * * * *

The room was quiet as Holmes ended his account of Mrs. Harding's unspeakable actions. It took several minutes before I could collect my thoughts.

"And the Bureau agent, Graham?" I asked.

"He would surely deny involvement, even if Mrs. Harding would accuse him, which she never would," Holmes responded. "She is obviously insane and has been for some time, perhaps stemming from the death of her son. Moreover, I have little doubt Director Burns might well have become aware of this plot and might have been persuaded to conceal the role of one of his agents so that he wouldn't be implicated in the premature deaths – to put it obliquely – of three American Presidents. Such a disclosure would hardly enhance his stature as the director of the Bureau of Investigations."

"What are you going to do?" I asked in amazement, the full weight of the incredible story sinking in.

"Mrs. Harding offered me one more piece of information that she believes is relevant," he said. "She is dying of kidney disease. Indeed, she has been suffering from it for many years, and now her doctors say she will be dead within a year." He took a deep pull on yet another cigarette, the orange tip burning furiously in the near dark of the room. "I suppose I must weigh the merits and drawbacks of revealing all I've been told against the terrible impact disclosure would surely impose on a people already bereft at the loss of their President.

"And to what end? Mr. Graham undoubtedly is a good enough investigator to have covered his tracks sufficiently. The Washington police would never be able to incontrovertibly connect him to these tragic events. The real perpetrator, the President's widow, would seem an implausible conspirator, and she appears likely to pay with her life long before a trial and sentence could be executed.

"Moreover, I don't think that I, as a foreigner, should be so deeply involved in disclosing a plot so heinous that it could have profound political implications for the Americans. No, Watson, I believe this is a case that will not only go unsolved but unrecorded, if you don't mind. Certainly I will inform our colleague, Mr. Moran, of my findings, but I strongly suspect he'll come to the same conclusion. The Americans have endured enough. We cannot serve the ends of justice by tightening the hand of guilt around the treacherous Mrs. Harding."

We used the few remaining hours of the night for a brief and, in my case, fitful sleep. Rising early, we ate our breakfast under the careful gaze of the Bureau agents. We were joined by Moran, whom Holmes quietly informed of his astonishing adventure in the White House the previous night. I doubt I have ever seen a man as shocked as was the Secret Service director as Holmes spun out his account of the sinister actions of Harding's widow and her Bureau of Investigations accomplice.

"Good Lord!" the astonished director cried. "She has accomplished as much as Booth, Czolgosz, and Guiteau combined! I will have to give all this some thought, of course, but I understand your hesitation to publicize Mrs. Harding's confession," he said. "But I have no choice but to bring your findings to the attention of President Coolidge. He'll have to make whatever decision he thinks warranted with respect to Mrs. Harding, Graham, and perhaps even Burns." He shook his head. "It's almost impossible to believe, Mr. Holmes. Let me ask you: Do you think it's all true, or has Mrs. Harding simply been confounded by her emotions upon losing her husband?"

"I believe her story, although I don't recall one I would so prefer to have never heard," Holmes said quietly. "Has your laboratory confirmed a trace of belladonna on the swab I inserted into Harding's mouth as he lay in the East Room of the White

House?" The director nodded tersely. "Yes, I thought so. Your diversion of the guards was most effective."

Moran rode with us to Union Station to await our train back to New York. There was a great crowd around the station waiting to bid farewell to the late President, for the train bearing the late President and his family and friends was soon due to depart as well. Indeed, as we waited to board our train, the automobiles carrying both the President's coffin and Mrs. Harding arrived.

A respectful silence fell over the crowd as she disembarked and turned to enter the station. As she walked past us, the widow caught Holmes's eye and they locked stares for a long moment. Then she was caught up in the rush of police and dignitaries and swept along to the crepe-draped train that would carry Warren Harding back to Ohio and his final rest.

Epilogue

"Do you remember mentioning how things have a way of happening in threes?" Holmes asked as we settled into our compartment for the ride to New York. "Well, that thought crossed my mind when I realized the unnaturally brief time span in which three presidents, all competing for the office in 1920, suffered strokes that left two dead and one an invalid incapable of running for office.

"True, it might be a coincidence, but experience has taught me that coincidences deserve, at a minimum, further investigation – especially when they involve unanticipated deaths and coveted positions.

"My research into the Secret Service's records of the death of Roosevelt and incapacitation of Wilson in 1919 revealed one point that immediately jumped out at me: In both cases," Holmes noted, "one particular Bureau of Investigations agent – Clayton Graham – was assigned to the potential victim. I asked Moran for a list of those in San Francisco with Harding just before he was fatally stricken, and again, Mr. Graham's name appeared on the manifest of names." He shook his head. "That was simply too coincidental, and it made me think that there must have been a conspiracy at work.

"But one point complicated my theory, and that was that Graham was nowhere near Mr. Harding for two days before the President's death. He certainly might have administered the poison earlier in the trip, which might have explained the President's confusing symptoms in Alaska and when he first arrived back in San

Francisco. But he was then not close enough to Harding to slip the nightshade into food or drink.

"Indeed, while he was bedridden in the Palace Hotel, only Mrs. Harding never had left his side, right up until the time he expired. And that caused a sudden and dismaying thought: Might his *wife* rather than Graham have administered the poison that caused President's death?

"But why would she have been an accomplice in the deaths of Roosevelt and Wilson?" I asked.

"Because, as she admitted to me, those two men stood between her husband and the office *she* intended that he occupy," Holmes said. "As to the relationship between the First Lady and Graham, I cannot be sure, but I would not be surprised if Dr. Freud would hypothesize that she viewed him as a substitute for her lost son and he, in turn, viewed her as a substitute mother he sought only to please.

"He became her agent, acquiring the belladonna berries and administering it to Roosevelt and Wilson, and then providing her the dose needed to kill her own husband," he concluded.

"And her motivation for doing so?" I asked.

"The dishonesty in the administration, the tawdry relationships, and the ignominy that would be her husband's certain legacy" Holmes answered. "Disclosure would surely have ruined a life of privilege that Mrs. Harding had carefully constructed from the tatters of her earlier marriage, if there even had been one. No, far better to have Harding depart as the martyr of a bereaved nation than the humiliated President driven from office in disgrace."

As Holmes had anticipated, his account of Mrs. Harding's confession was never made public, until now. As Holmes requested, my agreement with Cox and Company ensures that this story will remain confidential until 2020.

While they did not face trials, a judgment of another kind awaited the two key figures in the case, neither of whom survived 1924. Mrs. Harding was not exaggerating the hopelessness of her own medical condition. Shortly after returning to Ohio, she had fallen gravely ill with inoperable kidney disease and she died just weeks after Mr. Coolidge was elected to a full term as President in November 1924. As to Graham, he didn't live long enough to disclose whatever he knew of the crimes, if he could have been persuaded. Assigned by Burns to a group of special agents enforcing Washington's prohibition law, he was shot in the back in January – presumably by accident, by a fellow agent during a raid on a

160

speakeasy associated with "the man in the green hat" on Capitol Hill, only weeks after Holmes and I had returned to London. In February, Mrs. Harding's last victim, Woodrow Wilson, the former President who had suffered grievously since his stroke in 1919, died as well.

Of the others with knowledge of the great plot, Moran has continued to serve as director of the Secret Service. But I suspect word of Graham's treachery made its way to Coolidge, raising questions about the Bureau of Investigation's chief, Burns, the so-called "Sherlock Holmes of America". Both he and the Attorney General under whom he served, a Harding crony named Harry Daugherty, were soon implicated in the massive Teapot Dome scandal and were removed from office in 1924. The new Bureau of Investigation chief – a young, former librarian of our unfortunate acquaintance named J. Edgar Hoover – appears likely to be an interim replacement until a more experienced director can be appointed.

The only other people who know the story surrounding President Harding's sudden death are Holmes and myself. He was soon back tending his bees in Sussex and I returned to my writing desk in London, where this startling account of our adventure in America has been finally recorded for future readers to contemplate.

The Odd Event
by Kevin P. Thornton

"Watson, is there much of politics that interests you?"

Holmes had travelled down to London to do whatever it was he did when he visited the city. These trips became more rushed as the years passed, as if he had ten things to do and only time enough for five. He was still a vibrant and healthy man even as a septuagenarian – indeed I liked to believe we both were – but he had lost a smidgen of the spring and vitality he'd had when we first shared rooms together, well over forty years before. And yet, here we were, about to venture on an adventure once more. He had invited me to meet him at the Diogenes Club, and such an invitation almost always meant that his brother Mycroft was involved.

"I try not to," I replied to his question, "and I must say I am quite surprised that you do."

"Indeed? I may be retired, but I still have an interest in the human condition in its many meandering forms. And where do you think much of the crime in the world comes from? I will tell you that the corridors of power, from here and across the park, are the home of the biggest criminals in the world. It is the only place in the Kingdom where one may safely get away with murder, extortion, robbery, theft, kidnapping, and a multitude of other crimes."

"Now I am intrigued," I said. "How is that at all possible?"

"Because they are in power, and power corrupts. Whomever holds the majority in the Commons has a license to foment mischief and more, all under the banner of policy."

"Policy?" I said.

"Indeed," said Holmes. He paced up and down in the Stranger's Room, the only place in the building where one may speak. The Diogenes Club was founded by the most umcommon men in London. Clubs are normally sociable institutions, yet The Diogenes club members were distinctly un-clublike and cherished their quietude.

"Pay no attention to my brother, Doctor Watson," said a voice from the door and I turned in delight to greet Mycroft. "If he accuses the government of criminal behaviour, he might very well include himself. He has often consulted for us and has always been happy to pocket his exorbitant fees." There was no heat to his words, and both

162

brothers acknowledged each other with a brief raised eyebrow and a slight tilt of the head. Such scantness was the Holmes family equivalent of a Frenchman's ebullient hug and double kiss.

I was awarded with a warmer show of emotion as Holmes the Elder touched my arm as we shook hands. Sherlock Holmes watched in amusement as his brother demonstrated his limited social skills, and then interrupted.

"Come Mycroft, you didn't arrange for this meeting to warm Watson's heart with your care and concern for his kin. What troubles you, and how may we assist?"

"Have you asked Watson to accompany you to Epping?" said Mycroft.

"How did you know that I would go?"

"I would have thought that was self-evident. Mister Oxley the circus man has been in touch with you, has he not? You have helped them before – that little event in 1915. * Who else would he call?"

Sherlock nodded in agreement. "But Oxley and his issues are not what troubles you. It's Churchill. Someone has threatened him again, have they not?"

"Indeed."

"Why is he your concern? He hasn't been able to get himself elected again in the last three elections and five years. Why would a Labour-led Government care about him?"

Mycroft sat. For a man closer to eighty than seventy, he moved with grace and lightness and seemed to be untroubled by a great deal of the aches and pains that would afflict many of his age. "This is not a government request. It is from me. Churchill has attracted the ire of the Fenians, and they have threatened his life. I wish to keep him alive. In addition to two plainclothes policemen, I have other agents in place protecting him. That you will be in the region is fortuitous. Judging by Watson's account of what happened in 1915, Churchill trusts you both and will listen to your judgement. He is installed in a mansion called Warlies Park, the home of the Buxton Barons. In fact, the uncle of the fifth and current Baron was a minister in Ramsey MacDonald's recently dissolved Government, and I have arranged for you two to stay there as well while you conduct your other business."

"If you've read Watson's notes from Epping nine years ago," said Sherlock, "and I am impressed that he trusted you with them, as his tin box is well-guarded, then you will know that the Winston Churchill we knew then was foolhardy and not averse to risking his life. We barely saved him then, and may not manage to do so this time. Granted he is an impressive man, but why is he so important?"

Mycroft tapped the table briefly and ever so gently, as if the action helped him decide. "It will not surprise you to know that there are people in the varied governments of the world who are of more value than their position suggests. They are the far-seeing ones – the ones who, if listened to, maintain the balance of power and prevent chaos. I must emphasize here the words 'if listened to'. The conflagration of 1914-1918 was one such instance where reason was swept aside, and it was left to a few of us to pick up the pieces and guide the rebuilding of Europe once more. Sadly, we have been hampered with the unreasonable need for revenge that came from the Paris Peace Conference."

"I would have thought that burdening Germany and the Central Powers with the cost of the war was the best way to prevent them from getting ambitious again," I said.

"That is a popular opinion," said Mycroft, "but as we have seen from the crazed inflation their economy has suffered, there is clearly a point at which punishment and reparations can be too much. There was never the intention among sensible men to bring Germany to its knees, ruin their economy, and starve their nation. Yet people are dying, and it is too late, for now, to turn things around. This is worrisome." His words did not carry the meaning of his countenance, and for the first time I saw in his aged face the burden that the Crown had asked him to bear all these years.

At the time, I believed Sherlock Holmes misread the sympathy in my eyes for confusion. 'The easiest way to foment revolution is to give the people no other choice. Unfortunately, it is also a small step to autocracy."

"In other words," said Mycroft, "the treaty that was put in place to prevent another war may end up causing one. To that end, people like myself, in this country and others, are looking for strong leaders to protect and develop them so that they might see off the trouble ahead – or at least be in a better position to deal with it."

The brothers waited patiently for me to catch up.

"Oh," I said. "And Churchill is one of them."

"Yes," said Mycroft. "While you are up in Essex visiting your circus friends, it would be useful if you could prevent Churchill from dying. There are some of us who see a bright future for him."

Mycroft left us and I asked Holmes, "What of the other matter you mentioned – the Oxley circus family?"

"Mycroft pre-empted my request. I wondered if you would join me in a trip to Epping? It seems Oxley Senior is facing a bit of a mystery."

"Is that all he said? That alone would not normally be enough to stir you."

"How right you are. He telephoned me though, and I could hear it in his voice. He is frightened, and this is a man who has performed on the high wire and now makes a living as an escapist."

"An escapist?"

"It is as it sounds: One who escapes. A wily part of prestidigitation, and one that Oxley has perfected."

"Then what frightens him?"

"He believes someone in his own family is trying to kill him."

I left Holmes at the club. I suspected that he was staying there, as he had said on more than one occasion that the enforced peacefulness appealed to him – although he had been censured once for writing his evening meal order on the pad with a pencil that was too noisy.

I couldn't imagine enjoying such stillness so I returned to the hustle and bustle of normal life. The next morning I met Holmes at Liverpool Street Station and we caught the 9:21 to Loughton, and then on to Epping.

"I looked at my notes last night," I said. "If there is a member of his family trying to kill him, there is a fertile field of options. Back in 1915, he had his wife, his sister, his sister-in-law, his daughter, his daughter-in-law who was married to his son Daniel, and his other son David who was not married at the time, but may be now. Counting Oxley Senior, that is eight people out on his farm."

'It is less," said Holmes. "You're forgetting that Daniel did not come home from Ypres. He is buried in a foreign field, while the other son David left after his involvement in our last adventure and hasn't been seen since. The father, whose first name is Django, has five women in his home, and he thinks at least one of them is trying to kill him."

"Does Django Oxley still perform as *The Marvelous Merlini*? He must be a man of sixty-some years by now. Surely the ravages of time will have caught up with his performances?"

"We shall see, Watson, we shall see."

Holmes said nothing more on that topic – unusual for him – although he digressed into the personal. "Mycroft would not be able to withstand your pity. He respects you and sees you as a steadying influence on me."

"I thought you had misread me yesterday. I was wrong."

"Since when has that ever been possible? Even to this day you wear your heart on your sleeve." He tapped out his pipe to empty it, and began the idle refilling from his travel tobacco pouch. "Mycroft sees only his failures – all the times when he was unable to persuade people to do the right thing. He should be reminded of his successes, but I fear it would do no good at this late stage of his life."

"I thought he had retired from whatever his role within the Government was."

"The Mandarin of Mandarins? I believe he has retired several times by now. He could easily have gone at the end of the Boer War. Twelve years later when he was mandated to retire, the Kaiser changed the world. Since then he has been brought back so often I believe they have given up reassigning his office."

"Is he right about Versailles and its ramifications?"

"He is right to prepare for the worst, all the while hoping for the best. It says little for the state of the Government that the protection of one such as Churchill has been left to whomsoever Mycroft could muster, plus two old crocks from Baker Street."

"Two valiant old crocks," I replied, but Holmes, after what was for him almost a confessional conversation, relapsed into his more familiar silence. He stared out the window for the rest of the journey, though I doubted his gaze was on the scenery.

We were met by Marcombe, a chauffeur to the Buxton family, who carried our bags out to a gleaming limousine. "Holmes," I said in delight, "that is a Silver Ghost."

"Of a sort, sir," said Marcombe. "It is actually a Rolls Royce Mark I Armoured Car that was sold off at the end of the war. Sir Thomas, the fifth and current Baronet, bought several and had the coachwork restored to the standards of before."

The rear door creaked as it opened, very unlike a Rolls. Marcombe apologized. "Much of the body and underpinnings are still the original armoured plate," he said. "It is not as quiet as a factory model, but I do fancy our chances of survival should we run into a train."

Holmes gave Marcombe the address of the farm the Oxleys still used as their base and we set out. It was a bracing October day, and the vehicle had been restored as an open landau in the rear, so I was glad of the carriage blankets provided. Holmes did not even appear to notice.

"Oxley is expecting us in the guise of old friends enquiring if there is a show to be seen. He said that he is on the road less and less every year, and his wintering at the farm has already begun, save one last performance. We will collect tickets from him when we visit. It is the same evening of the day of the election: Two days hence, Wednesday the 29th."

"How do you plan to investigate such a fear? He's brave enough as it is to have so many women under one roof."

"My dear Watson, do I detect a morsel of chauvinism in your manner? Say it isn't so!"

"You may very well tease, but it's not chauvinism, it is fear. It has been my experience that a home has room for only one woman of the house. Django Oxley has five, all of whom have managed their own homes before, and all of whom will wish to exert their authority. I'm surprised he thinks that one of them is trying to do away with him. It's more likely to me that they would *all* be plotting against each other."

"It is one of your more plausible theories. It is still wrong, but it has the merit of drama to it. I believe you're wrong about Oxley's status in the household, and I already have an idea that needs only a small morsel of truth or evidence for verification. We'll know soon enough, for yonder lies the farm."

Django Oxley answered the door as if he'd been waiting for us, and he came out without a word to anyone else inside.

"Mister Holmes, Doctor Watson, so good to see you. Thank you so much for coming. Here, let us walk to the barn. You will see why in a minute." He scurried ahead and we nearly had to double-time to keep up with him.

We crossed to the barn, which seemed to be the centre of some activity.

"I never learns me lesson. I have another lot wintering here in my barn, an Irish bunch of travellers. Here to pick my brain, more like. Always wanting to know how I do this balancing act or that bit of escaping. I'm thinking I might show them. It's not like I have anyone to pass it onto, with both my boys gone. It's a shame, Mister Holmes. It broke my heart when Daniel never came back from the war. He died at Ypres, do you remember?"

"I do," said Holmes. "And what of your other son, David – the one who was involved with the anarchists?"

"He was always naïve, was Davey. He was horrified at what he had done, bringing them here. When he heard they had been shot as spies, a fate that could have been his were it not for your intervention, it seemed to unhinge him. He disappeared within the week and we've not seen him since." Django Oxley sighed as he stepped into the barn. He was still a fit looking man. He would need to be. As a circus *artiste*, he relied on his own strength and dexterity more than most, and he still looked capable and spry. But there was a weariness to him that was new since our last meeting.

We entered the barn and saw what Oxley meant. On the far side, two travelling caravans had been parked next to each, as if they were occupied. There were two young men and two women sitting outside the doors and they waved at Oxley as he walked past, heading towards a walled off area. Further along there was a small group practicing tumbling, and out the other side in the paddock, there were two women riding horses, falling off them and then jumping back on.

"I have been amusing myself these last years with escaping tricks," said Oxley. "They are very popular and draw large crowds. I don't mind admitting that after the loss of my two sons, and with the responsibilities of my household, I have worked hard and done very well since the war. I also don't mind admitting that when that American chap Houdini started catching everyone's attention, he left room below him for some of us to make a good living. I have worked out some of his tricks and will do them all, save the submersed ones." At Holmes's querying look he said, "I'm not partial to the cold water. It affects my dexterity and that can be crucial when you are upside down in a bolted chamber, holding your breath." He saw the look of astonishment on my face and laughed. "My dear Doctor Watson, you have no idea how magic is created, do you? I know from our correspondence that Mister Holmes has worked out most of our little tricks. Without breaking the magician's oath, I can tell you that most escape tricks involve nothing more than an agile mind and body, dexterity, and strength of fingers and toes, and the ability to hold one's breath. Take your own, for example. How long do you think you can hold your breath?"

"I once managed forty-two seconds," I said, "but I was much younger."

'And that is the approximate number that most members of an audience will have in mind. If I were to tell you that I can sit and hold my breath for nearly four minutes, and that, even working underwater, upside down, chained and blindfolded, I can safely

168

function for all but thirty seconds of that time, would you believe me?"

"I would, sir, because I know you, but I could see how an audience could be caught in a frenzy of anticipation."

"In particular if they have been told that the performer is only capable of holding his breath for only ninety seconds."

"Exactly, Mister Holmes. When I used to do my tricks underwater, the time between ninety seconds and two-hundred was where we made our living. The girls had this thing they did where they'd pass a hat in the audience. 'Buy the hammer' they'd call it, getting the spectators to pay for the use of a sledgehammer to break me out. It was a brilliant wheeze."

"Fascinating," said Holmes. "Now to your problem. You fear someone is trying to kill you."

"I know it," said Oxley. He unlooked the door to the room and led us in. There were three or four ungainly contraptions set up on benches, as well as decently equipped workspace.

"These are my tricks," said Oxley. "That contraption is a cell that I am locked into and suspended above the audience. That," he said, pointing to a large steel canister, "is my version of Erik's milk can escape trick, and this is the one I will do on Wednesday night, the 'upside down in a bag and cage' escape. It's the only one that hasn't tried to kill me recently."

"And yet tricks do not kill."

"I know," said Oxley. "We are very secretive about what we do and how we do it. These frames, if examined in close detail, could give up their stories to another magician. So they are locked up when we are at home, and guarded by the women of the family when we are at a show. Which means when they fail, it is either due to my carelessness, or . . . ." He seemed unable to say any more.

"But why?" I said, surprised that Holmes hadn't already asked. "You say you have been successful. Why would one of the women of the house try to kill you? It would be as if . . . ." I paused, not enjoying where I had led myself.

"Like killing the goose that laid the golden eggs?" said Holmes. I winced at his bluntness, but Oxley seemed unabashed.

"Exactly. Yet it can be no other."

"May we see your trick for the show?"

Oxley seemed reluctant, but he uncovered it anyway. It was a tubular steel frame, welded together with a strong eyehook on the top from which I assumed he would be suspended. The entire frame was bedecked in intricate filigree. Holmes took one look at the

169

design and smiled. "I see the capacity of mankind to be blind to the obvious has not diminished. I assume you are searched by the local constabulary or some-such before you are bound within."

"Of course," said Oxley. "I might have guessed you would see the secret."

"What secret?" I asked.

"This is a variation of one of Houdini's more famous tricks," said Holmes. "He is stripped as bare as socially acceptable and searched for any lock-picks before he is bound, bagged, and suspended. The trick is in the preamble, which leaves the audience to say 'How did he do it?' I, on the other hand, ask 'Where does a man with no place to hide a lock-pick hide a lock-pick?'"

"Erik Weiss received one from his wife's kiss, the last thing they did before he was locked away."

"Weiss is Houdini's real name," said Holmes for my benefit. "You could not do the same – hence the filigree pattern."

"Yes Mister Holmes, you have it. If my wife were to give me such a dramatic kiss in front of a staid British audience, people would want to know why, so I found another way to do it."

"The filigree, Watson – the detailed and ornate work of the filigree. Go and examine it, and then ask why so much work went into a frame that is hidden in a bag."

I examined it carefully, prodding and poking. "Were it not so finely put together, I could see each individual decoration serving another purpose, but I'm not sure."

"Lock picks," said Holmes. "Each individual part of the overall design could double as a makeshift lock pick."

"Except they are all firmly brazed to the frame."

"Not all," said Holmes. "Of the five-hundred or so attached to the frame, there will be at least one or two that are easy to twist off."

"Three actually," said Oxley. "They function as adequate lock-picks."

"To someone who knows how to use them," continued Holmes. "All you need to do is to make sure they are there immediately prior to your performance."

"Which still doesn't tell me who is trying to kill me, or why."

"Patience, my good man. Watson and I will make sure you survive your performance. I merely need to check one small detail."

We left Oxley in the barn with his promise of tickets for the show to be left at the theatre door. As we walked across the courtyard, I noticed a man out in the field tending to the horses. Every time he approached them, they shied away.

"Holmes, do you see the farmhand? Oxley said nothing about extra help."

"It is a farm, as well as a travelling circus home-away-from-home. There will be workers."

Even though the man was some distance off, we could hear him berating the recalcitrant animals, and he did so in the coarse brogue of an Ulsterman.

"Did Mycroft not warn of a possible Fenian danger? And now Oxley is wintering a circus troupe from Ireland, and a farmhand with no knowledge of animals who is quite patently Irish. Should we not find out more?"

"You may stay if you wish, but I am all for being taken to Warlies Park where good whisky, good food, and good conversation awaits."

If there one constant in this world it was my old friend's capacity to frustrate. I could see he that hadn't lost his touch. Normally I would've left him alone, but there was more that was unsaid.

"What of the women who are trying to kill him? Should we not talk to them?"

Holmes shuddered. "Feel free. If I felt there was any value to that, I would do so. I must make a telegraphic enquiry. From that I may find it necessary to talk to the five Oxley women, but until such is required, I would prefer to use what time we have in the company of amicable men rather than plotting women."

We stopped to send Holmes's telegram, reply to be sent onward. Warlies Park had originally been the home of the Abbot of nearby Waltham Abbey, a brotherhood with only a tenuous link to the vows of poverty. After Henry VIII's dissolution of the monasteries, the home had been owned by one or another supporter of the Crown until the middle of the nineteenth century. All this was told to us by our driver, Marcombe, who seemed far better educated than his position demanded. He volunteered that he'd had parents who had instilled in him a love of reading, with local history being one of his interests.

"I have also read all of your own writings, Doctor," he said, "and eagerly await more." This last left me inordinately pleased, and I moved closer onto the jump seat, the better to hear him.

"It has seen some changes since the Buxton family bought it," he continued. "It is now gothic in style, and the current Baronet continues the work of his late father, not long dead."

"I read of that," I said. "It was an automobile crash, was it not – the way the previous Baron died? How sad and unusual."

"Not that unusual," said Holmes. "Nine people died in England in car crashes last month."

"The Baronet's death was a terrible tragedy," said Marcombe. "He hit a tree and a sharp branch came through the body of the automobile and into Sir Thomas. I think that is why his son was so keen on these old armoured Rolls-es. He was quite affected by his Father's death. They were very close."

We were met at the door by Noel Buxton, until recently a Minister in Government.

"Please forgive my nephew for not being here to welcome you."

"Buxton! Have those two old rogues arrived? Bring them in, and let us dine and sup." The gravelly voice of Winston Churchill was unmistakeable, and we heard him some seconds before he turned the corner. The intervening years had added to his frame as it had taken from the top of his head, but his warmth and wit were still firmly in place. Even Holmes, who rarely found reason to show his delight, was forced to smile as Churchill gathered us into his lair as adeptly as if it were his own home. Buxton seemed used to Churchill, and he later told me they had been scions of the Liberal Party together before splitting left to right, and were still firm friends. "While I am campaigning for my seat in Norfolk, Winston is using my family home to campaign locally. Indeed, he even has three of the women of my family managing his campaign for him."

"Only two," said Churchill. "Your niece and one of your sisters. The other sister provides a far more useful service as a late night dispenser of port and advice. Besides, I am – like you – the poor relation of nobility, and I need all the help I can get. Don't forget I have lost my last three elections."

"Yet Baldwin has put you here in a seat that you will easily own come Wednesday," said Buxton. There was no malice to his comments though, and after some more small talk he excused himself.

"That is how politics should work," said Churchill. "I disagree with much of what Buxton believes, but because we can remain friends, we are able to find common ground. As you well know, that is not always the case."

"Indeed," said Holmes.

"No need to be coy," said Churchill. "I may be a little older and a little greyer, but I have not lost my mental faculties. I agree with your brother that we have created a storm in a whirlwind surrounded by a cyclone at the Paris Peace Conference. It is all very well to kick a nation when it is down. It is even understandable to apply some jackbooted pressure to the jugular while the kicking is taking place. But it becomes too much when we try to jump up and down on the burning torso simultaneously."

He paused to jot a note in a waistcoat notepad. "Hmm," he said. "Words grouped in threes have cadence and rhythm."

"*Veni, vidi, vici*," said Holmes.

"Indeed," Churchill replied. "*Omne trium perfectum.*"

"Yet we are not here for your oration, as delightful as it no doubt will be. Rather, tell us what you have done to irk the Irish."

"No more than usual," said Churchill. "I am an Englishman with an opinion and a platform. I have said some good things about Irish independence, which has perturbed Ulster. I have also said some good things about Northern Ireland, which has disturbed the Republicans. They all only remember the bad, and that is enough to inflame them."

"Do you think you are a target?" I said.

"Anyone can be a target. The first argument in history happened with the arrival of the second person. Nothing has changed since then except that for every person who says black, there is likely to be someone who picks another colour and defends it to the death." Churchill paused, took a puff of his cigar, and a slurp of brandy from his snifter. "Elections are odious parts of history as they are a license to argue, often absent the focus of rationality."

"I thought elections were about democracy," I said.

"No, they are about numbers. This, for me is a safe seat, and I should be elected come Wednesday. The statisticians and the mathematicians have done their calculations — I do not know how nor do I care — but the party has decided they want me back."

"Yet you stood in two by-elections and lost both," said Holmes.

"Arithmetic has never been my strongest discipline. When I was told not to run in those constituencies, I decided I had to find out for myself. They were right."

"Most politicians would not come back from so many defeats."

"Agreed, but I have my uses. Baldwin needs me as his conscience. He also needs someone to protect him by taking the brunt of the bad publicity. I will do so if what we are doing is right." He turned to me. "You asked if there are people ready to kill me.

Yes, there are. I just don't know if it is the turn of the Irish this week."

Our talk turned to other things. Churchill was interested in Oxley's perceived difficulties. "Django Oxley," he said. "I did not know his first name, but it explains much."

To my query, he replied, "It seems that the circus life is most suited to the Romany people, although I believe they call themselves travellers, and never gypsies, a term they find insulting. Django is a common name among their community, and many of them opt for the circus life, as it allows them to follow their peripateticism."

"How philosophical," said Holmes, "although I assume you meant their caravanning lifestyle as distinct from Aristotle's thoughts."

"Well spotted. As regards the women, I would show care in my dealings with them. They are known to be proud, passionate, and armed, often with sharp knives hidden about themselves. My biggest surprise is, if one of them wanted him dead, why hasn't it happened yet?"

"You have hit upon the most salient point of the entire affair," said Holmes.

At that moment Marcombe, whose duties when the house was busy seemed to include butling, told Holmes that there was a telephone call for him. He went away and returned with an air of slight discontent. "That was Mycroft. It appears that Oxley neglected to mention he is being followed."

"Maybe he doesn't know," said Churchill. "Not everyone is as suspicious of the world as the occupants of this room."

"How did Mycroft know?" I said. "He barely has enough people to make sure Winston is safe. How can he have Oxley followed as well?"

"Maybe it's not Oxley, Holmes," said Churchill. "Maybe he has *you* under watch. A bit of family care from big brother."

Holmes snorted. "I assure you that is the last thing on my brother's mind. However it does create some interesting variations on the question at hand."

"Which is?" pressed Churchill.

"Who is trying to kill *you*?" I said to him, "And which woman in his household is trying to kill Oxley? Should we not move him?"

"He is safe from his family until after the show," said Holmes. "And as for Winston, the only evidence is that there is talk the Irish are revolting. The Irish are always revolting, and if they were

174

looking for someone to kill, frankly there are bigger and easier targets."

"Well, thank you very much for putting me in my place," said Churchill, but he was nodding as he said so. "There is however one part of this concatenation that is not yet evident to you: At the end of voting on Wednesday, Gilbert Granville Sharp, James Ranger, and I – the three candidates – have all been invited to The Marvelous Merlini's performance. If anybody is trying to kill anyone, the theatre would be a good time and place."

As we retired that evening, Holmes had a telegram waiting for him. He said nothing more that night, and the next morning, he – not always the earliest of risers – was up with the sun, as he later told me at breakfast. "What a wonderful day to be alive, Watson! The countryside is glorious. I have been to the ruins of the abbey and across to the monument of Queen Boadicea's place of death. Now what are your plans for the day? I propose we go to the market. There is a specific type of honey from the area I would like to sample." He waffled on and on all day, and at the end of it, I felt he had made a special effort to be his most charming self. Naturally I responded, and it was only after dinner that Tuesday evening I was given time to ask him some questions, time I snatched from him in my grumpiest manner possible.

"Holmes, please stop. You invited me down here to investigate Django Oxley's fears."

"Which we did."

"Did we? I don't recall that happening. In the meantime, Churchill might be in danger, and we know of at least one Irishman who seems out of place. In addition to someone following Oxley, he will be doing a difficult show tomorrow night surrounded by people who want to kill him. Yet you do nothing."

"My dear Watson, you have excelled yourself. You have all the facts in front of you, yet you have drawn all the wrong conclusions."

"Not *all* the facts. What was in the telegram you received?

"An enquiry with Lloyds. They are the only company who insure the unusual. Circus performers fall into their bailiwick."

"And what did they say?"

"That The Marvelous Merlini is not insured."

"Why that's terrible!" I said. "So if he dies, his family is left with nothing."

Holmes actually shook his head in frustration. "My dear friend, you have spent too much time away from the world of the intellect."

"Then tell me: What have I not seen?"

"Everything. You have missed everything." He walked over to the table and pointed at the Irish linen tablecloth. "What colour is that?"

"It is white. What manner of question is that?"

"A benchmark. Given your run of luck today, I could nearly have believed you would have had it as black."

We missed Churchill and Buxton that evening, as the night before an election is a busy one. Maybe it was for the best as I was in a state of medium to high dudgeon with my friend. Holmes knew this and there was a touch of the same asperity of mood from him as when we first met and shared rooms in Baker Street. He knew he had vexed me and left me stewing, and I would not give him the satisfaction of asking him more questions. And so two stubborn old men went to bed, and when we woke it was Election Day and the house was all a bustle.

I wanted to go into the town to do – What? Something to show that I was trying to help Oxley or Churchill? Make ready to step in front of a Fenian bomb or a traveller woman about to stab the man of the house? I resisted only because deep down I knew that my friend was not insane, and if he chose to do nothing it was because he was confident there was nothing to do.

But by Jove, he was at his most irritating when his sanctimony leaked ever more into view.

Later in the day we arranged for Marcombe to take us into the theatre. We dined first at the King's Head, where the mutton pot was well cooked and the potatoes fresh out the cellar. Then we walked across to the theatre, collected our tickets, and went backstage.

Oxley was in a terrible state. When he saw us, he shouted for all to clear the stage. There were a couple of women reluctant to do so – "My wife and daughter," he told us – but he was persuasive.

"Look, Holmes," he said, "Do you remember this filigree cage I showed? I'm supposed to be searched before I am tied into the frame and the bag. Then when no one can see, I break off one of the three loose parts and pick my way out of trouble."

"And all three loose parts are missing."

"How did you know?"

"Because it is how I would have done it. Do you trust me, Django Oxley?"

"I do, sir, I do."

"Then make as if nothing is wrong, only announce me as the final check of your equipment. Having the greatest detective in the

176

world as an endorsement will seem believable, and I will come on stage and make a meal of it. Then the last thing I will do is shake hands with you and pass to you a replica of an Alfred Hobbs lock pick."

"Ho ho, Mister Holmes! They are the gold standard of the game. I won't ask where you availed yourself of one of those, but if you manage to do that, I will need to work much slower or else people will think I cheated."

"But you are cheating," I said.

"As opposed to what?" said Holmes. "Real magic? Of course he is cheating. All magic is cheating, but if you want to stand on the side and shout '*Simsalabim!*' at the appropriate moment . . . ."

"Holmes, Oxley, I apologize. It just seems unfair, that's all."

"My dear Watson, how could the Empire survive without men like you – so right in their wrongness?"

Thirty minutes later when the curtain went up, Holmes did his little part as if born to the stage, and then he came down into the audience and whispered to me, "Watch the reaction of the women. When he gets out, we must hurry backstage. There are things we need to do so make Oxley's life better."

We were in the second row at one end. In front of us, Churchill and the other two candidates sat among the local sycophants. Unlike the jolly man with the drink and cigar, this version of him was all business, as if he knew that the impression he left was almost as important as the work he did.

Up on stage, Oxley was chained at both ends within the filigreed frame and hung upside down before a large canvas sail sack was placed over everything. It was raised above the platform and the five women stood on the stage, arms pointed in the air as if in obeisance. Even though it was part of the act, it felt mocking, as if they were laughing at the death they promised the Marvelous Merlini.

Although I knew he would escape, and how he would do it, to see him flip the sack off and hang insouciantly off the outside of the cage was a triumph of art and spectacle. I remembered at the last to look at the women, and I saw the guilt in their eyes. "They had all planned it," I said to Holmes as we rushed backstage, but he did not answer me.

"You all planned it," said Holmes. We were behind the curtains and the stage was cleared, apart from Holmes, myself, the five Oxley

177

women, Django, and Winston Churchill, who was standing next to me enjoying the show.

"I read a novella the other week," he whispered, as Holmes paced up and down the stage. "It was a crime story, about a private detective who gathers all the suspects together at the end and explains who the murderer is. It was a bit contrived, and the detective was very eccentric. Still, maybe fiction is the way to go, now that your friend is less active."

'I'm afraid I'm too set in my ways to change now," I said. "I'll keep writing my true crime tales. I should look at the book though. Do you remember the name?"

"Something about a murder at Christie," said Churchill, "by Agatha Styles."

Holmes glared at the two of us as if we were naughty schoolboys. "You all planned it – planned for the trick to fail."

"They tried to kill me," said Oxley.

"No we didn't, you old fool!" said one of them. They were all dressed alike for the stage show, so I assumed it was his wife. "We're trying to keep you *alive*, but you're too stubborn to retire, and you won't listen to us."

"No," said Oxley. "You made the tricks fail."

'They did," said Holmes. "You're getting old and, dare I say it, cranky. By your own admission, you can't do the tricks submerged anymore because your joints seize up. Watson, what is that a sign of?"

"Arthritis," I replied, "and old age."

'Is there a cure?"

"No," I said, as I realized how wrong I had been about everything. No wonder why Holmes hadn't worried.

"They want you to stop for your own good, but you won't listen to them, so they tried to force you to quit in a panic."

'But, but – What are we going to do for money?"

"My dear foolish husband," said the same lady. "We have money saved, and as for the rest of it, whenever we're at home you're down in the barn teaching all those young travellers. Make it official: Start that circus school you've always wanted."

"Which is our cue to leave," said Holmes, guiding us to the stairs.

Oxley grasped him by the hand. "Thank you! Oh thank you, thank you! This is so much better than when I thought they were trying to kill me."

178

We left via the front door of the theatre. The streets were busy, the main polling office was across the road, and the local result was imminent. As we walked out I saw a man running towards us from about fifty yards off, holding something in his hand. As he reached back to throw it towards us, the useless Irish farmhand ran out of the crowd towards him. All I registered was a missile in the air arcing towards us before the farmhand tackled him and laid him on the ground with the style of a London Irish flank forward. I turned and dived for Churchill, knocking him down and blocking him from the blast that was surely to come, just as Marcombe rounded the corner in the armoured Rolls and placed it in between the projectile and the theatre.

There was no blast. Holmes, standing in his selfsame position, pulled me up before doing the same for Churchill. "It's not a bomb," he said.

Marcombe had tensed himself, foot on the brake, waiting for the blast.

"It's not a bomb?" he said. "Well, that's good. Bombs are hard to clean off limousines."

Holmes walked over to the farmhand and the madman, picking up the projectile along the way.

"You must be one of Mycroft's men," he said to the Irishman.

"I am, sir. Constable Simon McDevitt. Why did the bomb not go off, sir, and why are you still holding it?"

"Because it is not a bomb – it's a picture," said Holmes to the other man. "Of you, your wife, and your two children. You've been following your father, haven't you?"

"Yes," said David Oxley. "I have."

"You were both close to the mark when you wondered how Mycroft knew Oxley was being followed," said Holmes much later. We were sitting in front of the fire at Warlies Park. It was late and we were tired, but it had been an eventful day and we needed the whisky to dull our adrenaline. "He had someone on the Oxley farm."

"The Irish farmhand who knew nothing about horses," I said. "You knew he was Mycroft's man?"

"I suspected something. I looked at all the reasons why someone who knew nothing about farming was working on a farm. He had to be there with Oxley's knowledge – otherwise he wouldn't have lasted a day. Mycroft placed him on the farm after another one of his men checked out the theatre for the candidate's safety when it was announced that they would be attending the show during the election. He saw someone following Oxley and reported it. Initially it sounded as if Oxley's fears were real. In the end it turned out that it was his son, ashamed of himself, yet still wishing to let his father and mother know they were grandparents."

"Taping a picture of his family to a rock and throwing it towards a crowded theatre is not the best way to confer good news," growled Churchill. "What will happen to him?"

"He is in custody, but not for long," said Sherlock. "I sense the work of my brother in the background. I spoke to young Oxley in the aftermath. It seems he was so ashamed of himself that he vowed never to darken the family door again. It took a sensible woman, the mother of his two children, to see him right, although I'm sure she didn't know about the picture-attached-to-the-rock part of the plan."

"Don't forget the chauffeur's good work," I said. "Had that rock been actually been a bomb, Marcombe might very well have saved the day. The armoured Rolls-Royce would have absorbed much of the blast. Marcombe deserves much credit for his behaviour."

"He does," says Churchill. "There is a new department being recruited as we speak, a special branch of the constabulary. I will be taking to him in the morning."

"Speaking of which," I said, "did the results come in?"

"They did," said Churchill. "And it is just as I feared."

"You lost again?" I said. "I'm so sorry."

"I won," said Churchill, "which means I have to do an honest day's work again." He rose to get the decanter, and as he walked by he placed his hand on my shoulder. "You had no way of knowing that the projectile wasn't a bomb, yet you tried to save my life. You and Marcombe are both heroes. Thank you. But I must ask, why me? Why not Holmes?"

"Our time has been and gone," I said. "Mycroft fears your time is still to come. My only wish is that you face whatever is coming boldly, bravely, and gloriously."

"Boldly, bravely, and gloriously," said Churchill. He paused for a moment then stood in front of the fire in his best orators pose.

"Success is not final, failure is not fatal. It is the courage to continue that counts, and we shall do so boldly, bravely, and gloriously."

"Amen to that," said Holmes.

NOTE:

* See "The Odd Telegram", in *Part I: 1914-1918* of this collection.

The Adventure
of the Second Body
by Stephen Herczeg

As the years drew on in the lives of myself and my greatest friend in the world, Mr. Sherlock Holmes, it seemed that the gaps between our visits grew as well. Holmes had retired in the early part of the century to a tiny country cottage near Beachy Head in Sussex. There he continued to enjoy his researches into all things esoteric, whilst also keeping bees as a form of relaxation. I, however, maintained a life in the busy metropolis of London, though my days of medical practice were well behind me.

It was on one of the occasions that I journeyed south to call upon Holmes that he was once more dragged from his self-imposed retirement and into the world of crime.

We had been simply catching up over a sumptuous afternoon tea while I showered Holmes with questions about past cases in an attempt to fill in some of the gaps in my notes. I still maintained a healthy number of papers in my tin dispatch box. Though sadly the opportunities to ask Holmes about tiny details were becoming rarer, I hoped to at least compile as complete a record as possible, either to be published by myself or to leave them to a potential future biographer.

I could tell that he knew of my intent, and played along to his own amusement. He seemed to enjoy my company, and my questions sent him back to a more exciting time in both our lives.

It was during my questioning over the lost details of the mystery of the banker's wife that a knock on the door broke our concentration. Holmes's housekeeper answered and within a few moments showed a rather young and slightly scruffy-looking constable into the parlour.

The young man – just out of his teens, I could tell – held his helmet in his hands and glanced around with an expression of awe mixed with fright.

Holmes simply waited until the man composed himself enough to make his introductions.

"Hello, sir. My name is Kendrick Kesson. Ah, Constable Kendrick Kesson, that is," the young policeman added.

182

After a moment, Holmes spoke. "Well met, Constable. I assume you know that I am Sherlock Holmes." The man nodded. Holmes held out a hand to indicate me. "This is Doctor Watson."

Kesson's eyes lit up as he looked across at me. He nodded. "A pleasure, sir. I never dreamed I'd get to meet both of you. Together."

I nodded my thanks and let Holmes finish his assessment, which I assumed was coming. Kesson opened his mouth to speak, but Holmes held up a finger to silence him, before steepling his fingers before his face as he observed the young man.

"So, Constable, you have obviously come in a hurry. You have mud splashed on your boots and lower pants leg. Given the weather has been rather dry these last few days, I assume you were in a boggy field or a forested area which shielded the ground from direct sun."

The constable's mouth dropped open and he nodded.

"You have a small twig gripping the back of your coat, and two dead but wet leaves stuck there as well, so I can presume it was a forest."

Kesson nodded again. "Yes, sir."

"Now, the darkness of the mud suggests a sizeable forest with a lot of leaf litter. The only such forests in the area are Westdean, which is hardly far enough for you to have worked up such a level of perspiration." Kesson's face remained impassive. "Or, perhaps you've travelled quite far from somewhere like Ashdown?" Again, the young constable's eyes widened in disbelief. "Yes. That's it. Ashdown Forest." I saw a small smile come to Holmes's face. "You'd be from East Grinstead then? Working for Captain Neafsey?"

Kesson nodded, his mouth still agape and unable to form words.

I turned to Holmes. From his expression, I could tell that he was holding back a slight chuckle. "All right," I asked. "How?"

"I do apologise to the both of you. Captain Jules Neafsey has done this before. He once worked with Lestrade and moved down to East Grinstead about ten years ago. He takes great delight in sending his junior constables to me when asking for my assistance. He confessed that it was to engender in them a sense of wonder at the art of deduction. In this case, that foreknowledge has simply helped me to ascertain the location of our next adventure together."

The drive took us through the edge of nearby Eastbourne, then Hailsham and Uckfield before finally turning slightly northwest towards Ashdown Forest. Kesson's nervous demeanour kept up throughout the journey as he answered Holmes's questions with barely more than one or two words. He kept very quiet about the purpose of the trip, until Holmes posed a taunting question to the young constable.

"I do assume that the captain and the coroner will meet us at our destination?" Holmes asked, a wry grin on his face. "I haven't had the opportunity to talk with Dr. Grey for quite a while. It will be pleasant."

Kesson, turned around, a puzzled expression on his face. "How did you know?"

I glanced at Holmes, the same question on my lips.

"Oh, that was simple. You have been charged to collect me. Therefore, this must be a very irregular crime."

Even I nodded at that piece of deduction.

"We're heading to the midst of a great forest – not the normal site for a robbery, or any form of fraud. Therefore, I can only assume there is a body of some sort to be examined."

"Amazing," said Kesson, turning back in a nick of time to realign the car with the road ahead, much to my relief.

Holmes continued, "If there's a body, then the coroner, Dr. Grey, will need to be involved as some point."

As Kesson nodded his head, I could see a smile grow across his features – a smile I had seen on many a young policeman's face as they became astonished at Holmes's abilities.

"You are simply astounding, Mr. Holmes. Yes, yes, Dr. Grey will be there, and you are quite correct. A body was found deep in the forest. I won't say any more, as the captain expressed his wishes for you to form your own opinions once you arrive."

I became increasingly intrigued by these events and could foresee another publishable story building as we drove. After another mile, Kesson turned north once more into a small rough trail and travelled for another minute or so before stopping next to two other automobiles.

We stepped out and found ourselves deep within the heavily wooded area, with only small dirt trails providing any navigable pathways. Kesson indicated a winding pathway leading west. "Along this way, gentlemen. Please follow me."

The trail led deeper into the darker area of the woods, and within a few minutes we found a large congregation of people milling about amongst the trees. The two policemen were easily identified. One possessed a visible level of authority greater than the other. I assumed this was Captain Neafsey. Spying Holmes, he smiled and moved in our direction, thrusting a hand towards my good friend. Holmes introduced me and then asked about the goings on. "Apologies if I've interrupted anything, but this one seemed intriguing enough to interest you." Neafsey then turned and indicated a balding man, hunched down with his back to us. "Dr. Grey should be able to fill you in on what we know so far."

As we approached the doctor, I looked around and was surprised at the ages of the other folk scattered around. Only one other was an adult, while the rest, about ten in all, were children.

Holmes leaned in at that moment and spoke softly to me. "I've been wondering about the scout troup myself. Looking at the well-worn path through this area, it may be a regular trail that they follow."

Before I could say anything, we reached the coroner, who stood to face us. A broad smile broke out across his face as he saw Holmes. They shook hands like old friends, and Holmes introduced me as another medical professional.

Dr. Grey had a warm, friendly handshake and spoke enthusiastically about all the adventures of my friend that he'd read in *The Strand* over the years. It was then I finally noticed the body – or at least what was left of it.

Standing near an open grave, the coroner moved away, allowing Holmes and me full view of the object of our attention.

Lying before us, about a foot below the level of the surrounding ground, was a dirt-stained skeleton. The skull and bones of the shoulders and upper chest had been revealed. The rest was still covered in dirt and forest mulch.

"The scouts found this earlier today, as they were on a trek through the forest. Some of the poor mites are still a little shell-shocked by the whole incident."

Glancing around at the young boys, I noticed a couple had that hollow look I'd seen on the faces of others, not much older than they, coming off the field of battle. Death seen at a young age can have a profound effect on the mind.

Holmes's voice snapped my attention back to the skeleton. "Is this how it was found? Or was it initially concealed, and did someone unearth more of the body?"

"As far as I know, no one else has touched it."

"Good," Holmes said, stepping closer and squating down for a closer look. He pointed at the edge of the hole. "The sharp edge indicates that this was achieved with a shovel, or more likely the square edge of spade. It does leave one main question open."

"What's that?" I asked.

185

"Was the purpose to uncover this body, or to bury something else?"

I was surprised by Holmes's question. "What do you mean?"

Standing and moving to the end of the shallow trench, he pointed to the starting point, then at the skeleton. When I realised there was a vacant gap of some three feet, my own mind became confused.

"Good. You see it too, then," Holmes said, nodding at my perplexed expression. "Whomever dug this hole either didn't know the precise location of this body, or didn't know there was a body here at all." He crouched once more and looked along the edges of the trench. "In fact, I would submit the latter."

"Why?"

Pointing along the edge of the small trench, Holmes indicated the line and made a small deviation to his right when his finger came in line with the skeleton. "This hole has all the hallmarks of someone digging a grave, and then finding it already occupied."

I stepped next to him and glanced along the same direction. Indeed, the trench deviated slightly to the right as it reached the skeleton.

"I would conjecture that our grave digger began his excavation, possible to bury a body he had brought with him, given the dimensions of the hole at this point." Holmes pointed nearest to us. "Then he unearthed the skeleton. Being intrigued, he continued to uncover more until either time grew short or he was disturbed, possibly by the scout troup. Which leaves . . . ."

His voice trailed off as he scanned the area, before moving deeper into the underbrush. I examined the ground myself, but couldn't see what Holmes had, so waited until a familiar tone of enlightenment echoed back. Dr. Grey, the captain, and I followed after him and found him standing by a pile of dirt.

"What have you there?" I asked.

Holding a handful of dirt, he let it run through his fingers and examined the grains as they fell back to Earth. "This is freshly dug. The looseness of the soil suggests it hasn't had time to settle and become hard-packed once more." He scanned the immediate area, glancing down at a disturbed patch of grass and what appeared to be two ruts leading up to it. "The other body was dragged across to this area, and then laid here while the culprit dug a new grave. There is a second body here, Captain. You'll need to dig out both the skeleton and this one to give us more clews to go on." Holmes continued to walk around the area, murmuring to himself and studying the ground.

"Something disturbing you?"

As he walked, he thrust a finger up and waggled it in the air. "Yes, Watson. Yes there is. This is far too much of a coincidence. An unknown person chooses a secluded part of a forest, such as Ashdown, to bury a body, only to find *another* body already buried exactly there." He stopped and stared at me for a moment. "What do you make of it?"

I thought for a moment. "Either a wild coincidence as you say, or this was the most logical spot to bury a body in this location."

"Or?"

I tried to read Holmes's face, but he retained that stoic and almost-smug look that I sometimes found irritating, but knew it also meant he was well advanced in the solution. "The skeleton wasn't the first."

He smiled widely. "Well done, Watson, well done."

The captain standing nearby looked completely puzzled by our conversation. He didn't possess the long-standing connection that Holmes and I did. "What? I have no idea what the two of you are talking about."

"You can tell him," Holmes said as he continued to examine the ground throughout the surrounding area.

I turned to the captain and his confused constables and said, "This area is well-suited for nefarious means. It's secluded, probably rarely visited, and the ground seems quite pliable and easily dug." Their puzzled looks remained, so I concluded by adding, "It would make a prime location to hide a body, as we have already seen. Therefore, there are probably more buried around here."

As I finished, Holmes let out a familiar "A-ha!" from deeper in the trees. We hurried over and joined him as he pulled branches and leaves from another patch of ground. The fresh brown colour of the dirt had faded back to a deeper, less vibrant brown, but the unveiled patch was slightly elevated from the darker, more settled earth around it.

"I do believe this area marks yet another shallow grave," Holmes said.

"Blimey!" said the captain, turning to his nearest constable, "Dickerson – spades. Now!" The young policeman sped off without another word.

The next hour was a whirlwind of activity, with Holmes moving around the area, uncovering two more possible grave sites. Kesson and Dickerson followed him around and gently excavated the areas until it was confirmed that a body lay within each. The constables refrained from unearthing more than was required to determine that someone was buried there. The light was starting to fail, and Holmes wanted to concentrate on the number of sites rather than their contents at that stage.

As fascinating and horrifying as the uncovering of the cemetery was, I did notice out of the corner of my eye that Captain Neafsey took it upon himself to speak once more with the Scout leader, and within a few moments the scout troup left the area to, I presume, head back to their campsite.

I'm happy to admit that as my interest began to wane, just as the light in the forest, Holmes then joined me. "From what I can see, that is all of them." I glanced around and realised there were now five sites that had been found to contain buried corpses.

"Good Lord! This is horrible. A murder spree, I presume?"

"I'm not overly convinced of that. I've asked Dr. Grey to oversee the exhumation of the corpses. I don't believe that there's much more I can deduce from their interred state. The ones we've unearthed so far are similar in that they are laid out in the same posture. The age of the bodies differs by only weeks or months, giving me the impression that whomever has been using this area to dispose of these bodies has done so for possibly only the last year."

"And the skeleton?"

"Ah, now that's the most interesting. That has been here much longer. I think that is still the outlier and may be the clew that breaks this riddle apart."

I had no idea what he was on about, but that seemed to be a return to our time together many years previously. It was at that point that the captain stepped over to us and suggested that he return us to Holmes's house.

He agreed, but said he wanted to meet with Dr. Grey in the morning to examine the bodies. The captain motioned for Dr. Grey to join us and explained Holmes's request.

"This many bodies will need to be taken to the hospital. I simply don't have the room at the morgue. We'll use one of the wards – there haven't been many patients of late, so it should be fine."

"Excellent," said Holmes. Turning to the captain, he continued, "One thing troubles me, Captain, and that is the skeleton. I don't have enough data, and hope that an examination of all the bodies

188

will confirm, but something tells me that there should be more poor unfortunates buried here from the same period as that skeleton." Glancing at me he asked, "Watson, in your opinion, how long would you say that skeleton has lain here?"

I looked back at the first open grave, more as a way of focusing on the question rather than searching for information. "Given the lack of flesh, and no obvious clothing, I'd have to say over ten years. Possibly longer."

Holmes nodded. "That was my deduction as well, which piques my interest even more."

The captain drove us back to Holmes's cottage, assuring us that the bodies would be extricated and moved to the hospital by morning. It had been my intent to return to London the next day, but I decided to change my plans and stay until this affair played out.

That evening we enjoyed a sumptuous meal, and I had hoped to sit with him and continue our discussions well into the evening, but he busied himself amongst his old files while I wiled away the hours until bedtime, reading a novel I'd brought with me.

It was over breakfast the next morning that I asked Holmes about his previous evening's studies. As he sipped his coffee, he said, "The initial idea that this was all to do with a rampant murderer on the loose disturbed me somewhat. I wanted to delve into my files to find an occurrence of any other killers that took means to hide their victims' bodies in such a remote location."

"What concerned you so?"

"Murderers of this nature act mostly on impulse. Those that find they need to hide their victims will do so in locations nearby, or highly accessible to them, sometimes by necessity, sometimes so that they can visit their handiwork. The presence of that many bodies in such a location means that there was a large amount of forethought put into the act of murder and disposal of the corpses."

"Perhaps the perpetrator is a local? And the forest is quite close to his home. That would solve both problems."

Holmes thought about my statement for a moment. "That could be it, I suppose. We will need to establish the identity of the victims, or at least the area of their origin."

I started to speak again when the telephone rang in the other room. Holmes almost leapt to his feet and hurried to answer. I followed, quite intrigued by his determination to hear from the caller.

189

The conversation was rather short but consisted of many nods and affirmative mutterings from Holmes. Within a few moments he hung up. Turning to me, I could see a glint in his eye and a wry smile on his face.

"Watson, the game is indeed afoot."

It was only after we had driven north through the Sussex countryside and on to the growing town of East Grinstead, and finally entered the hospital, that Holmes's excitement began to make sense to me.

As he had suggested, Dr. Grey had set aside an entire ward to house the unearthed bodies from the forest graveyard. There were six in all. It turned out that another skeleton had been uncovered as part of the constables' excavations the previous evening. The other four bodies were all much more intact, and in line with Holmes's earlier observation, possibly dead for only twelve months or so.

My eyes scanned the bodies and skeletons and finally fell upon the object of Holmes's current scrutiny. Although the man's clothes were filthy with the dirt from his unchosen gravesite, I could see that he wore the deep blue, almost black, uniform of a London policeman. I gasped with the realisation. Suddenly, what had started as a possible localised murderer was now a case that would attract a much higher level of scrutiny from Scotland Yard.

I noticed Holmes take out his glass and begin a close examination of the policeman. I stepped over to observe. A stern voice from behind caused both of us to stand and glance around.

"I would much prefer if you would leave these bodies well alone."

At the doorway to the ward stood a tall, well-built man in a day suit. The stern look on his face, and the way he stood, betrayed his profession. A smaller man in a constable's uniform stood behind him, his expression was less grim and more full of wonder – a reaction to the display before him, I supposed.

Captain Neafsey stepped between the plainclothes policeman and the bodies. "And you are, sir?"

A greeting card was thrust in Neafsey's direction. "Inspector Jackson. Scotland Yard. I've been sent to take over this investigation."

"On whose authority?"

"Deputy Commissioner Andrew Black. London Bureau."

Neafsey nodded, and I noticed a wry grin come to his face. "Ah, Blackey, aye? We go way back. I'll have a word with him later then and sort out the lines of authority."

"And why would this concern you?"

"I am Captain Neafsey. Commander of the local precinct. Until these bodies are identified, this is still my case."

The two policemen locked eyes for a moment. The tension building between them, until Jackson finally spoke. "Understood, sir." He indicated Holmes. "And why are these civilians here?"

"This is Mr. Sherlock Holmes and Doctor John Watson. They are helping with this investigation and have already provided undeniable assistance."

"Doctor Watson is also assisting me with the preliminary autopsy examinations," piped up Dr. Grey, winking at me as I glanced in his direction. I smiled at the wily old country doctor's quick thinking.

Jackson looked from face to face, scrutinising each in turn before relaxing slightly. "Fine. Then you can bring me up to speed on what has occurred." He pointed at the dead policeman. "Starting with him."

Holmes and I backed away from the corpse as Jackson approached. It was then that the young constable accompanying him had his first good look at the body. I expected a touch of horror, but instead his entire body seemed to deflate as his eyes fell on the dead man's face.

"Oh, God, that's Smithy!"

"Out with it, man. Who is 'Smithy'?" asked Jackson.

The young constable stepped up to the gurney with the policeman's body and stared down at what seemed to be a close friend. "Albert Smith. We signed up together. Smithy was a bit older than me, and a bit more street wise. He grew up in the East End, so it was only natural they give him that beat." He shook his head in sorrow. "Last I knew he'd gone missing. About a month ago. He'd done it before though, usually turned up again after a week or two. Drunk out of his brain. The sergeant didn't really care. He'd dock him his pay for the time and then put him back to work. Apart from his drinking, Smithy was a good policeman. Knew the East End docks like the back of his hand."

"Interesting way of running your force up there in London," said Neafsey, his statement directed at Jackson, who harrumphed in reply.

191

"Well, that leaves me to wonder then," said Holmes, "whether we have another killer running around the East End, or is this something far more insidious." He turned to Dr. Grey. "Considering this case is still in your hands, Good Doctor, I would think it an appropriate time to begin a deeper investigation into the causes of death."

Doctor Grey nodded and then spoke to me. "It may speed things up if you could examine the skeletons first, then join me once I've finished with the first couple of fresher bodies."

I nodded and moved across to claim an apron and some gloves before stepping over to the first of the skeletons. Holmes joined me, I thought in part to avoid the tension exhibited between Jackson and Neafsey, but he mentioned in passing that the crux of the matter lay, not with the fresher bodies, but with the older.

To begin I, simply stood and examined the remains, murmuring some audible notes as I went. "Male. Approximately five-feet-eight-inches tall. Solid frame given the width of the shoulders." There wasn't much else left of the body. The skin and flesh had rotted away, along with the clothing. The skeletal junctures were still in place, but in moving the body it seemed that the constables had caused them to break, as one of the arms and a leg lay separated from the main frame.

As I examined the arm, I noticed the first peculiarity about the skeleton. All of the distal phalanges were missing. I quickly checked the hand on the attached arm. The same. I turned and called to Kesson to join us. As he approached I pointed to the hand and asked, "Did you find any free bones in the grave? The fingertips are missing."

Kesson's eyes grew wide as he studied the bones, but then he shook his head. "Not that I know of. We can go back out and look though. Take a couple of hours."

Meanwhile, Holmes had retrieved a pair of gloves and was studying the ends of the fingers with his glass. "What do you make of this?" I leaned in and stared at the magnified ends of the finger joints. Small scrapes ran along a couple of the knuckle bones.

"I don't know. What do you think?"

"We'll check the other skeleton, but those marks may be consistent with a common carpenter's chisel." He placed the free arm down and picked up the other, checking each middle phalange, and the proximal on the thumb. Again, a couple had distinct score marks across the knuckle, as if something sharp had gouged the surface.

"Why would he cut off the fingertips?"

"To make future identification of the corpse almost impossible, or perhaps as a way of claiming a bounty, or even as a token to add to a collection."

I screwed my face up at the last suggestion. "That's disturbing."

"Quite so, but it gives us a starting point." Holmes led me by the arm to the second skeleton and we immediately examined the fingers.

"It's the same," I gasped.

"Excellent," said Holmes. "A strong clew." A smile grew on his face, as confusion grew on my own.

"Care to enlighten me?"

"From your observations, you believe these corpses to be around ten years in the ground, yes?" I nodded. "Good. So we are looking for someone who operated around that time, and perhaps displayed a characteristic habit, such as the removal of the fingertips." I nodded again.

"Someone like Mad Dog Murgatroyd?" said a voice from behind us. We turned to find Captain Neafsey looking at the skeletons, with a wry grin on his face.

"Who?" I asked.

"Yes," said Holmes. "James 'Mad Dog' Murgatroyd. He was put away about eight years ago and then hanged not long afterwards – just before the end of the war. His execution was expedited to free up space in Wandsworth, I think."

Neafsey nodded. "That it was. The Yard felt that we were going to get a few coming back from Europe that might go straight to Wandsworth, so anyone who wasn't in for a long time was shuffled off, so to say." The captain stepped around the gurney and approached the left-hand side of the skeleton. "Now, if this is the work of Mad Dog, there's one more piece of evidence to prove it." Motioning for Holmes to join him, he continued. "If you would be so kind, Doctor, could you turn this poor unfortunate on his right-hand side?"

As I did so, Neafsey pointed at the skeleton's rib cage and said, "There – do you see it, Holmes?" Holmes nodded. I strained to see and was surprised by a pair of deep gouges on the edges of the fifth and sixth rib bones on the skeleton's left-hand side."

"He was a vicious blighter, was old Mad Dog," said Neafsey. "Used to carry around a nine-inch-long dagger, with an inch-wide blade. Favourite method of attack was a sharp thrust up into the heart from behind. He was left-handed too – made it so much easier for him."

"I actually read the coroner's reports of the day when Murgatroyd was arrested," said Holmes. "He was consistent and quite accurate. Each victim had identical scoring on the ribs. Made it so much easier to convict him." Holmes looked across to the first skeleton. "Now, if you are correct, Captain, as I presume you are . . . ." Moving across to the first skeleton, he let the last word hang, before carefully manoeuvring the corpse onto it's right side. "A-ha!" I hurried across to join him and was greeted with a similar set of score marks on the rib cage. "What say you, Watson?"

I nodded. "Both remains exhibit almost identical injuries. From these marks, I would surmise that a sharp, wide-bladed instrument was driven upwards between the ribs and into the victim's heart. Death would have been virtually instantaneous." Turning to look across at Dr. Grey, I muttered, "Do the modern victims bear the same wounds?"

Holmes, Neafsey, and I joined Dr. Grey as he examined the body of the unfortunate Smithy. The policeman's remains seemed fairly intact. No fingertips were missing, and there was no evidence of death by knife wound. Instead Dr. Grey pointed to severe discolouration and bruising around the man's neck.

"Strangulation?" I asked.

He nodded. "It would seem so, Doctor."

"Have you found similar on the other victims?" asked Holmes.

Dr. Grey nodded and pointed to the nearest and more-recent body. A rather pudgy man in his early fifties. "Yes. Notice the severe bruising on the throat of that man. Our perpetrator was incredibly powerful, with large hands, and with what seems to be an almost animalistic delight in inflicting harm."

"Why would you say that?" I asked.

"The large man's windpipe was crushed, and there are several bruises on the back of his head. He was either forced against a wall as he was strangled, or his head was hammered to engender his compliance in the act. The strangler kept the pressure up well after the man was dead – hence the damage to the internals of the throat."

"But it ain't Mad Dog," said Neafsey, "It wasn't the way he'd do it, plus he was hanged, so not someone copying him either."

Holmes nodded, but I could tell the wheels of his mind were spinning at a fast rate. He stood, staring at the corpses arrayed before him, a hand resting under his chin with one finger extended up his cheek. Neafsey stared at him for a moment, expecting a comment, but when none was forthcoming, he wandered away. I knew better than to break his concentration and did the same.

Some time later, once we had finished a wonderful meal and were settled in Holmes's parlour, he with a pipe and me with a cigar, that I finally decided to ask his thoughts.

"You've been withdrawn and pondering on this case since this morning. What is worrying you so?"

He drew deep on his pipe, then blew out a deliberately long and slow cloud of white smoke. "The facts aren't fitting into the narrative. The new bodies were found over some distance from their supposed origin. We know this from the lone policeman, who – still being in uniform – was possibly snatched while on duty in the East End. Everyone thought that he had simply abandoned his post. We'll have to wait for the identities of the other three before confirming that assumption." He took the pipe from his mouth and used the stem to punctuate his points. "Only someone who has applied a level of pre-meditation to their murderous activities would use such a remote location for disposal. But the style of death indicates someone with an almost palpable psychosis entrenched in his or her mind."

I nodded in agreement. The level of aggression was disturbing. "As to the two older bodies – and I am confident there will be more if the captain continues to search – they are the end result of a concerted effort at hiding the evidence of crime. Our probable perpetrator, this Murgatroyd, was a known factor, with a repeatable *modus operandi*, which resulted in his own demise. I presume these bodies were from his work as an enforcer with the Hoxton Mob."

He suddenly rose and moved to a nearby bookcase, extracted a thick volume, and walked to a nearby table. I jumped up, quite intrigued, and stood nearby as he opened the book. It was a series of news clippings and annotations, in Holmes's own spidery scrawl, about the goings on of gangs and mobs in London. I hadn't seen these pages before and realised they were part of Holmes's later researches and studies.

"This is information I've been building that concerns the growth and activities of criminal gangs in London and the surrounding areas. It seems that since the end of the war, the number of recruits have grown with the returning soldiers, and the boldness of activities is increasing as well. As we move deeper into the new century, I believe it will only increase further. These gangs have been building in confidence in line with the activities of their spiritual brothers in the United States, ever since Prohibition began."

"That seems to be a long bow you're drawing there, Holmes."

He paused to look at me with a wry smile before turning back to the tome on the table. Flipping through several pages, he stopped at one with the name *"Hoxton Mob"* written boldly across the top. Holmes pointed to a grainy photograph, clipped from a newspaper, pinned to the top of the page. It featured a bald man in a suit being helped into a black car.

"This is Ken Porritt, also known as 'Curly'." I chuckled, as the nickname was an allusion to his obvious lack of hair. "Yes, it's because he's bald – very dry humour these thugs have." Further below were two other written names, but no photographs. "Porritt has two known lieutenants, Rene Gibbison and Herbert Marginzer. Now, this gang became quite prominent across the East End before and during the early part of the war. They concentrate on running illegal betting rings out of few local pubs, and of course at some of the nearer racecourses."

"I'm assuming then that Murgatroyd was used to reclaim debts – or at least close them out anyway."

"Precisely. He was a little too enthusiastic, shall we say, and hence why he was eventually hanged."

"That perhaps explains the older bodies," I said, "but what of the newer ones?"

"That has been puzzling me also. I dislike the idea of a random killer utilizing the same dumping ground as an earlier murderer by pure coincidence – especially considering the size of Ashdown Forest. For now, I'd like to believe that our new man must have had prior knowledge, and perhaps is working in concert with our long gone Murgatroyd, almost unwittingly."

"You believe he may be employed by the Hoxton Gang?"

Holmes held up a single finger. "That is one theory."

"The open grave then?"

He held up a second finger. "And that brings us to another set of theories. Our mystery man's purpose was to bury a body. He unearthed a second body, but instead of covering it up again, he left it alone." He stood and began to pace around the room. "Was that act on purpose? If so, why? If he were working for the Hoxton Gang, he wouldn't wish to draw attention to his activities." Holmes stopped and stared at me, a wry grin on his face, and then stepped back to the table, flipping over several pages until another account of a London gang was shown. "What if our perpetrator *wanted* that second body to be found? What if he wanted to draw the authorities to that site so that they would end up unearthing the other victims?"

"But why? I'll admit that in hindsight the newer graves weren't very well camouflaged, but surely a murderer would wish to remain hidden."

"Yes, but what if this new murderer was working in competition to the original users of that dumping ground?" Holmes pointed at the page before us. It was similar to one for the Hoxton Mob, but was headed with the name "*Sabini Gang*". A similar photograph sat at the top of the page, the name Charles Sabini written beneath it. "Then there may be more to this whole adventure."

The next morning as I entered the kitchen in search of breakfast, I found Holmes sitting in the corner of the parlour, listening intently to a conversation on his telephone. I refrained from questioning him out of respect, and instead helped myself to the simple fare prepared by the housekeeper.

Luckily, there was coffee, toast, marmalade, and the morning's newspaper. Resigning myself to wait until Holmes joined me, I simply ate and read the news. I was slightly relieved to see that nothing of our grotesque find had made its way to any local reporter's ear. I was sure that he would be of the same opinion.

The local affairs in the paper were of a very trivial nature, which made for a much lighter read than those generally reported by the London press. I had almost finished the whole thing when Holmes finally joined me at the table.

He quickly poured himself some coffee and buttered a piece of toast. Before I could inquire about his telephone call, he said, "I presume you are heading back to London today?"

To be honest I hadn't even thought that far ahead. I had no train ticket, as I had no urgency to return. "I'm willing to stay while this adventure is still underway," I answered.

"Oh, that's precisely why I asked. I just spoke with Neafsey, it seems that our Inspector Jackson has returned to London, with three corpses in tow, including the poor unfortunate policeman. The others will be ferried north later today. I then made a call to a former colleague of Lestrade's: Chief Inspector Sheldon Wengert. He is now charged with keeping an eye on the criminal gangs running loose around London. I've arranged to meet with him later this afternoon."

I almost spluttered out my mouthful of coffee. "You're going to London?"

"Oh, yes. That's why I asked whether you planned to leave today. I thought we could journey together, and I was hoping I could reside in your abode tonight, and possibly tomorrow night as well."

"Of course, that is never a problem. I just didn't realise that you meant to leave almost this minute."

"Oh, there's no need for such haste," he said taking a sip of coffee before continuing, "The train from Eastbourne doesn't leave for another hour."

It was then I noticed that Holmes was already dressed ready to leave the house. I was still arrayed in my dressing gown. "Well, in that case . . . ." I quickly downed my coffee and left to pack my bags.

Several hours later, we were introduced to Chief Inspector Wengert, a tall slender man with blonde hair and prominent cheek bones. He didn't look like a policeman in any way, which I assume helped him no end if he was required to assume an undercover identity.

Greeting us both with obvious enthusiasm, but holding his eagerness in check, he expressed his desire to work with us in any small way possible. It was obvious that our reputation had preceded us – a common occurrence, especially since Holmes's retirement from active investigations.

"Have you heard about the six bodies found in Ashdown Forest?" Holmes asked.

Wengert nodded. "Yes, the news went through the Yard like wildfire. Jackson's handling that, isn't he?" We nodded in unison. "Hmm. Strange fellow. Very determined." I stifled a small chuckle. "Where do I fit in then?"

"Ah, we have one major clew that needs to be confirmed. Four of the bodies died fairly recently, but the two skeletons show signs of death consistent with the activities of a local gang soldier from about ten years ago."

A shocked expression ran across Wengert's face. "Do you know who?"

"Yes. James Murgatroyd."

"Mad Dog? Good Lord. He was hanged years ago, wasn't he? Spent most of the war in Wandsworth."

"That's our understanding."

A broad smile crossed Wengert's face. "I heard there were six bodies found. You mentioned two. You can't believe Murgatroyd had anything to do with the other four? I didn't see him hang, but I know some who did."

"No, no. The cause of death for the more recent victims is completely different. My theory, and it's only a theory at this stage, is that another person became aware of Murgatroyd's dumping ground and used it for his own purposes."

"Interesting. I still don't see why I'm necessary."

"I wanted to investigate the growing gang activities in London since the end of the war."

"Ah, yes. Precisely why I have my own team."

"Mostly, I wanted to find out any recent activity amongst the Hoxton Mob or their contemporaries."

Smiling, Wengert led us to a large map of London. Several areas had been marked with different coloured pins. Two small areas were shown in the East End, with the adjacent borders coloured in a thicker amount of ink. The Chief Inspector pointed at it. "The Hoxton Mob and the Sabini Gang both lay claim to this disputed area. There have been some assaults, arson, and even a murder or two, in that area over the last two years."

"Surely you've made a large number of arrests then?" I asked.

"Ah, that's the main problem." Wengert's smile slid from his face, as he became more serious. "It's amazing how few witnesses one finds in these matters. And those that come forward shut up or disappear before a trial can be held."

"What about the local bobbies? Do they keep a close eye on things?"

"Yes, they do, but a lot of them remain tight-lipped as well. We have another team working on that worrying little aspect."

"What about Constable Albert Smith? He was one of the bodies we found."

Wengert's face lit up in surprise. "Smithy, aye? Now that is interesting. He was high on the list of suspicious constables. I didn't even realise that he'd disappeared, but again, that's not my area. I'll have to check with the other team."

"What about the enforcers? Are there any in the Hoxton Mob that would be able to, say, strangle a man with his bare hands?"

The policeman laughed. "Oh, most of them. These enforcers, or soldiers, are chosen for their particularly large build. Most prefer to resort to their fists. For the most part, murder is bad for business. The soldiers' duty is to act as a warning to the populace."

"I assume the Sabini Gang has a similar predilection for well-built enforcers?"

"Yes. Again, they tend to only concentrate on threats and intimidation. Any violence is generally done through the use of cutthroat razors or knives. Sort of a signature to maintain their posture." He thought for a moment. "Murgatroyd was an interesting case. If I remember correctly, he overstepped the mark on several occasions. It was his boss that finally set him up, I believe, though it was never proven, just assumed."

"Interesting," said Holmes. "That's very interesting."

Departing Scotland Yard, we caught a cab back to my home and I settled Holmes into the spare bedroom, and then left him to his own devices while I retired to the parlour for a late afternoon cigar and perusal of any items of mail that had arrived in my absence.

When my housekeeper informed me that dinner would be soon, I realised that Holmes hadn't made an appearance and, presuming him to have fallen asleep, went to his room to wake him. To my surprise, the room was empty and the bed made and unused, except for a small depression where Holmes had obviously sat while putting on his shoes.

I smiled to myself as memories of old times flooded my mind. He may have retired, but when the smell of an adventure reached his nostrils, there was no stopping him.

After a wonderful repast, I once again returned to the parlour to read the papers and write up some notes surrounding our current endeavour, with the full hope that Holmes would fill me in on any future developments. I knew that I wouldn't be able to publish anything immediately, but held out hope that I would find a suitable candidate to carry on in my future absence.

I fell asleep in my chair and was shocked awake as footsteps in the hallway approached parlour. My eyes fell on a slightly bedraggled figure before me, fear rising within, before I realised it was Sherlock Holmes. "Good Lord, you look dreadful." His face looked sunken and sallow, and his normally tall frame stooped from fatigue.

"I do apologise, Watson. I wish that this was a disguise, but I'm getting old and quite unused to traipsing all across this large metropolis like my younger self once did." I rang the bell, mindful of the late hour, but hopeful that my housekeeper had yet to retire. Holmes took a chair near mine and visibly deflated into it.

I waited until he regained his composure before pressing him for details. "Well, was the effort at least worth it?"

He glanced over and smiled. "It was." He sat up just as my housekeeper entered. I asked for coffee and brandy. She took one look at Holmes and nodded. He waited until she left before sitting a little more upright and relating his tale.

"My first stop was to an old friend who had served as a guard at Wandsworth until recently. I plied him with questions concerning Murgatroyd: His actions in prison. His cell mates. His acquaintances. Any enemies he might have had. He was very forthcoming and spun a very intriguing story about this 'Mad Dog'."

"Yes?" I said, my own interest rising.

"Murgatroyd was indeed extremely upset with his employers. It was well known through Wandsworth that he felt 'stitched up'. His employer wanted a few people to vanish, so Murgatroyd murdered and buried them in Ashford Forest. My contact believes that he only told a couple of people the actual location."

"Did you find out any of their names?"

Holmes smiled, "I did. And one of them left Wandsworth several months ago and now works in the East End, for one of the gangs."

"Not the Hoxton Mob?"

"No. The Sabini Gang. That's why I'm so tired and grimy, I spent a couple of hours wandering around the Sabini's territory, looking for our possible culprit."

"And?"

"I found him. A huge man, with massive hands. And from the way he dealt with several people during that time, quite the temper."

It was then that my housekeeper returned with the coffee and brandy. I poured us both a good amount of the latter, and as Holmes was reviving himself asked, "Where does that leave us?"

"I think once we've finished and retired for a well-rested night, we can contact the Chief Inspector and see where that leads us."

I was relieved. I had half-expected Holmes to be off again into the night to confront this potential murderer, but as it seemed that age had slight wearied him and made him more mindful of his own limitations.

When I looked back, I realised he'd already fallen asleep, with his head resting on his breast – another reminder of days gone past.

The following morning was a whirlwind of activity, once Holmes's plans were enacted.

Upon awakening, I strode into the parlour to find it now empty. I presumed that Holmes had moved to his room at some stage during the night, only to be taken by surprise when I found him at the kitchen table taking some breakfast, while chatting amiably with my housekeeper.

As I sat and partook of my own meal, Holmes informed me that our first port of call would be back to see Wengert, to take him through the information gathered the previous night.

We were given entry purely through the officer on the front desk's recognition of Holmes and me. A young policeman was called to escort us to Wengert, and it turned out to be Constable Green, whom we'd met with Jackson. He and Holmes chatted amiably during our walk, with Holmes stopping our progress for a moment to have a more in-depth conversation before we reached Wengert's rooms. I couldn't hear what was discussed, but presumed that Holmes wanted to know more details about Jackson's investigation.

"You're talking about Duncan Hullar?" Wengert asked as Holmes laid out his information. "He's just a minor soldier in the Sabini Gang – works Raymond Mowler's part of the crew, who himself is just a minor lieutenant. They aren't even the main portion of Sabini's organisation."

"And that seems to be perfect for what they have planned."

Wengert moved across to his board with the Sabini Gang's names and hierarchy mapped out. He wrote Hullar's name well below Mowler's, stepped back and studied it, glancing across at the Hoxton Mob board from time to time.

"And you're 'old friend' places Hullar in Wandsworth at the same time as Murgatroyd?"

"Yes. In fact, they shared a cell for a period of three months, before Murgatroyd was moved into isolation in the weeks before his execution. I feel that he would have been at his lowest point at that time, and might have vented out as much information about the Hoxton Mob as he could, to all and sundry."

"And that's where Hullar comes into it?"

"Yes. Hullar was released only a year ago. He had been imprisoned for a violent assault. That sort of record would have left him with very few options when he was released."

"Wouldn't he have used his information to gain a higher-level position in the Hoxton Mob?"

"Or, on Murgatroyd's insistence, he used that information to wangle his way into an opposing gang."

Wengert nodded. "Yes, that makes sense. Even though there is an uneasy peace, these gangs wait for the chance to tear pieces out of each other and gain more territory." He glanced around at Holmes. "You want to talk with Raymond Mowler?"

"Oh, I believe we should try to go to the top of the organisation. If nothing else, the fact we have uncovered this information will unsettle Mr. Charles Sabini and make him think harder before attempting anything like this in the future."

A smile grew across Wengert's face and he nodded. "If I know Charles Sabini, he will be furious. This could be quite interesting."

In my long experience walking in the shadow of Sherlock Holmes, I've been exposed to many a criminal element, and at times been fearful for my life. That afternoon, however, was something completely different.

After the Great War ended, a void remained in London, a void created by the removal of so many good young men, and also an economic void caused by the closure of many businesses due to their owners and employees going off to war, and many not returning. There was a more recent void triggered by the number of men and women who had been diverted to the cause of war, finding themselves suddenly unemployed while the remaining businesses realigned their efforts back to normal service.

As in nature, humankind abhors a vacuum, and those voids were quickly filled with a new style of business – one based on various nefarious activities: Gambling, alcohol, drugs, sex, all in a more coordinated and focused way than they had been prior to the war. Criminals banded together into gangs to run these new enterprises, the heads of each taking on almost the same allure as movie stars.

One of the most notorious in London was the Sabini Gang, whose leader, Charles Sabini, had grown up in the East End and now ran several nightclubs and oversaw a large number of bookmakers at racecourses across the south of England.

Wengert informed us that even though Scotland Yard knew much of what the gangs were up to, there was an uneasy accord in place. The Yard's forces had been decimated by the war, and they were still recruiting – much slower than the gangs it seemed – so a level of tolerance was applied that dictated where the gangs could operate. I personally didn't like the idea that criminal gangs were basically operating unhindered in my beloved London, but I understood the pragmatic approach that the Yard took.

It was to one of Sabini's nightclubs that Chief Inspector Wengert took Holmes and me. It was only early afternoon, but the place was a hive of activity as preparations for the evening were underway.

The large man on the door knew Wengert, and after a quiet word was sent deep into the establishment, we were led to a large smoky room in the back that operated as Charles Sabini's personal office.

I was surprised, as Sabini's reputation hinted at the glamourous, but he was a simple looking man, albeit well built from the cut of his modest dark suit. The man standing behind and to his right was similarly dressed. I assumed this was his assistant or a bodyguard.

As we entered, Sabini remained seated, but obviously knew Wengert quite well. "Chief Inspector, to what do I owe this pleasure?"

"Thank you for seeing us at such short notice, Mr. Sabini. May I introduce my companions."

Sabini cut him off, looked us up and down and said, "Good Lord – Sherlock 'Olmes and Dr. John Watson, I presume."

Holmes replied, "I'm impressed. I thought the years of my absence would have dulled any recognition."

"It's the 'at and coat, sir. I've also read every single adventure that Dr. Watson published in *The Strand*. I'm quite the admirer, you know." He leaned back in this chair and took a deep draw on his cigar, blowing out a pall of smoke in one long languid release. "What can I do for one of my actual 'eroes?"

"I think it might be more of a question about what we can do for you," Holmes said.

"Oh, yeah, and what's that then?"

"The body of a policeman was found down south in a very remote forest."

A puzzled expression crossed Sabini's face. "And that 'as what exactly to do with me?"

"The policeman's beat was around this area, and across into Finsbury, Hackney, and sometimes Hoxton."

I watched Holmes's eyes glued to Sabini's face. I glanced across at the gangster, hoping to see what Holmes sought. Sabini simply shrugged. "Yeah, lots of coppers on that beat. What of it?"

"This one was taking money from one of your lieutenants. Mowler, I think his name was."

"I'd 'ate to tell you 'ow often that 'appens." Sabini held his hands out to emphasise his innocence. "It's the way of the game, isn't it? We keep our bobbies 'appy, and they don't make too many waves for us." He glanced at Wengert. "Isn't that right, Chief Inspector?"

"We have an agreement, yes. We turn a blind eye, but not when you murder our constables."

"Whoa, whoa. Murder? You can't blame my organisation for murder."

Holmes piped up. "You have a Duncan Hullar working for you, do you not?"

Sabini grimaced and spoke towards one of his assistants standing nearby. The assistant nodded and whispered back. A surprised expression broke out on Sabini's face. He smiled and glanced back at us. "It seems I do. 'E just so 'appens to work for Mowler." His face then turned sour. "'Ere, what are you suggesting? Mowler put 'im up to it?"

"Perhaps. I don't suppose we could talk with this Huller?"

Shrugging, Sabini picked up his telephone, requested a number, and waited. "Doris, can you track down Mowler and tell 'im he needs to be 'ere now, and to bring Duncan Huller. Yes, tell 'im I said now." I noticed Sabini lose the thick accent when pronouncing Huller's name. He replaced the receiver and held out his hands. "Well, we'll see, won't we?"

It took only three minutes for Raymond Mowler to enter Sabini's office. During that time, Holmes and I were plied with all sorts of questions about our adventures over the years. For the most part, Holmes simply smiled and allowed me to answer those that pertained to points of clarification. Several, however, were aimed at Homles's deductive methods and seemed to have relevance to our current situation. I kept an eye on my friend and realised he was enjoying the intellectual jousting.

Sabini held up a hand as Mowler began to ask a question. "All in good time, Raymond. Mr. 'Olmes and Chief Inspector Wengert 'ere 'ave some concerns about a particular bobbie that's come to some 'arm."

"A bobbie?" asked Mowler. "We don't do nothing to no bobbies. That's bad for business, init?"

"I've already alluded to that point of view, but a dead body's a dead body, and the Yard don't like no dead bobbies."

"Who was it?"

"Constable Albert Smith," said Wengert. "Known as 'Smithy'. Been around these parts for years."

"According to one of my sources," said Holmes, "he was receiving moneys from both the Sabini Gang and the Hoxton Mob. Playing both sides."

"Then it must 'ave been the 'Oxtons," said Sabini, "Case closed. Good night."

Holmes smiled. "You would think so, wouldn't you? Especially when the policeman's body was found in a shallow grave in an area of Ashdown Forest that was previously used by a Hoxton Mob enforcer."

Sabini held his hands out in surprise and he glanced at Wengert. "Again, case closed." He reached over to pick up the telephone. "I can call Curly Porritt for you if you like. 'E'd be just as fascinated as me, and possibly a bit more."

Holmes held up his hand. "There are a few more interesting points that need to be addressed."

Removing his hand from the telephone, but keeping his eyes fixed on Holmes's face, Sabini leaned back in his chair. "Go on, then."

"There were other bodies in that location. Five more in all. Two had likely been there for over ten years, but three others were as recently buried as the unfortunate policeman. All men. All strangled. By someone with larger than normal hands and incredible strength."

"Know anyone like that, Raymond?" asked Sabini, keeping his eyes fixed on Mowler's face.

The other man shuffled slightly in place, "Well, 'Ullar's a big fellar." Holding out his hands, Mowler stared down at them. "'E's got a pair of big mitts. But I dunno? If 'e's done in a bobbie, then we should be well shot of him."

"Did Mullar know this Smithy?" asked Holmes.

Fixing his gaze on Holmes's face, Mowler replied, "I only told 'im to keep an eye on Smithy. Nothin' more."

I watched Holmes stare at Mowler for a moment, his hand on his chin, his index finger extended. He then glanced across at Sabini. "Perhaps this Huller overstepped the mark? Or was he trying to impress his credentials upon you?"

Sabini shrugged. "I cannot answer that, Mr. 'Olmes. I've not even met this fellow. I do 'ave rather a lot of people in my organisation – a fact of which I am quite proud."

"Maybe it's time that you were introduced," said Holmes, a wry smile on his lips.

"Perhaps," said Sabini, motioning towards a man near the door. "Martin, show this Hullar chap in."

Martin opened the door and spoke to someone on the other side. Within seconds, an amazingly large man entered the room. As had been described to me already, Huller towered well above six-feet six-inches. I glanced at his hands and realised they were of such a size that they could easily surround a man's throat and crush the life from him.

"My word, you are a big one, ain't ya?" said Sabini as his eyes fell on Hullar.

I noticed the large man's eyes meet Sabini's and crinkle up in a questioning frown. Realising that at least one of this pair knew the other, I glanced at Holmes and saw a small grin cross his face. He saw it as well. Hullar's eyes flashed in Mowler's direction. The Lieutenant shifted his gaze towards his feet.

"Now, you'd be Duncan Hullar, is that right?" asked Sabini, "Just started working with Mr. Mowler 'ere, right?"

Hullar's eyes grew wide in disbelief. "Well, yeah. I've been working for two months. We met – "

Sabini cut him off, holding a hand towards Holmes. "Now, Mr. Holmes and Inspector Wengert have a few questions for you."

The big man's face turned towards Holmes. My friend looked him up and down, pausing for effect, before finally asking stating, "Mr. Hullar, let me first introduce myself. I am Sherlock Holmes, a retired consulting detective. I am assisting Inspector Wengert of Scotland Yard here in a disturbing case of multiple murders. I understand that you recently spent some time in Wandsworth Prison. Is that correct?"

"Yes, sir, I did. I am shamed by it, but I cannot lie."

"And you were a cell mate of James Murgatroyd." The big man nodded. "Did Murgatroyd discuss his time working for the Hoxton Mob with you?"

Nodding again, Hullar looked at Mowler and Sabini before turning back to Holmes and replying, "Yes he did."

"And he told you about a secret place down in Ashford Forrest?"

Hullar's eyes suddenly looked frightened and darted between his bosses once more, settling on Mowler. "Yes, I told Mr. Mowler about it. He said it would be a good dumping ground."

Mowler looked shocked. To me, his expression appeared a little rehearsed. "I don't know about that. I might have said that explains why the 'Oxtons used it, and maybe it was a good idea, but I didn't say that *we* should use it."

Holmes stepped across the room and stood before Hullar. I was quite worried. Hullar towered over him, something that could not be said of a lot of men. "Would it surprise you, sir, to know that we found the body of Constable Albert Smith, a local policeman, in a shallow grave in that forest?"

The large man's eyes darted around the room once more, locking on Sabini's for a moment, before dropping to the gaze at the floor. He shuffled on the spot, a sign of nerves – a very strange thing to see in a man of his size.

"Come to think of it, I do know you, don't I, Duncan?" All eyes turned to Sabini. His gaze was fixed on Hullar's face. The man sat forward and clicked his fingers, pointing at Hullar. "I do apologise. We have met before. A couple of months ago, just after you started with Randall. You have a mother that lives down in Ratcliff, isn't that right?"

Hullar nodded mutely.

Shaking his head slowly from side to side, Sabini continued. "That's a nasty part of town that is. If I was you, I'd be keeping a very close eye on her. There's some nasty villains that roam that area. Nasty villains."

I don't think I've ever seen anyone turn so white before as Hullar did. His mouth dropped open to answer, but nothing came out.

"So, do you know anything about these murders 'Ullar?" asked Sabini, "These gentlemen seem to think that it was you."

Terror crossed Hullar's face. He tried to step back but came up against the wall and simply stopped. His hand shot out to the side and pointed at Mowler. "He told me to do it. And the others too."

Throwing up his hands in defence, Mowler retorted, "Whoa, whoa! I said no such thing. I said something should be done about the constable playing the Hoxtons off against us, but I never suggested he should be killed! And I have no idea what others you're talking about."

"You did! You said I should fix him and dump him in Ashford. That way the Hoxtons would get the blame." Moving suddenly towards the exit door, Hullar pushed up against Martin. The shorter man was wider and had a look on his face that begged Hullar to try and get past him.

Almost shouting at Mowler, the desperate man pleaded with his him. "You did! You told me to do it! I only done it on your orders."

"I never said to kill anyone!" Mowler replied, his face stern.

"There you go, Mr. 'Olmes," said Sabini. "'E just confessed. Must 'ave misunderstood poor Randall's orders and become a little too *enthused*." He shrugged. "It will be sad to lose a valid employee, but you can take 'im away, Inspector."

"What?" hollered Hullar, stepping again towards the doorway.

"I'm sorry. Duncan, is it? But I can't 'ave no killers in my gang. I'm an upstanding member of society. I 'ave my reputation to consider." Sabini's face grew grim once more. "And do remember your lovely mother."

The big man stopped, staring at the gang boss in disbelief. "But . . . you told me to do it."

Sabini stepped out from around his desk and stood before the huge man. "As we 'ave already established, you 'ave misunderstood what Mr. Mowler 'ere said, and have gone a little off the deep end. I think you should accompany the good inspector 'ere to the Yard and 'elp with 'is investigations." Nodding in the big man's face, Sabini said, "Is that understood, Duncan?"

Hullar dropped his gaze to the floor and nodded meekly.

Turning towards Wengert, Sabini indicated Hullar over his shoulder. "It's a shame to lose such a fine specimen, but we can't 'ave no murderers running around loose in our ranks, now can we?"

Colour seemed to return to Hullar's face as Sabini's words sunk in. He stood to his full height and spoke. "What do you mean?"

A cruel smile crossed Sabini's face as he turned. "Well, you'll probably end up back in Wandsworth for a stint. Shouldn't be too long though. They don't keep murderers around for long." The intent of that last statement wasn't lost on anybody in the room.

"No!" bellowed Hullar, "No! I'm not going back there! You told me to do them in! I was just following orders!"

It was then that everything went mad.

Hullar howled in rage at Sabini. His face turned to pure frenzy. Stepping forward, he brought up those massive hands, grabbing Sabini around the neck and dragging him across the room before anyone could react. Sabini was thrust against the wall, gasping for air as the tall man crushed his throat.

Mowler leapt at Huller, but a simple shrug saw him thrown aside. Sabini's assistant ran from the room. I presumed he went for help, but he could have left out of simple self-preservation. Wengert moved forward to grab at Huller, but received an elbow to the midriff, knocking the wind from his lungs.

From pure instinct, Holmes and I reached for our pistols, but we both realised that those days were gone, and we hadn't brought them with us.

But the sudden shock of a gunshot in that small room stopped us in our tracks. All eyes fell on Hullar's back. The large man's hands dropped away from Sabini's neck and he slumped to his knees before collapsing to the ground.

Sabini held a small revolver in his right hand, a slender trail of smoke rising from the barrel. He looked from me to Holmes. "I always keeps this on me. You just never know when you'll need it. I picked that one up from you and the good Doctor."

Back at my house, Holmes and I reposed in the parlour with coffee and a mid-afternoon brandy – something I felt was well-deserved after the day's events.

"That didn't quite go as planned, did it?" I asked him.

Taking a sip of coffee and placing the cup down, he smiled in my direction. "No, Watson, frankly it didn't, but the outcome was as expected."

"How so?"

"Sabini is no fool. He may not have damaged the Hoxton Mob's hold on any territory as he hoped, but he did remove a troubling element within his ranks. Both Hullar, who verged on the uncontrollable due to his anger problems, and Smith, who was playing him against the Hoxtons."

"But Sabini got away with murder."

"Did he?" Holmes said. "We believe that he did, but we only have circumstantial evidence to tie him to the murders. In the eyes of the law he is free. Hullar's death was self-defence. All the murders can be attributed directly to him. The Sabini Gang is reknowned for the use of knives and blunt force trauma via hammers, but never strangulation. Therefore, there is no direct correlation to their methods."

"I still feel a little unnerved by all this."

"As you should ,Watson. Theoretically, we uncovered a strange plot to undermine one criminal gang by another gang and put a stop to it. We found a murderer and he found his just deserts. Sabini and his crew are well in the sights of Chief Inspector Wengert, so they will have to play it safe for a while yet. Overall, actually a quite successful adventure."

"If you say so." I thought for a moment. "I wonder about writing this up for *The Strand* . . . ."

"If you do, make sure that it's clear that I'm still retired. This was but a momentary reprieve, and to be honest, a most enjoyable – though tiring – one."

The Case of the
Troubled Policeman
by Daniel D. Victor

All writers are vain, selfish, and lazy,
and at the very bottom of their motives there lies a mystery.
– George Orwell "Why I Write"

Chapter I

"Y ou have been in Burma, I perceive," said Sherlock Holmes.

Thus my friend greeted the younger of the two men who entered my sitting room on a chill November afternoon in '27. Holmes rose from his chair to welcome the visitors, and I, with the aid of my stick, stood up and joined him. The older man remained by the door, however, and his younger companion moved toward the fire in the hearth.

"That Burma business, Mr. Holmes," the younger man replied with the nod of his head. "Very clever indeed. But you see, I've read *A Study in Scarlet*. I know the details of your initial meeting with Dr. Watson. How you inferred from his darkened skin, his haggard look – and what else was it? – oh, yes, his military bearing – that he had recently returned from Afghanistan."

My friend drew deeply on his black briar. Though his hair had silvered, I knew that he too recalled that most memorable of meetings, now close to fifty years removed.

"Your companion – " Holmes tried to explain, but the young man would not be stopped.

"Obviously," he went on, "you reached a similar conclusion by looking at me."

My hearing has declined during the past few years, yet my vision remains sharp, and I could clearly see that this younger man – a tall, thin, gangling fellow with tousled dark hair, a weathered mien, and a black-toothbrush moustache – looked nothing like the Imperial Policeman I had been informed that he was. What is more, though his accent was that of a gentleman, his clothing was anything but. He was dressed in a worn tweed coat – too short at the sleeves – a faded-blue shirt, and lifeless, brown corduroy trousers. As he stood before us, his gaunt figure swayed back and forth in an awkward attempt to remain erect.

"I am certain that you noted my own tinted skin, Mr. Holmes," he continued, "but I should imagine that it is from my unfortunate appearance – my slight frame, my lapses of breath, and my rather clumsy effort to remain upright – that you deduced I am recuperating from Dengue Fever, an affliction which you rightly associated with Burma. In a word, sir – " Here he pointed an accusatory finger at my friend. " – though you reached the correct conclusion, I refuse to be impressed by it. I may have been schooled at Eton, but I have also attended the Provincial Police Training School in Mandalay. I know a thing or two about how deductions such as yours are drawn." Despite a blank expression, there was directness in the young man's light-blue eyes.

His companion, on the other hand, grunted impatience. "Stuff and nonsense," he growled from behind heavy eyebrows and side-whiskers. This second gentleman, having failed to relinquish his hat and coat to my housekeeper, appeared eager to take his leave. "It was I who furnished Watson with your background – over the telephone wire – and doubtlessly he shared the details with his friend here. No cleverness required."

I nodded in confirmation while Holmes produced more puffs on his black briar. "I tried to explain," he shrugged.

"That said," the curmudgeon continued, "I have completed my task. I have delivered to you gentlemen my former student, and I now bid you, 'Good day'." With those words, the fellow performed a quick about-turn and made his way back to the entry hall. Behind him, my housekeeper, the indefatigable Miss Ross, closed the twinned pocket-doors of the sitting room and ushered Mr. Gow to the exit.

In point of fact, the man's abrupt departure was the last either Holmes or I ever saw of the chap. He had fulfilled his obligation as he said he would when he had rung me a week earlier to establish this very meeting.

I remember the call so distinctly because the telephone line had been rich with static, and I had difficulty in hearing the voice at the other end.

"Is that Dr. John Watson?" I could barely discern over the crackles. "The author of the Sherlock Holmes sketches?"

I answered in the affirmative, and he offered his name. I could not make it out, however, and asked him to repeat it.

213

"Andrew Gow," I heard. "Gow – *G-O-W* – formerly an Assistant Master at Eton and now," he proudly emphasised, "a Fellow of Trinity College."

I suppose I did not respond quickly enough, for he added even more proudly, "Cambridge."

Eton and Trinity – both schools at the top of anyone's list. And yet Eton had educated two of Holmes's most formidable adversaries, the ever-dangerous Colonel Sebastian Moran and the always-scheming John Clay. As for Trinity, it had figured in one of our most distressing investigations.

"Sherlock Holmes had a case involving a student at Trinity," I said into the mouthpiece. "Godfrey Staunton, who played rugger for Cambridge back in '96." It had been many years earlier; but as an old rugger myself, I recalled with great clarity the tragedy which had prompted Holmes to seek out the missing three-quarter.

"No interest in athletics," I heard Mr. Gow reply. In spite of the static I could feel the coldness in his voice. "But you may have cause to remember me in connection with another of your old cases, the one involving some bad business at Dulwich College." (I had originally disguised the name of the school as St. Luke's.)

In fact, now that he mentioned it, I did recall Gow's name. Although I had never met the man, I remembered the favourable letter he had sent to *The Strand* in response to the magazine's publication of the sketch I titled "The Adventure of the Three Students." If memory serves, the narrative appeared in June of '04.

"The cheating scandal related to the Fortescue Scholarship," I said into the telephone. "The examination required a translation from some odd bit in Greek – "

"Half a chapter from Thucydides," Mr. Gow was quick to remind me. A student of Greek at the time, he took such special interest in the subject that he went on to teach Classics at Eton and Trinity. His letter touted my account of Holmes's success. "A clarion call for fair play in academics," he had claimed. I remember relishing the praise and storing the letter along with my other papers in the vault of Cox and Company, Charing Cross.

And yet the sketch and letter had appeared more than two decades earlier. What the Cambridge Fellow had to say to me on the telephone that day I could not imagine. "Yes?" I said, hoping he would get to the point.

Mr. Gow cleared his throat. At least, I believe it was he I had heard and not more static on the line. "I promised a former student of mine – Mr. Eric Blair, a Colleger home on leave from service in

214

Burma – that I would set up a meeting between him and the two of you."

"The *two* of us?"

"Quite so. You and Sherlock Holmes."

Now Collegers were the boys who displayed exceptional promise at Eton, so I recognised that the young man must have possessed several qualities of note. Save for some vague worries concerning the student's future, however, Mr. Gow told me nothing about the reason for such a meeting.

Which is not to say that the matter failed to interest me. As I am certain my faithful readers can attest, endeavouring to set people on their proper paths is part of my nature, and the notion of helping an Old Etonian appealed not only to my conscience but also to my vanity. As a consequence, I rang Holmes at his retirement cottage in Sussex as soon as my conversation with Mr. Gow had ended.

Like myself, Sherlock Holmes is now in his seventies; but ever since his retirement in '03, he has steadfastly resisted coming up to London. Even now, though he moves much more spryly than I, he prefers to remain at home. As a result, I decided to rely upon the air of mystery surrounding Eric Blair's clouded future to entice Holmes to my house for the meeting with the young man.

Happily, my friend was most accommodating. "A provocative diversion," he cried, agreeing to a visit that would include a day with the young man. Immediately thereafter, I rang Trinity College to confirm the date with Mr. Gow.

No sooner had the Cambridge Don left my sitting room that November afternoon than Holmes returned to the armchair he had been occupying earlier. I indicated that Eric Arthur Blair – for that, as he informed us, was his full name – should take the seat next to Holmes, and I resumed my own place behind the writing desk in the middle of the room. Years earlier, I had arranged that my desk and rolling chair be set up in that central location to decrease the exertion I experienced climbing the stairs to my study. In addition to easing my labours, the new site provided me with an excellent view of the fire crackling in the hearth, even as my visitors sat with their backs to the grate.

As I stared into the flames, I could not avoid contemplating the irony. The culprit in the cheating scandal which had so interested Mr. Gow had quit his schooling and gone off to join the Rhodesian Police. Here before us sat Mr. Gow's former student at Eton who had gone off to Burma as an Anglo-Indian member of the Imperial Police.

215

It was Blair himself who interrupted my thoughts. "With your permission, Doctor?" he asked, producing a pouch of dark tobacco and a small square of rolling paper.

I nodded and, noting the flecks of tobacco already hitting the carpet, offered him a glass ashtray. I knew from experience that it was not unusual for men returning from their stations in India to be so accustomed to their native servants' picking up their droppings that they became oblivious to the detritus they left in their wake.

"In truth, Mr. Holmes," said Blair, "I am pleased to meet you at last."

"At last?" Holmes questioned.

The policeman nodded as he began to roll the cigarette. "I first heard of you when I was a lad at St. Cyprian's."

"The school near Eastbourne."

"Of course, you would know of the place. St. Cyprian's was but a quarter-mile from your home at Beachy Head. We would wander past your digs on the way to the cliff. The headmaster, Mr. Vaughan Wilkes, told us a retired detective lived in the cottage, and now I finally have the chance to meet him."

Holmes bowed his head in response.

"Such were the summer days," Blair went on, "when we would walk in a crocodile across the Downs to pick blackberries or simply explore. Sometimes we marched all the way up the steep chalky trail to the top just so we could risk cuts and bruises climbing down to the water and swimming among the rocks."

Holmes offered a smile of recognition. "I still notice groups of schoolboys crossing the Downs. Perhaps I might even have seen you."

Tapping his cigarette on the back of his hand, our visitor turned in my direction. "In your case, Doctor, allow me to begin with an apology."

I could not imagine for what the policeman might be apologizing. We had never met before, and I had no knowledge of him personally.

"You have the right to look puzzled," he said, lighting his cigarette. "But allow me to explain. In my days at Eton, I contributed bits and pieces to a small magazine we called *The Election Times*."

"Good work," I beamed. "Nothing to apologise for in that."

"One hopes," Blair said sheepishly. "You see, months before the Great War ended, I misplaced my ration-book. Looked high and low, but couldn't find it. I had to borrow from friends."

"A difficult situation," I said, "but you seem to have managed."

"Oh, I did. But the situation prompted me to write a story about my dilemma, and I'm rather afraid that I composed a parody in the style of your accounts of Mr. Holmes's investigations."

"A parody?" I cried, my good feelings suddenly draining from me.

"I called it '*The Adventure of the Lost Meat-Card*'."

"'*Lost Meat-Card*'?" I repeated in disbelief. Though from the corner of my eye, I could detect a smile on the lips of Sherlock Holmes, I was not to be placated. "Mr. Blair," I told him in no uncertain terms, "I do not *compose* stories. I write narratives based on fact."

"Oh, I know that, Doctor. One could easily tell that my story should not be mistaken for Truth. Why, I presented your Inspector Lestrade as the villain of the piece."

Holmes produced a dry laugh. "Lestrade could be called many things, Blair," said he, "but 'villain' is not among them."

"Of that I am quite certain," said the policeman. "I have read Dr. Watson's accounts of the inspector's bulldog nature, and while I am aware of the man's limitations, I had no intention of belittling him."

Blair's honesty helped calm me down. His confession sounded heartfelt, and it had been almost a decade since this so-called parody had been produced. Though it rankled to consider my work treated in so cavalier a fashion, I decided it was time to forgive the young man and to deal with the matter at hand.

"Let us return to the present, shall we?" I said.

"Indeed," Holmes offered. "How it is that you came here today?"

"You already know that Mr. Gow was m'tutor at Eton," he said. "Following my return from Burma, he rang my father in Southwold. Mr. Gow didn't know my whereabouts at the time – I have a small room in Portobello Road about three miles from here in Notting Hill – and he asked my father to deliver the message that Mr. Gow wanted to meet with me in Cambridge. That was actually the start, though indirectly, of how you two gentlemen got involved."

Chapter II

Eric Blair leaned back in his chair and filled his lungs with cigarette smoke. Closing his eyes to enjoy his tobacco, he blew the smoke ceiling-ward and emerged from his brief reverie with a series of peppering coughs.

217

Not yet rid of the fever, I remember thinking.

"I must say," Blair continued once he had settled down, "that it was a bit of a surprise when my father reached me. I'd had no communication with Mr. Gow when I was in Burma – in fact, not since I'd left Eton. We used to call him 'Granny' Gow back then because of his old-lady ways, and I can tell you that he was none too enthusiastic about my academic future. I suspect he considered me a slacker – probably still does. No doubt always will."

"Hard to believe," said I. "A member of the Imperial Police a slacker?"

"Mr. Gow recognised I had little interest in academics. He warned my father that I would bring disgrace to Eton if I, like so many of my successful mates, sought a scholarship to Cambridge or Oxford. Which, incidentally, would have been the only way my father might have tolerated my attending university at all. None the less, I did remember some of the pleasant Sunday evenings we spent with 'Granny' discussing literature and such – Milton, if I recall correctly – and so not long after receiving Mr. Gow's invitation, I decided to accept. I took a train to Cambridge, found Trinity College, and ultimately located Mr. Gow in his rooms.

"'You are still a policeman,' were Mr. Gow's first words to me."

"Right to the point," I observed. "Not too warm a fellow, eh?"

"You're right about that, but then you saw him yourself this afternoon and got a measure of his coldness."

"You say he immediately identified you as a policeman," Holmes said.

"Indeed. 'A member of the Indian Imperial Police,' I told him, 'currently on leave.' You've already noted that I'm stationed in Burma, Mr. Holmes. I spent some time in Rangoon and Mandalay, but my official postings were elsewhere – most recently in Katha."

"You must have had your hands full out there," I said. "I recall my own experiences in Afghanistan." Just thinking about those days so long ago made my leg throb.

"Ah, yes, Doctor," Blair said, blowing out a cloud of white smoke, "but you were military. I am police. We are responsible for the entire population of Burma – all thirteen-million of them."

"I assume," said Holmes, "that Gow hoped to take advantage of your expertise."

"Correct again. In fact, I soon learned that my police training was the sole reason for his invitation. It seemed that some of his colleagues had reported items missing from their rooms – a watch here, a fob there – and he wanted to enlist my aid in finding them.

What's more, my arrival was most fortuitous for, just that morning, he'd discovered that his own gold signet ring – a parting gift from Eton, he told me – had gone missing. At first, he thought he might simply have misplaced it, but after turning his rooms upside down in search of the thing, he had to admit to failure."

"That is why he welcomed your aid," I observed.

"I must say," Blair replied between puffs on his cigarette, "that I was reluctant to become involved. You see, gentlemen, though I haven't decided for certain, more and more I expect that my policing days are over. Discontent with the job, you might call it, but the slow recuperation from the illness I caught over there is also convincing me to pack it in. Even so, I decided to help 'Granny' – for old time's sake, if nothing else."

"Quite understandable," I said. "But why did your tutor call on you in the first place? He could have summoned the local authorities to find his missing ring."

Holmes laughed drily. "When a lecturer at Cambridge seeks to avoid the locals, old fellow, it generally means that he wishes to keep the college's soiled linen from public view. I daresay these thefts were an internal matter."

"Exactly," said the policeman. "Unable to find the ring himself, he concluded that, like his colleagues' missing objects, it must have been stolen. And the bedder who had just finished her work in his rooms became his chief suspect.

"Since his was the last room she had cleaned, he reported to me how he was able to follow her to the town centre. Despite the crowded walkways, she moved quickly down Trinity Street to Fitzbillies, a bakery in Trumpington Street where, as Mr. Gow soon discovered, the woman's paramour worked. Only after the man had put the latest batch of sticky buns into the oven would he talk to Mr. Gow. As you might expect, the baker said he knew nothing of any stolen items that day or any other."

"So Gow was stymied," said I.

"Correct. When I arrived at his rooms not long thereafter, an eager Mr. Gow immediately marched me down to Fitzbillies so I might be the one to have a go at the baker."

Holmes's eyes suddenly lit up.

"I can see it in your expression, Mr. Holmes," said our visitor. "You are one step ahead – though it is really to Dr. Watson that I owe my success – that is, to his account of a similar case."

I looked at Blair in bewilderment. "A stolen ring? A bakery? I fail to see a connection."

Sherlock Holmes uttered a single word. "Beppo."

The policeman nodded. "Do you not recall 'The Adventure of the Six Napoleons', Doctor? Beppo, the man who stole the Black Pearl of the Borgias, hid it inside a wet plaster bust of the Emperor and wound up having to locate and then crack open the hardened statues to recover the pearl."

"A process that led to murder," Holmes reminded us.

"Indeed," said I, "but Blair has mentioned no statues in his tale."

"The dough, Watson, the dough," said Holmes. "Is that not the correct explanation, Blair?"

"That's right, Mr. Holmes," answered the policeman. "In this case, I had to wait for the buns to bake. But when they were removed from the oven – smelling sweet and coloured deep-caramel, I should add – I discovered the truth. With Mr. Gow fresh on the woman's trail, the baker had to hide the ring as quickly as possible. With no other alternative in sight, he placed it in the middle of a square spiral of wet, syrupy dough and proceeded to bake the bun along with the others. But once I recalled your account of "The Six Napoleons', Doctor, it took but a few moments to tear open some fifteen of the forty freshly baked rolls before I found Mr. Gow's ring nestled among the currants within the centre of one of the buns."

"Well done," said I. "But what happened to the miscreants? How did they fare?"

The policeman puffed on what was left of his cigarette. "Faced with the crime, the baker confessed that the woman had given him everything she had stolen. They were afraid of being found out in Cambridge, and though they were planning to sell their loot in London, they still had the stolen goods in their digs. Once caught, the baker agreed to return it all."

"And no police were involved," Holmes observed.

"To be sure. Oh, the baker did have to make amends for the buns that were wasted, but he turned out to be too valuable a pastry-maker for Fitzbillies to sack him. The same could not be said for the woman. She lost her position at Trinity. As for me, I confiscated all the buns I had ripped asunder and presented them to my mother in Southwold."

"Bravo!" said Holmes with a clap of his hands. "I know of detectives at Scotland Yard this very day who might only have located the missing ring accidentally – by breaking a tooth on one of those buns."

Blair laughed. "Maybe someday, Mr. Holmes, I'll write a piece about Napoleon in honour of the case that inspired me." He laughed again, and as he dropped the fag end of his cigarette on the floor, his laugh turned into a cough. Suddenly, the policeman remembered where he was, picked it up, and proceeded to snuff it out in the ashtray I had given him earlier.

Chapter III

"An entertaining story, Blair," I said, "as far as it goes. But you still have not explained what any of this has to do with Holmes and me."

Blair sighed. "It was Mr. Gow's idea to set up this meeting with you. 'Granny' was never one to take an interest in my private life, but before I left Cambridge that afternoon, he did ask how I was getting on. I told him the truth – that for some time now I've been questioning my role in Burma and that I was using my current leave to consider an alternative career in writing."

"And his response?" I asked.

"Mr. Gow took a minute or two to absorb what I'd said. Finally, he nodded as if he'd made up his mind. He said he reckoned he just might be able to recommend two people from whom I should get advice. That was when he suggested the two of you. In point of fact, I believe that arranging today's meeting was Mr. Gow's singular way of thanking me for helping locate his ring."

"You have already spoken of your concerns about continuing with the Police," said Holmes. "Pray, explain more fully."

Blair ran his hands along the sides of his corduroy trouser legs. "In a word, Mr. Holmes, though duty, along with my father, calls for it, I have come to consider as odious the thought of resuming my career in Burma. If you must know, I consider myself unsuited for the job.

"At the same time, I find most compelling the challenge of testing my writing skills. Yet I remain hesitant about making a final decision. I suspect Mr. Gow believed that owing to your particular talents, you two gentlemen – my *yin-yang*, so to speak – might be the very ones able to help me sort things out."

I knew little of *yin* or *yang*, but I believe I understood the reasoning behind the tutor's suggestion. Holmes was a retired detective, who, however infrequently, still entered the fray. I was his Boswell, who, however humbly, still occupied myself with the business of writing. Mr. Gow must have believed that Holmes and I

221

personified the contradictory forces in Blair's future. Presumably, he thought that Holmes could address the police issues and that I could enlighten Blair about the demands of a career in writing.

The young man's gaze travelled from Holmes to me and back again. He brushed aside a shock of dark hair that had fallen across his brow. "So where do we begin?"

Sherlock Holmes put down his briar, leaned back in his chair, and steepled his fingers beneath his chin. "Why not tell us what has prompted your decision to leave the Imperial Police?"

Blair stretched out his long legs, slouched in the chair, and exhaled audibly.

Not the attitude of a policeman, I remember thinking. This entire drama might be embodied in his pose.

"It was a little more that two years ago," Blair said, "when I first realised my own concerns were hampering me. In September of '25 I was posted to Insein, and a month later I failed to get to the bottom of a drugs investigation. Clues were there, but I was so distracted by my inner conflicts that I could make nothing of what I was seeing." He rubbed his chin. "The investigation was one of my first in Insein. I had a stickler of a District Superintendent, and I hoped to create a good impression. To this day, the shambles I made of it still sticks in my craw."

"I realise that time has passed," said Sherlock Holmes, "but perhaps, I can help. What are the facts?"

"It wasn't the most infamous of affairs," the policeman explained, "but the Dangerous Drugs Act had been passed, and we'd been told by the Foreign Office that an English drugs trafficker named Thrush would soon be arriving in Rangoon via a P. and O. steamer. Insein is but a brief railway ride of ten miles, and I was called in. Thrush was presumed to be coming to Insein to meet a certain *naïf*, an innocent who had agreed to sell cocaine for him. We knew the time Thrush's ship was due in port, and once I identified him – a wiry ferret of a man, he was – I followed him back to Insein and a boarding house where we suspected his mark was staying. I had my men surround the building."

"Good," said my friend.

"Here's where it gets strange, Mr. Holmes. Outside the building, we discovered a light-coloured powder coating the purple flowers of a bougainvillea that was climbing along the wall."

"Cocaine," I suggested, "'unquestionably, tossed out a window. You must have been seen arriving."

"My thought, exactly," said Blair with a wry smile, "but when I had one my of Burmese policemen taste the stuff, he shook his head and spat it out. 'Face powder, I should judge, sir,' he said with a scowl.

"'Nothing to do with us,' I thought."

"And yet," Holmes offered, "one assumes that you purposely searched the rooms whose windows overlooked the discarded powder."

"I did. Maybe there had been a replacement somewhere – cocaine for face powder. I couldn't be certain, but having followed this Thrush fellow, I believed that locating him inside the boarding house would reveal the cocaine and the proof we needed to arrest him."

"And?" I asked.

"In fact, we started our search on the ground floor and finally found Thrush on the third. He was with another Englishman, an older chap whose room it was. I should say that Insein has many Europeans lodging there and a particularly strong British influence. Strange to say, this other fellow, Burnham by name, had a half-dozen tins of face powder in plain view on a table."

"Out in the open like that," I said. "Surely, too obvious a hiding place. Like Poe's purloined letter."

Blair nodded. "That's what I thought as well, and so we didn't even bother to open the tins. Instead, we searched the room from top to bottom. We overturned the drawers, examined a valise and Gladstone. We searched the little clothing there was – without success."

"And during this time," Holmes observed, "I imagine that Thrush was quite calm while Burnham grew more agitated the longer you searched."

Eric Blair raised his eyebrows. "Why, that's right, Mr. Holmes. Burma is five-thousand miles from here, and this business occurred two years ago. Yet you are able to describe the scene with great accuracy."

Holmes smiled. "I have my methods, as Watson can attest."

I dismissed Holmes's comment with a wag of my hand. "What happened next?" I asked. "I presume you finally did check the face-powder tins."

"Indeed we did," Blair said. "No other choice, really."

"And found they contained face powder," Holmes added, steel-grey eyes ablaze.

Blair's own blue eyes opened wide. "Why, yes, Mr. Holmes!"

"One presumes," said my friend, "that Burnham's anxiety reached its height when you made for the tins. And when you finished examining them, he seemed remarkably relieved."

"Right again," said Blair, now sitting up straight. "We had no evidence, no proof, and with Thrush smirking all the while, we left the premises. I felt quite cross with myself for not producing a solution. The District Superintendent shared my displeasure. You, on the other hand, seem to have deduced what actually happened."

My friend leaned forward and picked up his briar. "Mind you, Blair, I can't be certain." Whilst Holmes spoke, he gestured with the pipe stem as if it were a pointer. "What I believe you uncovered was a dastardly scheme by Thrush to cheat Burnham two-fold. I can only assume that Thrush had talked Burnham into buying – and then selling – the illicit narcotic.

"Being a novice, Burnham took the villain at his word and believed that what he'd purchased from Thrush was the promised cocaine. To make room in the tins for what he thought was the genuine narcotic, Burnham dumped the face-powder out the window. The growing anxiety you saw Burnham exhibit was based on his fear that once you had concluded that the contraband could be nowhere else, you, a representative of the Crown, were about to discover it in the tins where Burnham thought it to be."

"But there was no cocaine," I pointed out.

"Ah, the beauty of Thrush's plan," Holmes said, now directing his pipe stem at me. "Thrush never sold the narcotic to Burnham – never intended to. Though Burnham paid him the high price of cocaine, all he really purchased was face powder. Thrush knew you wouldn't find any narcotics, and so he had nothing to fear during your search. Burnham, on the other hand, lacked that knowledge, and the closer you got to inspecting the face-powder tins, the more his dread grew." Holmes allowed himself a quick smile upon completing this analysis.

I sat in silent appreciation. I am sure Blair felt the same.

"Most cunning indeed, Mr. Holmes," the policeman said at last, a shadow darkening his brow. "But, you see, I should have figured it out at the time. Your success merely underscores the correctness of my decision to leave the Imperial Police. I am a failed copper."

"Now, Blair," I said, "I think you are a bit too hard on yourself. You've said you were distracted. You must have had too much on your mind."

"That was indeed the case, Doctor. I was distracted. Still am."

"Let us change the emphasis," said Holmes. "Why not tell us of your accomplishments in Burma?"

"Surely," I suggested, "some aspects of your work there must still beckon."

"Beckon?" Blair spat out the word. "I was an Assistant Superintendent of Police who did my duty. I faced murders and native uprisings, and I shall never forget the hanging of a poor fellow I witnessed in Insein's prison. Men sentenced to death in a language they couldn't understand. Nor can I forgive myself for shooting a rogue elephant during my posting in Moulmein. The poor creature had calmed itself down by the time I arrived, but I had to show the natives who was boss. Oh, I did my job, gentlemen, but I'm not certain there are any accomplishments to boast of.

"You see, the longer I remained in Burma, the more I questioned virtually every action we took. Why should so few British officers – there were ninety of us overseeing some thirteen-thousand native policemen – why should so few of us be enforcing English law upon millions of people whom we neither knew nor – at least, as far as I could tell – cared about?"

"Why, to preserve our way of life," I answered.

Darkness clouded Blair's face. "I too felt that patriotism when I originally went out there. But I am no longer that naïve youth. The more I saw of British authority, the more disenchanted I became. Based on the behaviour I witnessed of the English *pukha-sahibs* – their arrogance, their prejudice, their sadism – the more sympathetic I grew towards the people we were oppressing.

"As a result, I learned the Burmese and Hindustani languages, and soon I found myself succumbing to the charms of a certain class of Burmese women. In Rangoon, I took to mingling with a former officer of the Imperial Police – the cashiered ex-Captain H.R. Robinson – who'd ultimately 'gone native'. His mates called him 'Robbie', and opium and women consumed much of his time and that of the people round him. It was then, I believe, that my superiors became suspicious of me."

"I should think so," I muttered. To myself I said, "Quite the Bohemian, this Eric Blair."

"But there's more," the young man continued. "I don't believe that leaving the Imperial Police will be remedy enough."

I missed his reference. "Remedy enough for what?" I asked.

"Remedy enough to rectify the profound injustices I have seen. It is clear to me now that our upright British society is nothing more than the enemy of impoverished people – not only in Burma, but round the world."

Dark thoughts indeed, I feared.

Holmes pointed his pipe. "You are not alone in your concerns, Blair. Watson and I heard of such horrid conditions ourselves from the American Jack London when he came round Baker Street many years ago. He was reporting the plight of the poor in the East End. Sad to say, the bleak situations he described have changed very little"

"*The People of the Abyss*," Blair noted eagerly. "One of my favourites. But Burma's not Whitechapel, Mr. Holmes. There's no class-friction out there. All that truly matters is whether your skin is white. It's the sort of thinking that promotes the most worthless of individuals to positions of authority. That is my dilemma. I recognise the inequities, and yet, as a policeman, I must help to maintain the system."

"*A policeman's lot is not a happy one*'," I said, citing W.S. Gilbert's familiar lyric. I spoke the words, and yet I sensed that Blair's lamentations had more to do with the mistreatment of natives than with the familiar complaints of an overworked copper.

Blair shook his head. "In the police force you witness first-hand the dirty work of empire, and I was never trained to hide my reactions to human misery. In a word, I got tired of arresting people for doing what I would have done if I were in their place. Don't you see? Once you start believing a Truth like that, you start understanding what leads people to commit crimes. You may even begin rationalizing the role of the criminal. I tell you, gentlemen, it was getting so that I couldn't enter a jail without feeling that I belonged on the other side of the bars. However prevalent such theories may be among academics and intellectuals, they are not the sort of ideas to be entertained by policemen."

"Quite so, Blair," said Holmes. "And yet you remained in Burma for how long?"

"Five years. No choice, really. Eventually, I was struck with fever. Though I was entitled to a five-month leave at the end of the year, owing to my medical condition, I was able to shorten my posting by six months. In July I was on one of those P. and O. steamers on my way back to England. What is more, gentlemen, it took only one sniff of English air to convince me that I should remain here. Of one other thing I can also be certain – there are many in Burma who will not be disappointed if I never return."

"So I should imagine," I said.

226

At those words, our visitor raised his chin defiantly.

"Which brings us back," said Holmes with another clap of his hands, "to the future of Assistant Superintendent of Police Eric Blair. What is it that you plan to do instead?"

Chapter IV

At last, it was my turn. Blair's unhappiness with life in Burma might have been the catalyst for his overall discontent, but Holmes's question provided me the opportunity to discover more about the young man's interest in writing. At that moment, however, Miss Ross knocked loudly on the sitting room doors. As it was nearing four o'clock, I knew she was bringing us tea.

"Enter," said I, and after sliding the wooden doors apart, she came in bearing a tray complete with tea service and chocolate biscuits. Miss Ross poured for the three of us and then, noting the diminished flames in the fireplace, employed a poker to rearrange the coal. Only after the blaze leapt up again did she leave us to continue our discussion.

At the moment, however, Eric Blair was contentedly inhaling the aroma from the steaming teapot. "Darjeeling," he said with a smile. "I have a keen sense of smell."

"Actually, a strong Darjeeling," I offered. "There's a touch of Lapsang Souchong for Holmes. He likes the smoky flavour."

"I do enjoy a rich cup of Indian tea," Blair said. "The Chinese addition, not so much. I tell you that in Burma I longed for the tea we used to get from Fortnum and Mason." With the fire now crackling behind him, he held up the white porcelain cup, it was part of my late wife's set, and I'm afraid she would not have tolerated the cracks and chips so obvious in the glow of the flames.

"I prefer a cylindrical cup," Blair said, taking a drink.

However one judged the policeman, he certainly had definite opinions. "You have said that you want to write," I reminded him as I sampled my tea. "Heaven knows, you have the material – the ring in the bun, the face-powder tins. Grand stories have come from less." I remembered Holmes's solution to the Abernetty business based on how far a sprig of parsley had sunk into butter.

"You're right about the material, Doctor. Anything one observes is fair game, and I am a grand observer." He reached for a biscuit and took a bite. "For the past twenty-five years, I've been composing stories in my head, stories that describe my own actions while they are actually happening."

"A sort of mental diary," I suggested.

"Exactly. In Burma I would detail in my mind our various police activities: The beatings, the round-ups, even my evenings with Robinson. I've always been fascinated with laying out a scene and describing the action. Sometimes I even invent invisible characters with whom I converse."

Clearly, the man had quite the imagination.

"And yet," said Holmes, "you eschewed university where you could have pursued your literary talents. Instead, you travelled off to Burma."

"Good point, Mr. Holmes," said Blair, finishing up the remainder of the biscuit. "But, you see, at that stage in my life, I was trying to give up the idea of being a writer – too many ties to my childhood feelings of loneliness. I reckoned that serving the empire would rid me of such worries."

"Yet you say you still want to write," I reminded him.

"That does seem to be the case," Blair nodded, clasping his hands together as if in supplication. "I can't eliminate the urge. Oh, I know there are all sorts of reasons that people want to write, and I can sympathise with all of them. Who doesn't want to show off his facility with language? Who doesn't want to reflect the beauty in the world? Who doesn't want his name to be remembered? Right, Doctor?"

I certainly could not disagree. "But what is it that you want to write about?" I asked. "What is it that moves you? "

The policeman responded with a look of solemnity. It took only a few moments, however, for his straight lips to form the broad grin that comes with understanding. "I seek to push the world in a certain direction," he proclaimed.

Holmes shook his head. "Not in the direction your District Superintendents would have you lead them, I should imagine."

"No, Mr. Holmes. Though I do love the beauty of words, I feel less compelled to play with the aesthetics of language than to share my observations about our society. It is not an appreciation of art that I am striving to create, but rather the need for justice. Take my vision for a grandiose novel about my Burmese days. As of now, I envision it a love story. But even so, I am committed to depicting the evils of empire I witnessed over there – the racial intolerance, the cultural contempt, the disregard for rectitude – all of it responsible for my growing hatred of authoritarian rule." He clenched his fists as he delivered this last comment.

228

Dangerous waters, I thought. *Extrapolating generalities out of personal experience.* Perhaps I might direct his interests to safer ground. "Rather than writing about Burma," I said, "I am sure you can find more fitting subjects closer to home."

Blair's eyes lit up. "Don't you see, Doctor? They are one and the same. We British are quick to recognise the oppressed in foreign lands, but blind to how we treat the outcasts who walk among us right here in London – the poor, the beggars, the prostitutes."

"A bit of a stretch, don't you think?" I countered.

"Not in the least. Why, in threadbare clothes I myself have slept on the streets. And I'll have you know that I've met some noble souls out there with whom I feel most honoured to share my time."

"Like a common vagrant?" I cried, almost spilling my tea.

"More like Jack London. My intent is to write about what I see, gentlemen. Spending nights in Trafalgar Square can produce some memorable adventures, I assure you – getting arrested for drunkenness, to name but one. Soon I shall head east to Whitechapel. Maybe I'll find a kip in Limehouse Causeway, then travel north and do some begging. I may even turn to Paris."

I shook my head in disbelief. Holmes, however, was much more sympathetic. "Come now, old fellow," he said to me. "As you are well aware, much can be learned while dressed in unfamiliar robes."

He was correct, of course, as I knew from his own varied performances. Many were the cases in which he might show up as a plumber, a vicar, or even an old woman.

Blair drank more tea and put down the cup with a clatter. "And yet, gentlemen, still I hesitate. My plan is sound, but I fear that I may not be suited for such a vocation. It began at St. Cyprian's when I was a lad. I was led to believe that I could never become a member of the upper crust, and that as a result any course of action I might take would ultimately end in defeat. I earned two public-school scholarships and attended Eton, and yet those early predictions of failure are difficult to forget. What if I simply lack the talent?"

"Therein, Blair," offered Holmes, "the patient must minister to himself. You are the policeman. I can only imagine that some sort of detective work went on in the infamous parody you described. I see before me a young writer with an investigative bent. You must seek the solutions to those mysteries on your own."

The young man furrowed his brow. "I'm still unsure, Mr. Holmes. I admit that having my parody published – if only in a student magazine – did give me the confidence to go on. Yet I worry that any disparagement I suffer personally shall bring shame to my family. When we vacationed in Cornwall just two months past, I hinted to my mother of my plans. She seemed understanding. But my father is another story. He already views with scepticism my dreams of being a writer. He would be worse than sceptical were I to become the kind of writer who exposes British injustice."

Author that I am, I realised it was time to support the young man. "Though I do not share your theories," I told Blair, "I must encourage you to write if that is what you wish to do. It is always difficult at the start, and you will always have your critics. Why, Holmes himself never tires of complaining about my narratives. They ignore the complexities of his investigations, he rants. I am far too concerned with what you just called one's facility with language. Why, my good friend here might even agree with the proposition that I record his cases so that it is *my* name which is the one remembered."

Sherlock Holmes held up his hands in mock surrender. But then he leaned forward again and directed his comments at our visitor. "I have an idea which you may take or leave. But hear me out. There is a way to shield your family from any scurrilous barbs hurled at you by your critics. As Watson can attest, upon many occasions, I have employed an alias to confuse my adversaries. Just before the start of the Great War, for instance, I called myself Altamont while spying on Germans working in Harwich. And during the three years that I spent incognito travelling to places like Tibet and Mecca, I was Sigerson, a Norwegian explorer."

"Don't forget Igor Nikolayev, your Russian violinist," I reminded Holmes, recalling the murder he solved at Cloverwood House in Hampstead.

"Quite," he said. "In any case, Blair, you might try the same. Why not take on a pseudonym, a *nom de plume* – or if you prefer, a *nom de guerre*?"

Blair rubbed his chin. "I must confess that on occasion I too have entertained such a plan."

"Do you have any names in mind then?" I asked.

The policeman nodded. "There is a river not far from where I grew up in Suffolk that has always appealed to me. I like its sound – the Orwell."

"Capital!" I exclaimed. "And your first name?"

"I'm thinking of George. It is common enough, and yet it is also the name of our king."

"To me," I said, "it sounds as if you have made up your mind."

Blair flashed a smile. "I believe I have, Doctor. And thanks in great part to you and Mr. Holmes, I can even see how my police training will fit in. I have been taught to solve crimes. As a writer, I will attempt to reveal them." His voice now filled with passion. "I will describe for readers the government's criminal actions against the oppressed, criminal actions performed in the name of the people. The clues are there, hidden in the labyrinth of official language intended to defend what is defenceless. Why, in Burma, we robbed the natives of their land, sent them on their way, and called it the 'rectification of frontiers'. Such criminal action must be unmasked, or it will grow even more malign in the future."

Holmes and I exchanged glances. I believe we both were pondering where our advice might lead this young man and what effect his writings might have.

For his part, Eric Blair rose from his chair and extended his hand.

Rather than shaking it, however, Holmes turned it on its side so Blair's palm faced down, an action that Holmes performed with the policeman's other hand as well. "When you speculated earlier on how I knew you had been in Burma," Holmes said, "you neglected to mention your tattoos."

I myself had not noticed them before, but I now saw a tiny blue spot on each of the knuckles of Blair's two hands.

"To the Burmese, Watson" Holmes explained, "symbols of good fortune."

"Spot on, Mr. Holmes," said the policeman. "They're supposed to protect their wearers from British bullets."

The three of us broke into rich laughter at the prospect. "Not too popular among your colleagues, I should think," said I.

"No, indeed, Doctor." Again Blair extended his hand. "I should like to thank you both for helping me solidify my views."

I picked up my stick, and together Holmes and I walked young Blair to the front door.

"Quite an interesting fellow," Holmes observed as we watched the tall, gangling figure wander off into the cold night beneath the glow of the electric streetlamps. Cadaverous as the troubled policeman might appear, he seemed to be standing a bit taller.

Chapter V

Save for a note I received in early December, we learned no more of Eric Blair. I rang Holmes in Sussex to convey to him the policeman's final message.

"Blair thanked us again for listening to him," I told my friend, and I read into the mouthpiece verbatim the young man's final words: '*I submitted my resignation from the Imperial Police on 26 November, to take effect 1 January, 1928.*'

"The New Year is but a few weeks away, eh, Holmes? Blair will be on his own with no one to shape the time ahead but himself. From the discontent brewing within him, one can envision the dangerous future he fears – powerful images of the helplessly oppressed put upon by their mighty oppressors." I allowed myself a brief chuckle. "Sounds like Socialist clap-trap to me."

Besides the usual electronic clicks and clacks, the telephone line remained silent for a few moments; and during the interim I could well imagine Holmes contemplating my words.

"Whatever anyone has to say about it, old fellow," he opined at last, "there's a future coming all the same, such a future as only a few can contemplate. If it's the grim tomorrow that Eric Blair has suggested, many may wither in its wake. But regardless of how long the likes of you or me may dwell in it, there will be some kind of future none the less, and if we can recognise the reality in what a former policeman has already decried – the power of authority, the corruption of language, the exclusion of the weak – then you can be sure, thanks to 'George Orwell', a safer, more just road to that future will most certainly roll out before us."

Then the line went dead.

NOTES

The importance of Watson's posthumously-published manuscript cannot be overemphasized. No biographies of George Orwell mention his seminal meeting with Holmes and Watson, the meeting that helped define Orwell's future. In addition, until now no substantial reason has been offered to explain Blair's trip to see Gow at Trinity College following his return from Burma.

It is clear that Holmes's influence began early in Blair's life. As Watson has informed us, "The Adventure of the Lost Meat-Card", Blair's parody of a Holmes story, appeared in a student magazine co-edited by Blair. (It sold for 1d and is listed at the University College Library as *The Election Times No. 4. Eton Magazine. ORWELL/A/1/c Jun 3 1918 lost meat-card*!)

In 1933, six years after revealing his intentions to Holmes and Watson, Blair assumed the name of George Orwell in publishing his first full-length work, *Down and Out in Paris and London*. The book depicts Orwell's exploits among the lower classes, and early in Chapter 7 he describes reading *The Memoirs of Sherlock Holmes* in a cheap hotel in Paris. Chapter 15 presents Orwell's account of the stolen ring baked in a bun, and Chapter 23 tells of the face-powder tins containing only face-powder. The astute reader will note that the book places both of those events in Paris – not in Cambridge and Burma, as Watson had reported – but four years later Orwell would admit in Chapter 9 of *The Road to Wigan Pier* that while "*nearly all the incidents* described [in *Down and Out*] *really happened . . . they have been rearranged.*"

It is also interesting to note that Gordon Comstock, the protagonist of Orwell's novel, *Keep the Aspidistra Flying* (1936), considers *The Adventures of Sherlock Holmes* his "*favourite of all books*", citing in particular Watson's account of "The Adventure of the Speckled Band."

The novel, *Burmese Days* (published in 1934), dramatizes Orwell's experiences in Burma. Though he fictionalized the events, they remain close enough to the truth to have upset some of his former police colleagues.

Watson did not live long enough to learn of the author's achievements, but Sherlock Holmes lived well into the 1950's (in fact, outliving Orwell) and took great pride in his and Watson's role in helping guide the former policeman to becoming so prescient a social critic. Thanks to such novels as *1984* (published in 1949) and *Animal Farm* (published in 1945 with a major character named Napoleon, as Blair had predicted to Holmes), George Orwell is now regarded as one of the most influential authors of the twentieth century.

In 1976, decades after Orwell's death, a still angry Andrew Gow remembered the young Eric Blair as "*slacking*" and "*wasting time*". (See Bernard Crick's biography, *George Orwell: A Life*, p. 63.) In more recent years, Gow's cold and reticent nature, as well as his reported pro-Soviet political views, not only has led to speculation that he may have been the "handler" at Cambridge for the Soviet spies Philby, Burgess, Maclean, and Blunt, but also has raised sinister questions surrounding the nature of Gow's visit to the hospitalized Orwell a short time prior to the writer's death. Orwell was said by some to be recuperating. Not long after Gow had arrived, Orwell was dead. To this day, critics continue to question the motives of Orwell's former tutor, which remain very much a mystery – a mystery whose possible origins George Orwell himself would certainly have understood. For more information on the recent speculation concerning Gow, see:

https://www.the-tls.co.uk/articles/old-school-ties/

The Unpleasant Affair
in Clipstone Street
by David Marcum

With each passing year, I'm able to look back and see connections that would have escaped me while in the midst of events. When I assisted my friend Sherlock Holmes on his notable investigations, it was only by way of his explanations – through his awareness of the bigger picture – that I was usually able to keep up with what was happening. In addition to his notable gift of being able to observe what others only saw, he had also cultivated a rare collection of friends and associates, and sometimes even enemies, who had either been able to instruct him in his youth as he prepared for his most unique profession, or to provide an important fact here or there in the course of an inquiry. His cases, and the individuals associated with them, formed threads in something of a "Great Tapestry". Some were self-contained and tied off neatly, while others twisted throughout the overall design, initially appearing for a moment, calling for attention before being subsumed back into the greater pattern, only to reappear quite far away – sometimes with no more than a quick bow or passing appearance, and others with much more serious and even tragic results . . . .

Our return journey from Ewelme had been something between quite tedious and rather unpleasant, first by way of an open carriage ride through the cold October mist, and then on a series of local trains. It could have been worse, I supposed, as we just made it into a small station in time to catch the departing train for the last leg into London. Holmes wouldn't have been happy to tarry any longer than necessary while waiting for the next train to arrive.

A couple of days before, a terse wire from one of his old school chums had resulted in Holmes's journey from Sussex up to London, where I joined him, before we continued together to that normally lovely part of Oxfordshire. The discovery of a hoard of Roman coins had resulted in an assault – a mysterious robed figure had violently stolen the collection and fled to Didcot. Holmes had initially been intrigued, but after reaching his solution following an examination of a nearby chalk pit and then a short interview with the wife of the man who managed the local almshouses, the culprit was quickly revealed, with the solution tawdry and seamy and embarrassing all at once. All told, Holmes's investigation, carried out with his typical skill, insight, and efficiency, had been remunerative and reputation-enhancing – none of which he needed at that age.

Because of the initial description of that problem, I had expected that we would be gone longer. Instead, it almost seemed that we had spent more time traveling there than what was required for the actual investigation. I wouldn't have minded rusticating in the countryside for a day or so, in spite of the autumn weather, but I could see that Holmes was only interested in leaving as fast as possible. It was only as we were stepping out of the inn where we had retrieved our bags that the local constable had stopped us, announcing that the thief had just been murdered – poisoned in his cell – and the cache of coins taken once again. I think that the solution, when it came, surprised even Holmes, and had left us both in a bitter mood – me with the realization that I'd never be able to share the truth of this adventure, and Holmes with a vast disappointment in his old school friend.

Upon our return to the capital, Holmes, having packed for several days, agreed with my invitation to stay at my Queen Anne Street home. Although my housekeeper was surprised to see us, as I had given the impression that we might be gone for a while, she was able to pull together a rather fine evening meal. Holmes was quiet for much of the evening, and soon after we ate he said good night and retired to his room, carrying with him a borrowed volume relating the history of the Romans in Britain. I read for a while before closing my own book, a recently published narrative regarding our friend Poirot's investigation concerning a murder on *Le Train Bleu* which had occurred the previous year. I turned down the gas and then made my way upstairs. As I grew older, I found that it was too easy to stay up late every night.

Back in the days when Holmes and I had shared lodgings in Baker Street, it was normal that he would receive unexpected visitors at all hours. I cannot count the dramatic entrances that ranged from the simply intriguing to the truly threatening, the initially innocent to the most portentous. Much less frequent were those occasions when a caller sought my assistance in some matter.

Thus, it was still a surprise, even after all those years that I'd been living in Queen Anne Street – twenty-six years by then, and several years longer than I'd spent in Baker Street – when a pounding at the street door sometime in the night resulted in the housekeeper being knocked up, causing her to climb the stairs to my room.

I'd already been awakened by the noise at the door and had glanced at my clock with a groan to determine that the hour had just reached six, meaning that I'd at least had more hours of sleep than I'd thought. For some reason in my half-wakened state, I'd expected that the housekeeper would stop at Holmes's bedroom, assuming that this was some sort of request for his attention. Even if that were the case, I would also soon be up and involved, regardless of the reason, but I certainly didn't anticipate that I would be requested first, or what followed afterwards.

With a solid knock upon my own door, I was informed that there was a man downstairs who wished for me to go with him, requiring my services as a doctor. I acknowledged this with something that resembled words. Raising my eyebrows to the empty room, I threw back the covers and looked out of my bedroom window. From that vantage, I could see that some of the neighbors were also already up, as evidenced by faint light thrown from their various windows. It was just enough to illuminate the ice that delicately limned the branches of the plane tree that grew in the bare little yard behind my house. An unseasonable plunge in the temperature had created a freezing mist, coating the surface with a thin rime of ice that resembled fairy tracery.

I could feel the cold through the glass, and the idea of going out was quite unpleasant. Still, I felt the obligation of my profession resting upon me and, having quickly made myself ready, I descended, stopping only to retrieve my medical bag. There was no sign of Holmes, so apparently he had wisely remained asleep. I continued on to the front door, where I found a tall man anxiously awaiting me, his hand on the door knob as if he were ready to bolt at the second of my arrival. "Doctor," he said, with a rather high-pitched whisper. "We need your help."

"Certainly. What's the problem?"

"It's our daughter, sir. She's taken sick in the night."

I had pulled on my coat during this short conversation and then reached for my hat and stick. Gesturing that he proceed me, I asked, "How old is she?"

I turned back to lock the door while he replied. "She'll be seven early next year."

There was no sign of a waiting conveyance, leading me to understand that my caller was from the local neighborhood. We set off down the street, stepping carefully along the slick pavement. "What are her symptoms?"

He described a fairly common set of gastronomical complaints that had been spreading throughout the city for a few weeks. His wording was rather vague, in the way that some laymen use when describing the less pleasant aspects of an ill human body. In the case of his daughter, it sounded as if her condition might be a bit more severe than normal and that she could be dehydrated, and I indicated that he was wise to have sought my help.

Along the way, he introduced himself as Tom Birch. I could see that he looked to be around thirty years of age. He informed me that he and his wife were caretakers at the house of a Mrs. Waltham, recently deceased. Birch's father had been one of the old woman's servants years earlier, when the lady's husband was still alive and the household had been much more vital. More recently, she'd spent her widowhood living quietly with only Birch and his wife Ivy to care for her. The Birch family consisted of just the father, mother, and one daughter, and they had their own apartment in the lower level of the house. When the old lady had died a month or so earlier, her attorney had asked Birch and his wife to stay on and look after the place until the estate could be settled, as there was some difficult in locating the heirs.

We walked farther than I would have expected, and it crossed my mind that in that neighborhood there were certainly other doctors much closer to where the Birch family lived. Why did he seek me out? I asked myself, but I kept those thoughts to myself. We hurried along Cavendish Street, and then for a short time north by way of Great Titchfield Street to Clipstone Street, where Birch led me into a mews, and so around to a set of steps leading down into the lower levels of one of the buildings that we had just passed. At the bottom was a solid-looking door with a small window at eye level, obscured by a curtain. The door was standing ajar. "That's not right," Birch muttered, pushing his way in. I followed.

Almost immediately we were in a little hallway, quite dark. There was a damp smell, as if laundry had been done recently and floors had been mopped. I sensed that my guide was moving deeper into the building, and I tentatively followed. Beyond him, I heard a door open, and then a light appeared ahead and to our right. Birch came to a sudden stop, and I barely avoided running into him. I was unable to see past him, but I heard a woman's voice. "Tom," she said. "He took her!"

238

Birch sagged and leaned a shoulder against the wall, allowing me to see beyond him. The hallway had several closed doors, and thus my eyes were drawn to the source of the light, a doorway that opened into what appeared – from my narrow view – to be a sitting room and kitchen. It was dimly lit, but I could see that there was very little taking up the space – not much furniture, and counter-tops that held only a few basic implements – a teapot and a few cups.

A woman was standing just outside the door, highlighted by the lamplight from within room. Setting down my bag, I laid a hand on Birch's shoulder, steadying his frame, and then stepping around him to face the woman.

"Mrs. Birch?" I said. "My name is Dr. Watson. Who has been taken? Your daughter?"

In the weak light I could see that she seemed to be around the same age as her husband – assuming that this was, in fact, Mrs. Birch. However, she seemed to acknowledge my statement, as she nodded. "Her name is Erin."

"And who took her?"

Her features tightened as she seemed to be trying not to cry. She covered her face and turned away. Apparently she had kept herself strong long enough for her husband to return, but now whatever had happened was overwhelming her. I sensed Tom Birch step up behind me. "Michael Whaley," he said. "It must be him – I don't know who else it could be."

The name sounded vaguely familiar, although I couldn't place him. Time enough to think of that later. I looked from one of them to the other, each showing a marked level of fear. "She has been kidnapped?" I clarified.

Birch nodded. "It seems so."

"But why?" I asked. "It sounds as if you know this man. What could he hope to accomplish?"

Birch looked at me. "You don't know Michael?" He ran a hand over his face and shut his eyes for a long moment. I shook my head, declining to explain that the name had triggered some vague sense of awareness. Then Birch continued. "It would be best, Doctor, for us to summon your friend, Mr. Holmes. We can explain it then."

"You know Holmes?"

"In a sense. Can you send him a message? Asking him to come up from Sussex?"

I considered arguing with him first. I wanted to press him for details, if only to satisfy my own curiosity. A part of me nearly said that we should summon a constable immediately, but I had known

Holmes long enough by that point to realize that no one would be better able to help these people than my friend.

"There's no need for that," I said, and Birch immediately frowned, but I raised a placating hand. "He's in London now – staying with me. Are you on the telephone?" Birch looked toward his wife, who lowered her hands and shook her head sadly, so I added, "I'll go and fetch him immediately."

Mrs. Birch shook her head. "Please, no, Doctor. Stay. You've long been associated with Mr. Holmes – perhaps you can think of something while we wait for him to arrive."

"I can deliver a note," added her husband, eagerly. "It won't take long at all."

I could think of better alternatives, but I frowned and nodded.

After urging them to move into the room with the light, I followed and saw that it was indeed a combination sitting room and kitchen, with chairs and a sofa placed in the area behind the door, and a dining table closer to the utilitarian countertop. There were unlit gaslight brackets set over the fireplace, and the room was instead illuminated by a lantern sitting on the table and a cheery little coal fire in the grate, its mood contrasting the tragedy that I had just entered. I could see that the room would always be rather dark, being mostly below ground level, with only a couple of small windows high on a far wall over the kitchen area. Near the door where we'd had entered were another couple of doors that opened into darkened chambers that appeared to be bedrooms.

I stepped to the kitchen counter, where I set my bag. I glanced around the room while I searched through it for one of the pads that I always carried, and then wrote a quick note, choosing my words carefully and succinctly. As I wrote, it occurred to me to see if there was a possible alternative to sending the message with Birch. When I finished, I turned and, to their surprise, told them that I'd be back in just a moment. I returned to the mews and walked briskly back out to Clipstone Street, lined on all sides by grim brick buildings, and where it was only slightly less dark than the Birch's doorway. The icy mist hung in the air without a hint of breeze, and I gave a shiver as it slipped between my neck and scarf. My breath formed and hung in the freezing air before me as stood on the street, looking left and right.

If there had been one of the pay telephones somewhere on the street, I would have called Queen Anne Street, but as expected, there wasn't, and I didn't know how far I'd have to walk before spotting one. Instead I was looking for a certain type of person – although the likelihood of finding such a one at that hour was uncertain at best. It had been years since Holmes had made use of those lads and lasses that he called his Baker Street Irregulars – and yet I didn't see why I couldn't do something similar. It had been nearly ten years since the war ended, and London had changed incredibly in that time, but one still occasionally saw those same rootless children of the type that Holmes had first started recruiting in the 1870's, when he'd lived in Montague Street and had decided to become a consulting detective. All of those original assistants had long since grown to adulthood and were now approaching old age. Even some of their children had served as Holmes's next generation of Irregulars before he left London in 1903. Yet, long after that he'd still made use of them, as his "retirement" was a rather misleading term, and he continued to carry out investigations regularly in those years leading to the war. But after the peace had been signed, he truly had retired, taking only occasional cases, such as the one that had led us to Ewelme the day before.

There was no one to be seen, and I kept walking, turning into Great Titchfield Street and thinking that this might not be the neighborhood or time of night to spot a potential messenger. I could very well end up going as far as Queen Anne Street and fetching Holmes myself before I was through. Yet I was fortunate that in just a moment, I saw a boy of ten or twelve looking cautiously toward me from out of one the small alleys to the west. I raised an arm and approached this early-riser (or possible night owl) slowly, with the wry feeling that I was doing so in the same slow manner that one uses when trying to gain the trust of a stray dog. The boy made no move to turn away, and listened intelligently as I explained what I needed – without mentioning Holmes's name. I didn't know if he would recognize it, but if he did, I didn't have time to convince him that Holmes would truly be the recipient of the message.

I dropped the note and a coin in the boy's hands and sent him on his way, confident that it would be in my housekeeper's possession in mere minutes, and then into Holmes's hands soon after. Then I made my way back to the Birch house and through the mews, down the steps, and to the entryway. Once my eyes had readjusted to the darkness, I took a moment to look at the heavy door, but there was no sign of forced entry. Inside the dim apartment, I found Birch and his wife sitting at the table, heads leaned toward one another. Mrs. Birch had been whispering, but she stopped when I entered the room. I had the sudden sense that she seemed uncertain as to what could be said in front of me.

241

"Did you send the message?" asked her husband.

"I did. I found a lad to deliver it."

"I could have taken it," he continued, almost sullenly. Mrs. Birch laid a hand on his arm.

"Better that you stay here with your wife," I said. "Holmes should be here shortly. While we wait, Mrs. Birch, can you tell me what happened?"

She closed her eyes, and Birch spoke instead. "We should . . . we should wait for Mr. Holmes, I think. And just tell it once. No offense intended, Doctor."

I nodded, with none taken. There was silence for a moment, and I listened to the great house stacked above us, but heard nothing. Only the crackle of the coal in the fireplace broke the otherwise absolute silence. Even noises from the street were non-existent – not surprising at this hour, and on such a quiet byway.

I tried to see what I could by observing my hosts, but the light didn't reveal much more than what I already knew – a couple around thirty years of age, he rather brawny, and she petite and blonde. Her hair would probably have an almost-white cast in bright light – not the gray of premature old age, but rather that of platinum, with a shine that would definitely attract second glances. Her face was set in a frown – no surprise for someone involved in such a matter, but I could tell that such an expression came naturally to her, and wasn't simply caused by the current tragic events.

"May I see your daughter's room?" I asked abruptly.

"Why?" asked Mrs. Birch sharply, as if yanked back from wherever her thoughts had led her.

"To get a sense of her. When Holmes and I find her, she may need to trust us immediately. Knowing something of her likes and dislikes – a favorite doll, perhaps – may help win her over." It sounded feeble saying it aloud, but the woman nodded, took her hand from her husband's arm, and rose, leading me to one of the side doors after lifting the lantern from the table.

"Would you mind lighting the gas?" I asked Birch as I turned to follow. "For when Mr. Holmes arrives?"

Birch shook his head. "We generally do without. Ivy gets headaches from it."

I let that statement stand, considering whether to request that they light another lantern, but not wanting to disrupt what was happening, and wondering why the strong kerosene smell that currently hung about the lantern didn't also cause headaches. Mrs. Birch held the lantern just across the threshold to the bedroom, allowing me to see inside just a bit, but also blocking my way. When I made to move past her, she said, "I've heard of Mr. Holmes and his methods. Perhaps we should wait for him to go in – to see if there's any kind of clue. After all, Michael went in there in order to take Erin."

I hadn't been told that fact, but I nodded, although not necessarily agreeing with her reasoning. I could see a rumpled bed and some clothing on the floor nearby. The rest of the room was in darkness. I stepped back, and then Mrs. Birch reached around me and pulled the door solidly shut.

We returned to the table. I surreptitiously observed Mrs. Birch to adjudicate the state of her nerves, deciding that no offer of a sedative was required. They were both tense, but Tom Birch seemed to have turned inward, while his wife exhibited a brittleness that would bear watching. The silence between us grew, and I found myself quite curious about Birch's apparent knowledge of Holmes, and wondered again where I'd heard of Michael Whaley. I tried several times to recall something about him, but it wouldn't come to me.

There were any number of questions that I wanted to ask, but each seemed as if it would quickly lead back to whatever it was something that should best be told to Holmes first. Finally, however, I thought to quiz them more about the arrangements of the household.

"How long did you serve Mrs. Waltham?"

Birch's eyes took on a grateful look, as if this topic could help fill the awkward silence, and he had an answer to this question. As he spoke, his wife began to twist a handkerchief in her hands.

"About seven years," said Birch. "My father was her driver long ago, and my mother her companion upstairs. I grew up here – in these very rooms. Thirteen years ago – back in 1915 – Mr. Waltham passed suddenly. A terrible stroke they said it was, and the life seemed to go out of his wife. She released all of the servants and became a hermit. After that, my parents left to find another position – although they weren't nearly as happy as when they'd lived here. They were both killed nine years ago, in a rail accident.

"I was seventeen in 1915 when Mr. Waltham died, and long gone by then – serving in France. Lied about my age. After I came back, I found work at a hotel in Upper George Street. That's where Ivy and I met, a couple of years later when she started there as a maid." He reached over and squeezed the back of his wife's hand. She raised her eyes to his, but then looked away once again.

"Not long after, I heard from a grocer friend that Mrs. Waltham was in sad shape, living here like a hermit. I went to check on her, and found that it was worse than I'd heard. Her husband's death had fairly broken her. I started to look in more often, and doing little odd jobs around the place when I had time – repairing leaks, and cleaning the place where I could. It wasn't long before she perked up and offered me a position as caretaker, for lack of anything better to call it. With this opportunity, Ivy and I had a chance to marry, and then Erin came along."

"And you've lived here since then," I asked, and then, with possibly with less tact than I should have shown, I added "Below stairs, while Mrs. Waltham occupied all the floors above, alone?"

Birch looked at me without comment, and his wife replied for him. "She offered to let us have rooms upstairs, but we . . . we didn't want to be seen to be taking advantage." She glanced at her husband. "And this was where Tom was raised – here in the servants' quarters. It seemed right to stay down here."

"After she died," continued her husband, "her lawyer asked if we could stay on until things were settled. He didn't want the place standing empty, and he believes that it will be quite a bit of time before he can locate an heir. There were no children, you see . . . ."

His voice drifted off, and I felt as if I should do more to keep the conversation moving forward, but the awkward silence returned, and every question that occurred to me related to the couple's missing child and the involvement of the mysterious Michael Whaley. Mrs. Birch rose and made some tea, which we all drank in silence. I considered how long it would take for Holmes to receive my message, and then cross the distance from Queen Anne Street to Clipstone Street. Not long – assuming that I had chosen wisely when hiring my unknown messenger. Fortunately, it was only a few more uncomfortable moments before we heard the outside door open, and then footsteps along the dark corridor, stopping outside the living quarters where we waited. My directions had led my friend to this place. What would happen next?

Birch stood. "Mr. Holmes?" he said, as a tall thin shadow appeared in the doorway. Even as Birch spoke, his wife stood and pushed past him.

"It's Michael Whaley," she breathed. "He took our daughter."

Holmes stepped into the dim light, his face was grim, his mouth a tight straight line, and a deep *V* between his brows. He walked closer, nodded to Mrs. Birch, and pulled out a chair. He sat on the edge, leaning forward, concentrating intently – so different from how he sometimes listened to a client's story during those long-ago days in our Baker Street sitting room, where he would settle back with his eyes closed, fully engaged but seeing everything play out within his mind. He motioned and the couple sat back down. "Are you certain that it was him?" he asked.

Both nodded, and Mrs. Birch hurriedly said, "Not long after Tom went to fetch the doctor, I heard a noise at the door. It seemed too soon for him to have gone to Queen Anne Street and back, so I thought that he might have forgotten something. But it wasn't Tom – it was Michael. I gave a little cry, and he took a step toward me. I feared what he might do, but then Erin coughed in the other room. He stopped and smiled, and then turned that way. I knew then what he was going to do, and I ran at him, but he pushed me away, and before I could get up, he was back with her, bundled in his arms. She didn't wake up – she's feeling too poorly, I suppose. He told me to remain quiet, or that he would hurt her. How could he threaten that? A child – ? He . . . he left then, and . . . and I didn't know what to do. I just stood there, wanting to move, and yet afraid that I might anger him, or that he would hurt her if I chased him and he started to run, and maybe tripped and fell on top of her. And I needed to tell Tom, but . . . ." She broke off and put the twisted handkerchief up to her eyes.

Her husband spoke. "He must have been watching, and he must have known when I stepped out." He leaned forward. "What can we do?"

His tone implied that since Holmes had now arrived, all would be well. In truth, in the years that I've known Sherlock Holmes, I've seen that he is one of the most capable people that I've ever met. And yet, I knew that in spite of his many gifts and abilities, both naturally occurring and rigorously trained, he was capable of failure. I recalled the times that we had been asked to find a taken child – instances that sometimes ended in tragedy, such as the affair of the Salisbury bug-hole, and also in the much grimmer Amersham Substitution. Yet there had been triumphs as well – for instance, the shocking revelations concerning the Dunblane Bodach came to mind. But from what I had already seen, this matter was quite different.

Holmes looked at Birch. "I remember you from the old days, Tom. How did you know Michael?"

The man started to speak, apparently surprised, but found himself at a loss for words. It was his wife who answered.

"I was the one who knew Michael. During the war. Later, he would sometimes . . . he would come around to see me – after Tom and I married. He – " She looked at her husband. "He insisted that Erin was his child."

I glanced at Tom Birch, but he showed no reaction, keeping his eyes forward and onto the tabletop.

I thought that Holmes might ask her if it was true – such delicate subjects had never prevented him from doing so before, and any knowledge about the motivations of this Whaley fellow would certainly be welcome. Yet even as I pondered this, Holmes appeared to have already heard enough. Perhaps my short note had given him enough perspective before he even arrived.

He rose abruptly, causing Mrs. Birch to give a slight and surprised gasp. Then he set about examining the room, crossing this way and that, but without bothering to bend over, or drop to his knees and crawl, as he had done so often in the past. Then he returned to the table and took the lantern, expanding his investigation into Erin's bedroom. Mrs. Birch rose then, as if she meant to join him, but I raised a hand. I thought that she might argue the point – an angry look flashed across her face – but then she held her place.

I stood then and I moved over to the other side of the room, near the fireplace, as if to stay out of Holmes's way. Except for Holmes's own movements, there was silence.

Without comment, Holmes reappeared out of the girl's bedroom and then abruptly opened the door to the hallway. He paused for a few seconds as if listening, and then took the lantern with him, leaving us in darkness only opposed by the dim light from the windows and the red glow from the fireplace. I tried to imagine a child being raised in such a dark chamber. Birch said that he'd been brought up here, but somehow it seemed worse to imagine a young girl in these circumstances.

From my position somewhat behind the door, I couldn't see Holmes's actions, but I could tell by the movement of the lantern light that he'd turned away from the outside door and deeper into the basement. He was only gone for a moment or two in that direction before swiftly walking back down the hall and then outside. He was gone longer before returning, and during that time, none of us that dark room spoke. However, I could sense some sort of tension arising between the couple, as if Mrs. Birch wished for her husband to do something. Yet he simply stood, pondering his own thoughts and looking toward the floor. Finally Holmes returned, leaving the door to the hallway open and replacing the lantern on the table. Everyone remained standing.

Holmes was shaking his head. "I found where he stood outside, watching this house." The Birch's glanced at one another, seemingly surprised. "The signs indicate that he was out there for several hours – likely since sunset. There's no indication of where the trail leads when he and your daughter departed. We cannot trace him physically, but instead will rely on what we can learn of his associates and habits." He took a step closer, his expression most sincere. "We will find your child."

Birch cleared his throat and asked, "How can I help? Shall I go with you?" His wife turned her head sharply toward him and frowned.

"No. Stay here. Await any messages that Matthew might send. I'll locate someone to remain nearby so that you can send word if you hear something." He glanced at the distraught mother, and then looked at me. "Watson, I'll need your help."

"Of course." I stood and, with a nod to the Birchs, walked over to the counter to retrieve my bag and then quickly followed Holmes outside. He led me briskly back along Clipstone Street, seemingly heading toward my home and practice. He was silent and set a pace that would have made conversation difficult, even if he was in the mood. I glanced from side to side, wondering if anyone was observing us. However, even though the first hint of false dawn was showing in the east, the icy mist perhaps a bit more pervasive, and there was no one visible on the street besides the two of us. We had just rounded the corner when he suddenly paused. "Slip back and watch the entrance to the mews," he said softly. "See if anyone enters or leaves." He reached for my bag. "I'll hold this for you. I'm going to use the telephone at the synagogue in Great Portland Street." He smiled. "I wonder if Rabbi Liebman still arrives with the sunrise."

I made my way back to where I could watch the entrance to the mews from an areaway across the street, hoping that no one had slipped in or out during the short time we were away. I stood there for ten or fifteen minutes, aware at some point that the occupants of the house behind me seemed to be waking up, and wondering what I would tell them should I be asked why I was trespassing ever so slightly upon their property. My concern was negated when I saw a man in a suit walk into the block and slip into a similar hiding place a few doors closer to the old house where we had interviewed Mr. and Mrs. Birch. At that point, I heard a distinct whistle. Recognizing it as one of the long-established ways that Holmes and I communicated, I left my hiding place and joined him in the next street.

He handed back my bag and told me that the old rabbi had been glad to let him in, and sent greetings to me as well. I knew that the old man was fond both of us – Holmes more than me, for I had only untied the rabbi after Holmes discovered his whereabouts once long ago, while my friend had been responsible for taking down two of the captors to my one in the brawl beforehand.

We had to walk to Cavendish Square before finding a cab at that time of morning, pausing along the way to drop off my bag in Queen Anne Street. When we were settled inside, Holmes directed the driver to take us to an address in Chelsea.

"Latham was at home," Holmes said, referring to a high-ranking government agent with whom we'd worked closely during the war. "He answered himself – no surprise there. It was he who sent the agent to watch the house while we're away."

"I wonder that the Birches let us leave," I said. "Considering the effort to get us both there and into that spider's web."

"They didn't have much choice – neither of us seemed inclined to step together into the trap, and once they had us, they seemed most unwilling to take any additional steps to prevent us from leaving. I suspect that there is more to this than simply luring us into an otherwise abandoned house."

"I wonder what the original plan was. They clearly expected that I was to summon you from Sussex, and that it would have taken hours for you to arrive. They were surprised to hear that you were just a few blocks away – although they took care not to show it."

"I thought that after you summoned me, you might have been locked up when I arrived." He didn't add, "Or worse."

"I thought so too – I even gave them the chance, offering to look in the bedroom – but Mrs. Birch stopped me, saying that you should examine it first for clues."

"If they had locked you in there," said Holmes, " – assuming they didn't knock you unconscious or kill you – then you would have made noise which would have made it harder to incapacitate me, or they would have had to open the door to put me in with you. It was apparently easier to simply wait and trick us both into entering that windowless room – which I doubt ever was actually a bedroom – where they could then slam the door shut and lock it behind us. I appreciated that you didn't join me in there."

"I wonder that they didn't try to force me," I said.

"Perhaps they saw that you're armed."

I felt the weight of my service revolver. "I never leave without it."

"Still."

"Always." I shifted in my seat. "I had seen that new lock on the supposed bedroom door," I replied. "On the sitting room side. If there had actually been any signs of a child truly living in that grim basement, then I would have suspected they were cruelly shutting her up in that windowless chamber. When I heard that they wished for you to join us, I began to suspect a trap." I described what I'd found when I'd first arrived at the basement – all the signs that negated the couples' story of truly living there, and how rehearsed and awkward their actions had seemed. I particularly remarked how Birch had almost seemed to expect the news about the kidnapping before he heard it from his wife upon our arrival. "I assume that my note was clear enough?"

"Indeed. Your oblique reference to the Eastcote House matter was more than effective."

When I'd first entered the Birch's chambers, I had been struck how unlivable it appeared. The odor of recently washed clothes and mopping wasn't enough to cover the overall scent of abandonment about the place. And while the sitting room itself was clean enough on the surface, there was evidence in places – the back of the counter, for instance, where I'd stood to write my note – that showed indications of long-accumulated grime. That, and the lack of furniture and other accumulated possessions that one would expect to see, made it quite apparent that these people didn't truly live there, and if they were lying about that, then there were likely other lies as well. In my note, I had requested that Holmes come 'round at once, and to leave a note for Mrs. Eastcote that I would be unavailable. That reference, to a case that had occurred in Wrexham in the early eighties involving both of us being lured into a mine that was ready to collapse, had been enough for him to understand my warning.

"The bedroom – " I said. "Had it ever been occupied by a child?"

"Not at all. The bed had been slept in, but the form doing so was over six feet in height. It's probably where Birch has been sleeping."

"Not with his wife, then? Are they even married?"

"It's likely but unconfirmed. They were comfortable with one another, even if the situation itself was causing them tension. In any case, there was no sign of an actual child having been in that room.

A few children's clothes had been piled beside the bed, but there was dust on them, and the same for an old rag doll lying nearby."

"So it was never meant to stand up to a real test," I said. "Just enough to look like a child's bedroom so that we would enter, and then the door would slam shut behind us."

"But I believe that there was some validity to the items, nevertheless," said Holmes. "Several of the pieces of clothing had 'E.B.' marked inside them, and the name 'Erin' was written on the bottom of the doll's shoe. The doll itself seemed to have been treated with a bit more respect."

"After they had locked us in – assuming we'd both willingly entered that room – what then? Would they have left us there to starve, on the assumption that we couldn't exit? Were they considering burning down the house around us? Did they plan to let some kind of poison gas under the door to asphyxiate us? Was there someone else in the house – upstairs – waiting to rush in and club us? I listened while we waited, but heard no indications."

"All good questions, Watson. There were a number of footprints that seemed to belong to Birch in the hallway dust, leading in and out of that sitting room and back to a closed door at the rear of the hall. While they were recent, there was no way to ascertain that they were fresh. That closed door was wider than the others on either side of it, and it certainly went upstairs to the main part of the house. I didn't hear anyone waiting on the other side, but just in case, I used one of my picks and quickly locked it before making sure the other rooms nearby were empty – all had been used in the past for storage, but are now long empty." He frowned. "It's likely that no one else was there. If it was assumed that I was still in Sussex – and no one had bothered to ascertain this ahead of time – other people may have meant to be there later when I arrived. Or this may be a little plot that the Birches have cooked up on their own."

"It certainly seemed to surprise them terribly when you came back after your search and announced that someone had been watching the house from outside."

"The merest moonshine. I knew that they feared that I'd walk in and dramatically denounce them – how could anyone not? There was no sign that anyone actually lived there – no clothing, no food. The rest of the basement hadn't even been cleaned. Maybe there wasn't any time to worry about being caught out – I'd arrived too soon, and we didn't cheerfully walk together into the trap.

"I wonder," he continued, "how they would have reacted if I had given away what we'd seen? Denial? More false tears from the lady? Some hastily fabricated alternative? Instead, I agreed with their claims, and elaborated upon them with a tale of a watching man. They must think me a doddering fool."

"I expect not. But you've certainly put them off-balance." I glanced at him. "I take it that you know them?"

"I know Birch – he was an Irregular once, but only for a month or so, when he was in his mid-teens during the war.

"He said that he fought in France."

"I have no reason to doubt it. When he worked for me, it was still early days – late 1914, I think. He didn't do very much, or last very long. You'll recall that there were always some that were like that – Irregulars recruited, never main players on the stage, only to drift away. What else did he tell you?"

I related what the two of them had shared with me sitting around the table. "Some of that may be true," judged Holmes. "The parts about Birch's parents, and Mrs. Waltham's history. He may have even worked for her for a time – but they certainly haven't been living there for years as they said. More likely when this plan was being concocted – whatever it turns out to be – they needed an empty house, and Birch remembered this one from his past association with it."

"And Michael Whaley?" I said. "He must have been an Irregular then, too. The name sounded familiar, but I can't place him."

Holmes pinched his nose as if he had an unpleasant headache, giving me a short biographical *précis* of the fellow in question.

"He was born in 1898 and raised in Lambeth," he said, as if reading from a document that only he could see. "Both his parents were alive, but he had little contact with them, and he was in and out of judiciary detention for various minor offenses throughout his formative years. Yet overall he never caused much trouble. Although I had moved to Sussex by the time he came of age, I still maintained my London network, as it continued to be most useful as I carried out those various tasks requested of me by Mycroft in the days and years leading to the war. Michael was a part of that little informal organization, still functioning in many important ways like the Irregulars of old.

"Having bought the lease to 221 Baker Street from Mrs. Hudson several years before, it was still known as a location where I could be reached if needed. As you know, I stayed there on occasion when I was in London, and it was during some small crisis, that I was introduced to Michael. He was just seven or eight then, and brought to Baker Street by one of the other Irregulars.

"Over the years, he was of some use, and I always found him trustworthy. But there came a time when something changed. I was following up on a little matter for Mycroft, and a few of the Irregulars had been sent to trail after a man named Lyons when he carried a stolen document from London to Reading – simple enough. While he was away, Michael's mother was struck by a carriage and killed in Berners Street. His father had died by then, and his older brother, his only sibling, had run away to sea a year or so before, so there was no one else left to him. He didn't find out about the tragedy until he returned to the city, having first presented himself at one of my hidey holes where I was staying in order to make his report. He left with a few shillings in his pocket for a job well done. But when he arrived home, he learned the terrible news . . . .

"After that, something in him changed. I still used him when I needed that type of help, and he was always one of the brighter lads, asking questions about what I was doing – my methods, and the reasons for this-or-that assignment – but there was now a . . . a slyness about him. A darkness, as if he had acquired just the faintest hints of contempt for those things on the right side of that line that divides and defines legalities. I didn't realize it, but he was already being courted, so to speak, by some within the Kyle Gang. I only learned the truth when he was watching a witness named Cosford at my direction, in order to protect him, and he and his new friends sold Cosford's location to the man who was seeking him. I was able to pull the fat from the fire before Cosford was killed, but I knew then that my trust in Michael was at an end. Of course, withdrawal of my support only served to send him further into the embrace of the gang.

"I followed his progress from a distance, and that of the gang as well, but neither ever amounted to much. The Kyle Gang, still named that even though Kyle himself was killed by falling into a drain in 1909 while running from a dog, have tried to maintain themselves as a separate organization, never subsumed into the bigger organizations that pervade London, but in actuality they've never been anything but foot-soldiers for some of the more successful and better-run groups.

"One would have thought that a lad like Michael would have used his gifts to rise within the gang, providing it with a bit more success than it had over the years, but there was never any sign that he was more than a second-class lieutenant, doing the bidding of others who had no true vision or ambition – or so I thought. As the years passed, in spite of their public ineffectuality, they somehow – suddenly and right under everyone's noses – became the controlling force for a narrowly defined smuggling ring, specializing in certain rather rare French liqueurs. In spite of their sudden success, I still could detect no signs that Michael was adding anything of value to the gang's growing reputation.

"As the war approached, and my time was directed elsewhere, my activities in London diminished greatly. After 1912, when I left for the United States for my extended tour as that rogue 'Altamont', I lost track of a number of people, including Michael. I'll admit to having given him no thought for years, until his name surfaced in connection with a more serious crime. In 1921, he was one of the birds who slipped away following the Rothsay Street raid in Bermondsey, in which a great haul of smuggled goods was recovered. You'll recall that I was consulted regarding locating the cache, but I wasn't actually in attendance when the police invaded the smugglers' warehouse, as I was involved at the time with two other affairs of greater interest: The Brakebill Endowment, and that of the five Russian grandmothers."

I recalled the latter, and the ridiculous trail that was laid down for us both to follow through the neighborhoods of Hackney, but I had no memory of the former, and admitted as much. "You had other matters to attend to at the time," he said, explaining simply that the affair involved a message carved into a blackened mantelpiece of ages past.

"The raid on the smugglers' lair should have passed as routine," continued Holmes, "except that one of the Kyle Gang's lieutenants, a bruiser named Haddenham, cracked the skull of a policeman – most likely by accident. He was always a clumsy and lumbering brute. Whaley, in a case of split-second misplaced loyalty, threw himself into the fray. Some thought it was to help Haddenham escape, but I suspect it was because he wanted to injure an officer. Nevertheless, he was recognized in the process. He then fled himself, successfully escaping to parts unknown. The policeman lived, but has never fully recovered, and the law's vengeance was quick to declare that Whaley would certainly pay the penalty when he was eventually caught.

"And caught he was," Holmes noted. "He was quickly arrested a month later after he slipped back into London. He was sentenced to ten years, but was released after five. That was two years ago. He came to Sussex and looked me up. He truly seemed to have learned his lesson, and through some of my contacts, I was able to arrange that he find a job working for a little known government office in a house off the King's Road in Chelsea. I understand that in the intervening couple of years, he's gained a great deal of trust, and been quite useful on occasion as well. He lives not too far west of there, in that tangle of streets near the Ebury Bridge and the Grosvenor Canal."

That was the area that we had entered as Holmes finished his story, and the cab pulled smoothly to a stop in front of No. 85 Alderney Street, a narrow but rather handsome little structure of three stories. We parked behind a waiting police car and a man in a suit who was standing beside it, while two others – a shorter man also in a suit and the other in a constable's uniform, were just stepping out of the building. The second constable joined the first. I recognized the shorter man as Superintendent Cable, an old acquaintance. Even as we climbed from the car, another vehicle slid behind us and Latham, by then in his forties but still as fit as the college athlete he'd once been and exuding a sense of danger that he could never hide, sprang out to join us.

"I took the call from Mr. Latham," Cable said, explaining to us while nodding toward the man from British Intelligence. He bounced a bit on his toes and a very grim expression tightening his lips. "We mobilized immediately." His eyes cut toward the building. "It isn't pretty."

He was right. The corpse was in what had been a plain white shirt and dark trousers. He was sitting slumped back in a dining chair, itself pulled back two or three feet from the table. His throat had been viciously cut, and blood had shot outward, apparently in great gouts, soaking his clothing and landing as well on the floor and tabletop in front of him. There was nothing on the stained surface itself but an empty cup, heavy white ironstone. Inside were the dried dregs of what appeared to be coffee, while the outside was stained with dried and clotted blood.

The man himself – who must have been Michael Whaley from Holmes's grim nod in my direction – was around thirty, with a small paunch. He would have been rather unassuming in life. His sunken eyes were still staring straight ahead toward whatever he'd seen as his soul passed. His thinning hair was combed toward the back of his head, and it seemed to be gathered there into something resembling a short handle. Long experience told me that it had been held to jerk his head back by whomever had stood behind him and slit his throat. The cut was clean and deep, from left to right by a right-handed person. Whaley would have died instantly.

"Three days, Watson?" Holmes said after examining the body. I concurred. The man had clearly been dead at least that long.

"I wonder why they waited so long between killing him and this morning to set the plan into motion," asked Latham.

"Plan?" asked Cable. "Is this something that I need to know about, gentleman?"

"I'm not sure, Superintendent." Holmes went on to explain my early-morning summons, what I had seen to make me suspicious, and my subsequent message to Holmes. "While we think the intent was to trap us at the very least," he continued, "the rest makes no sense as yet. It seems that my already being in London, and ability to arrive within minutes instead of hours, threw grit into the works, and they were unable to adapt – or perhaps they simply got cold feet. I would wager that they didn't expect for us to be here in this room now, either. I doubt if many people – and probably not the Birches – knew that I was still in touch with Michael regarding his work or could make this connection so quickly."

"And what work was that?" asked the Superintendent. "If you don't mind me asking, that is," he added. He glanced at Latham, who was wandering further afield, looking at various objects in the room with a grim expression. "I know that if Mr. Latham is involved, it may not be any of my business."

"In the time since he was recommended our way," said Latham, glancing at Holmes, "Michael had discovered an aptitude for recruiting minor agents to fulfill small but necessary tasks. He went forth on a regular basis to establish connections with these people – gatherers of fragments of information for a small regular payment. Confirming whether such-and-such fellow made regular visits to a certain postal box, for instance."

He finished circling the room and stopped before us. "He was rather good at what he did, and had increased his responsibilities with every passing month. It was by way of a chance conversation that he became aware of a threat related to the introduction of Irish coinage later this year. I fear that something associated with that has blown up in his face."

Holmes frowned but didn't say anything.

Cable nodded, as if the murder by some espionage-related intrigue would lift the responsibility of the investigation from his shoulders. "Any idea who else might be involved?" he asked, almost hopefully, perhaps wishing it was some foreign agent who would fall under Latham's vengeance.

Holmes shook his head. "It's a mistake to jump to conclusions without data. We haven't even made an examination of the premises. The most telling factor is staring us in the face."

"He trusted his killer," I said.

"Exactly," replied Holmes. "Michael had become an experienced agent. Even if he'd allowed a meeting to take place here, in his own rooms, he wouldn't have let that person get behind him so easily." He pointed to the dead man, slumped in the chair. "There's no sign of a struggle. He just sat there until his hair was grabbed, yanking back his head and exposing his throat. Then the killer cut without any hesitation."

"What you say may be so," said Latham, "but we can't take the chance. I'm going to issue an alert. In the meantime, see what you discover otherwise."

He stepped outside while Holmes began to prowl around the dead man's quarters, first examining the area near the body, and then moving elsewhere, going through the man's papers, and then entering his bedroom. Soon he made his way deeper into the building. Meanwhile Cable and I were left beside Whaley's corpse, both having known Holmes long enough to realize that it was best that we not offer to help, and instead find a spot and stay there. I asked Cable about his two sons, both now at university, and he in turn got me talking about a trip I'd taken the previous summer to Edinburgh. Both of us made a point not to glance toward the gaping wound, covered in dried gore, that faced us from just a few feet away.

Holmes came back a few minutes later, a small stack of letters in his hand and a sad expression on his face. He seemed surprised that Latham hadn't yet returned.

"Some aspect of Michael's professional work may very well be the cause of this, but I think otherwise – that it's a much smaller and unhappy plot. Superintendent, will you join Watson and me as we return to Clipstone Street?"

Cable nodded and we went out to where the cars still waited. Latham was talking to several more men in dark suits who had arrived while we were upstairs. He turned to us, and then he and Holmes stepped to one side. Holmes let him read a few of the letters, pointing specifically to one in particular. Latham nodded, and then they separated.

"Latham is going to continue following up on his side of the business," said Holmes. "It would be unwise to do otherwise. But I think that we'll soon see an end to it."

256

We paid and dismissed our cab and joined Cable in his roomy official car, quickly traversing across London, now in the full throes of a typical mid-morning. Holmes explained what he'd found in the letters, and what he'd deduced from them. I shook my head for the thousandth time at the unhappiness in the world.

We parked on Clipstone Street and stood beside the car for a few minutes until the man whom I'd seen arrive and hide earlier stepped out. He and Holmes seemed to know one another, and it took but a few seconds for us to learn that no one had been in our out of the mostly abandoned house while we were gone. Holmes nodded, unsurprised, and then asked the man to move closer, keeping watch within the mews itself. "I'm not sure what to expect, but be prepared for anything, and protect yourself if anyone should suddenly emerge – especially if it's the woman."

The agent nodded, and then we walked through the mews and over to the basement door, which was now closed. Holmes knocked, and then again, but with no response. Looking at Cable and me, he gave a little nod and reached for the knob. It turned, and we walked through into the darkened hallway.

The damp smell still hung in the air, but now there was something else, all too familiar. I'd first been introduced to it early in my medical training. It was readily obvious and often encountered during decades of Holmes's investigations. And most recently, although somewhat different due to being several days old, we'd found the same odor hanging in the air of Michael Whaley's apartment: The coppery tang of blood. A great deal of it.

The door to the little sitting room was open, and while the fire had gone out, the lantern was still lit, and there was now more light coming through the windows over the kitchen counter. That actually served to make the room seem darker at first, as our eyes tried to adjust from the sudden glare and take in the other darker side of the room, where both Mr. and Mrs. Birch sat around the table. The woman was looking at us, her head turning as we moved from the door to a spot across from her. But her husband simply slumped in his chair. Unlike Michael Whaley who had faced eternity looking straight ahead, Birch had been met death staring at the floor. But even though his head was dropped forward, there was no mistaking the same type of wound across his throat. It was his blood that I had scented as we entered the building.

Mrs. Birch's left hand was lying cupped against her abdomen, while her right was on the table, holding a thin and rather keen-looking knife. It suggested something foreign, such as would have

257

been used in ages past in assassinations of Italian nobles, being pulled out every generation or so to let it have another lick of misery. How it came to this dark basement was something that we would never learn.

"Tom was in the Kyle Gang, too, Mr. Holmes," the lady said, glancing toward the dead man beside her. "He thought when he became one of your Irregulars that it was the best thing that ever happened to him, but then you dropped him – you never sent for him, and he never heard a word from you."

Holmes cleared his throat. "I only dealt with a few specific lieutenants – usually members of the Wiggins family, brothers and sisters and cousins, who rotated in and out as leaders of the group. I remember Tom, but I thought that he'd simply lost interest, or had something else to do. It was one of the other boys who stopped using him."

She shook her head. "He always blamed you, though. Poor stupid Tom. It was only worse after he got into the gang. He wasn't ever very good at it, you know. He was arrested early on, just for being slower than the ones who outran him and got away. But he never peached on the rest of us. That was one good thing about him. He'd do anything for those that he cared about."

"Us?" Holmes asked. "Then you were a member of the gang as well?"

"In a sense," she said. "My father was Amos Sykes Kyle, who founded the gang. He died, you know. You killed him."

Holmes shook his head. "Not true. I was responsible for notifying the police where the warehouse containing the fenced goods was located. It was your father who took it upon himself to flee from the policeman's dog, abandoning his own troops, and then tripping and falling into the drains that were torn up in the adjacent street."

The woman sat up a little straighter then, angry now. "You lie! If you hadn't interfered, my father wouldn't have died, and things would have turned out much differently. Father was grooming Michael – without him, Michael was never able to get ahead. He never would have allowed things to get to the point where the gang was broken and he was arrested. It all goes back to *you*, Mr. Holmes!"

"If you still knew Michael after all these years," Holmes responded, "then you know that I was able to point him toward a better future after he was released from prison."

"A future without *me!*" she said, her voice breaking a bit. "That's why I had to settle for Tom." A sneer crept into her voice, a trace of contempt, and this time she didn't bother to glance toward the corpse beside her.

"We've read the letters," said Holmes, holding up the little packet that he'd brought with him from Alderney Street. "They were in Michael's bedside table."

She gave a little gasp, her surprise palpable. "He kept them then? Ever since he came back, he was . . . he acted so . . . so indifferent."

"He probably was," said Holmes, rather coldly. "Michael Whaley had a deficiency. Of character. People were never real to him – they were game pieces. It was useful in his new work, but for you to have believed otherwise, even as the mother of his child, was a mistake."

Ivy Birch sat up straighter then. "He loved me! In his own way! And he would have loved Erin too, if he'd had the chance to meet her. But when he got out of prison, she'd already died! He never had the chance!"

"I'm sorry for the loss of your daughter. I hope that she had a good life. Was it an illness that took her?"

Ivy Birch didn't answer. Instead, she glanced around the dark basement. "We have a place in St. John's Wood. Not so very different from here. Tom was never able to hold much of a job. He was in and out of jail too, after the war." She looked at me. "That story about us meeting at the hotel was true, but he wasn't there for very long before he was fired for stealing. And his parents did work for the old lady that owned this house, but we weren't ever her caretakers. Tom just knew that she'd died, and that this house would be an empty place we could use for a while."

She shifted a bit, as if in pain, and then settled back and rubbed her abdomen again. "But Tom always said that he loved me, and when Michael was sent away, and I needed a father for the baby, he was willing enough to take us on. He even loved her like his own – or seemed to want to, on most days."

"And he didn't mind when you tried to resume your association with Michael Whaley after his release from prison?" He held up the letters again, as if to remind her that the whole sorry business was known.

"It was none of Tom's affair! Michael was still willing to see me sometimes, and Tom just had to live with it. He never complained."

"And when you became sick?" asked Holmes. "Did he mind that you approached Michael again – this time for help with your medical expenses?"

"What choice did he have? Tom said he loved me. To prove it, he had to take what came – including the fact that my heart always had belonged to Michael."

"And yet you killed him," countered Holmes. "That isn't quite clear to me. There's nothing in these – " He held up the letters. " – that explains why you would change your feelings so quickly, after so long."

"I'm not sure myself. I went to see him the other day. To ask for more help. You see, it's not just that the cancer is spreading. It's the baby – Tom's baby, this time. I'm three months along, and I wanted to tell Michael that this one could be his too – it could make up for the one that had died, and for what he missed while he was gone – if only he'd take me back.

"I waited for hours for him to show up, standing in the street, trying not to be seen. When he did come back, he said he'd been traveling for work. He looked more tired than I'd ever seen. He'd aged, and he didn't seem to want to talk to me. But he invited me up anyway, and he made a cup of coffee – I suppose to stay awake. He didn't offer me any. I guess he hoped that I'd speak my peace and go away.

"I told him about the baby – I hadn't seen him in several months, which was how he knew it couldn't be his. Otherwise, I would have told him that it was. I explained how he could be the father this time anyway, since he'd missed his chance before. But I needed money for the doctors – they want to do an operation, for the cancer. He drank his coffee and let me talk, but I could see that he wasn't even really listening – just waiting for me to finish and be gone. I got up and started pacing, but the more excited I became, the less he seemed to care, and he seemed to be getting ready to stand up put me out. He pushed his chair back, and that's when it snapped. *I* snapped. I was behind him, and I pulled out my knife – my dad gave it to me long before he died, and told me how to use it. I stepped up and grabbed his hair – that fine dark hair I'd always loved so – and pulled his head back. I'd made the cut before I gave it another thought – like I'd been taught – and before he could even raise a hand to stop me.

"He made a noise like a little puff of wind, and then it was done. And I walked out."

260

"But what of the rest of it?" I asked, barely staying even with what they were discussing. "Why lure Holmes and me here? Why contrive this ridiculous plot to seem as if you lived in this empty house, and that your child had been kidnapped?"

"It was Tom who thought of it. I knew it wouldn't work, but what else could we do? He'd always hated you, Mr. Holmes. You helped Michael after prison, but you never did anything for him. And you were the closest thing to a famous man that he'd ever met. He thought that if we could grab you, someone would pay to get you back." She looked my way. "It was me who thought of you, Doctor. I knew that you lived nearby, and that if we took you first, Mr. Holmes would have to come looking.

"After I . . . after Michael died, I came back and told Tom that there was no hope for any money from that direction. I didn't want him to see how upset I was, but I didn't want to see how secretly happy he was either. He tried to hide it, but his eyes lit up – him, a man never fit to wipe Michael Whaley's boots!" Yet even as she said it, she didn't waste a glance upon the corpse beside her. I wondered if he was listening somewhere, thinking of a life wasted as this woman cataloged her contempt for him.

"We thought to lure you here, Doctor, and have you then summon Mr. Holmes. Tom had remembered this place, and we spent a day moving in some things and cleaning enough to seem as if we lived here. We rehearsed our stories and decided that we couldn't take you outright – Mr. Holmes wouldn't walk in by himself. Instead, he'd have the entire police force at his back, searching for you. So we came up with the kidnap plan, because that would need to remain a secret.

"Tom was for killing you as soon as you'd sent a message to Mr. Holmes, but I thought different. I thought we should wait and lock you both up together. That's why I didn't let you go in there this morning with that talk of protecting clues. I thought that Tom might still rush over and lock the door, ruining everything. But then Mr. Holmes was already in town, and it was rushing by much faster than we'd thought – or planned. And then we both saw you had a gun, and you didn't both go in the bedroom together, so we couldn't lock the door behind you without first having to get into a fight. And then our chance slipped away and you'd both gone."

"And so you both sat here and stewed in your own failures," said Holmes, "before you eventually killed Tom Birch as well."

"I was tired of listening to him. He'd let you both get away, and how would we get another chance? Before, when we were planning it, Tom was full of confidence. He fixed up the room with the lock, and he was going to make up some gas by way of a recipe he'd learned in the war, using ammonia and bleach. When you were in the room, we would let it in under the door and finish you off so there wouldn't be any more trouble. Then we'd find out where to send a message and let them buy you both back – thinking that you were still alive, of course. But after you both left, he was the same failure that I've known for fifteen years. He just sat around whining about 'If only' and 'What if?', and trying to reach and hold my hand. I realized that I'd be better off on my own – me and the baby. I walked behind him and finished it, and then I was resting here, trying to gather the strength to leave, when you came back."

She stopped speaking then. She carefully laid the blade on the table and simply continued to rub her abdomen.

The doctors somehow kept her alive long enough for the baby to be born. I made sure that it went to a good home.

Holmes looked upon the whole episode with distaste, and I couldn't blame him. After the woman's confession, he'd distracted himself by searching the house until he found the materials upstairs that would have been combined to make deadly chlorine gas. He commented that in that terrible basement, it was just as likely that Tom Birch would have also killed himself and the woman he loved.

Latham had stopped by Queen Anne Street that night to learn the details that he'd missed. He was quite relieved that whatever Michael Whaley had been investigating wouldn't be affected by the man's death, and pleased that the individuals whom Whaley had identified and cultivated on his last mission – enemies of the Government intent on as much mayhem as they might create – would be allowed a great deal more rope before hanging themselves, instead of being arrested for a seamy little murder.

When he was gone, I poured a couple more brandies for Holmes and myself, deciding that it wasn't unwelcome after such a day. I could see that Holmes had been bothered by the recent events.

"None of this was your fault," I said. "In spite of what she said. Events are too intertwined and tangled to be able to follow along a clear path back to the death of Ivy's father as some certain point where her life went wrong. The same for Tom Birch. I would venture to say that you didn't help him after his own time in jail because he never sought you out to ask."

Holmes sighed and took a long swallow of the brandy. Then pursing his lips for a moment, he replied, "I suppose you're right.

Still, one is tempted along the way to feel responsible for things, and while I logically know that I cannot be the reason for Tom Birch's sad life, I still wish that I'd thought to make sure that everything was all right with him." He shook his head. "I keep seeing him, dead and defeated in that chair in a filthy basement – the inevitable culmination of a wasted life."

I set down my brandy. "Holmes, you are not God." I considered elaborating. I had done so in the past when he felt too much guilt for a burden that he had wrongly shouldered. I had sometimes realized afterwards that I'd hurt my argument by continuing to press it, always seeking some better way to say it that might, this time, find a way into his thoughts. But anything else that I might have said had already crossed his mind. I picked up the delicate snifter and took another sip.

Finally Holmes finished his own brandy and stood. "It didn't escape my attention that you seemed in the mood for a holiday when we set out for Ewelme." I nodded and he continued. "I find that I don't feel the immediate pull to return to my cottage. Perhaps we could set off on some other small journey the morning."

I raised my eyebrows. "No plans? No tickets or reservations?"

He nodded. "Wherever the wind takes us – or in this case, the exceptional British railway system. Right now, I think that such a trip would suit me down to the ground. Think of someplace you'd like to visit – any direction will do."

And with that he said good night, leaving me there with no chance of going to sleep anytime soon, a plethora of possibilities now spread wide before me, and the responsibility of making a wise choice. I stood up. Clearly more brandy would be required.

About the Contributors

The following contributors appear in this volume:
After the East Wind Blows
Part III: When the Storm Has Cleared (1921-1928)

Brian Belanger is a publisher, editor, illustrator, author, and graphic designer. In 2015, he co-founded Belanger Books along with his brother, author Derrick Belanger. He designs the covers for every Belanger Books release, and his illustrations have appeared in the MacDougall Twins with Sherlock Holmes series, as well as *Dragonella, Scones and Bones on Baker Street*, and *Sherlock Holmes: A Three-Pipe Problem*. Brian has published a number of Sherlock Holmes anthologies, as well as new editions of August Derleth's classic Solar Pons mysteries. Since 2016, Brian has written and designed letters for the *Dear Holmes* series, and illustrated a comic book for indie band The Moonlight Initiative. In 2019, Brian received his investiture in the PSI as "Sir Ronald Duveen". Find him online at *www.belangerbooks.com, www.zhahadun.wixsite.com/221b*, and *www.redbubble.com/people/zhahadun*

Derrick Belanger is an educator and also the author of the #1 bestselling book in its category, *Sherlock Holmes: The Adventure of the Peculiar Provenance*, which was in the top 200 bestselling books on Amazon. He also is the author of *The MacDougall Twins with Sherlock Holmes* books, and he edited the Sir Arthur Conan Doyle horror anthology *A Study in Terror: Sir Arthur Conan Doyle's Revolutionary Stories of Fear and the Supernatural*. Mr. Belanger co-owns the publishing company Belanger Books, which has released numerous Sherlock Holmes anthologies including *Beyond Watson, Holmes Away From Home: Adventures from the Great Hiatus, Sherlock Holmes: Before Baker Street, Sherlock Holmes: Adventures in the Realms of H.G. Wells, Sherlock Holmes and the Occult Detectives, Sherlock Holmes and the Great Detectives*, and *Beyond the Adventures of Sherlock Holmes*. Derrick resides in Colorado and continues compiling unpublished works by Dr. John H. Watson.

Sonia Fetherston BSI is a member of the illustrious *Baker Street Irregulars*. For almost thirty years, she's been a frequent contributor to Sherlockian anthologies, including Calabash Press's acclaimed *Case Files* series, and Wildside Press's *About* series. Sonia's byline often appears in the pages of *The Baker Street Journal, The Journal* of the *Sherlock Holmes Society of London, Canadian Holmes*, and the Sydney Passengers' *Log*. Her work earned her the coveted Morley-Montgomery Award from the *Baker Street Irregulars*, and the Derek Murdoch Memorial Award from *The Bootmakers of Toronto*. Sonia is author of *Prince of the Realm: The Most Irregular James Bliss Austin* (BSI Press, 2014). She's at work on another biography for the BSI, this time about Julian Wolff.

Tim Gambrell lives in Exeter, Devon, with his wife, two young sons, three cats, and now only four chickens. He has previously contributed stories to *The MX Book of New Sherlock Holmes Stories*, and also to *Sherlock Holmes and Dr Watson: The Early Adventures* and *Sherlock Holmes and The Occult Detectives*, also from Belanger Books. Outside of the world of Holmes, Tim has written extensively for Doctor Who spin-off ranges. His books include two linked novels from Candy Jar

Books: *Lethbridge-Stewart: The Laughing Gnome – Lucy Wilson & The Bledoe Cadets*, and *The Lucy Wilson Mysteries: The Brigadier and The Bledoe Cadets* (both 2019), and *Lethbridge-Stewart: Bloodlines – An Ordinary Man* (Candy Jar, 2020, written with Andy Frankham-Allen). He's also written a novella, *The Way of The Bry'hunee* (2019) for the Erimem range from Thebes Publishing. Tim's short fiction includes stories in *Lethbridge-Stewart: The HAVOC Files 3* (Candy Jar, 2017, revised edition 2020), *Bernice Summerfield: True Stories* (Big Finish, 2017) and *Relics . . . An Anthology* (Red Ted Books, 2018), plus a number of charity anthologies.

Sir Alfred Gilbert RA (1854–1934) was an English sculptor and illustrator. He also explored other techniques such as goldsmithing and damascening. Additionally, he painted watercolours and drew book illustrations. He was made a member of the Royal Academy of Arts in 1892, but his efforts declined around that time as he took on too many commissions and entered into debt, whilst at the same time his wife's mental health deteriorated. In 1892, he received a royal commission for the tomb of Prince Albert Victor. However, he was unable to complete it and complaints from other dissatisfied clients began to accumulate. Eventually, Gilbert was forced to declare himself bankrupt and to resign from the Royal Academy. However, in the 1920's his career was rehabilitated, and he returned to England and completed the tomb of Prince Albert Victor, as well as the Queen Alexandra Memorial. In 1932, Gilbert was knighted and reinstated as a member of the Royal Academy.

Stephen Herczeg is an IT Geek, writer, actor, and film-maker based in Canberra Australia. He has been writing for over twenty years and has completed a couple of dodgy novels, sixteen feature-length screenplays, and numerous short stories and scripts. Stephen was very successful in 2017's International Horror Hotel screenplay competition, with his scripts *TITAN* winning the Sci-Fi category and *Dark are the Woods* placing second in the horror category. His two-volume short story collection, *The Curious Cases of Sherlock Holmes*, was published in 2021. His work has featured in *Sproutlings – A Compendium of Little Fictions* from Hunter Anthologies, the *Hells Bells* Christmas horror anthology published by the Australasian Horror Writers Association, and the *Below the Stairs*, *Trickster's Treats*, *Shades of Santa*, *Behind the Mask*, and *Beyond the Infinite* anthologies from OzHorror.Con, *The Body Horror Book*, *Anemone Enemy*, and *Petrified Punks* from Oscillate Wildly Press, and *Sherlock Holmes In the Realms of H.G. Wells* and *Sherlock Holmes: Adventures Beyond the Canon* from Belanger Books.

John Lawrence served for thirty-eight years as a staff member in the U.S. House of Representatives, the last eight as Chief of Staff to Speaker Nancy Pelosi (2005-2013). He has been a Visiting Professor at the University of California's Washington Center since 2013. He is the author of *The Class of '74: Congress After Watergate and the Roots of Partisanship* (2018), and has a Ph.D. in history from the University of California (Berkeley).

Gordon Linzner is founder and former editor of *Space and Time Magazine*, and author of three published novels and dozens of short stories in *F&SF*, *Twilight Zone*, *Sherlock Holmes Mystery Magazine*, and numerous other magazines and anthologies, including *Baker Street Irregulars II*, *Across the Universe*, and *Strange Lands*. He is a member of *HWA* and a lifetime member of *SFWA*.

266

David Marcum plays *The Game* with deadly seriousness. He first discovered Sherlock Holmes in 1975 at the age of ten, and since that time, he has collected, read, and chronologicized literally thousands of traditional Holmes pastiches in the form of novels, short stories, radio and television episodes, movies and scripts, comics, fan-fiction, and unpublished manuscripts. He is the author of over eighty Sherlockian pastiches, some published in anthologies and magazines such as *The Strand*, and others collected in his own books, *The Papers of Sherlock Holmes*, *Sherlock Holmes and A Quantity of Debt*, and *Sherlock Holmes – Tangled Skeins*. He has edited over sixty books, including several dozen traditional Sherlockian anthologies, such as the ongoing series *The MX Book of New Sherlock Holmes Stories*, which he created in 2015. This collection is now up to 27 volumes, with more in preparation. He was responsible for bringing back August Derleth's Solar Pons for a new generation, first with his collection of authorized Pons stories, *The Papers of Solar Pons*, and then by editing the reissued authorized versions of the original Pons books, and then volumes of new Pons adventures. He has done the same for the adventures of Dr. Thorndyke, and has plans for similar projects in the future. He has contributed numerous essays to various publications, and is a member of a number of Sherlockian groups and Scions. His irregular Sherlockian blog, *A Seventeen Step Program*, addresses various topics related to his favorite book friends (as his son used to call them when he was small), and can be found at *http://17stepprogram.blogspot.com/* He is a licensed Civil Engineer, living in Tennessee with his wife and son. Since the age of nineteen, he has worn a deerstalker as his regular-and-only hat. In 2013, he and his deerstalker were finally able make his first trip-of-a-lifetime Holmes Pilgrimage to England, with return Pilgrimages in 2015 and 2016, where you may have spotted him. If you ever run into him and his deerstalker out and about, feel free to say hello!

Frederic Dorr Steele (1873-1944) was born in Marquette Michigan, and studied at the National Academy of Design before becoming a free-lance illustrator. In 1903, he received the commission from *Collier's Weekly* magazine to provide the illustrations for *The Return of Sherlock Holmes.* Rather than base his likeness on Holmes's true appearance, as shown in Sidney Paget's drawings, he instead modeled his drawings on William Gillette, whose portrayal of The Great Detective was very popular during that time, particularly in the U.S. This led to the American perception for a generation that Holmes mistakenly resembled Gillette. Steele passed away in New York on July 6, 1944.

Kevin P. Thornton is a seven-time Arthur Ellis Award Nominee. He is a former director of the local Heritage Society and Library, and he has been a soldier in Africa, a contractor for the Canadian Military in Afghanistan, a newspaper and magazine columnist, a Director of both the *Crime Writers of Canada* and the *Writers' Guild of Alberta*, a founding member of *Northword Literary Magazine*, and is either a current or former member of *The Mystery Writers of America, The Crime Writers Association, The Calgary Crime Writers, The International Thriller Writers, The International Association of Crime Writers, The Keys* – a Catholic Writers group founded by Monsignor Knox and G.K. Chesterton – as well as, somewhat inexplicably, *The Mesdames of Mayhem* and *Sisters in Crime*. If you ask, he will join. Born in Kenya, Kevin has lived or worked in South Africa, Dubai, England, Afghanistan, New Zealand, Ontario, and now Northern Alberta. He lives on his wits and his wit, and is doing better than expected. He is not one to willingly split infinitives, and while never pedantic, is on occasion known to be ever so slightly punctilious.

Nicholas Utechin BSI joined *The Sherlock Holmes Society of London* in 1966, aged fourteen. Ten years later he became Editor of *The Sherlock Holmes Journal* – a position he held for thirty years. The year 1976 also saw the publication of two Holmes pastiches he co-wrote: *The Earthquake Machine* and *Hellbirds.* This is his first venture in the field since then. He is a *Baker Street Irregular*, an honorary senior member of *The Sons of the the Copper Beeches* scion society, a founding member of *The John H. Watson Society*, and has contributed extensively to Sherlockian scholarship over the decades. The fact that he is related to Basil Rathbone could have something to do with this madness. In another life, he was a senior producer and occasional presenter for BBC Radio in the field of current affairs. Now retired, he lives in Oxford, UK with his wife, Annie, follows the careers of their two sons with interest, and the lives of their two grandchildren with love. He believes he knows quite a lot about fine wine and silent films (meeting and interviewing Lillian Gish was something special,) and is lucky enough to own a Sidney Paget original (sadly not one for a Sherlock Holmes story.)

Daniel D. Victor, a Ph.D. in American literature, is a retired high school English teacher who taught in the Los Angeles Unified School District for forty-six years. His doctoral dissertation on little-known American author, David Graham Phillips, led to the creation of Victor's first Sherlock Holmes pastiche, *The Seventh Bullet*, in which Holmes investigates Phillips' actual murder. Victor's second novel, *A Study in Synchronicity,* is a two-stranded murder mystery, which features a Sherlock Holmes-like private eye. He currently writes the ongoing series *Sherlock Holmes and the American Literati.* Each novel introduces Holmes to a different American author who actually passed through London at the turn of the century. In *The Final Page of Baker Street*, Holmes meets Raymond Chandler; in *The Baron of Brede Place,* Stephen Crane; in *Seventeen Minutes to Baker Street*, Mark Twain; and in *The Outrage at the Diogenes Club,* Jack London. His most recent novel is *Sherlock Holmes and the Shadows of St. Petersburg* and *Sherlock Holmes and the Pandemic of Death* will be published later in 2021. Victor, who is also writing a novel about his early years as a teacher, lives with his wife in Los Angeles, California. They have two adult sons.

Joseph S. Walker is an active member of the *Mystery Writers of America.* His fiction has appeared in magazines, including *Alfred Hitchcok Mystery Magazine, Mystery Weekly,* and *Dark City*, and in anthologies such as *Seascape, Day of the Dark*, and the MWA collections *Scream and Scream Again* and *Life is Short and Then You Die.* In 2019, his story "Haven" won the Al Blanchard Award, and his story "The Last Man in Lafarge" won the inaugural Bill Crider Prize for Short fiction. He lives in Indiana and teaches college literature courses. Follow him on Twitter (@JSWalkerAuthor) and visit his website at: *https://jsw47408.wixsite.com/website*

Richard W. Wallace was an American illustrator who, in 1919, provided images for three Holmes stories in *Lectures Pour Tous*, a French magazine. These included "His Last Bow", "The Dying Detective", and "The Red Circle"

The following contributors appear
in the companion volumes:
Part I: The East Wind Blows (1914-1918)
Part II: Aftermath (1919-1920)

Wayne Anderson was born and raised in the beautiful Pacific Northwest, growing up in Alaska and Washington State. He discovered Sherlock Holmes around age ten and promptly devoured The Canon. When it was all gone, he tried to sate the addiction by writing his own Sherlock Holmes stories, which are mercifully lost forever. Sadly, he moved to California in his twenties and has lived there since. He has two grown sons who are both writers as well. He spends his time writing or working on the TV pilots and patents which will someday make him fabulously wealthy. When he's not doing these things, he is either reading to his young daughter from The Canon or trying to find space in his house for more bookshelves.

Nick Cardillo is the author of *The Feats of Sherlock Holmes*, as well as several short stories that have appeared in collections for both MX Publishing and Belanger Books. A devotee of Sherlock Holmes since the age of six, Nick is also a lifelong fan of the Golden Age of Detective Fiction and Hammer Horror. He is a recent graduate from Susquehanna University and earned his ShD – Doctorate of Sherlockiana – from the Beacon Society in 2019.

Chris Chan is a writer, educator, and historian. He works as a researcher and "International Goodwill Ambassador" for Agatha Christie Ltd. His true crime articles, reviews, and short fiction have appeared (or will soon appear) in *The Strand*, *The Wisconsin Magazine of History*, *Mystery Weekly*, *Gilbert!*, *Nerd HQ*, Akashic Books' *Mondays are Murder* web series, *The Baker Street Journal*, and *Sherlock Holmes Mystery Magazine*.

Craig Stephen Copland confesses that he discovered Sherlock Holmes when, sometime in the muddled early 1960's, he pinched his older brother's copy of the immortal stories and was forever afterward thoroughly hooked. He is very grateful to his high school English teachers in Toronto who inculcated in him a love of literature and writing, and even inspired him to be an English major at the University of Toronto. There he was blessed to sit at the feet of both Northrup Frye and Marshall McLuhan, and other great literary professors, who led him to believe that he was called to be a high school English teacher. It was his good fortune to come to his pecuniary senses, abandon that goal, and pursue a varied professional career that took him to over one-hundred countries and endless adventures. He considers himself to have been and to continue to be one of the luckiest men on God's good earth. A few years back he took a step in the direction of Sherlockian studies and joined the *Sherlock Holmes Society of Canada* – also known as *The Toronto Bootmakers*. In May of 2014, this esteemed group of scholars announced a contest for the writing of a new Sherlock Holmes mystery. Although he had never tried his hand at fiction before, Craig entered and was pleasantly surprised to be selected as one of the winners. Having enjoyed the experience, he decided to write more of the same, and is now on a mission to write a new Sherlock Holmes mystery that is related to and inspired by each of the sixty stories in the original Canon. He currently lives and writes in Toronto and Dubai, and looks forward to finally settling down when he turns ninety.

John William Davis is a retired US Army counterintelligence officer, civil servant, and linguist. He was commissioned from Washington University in St. Louis as an artillery officer in the 101st Air Assault Division. Thereafter, he went into counterintelligence and served some thirty-seven years. A linguist, Mr. Davis learned foreign languages in each country he served. After the Cold War and its bitter aftermath, he wrote *Rainy Street Stories, Reflections on Secret Wars, Terrorism, and Espionage*. He wanted to write about not only true events themselves, but also the moral and ethical aspects of the secret world. With the publication of *Around the Corner*, Davis expanded his reflections on conflicted human nature to our present day traumas of fear, and causes for hope. A dedicated Sherlockian, he's contributed to telling the story of the Great Detective in retirement.

Margie Deck (Spanaway, Washington) lives in the Pacific Northwest with the books, the husband, and a dog. She whiles away her time talking about Sherlock Holmes on Twitter (*@pawkypuzzler*) and volunteering for *The Sound of the Baskervilles* and *The John H. Watson Society.*

Sir Arthur Conan Doyle (1859-1930) *Holmes Chronicler Emeritus.* If not for him, this anthology would not exist. Author, physician, patriot, sportsman, spiritualist, husband and father, and advocate for the oppressed. He is remembered and honored for the purposes of this collection by being the man who introduced Sherlock Holmes to the world. Through fifty-six Holmes short stories, four novels, and additional Apocryphal entries, Doyle revolutionized mystery stories and also greatly influenced and improved police forensic methods and techniques for the betterment of all. *Steel True Blade Straight.*

John Linwood Grant is a writer and editor who lives in Yorkshire with a pack of lurchers and a beard. He may also have a family. He focuses particularly on dark Victorian and Edwardian fiction, such as his recent novella *A Study in Grey*, which also features Holmes. Current projects include his *Tales of the Last Edwardian* series, about psychic and psychiatric mysteries, and curating a collection of new stories based on the darker side of the British Empire. He has been published in a number of anthologies and magazines, with stories range from madness in early Virginia to questions about the monsters we ourselves might be. He is also co-editor of *Occult Detective Quarterly*. His website *greydogtales.com* explores weird fiction, especially period ones, weird art, and even weirder lurchers.

Arthur Hall was born in Aston, Birmingham, UK, in 1944. He discovered his interest in writing during his schooldays, along with a love of fictional adventure and suspense. His first novel, *Sole Contact*, was an espionage story about an ultra-secret government department known as "Sector Three", and was followed, to date, by three sequels. Other works include six Sherlock Holmes novels, *The Demon of the Dusk, The One Hundred Percent Society, The Secret Assassin, The Phantom Killer, In Pursuit of the Dead*, and *The Justice Master*, as well as two collections of Holmes *Further Little-Known Cases of Sherlock Holmes*, and *Tales from the Annals of Sherlock Holmes*. He has also written other short stories and a modern detective novel. He lives in the West Midlands, United Kingdom.

270

Paula Hammond has written over sixty fiction and non-fiction books, as well as short stories, comics, poetry, and scripts for educational DVD's. When not glued to the keyboard, she can usually be found prowling round second-hand books shops or hunkered down in a hide, soaking up the joys of the natural world.

Paul Hiscock is an author of crime, fantasy, and science fiction tales. His short stories have appeared in several anthologies and include a seventeenth century whodunnit, a science fiction western, and a steampunk Sherlock Holmes story. Paul lives with his family in Kent, England, and spends his days chasing a toddler with more energy than the Duracell Bunny. He mainly does his writing in coffee shops with members of the local NaNoWriMo group, or in the middle of the night when his family has gone to sleep. Consequently, his stories tend to be fuelled by large amounts of black coffee. You can find out more about his writing at *www.detectivesanddragons.uk.*

Naching T. Kassa is a wife, mother, and writer. She's created short stories, novellas, poems, and co-created three children. She lives in Eastern Washington State with her husband, Dan Kassa. Naching is a member of the Horror Writers Association, Head of Publishing and Interviewer for *HorrorAddicts.net,* and an assistant and staff writer for *Still Water Bay* at Crystal Lake Publishing. She has been a Sherlockian since the age of 10 and is a member of The Sound of the Baskervilles. You can find her work on Amazon:
https://www.amazon.com/Naching-T-Kassa/e/B005ZGHTI0

John Lawrence *also has a story in Part I*

David Marcum *also has stories in Parts I and II*

Will Murray has been writing about popular culture since 1973, principally on the subjects of comic books, pulp magazine heroes, and film. As a fiction writer, he's the author of over 70 novels featuring characters as diverse as Nick Fury and Remo Williams. With the late Steve Ditko, he created the Unbeatable Squirrel Girl for Marvel Comics. Murray has written numerous short stories, many on Lovecraftian themes. Currently, he writes The Wild Adventures of Doc Savage for Altus Press. His acclaimed Doc Savage novel, *Skull Island*, pits the pioneer superhero against the legendary King Kong. This was followed by *King Kong vs. Tarzan* and two Doc Savage novels guest-starring The Shadow, and *Tarzan, Conqueror of Mars*, a crossover with John Carter of Mars. He is the author of the short story collection *The Wild Adventures of Sherlock Holmes. www.adventuresinbronze.com* is his website.

Robert Perret is a writer, librarian, and devout Sherlockian living on the Palouse. His Sherlockian publications include "The Canaries of Clee Hills Mine" in *An Improbable Truth: The Paranormal Adventures of Sherlock Holmes*, "For King and Country" in *The Science of Deduction*, and "How Hope Learned the Trick" in *NonBinary Review*. He considers himself to be a pan-Sherlockian and a one-man Scion out on the lonely moors of Idaho. Robert has recently authored a yet-unpublished scholarly article tentatively entitled "A Study in Scholarship: The Case of the *Baker Street Journal*'. More information is available at:
www.robertperret.com

Tracy J. Revels, a Sherlockian from the age of eleven, is a professor of history at Wofford College in Spartanburg, South Carolina. She is a member of *The Survivors of the Gloria Scott* and *The Studious Scarlets Society*, and is a past recipient of the Beacon Society Award. Almost every semester, she teaches a class that covers The Canon, either to college students or to senior citizens. She is also the author of three supernatural Sherlockian pastiches with MX (*Shadowfall*, *Shadowblood*, and *Shadowwraith*), and a regular contributor to her scion's newsletter. She also has some notoriety as an author of very silly skits: For proof, see "The Adventure of the Adversarial Adventuress" and "Occupy Baker Street" on YouTube. When not studying Sherlock, she can be found researching the history of her native state, and has written books on Florida in the Civil War and on the development of Florida's tourism industry.

Roger Riccard of Los Angeles, California, U.S.A., is a descendant of the Roses of Kilravock in Highland Scotland. He is the author of two previous Sherlock Holmes novels, *The Case of the Poisoned Lilly* and *The Case of the Twain Papers*, a series of short stories in two volumes, *Sherlock Holmes: Adventures for the Twelve Days of Christmas* and *Further Adventures for the Twelve Days of Christmas*, and the ongoing series *A Sherlock Holmes Alphabet of Cases,* all of which are published by Baker Street Studios. He has another novel and a non-fiction Holmes reference work in various stages of completion. He became a Sherlock Holmes enthusiast as a teenager (many, many years ago), and, like all fans of The Great Detective, yearned for more stories after reading The Canon over and over. It was the Granada Television performances of Jeremy Brett and Edward Hardwicke, and the encouragement of his wife, Rosilyn, that at last inspired him to write his own Holmes adventures, using the Granada actor portrayals as his guide. He has been called "The best pastiche writer since Val Andrews" by the *Sherlockian E-Times.*

Dan Rowley practiced law for over forty years, both in private practice and with a large international corporation. He is now retired and lives in Erie, Pennsylvania, with his wife Judy. He inherited his writing and creative abilities from his children Jim and Katy.

Andrew Salmon has won several awards for his Sherlock Holmes stories and has been nominated for the Ellis, Pulp Ark, Pulp Factory and New Pulp Awards. He lives and writes in Vancouver, BC. His novels include: *Fight Card Sherlock Holmes: Work Capitol*, *Blood to the Bone* and *A Congression of Pallbearers* (collected in the *Fight Card Sherlock Holmes Omnibus*) *The Dark Land*, *The Light of Men*, and *Ghost Squad: Rise of the Black Legion* (with Ron Fortier) and his first children's book, *Wandering Webber*. His work has also appeared in numerous anthologies covering multiple genres. His tales from the *Sherlock Holmes Consulting Detective* series were collected in *Sherlock Holmes Investigates*. He is currently at work on the first in a series of Eby Stokes novels, the female pugilist turned Special Branch agent, who debuted in the *Fight Card Sherlock Holmes* trilogy, as well as a myriad of other projects. To learn more about his work check out:
amazon.com/Andrew-Salmon/e/B002NS5KR0

Frank Schildiner is a martial arts instructor at Amorosi's Mixed Martial Arts in New Jersey. He is the writer of the novels, *The Quest of Frankenstein*, *The Triumph of Frankenstein*, *Napoleon's Vampire Hunters*, *The Devil Plague of Naples*, *The*

Klaus Protocol, and *Irma Vep and The Great Brain of Mars*. Frank is a regular contributor to the fictional series *Tales of the Shadowmen* and has been published in *From Bayou to Abyss: Examining John Constantine, Hellblazer*, *The Joy of Joe*, *The New Adventures of Thunder Jim Wade*, *Secret Agent X* Volumes 3, 4, 5, and 6, *The Lone Ranger and Tonto: Frontier Justice*, and *The Avenger: The Justice Files*. He resides in New Jersey with his wife Gail, who is his top supporter, and two cats who are indifferent on the subject.

Shane Simmons is the author of the occult detective novels *Necropolis* and *Epitaph*, and the crime collection *Raw and Other Stories*. An award-winning screenwriter and graphic novelist, his work has appeared in international film festivals, museums, and lectures about design and structure. He was born in Lachine, a suburb of Montreal best known for being massacred in 1689 and having a joke name. Visit Shane's homepage at *eyestrainproductions.com* for more.

Robert V. Stapleton was born and brought up in Leeds, Yorkshire, England, and studied at Durham University. After working in various parts of the country as an Anglican parish priest, he is now retired and lives with his wife in North Yorkshire. As a member of his local writing group, he now has time to develop his other life as a writer of adventure stories. He has recently had a number of short stories published, and he is hoping to have a couple of completed novels published at some time in the future.

Kevin P. Thornton *also has a story in Part I*

I.A. Watson, great-grand-nephew of Dr. John H. Watson, has been intrigued by the notorious "black sheep" of the family since childhood, and was fascinated to inherit from his grandmother a number of unedited manuscripts removed circa 1956 from a rather larger collection reposing at Lloyds Bank Ltd (which acquired Cox & Co Bank in 1923). Upon discovering the published corpus of accounts regarding the detective Sherlock Holmes from which a censorious upbringing had shielded him, he felt obliged to allow an interested public access to these additional memoranda, and is gradually undertaking the task of transcribing them for admirers of Mr. Holmes and Dr. Watson's works. In the meantime, I.A. Watson continues to pen other books, the latest of which is *The Incunabulum of Sherlock Holmes*. A full list of his seventy or so published works are available at:
http://www.chillwater.org.uk/writing/iawatsonhome.htm

Also from Belanger Books
Edited by David Marcum
Holmes Away From Home:
Adventures from The Great Hiatus
Volumes I and II
With Forewords by Mark Alberstat, Ron Lies, and David Marcum, and an
Afterward by Derrick Belanger

Volume I – 1891-1892
The Final Problem – by Sir Arthur Conan Doyle
Over the Mountains in the Darkness – by Sonia Fetherston
An Englishman (or Two) in Florence – by David Ruffle
The Secret Adventure of Sherlock Holmes – by Diane Gilbert Madsen
The Harrowing Intermission – by Craig Janacek
The Adventure of the Indian Protégé – by Jayantika Ganguly
The Incident at Maniyachi Junction – by S. Subramanian
The Adventure on the Road to Mecca – by Deanna Baran
The Adventure of the Dragoman's Son – by John Linwood Grant
A Murder on Mount Athos – by Katie Magnusson
The President's Roses – by Stephen Seitz

Volume II – 1893-1894
The Adventure of the Old Brownstone – by David Marcum
The Adventure of the Flaked Breakfast Cereal – by Mark Levy
For Want of a Sword – by Daniel D. Victor
The Case of the Fragrant Blackmailer – S.F. Bennett
A Case of Juris Imprudence – by Robert Perret
A Most Careful, Strategic, and Logical Mind – by Derrick Belanger
The Aviator's Murder – by C. Edward Davis
The French Affair – by Mark Mower
The Woman Returns – by Richard Paolinelli
The Adventure of the Melting Man – by Shane Simmons
The Adventure of the Empty House – by Sir Arthur Conan Doyle

Also from Belanger Books
Edited by David Marcum
Sherlock Holmes: Adventures Beyond the Canon
Volumes I, II, and III
With Forewords by Nicholas Utechin, Derrick Belanger, and David Marcum

Volume I – 1887-1890
The Swamp Adder (*A Poem*) – Rhea Belanger
A Gentleman's Disagreement – Narrelle M. Harris
The Incident of the Frantic Countess – Arthur Hall
The Ten Orange Pips – Jayantika Ganguly
The Adventure of the Spectral Menace – Benjamin Langley
The Greek Murder – Katie Magnusson
The Adventure in Nancy – Stephen Herczeg
The Shadow of Malice – Brenda Seabrooke
The Adventure of the Upright Man – Nick Dunn-Meynell
A for *Argentina* – Mike Hogan

Volume II – 1894-1902
The Great Detective (*A Poem*) – Rosie Mower
The Adventure of the Empty Cell – Kevin P. Thornton
The Case of the Mysterious Horseman – Roger Riccard
The Adventure of the Third Traitor – Craig Janacek
A Frail Thread – Jacquelynn Morris
Mercy Unwilling to Trust – Thomas Fortenberry
The Officer in the Duke of Wellington's Regiment – Tim Symonds
The Fear of Retribution – Craig Stephen Copland
The Case of the Stratford Poisoner – Mark Mower
The Musgrave Burden – John Linwood Grant
Another Man's Poison – Paul Goodenough
The Mysterious Client – Derrick Belanger

Volume III – 1903-1921
Sherlock Holmes (*A Poem*) – Phoebe Belanger
The Unsettling Matter of the Graveyard Ghoul – Will Murray
The Adventure of the Star-Crossed Lovers – Daniel D. Victor
The Pearls of Great Price – Deanna Baran
The Adventure of the Crown Diamond – Sir Arthur Conan Doyle *and* Ann Margaret Lewis
The Adventure of the Gnarled Beeches – Robert Perret
A Ghost from the Past – Nick Cardillo
Another Problem at Thor Bridge – Geri Schear
The Pegasus Affair – Tim Symonds
The Brook Street Mystery – David Marcum

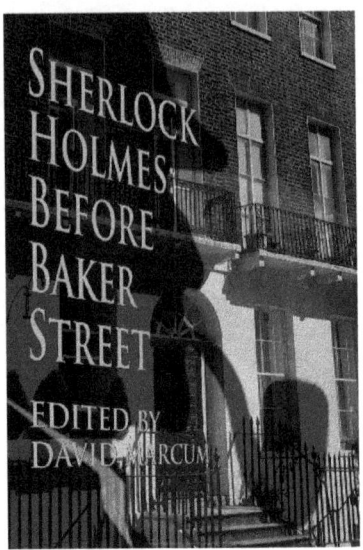

Also from Belanger Books
Edited by David Marcum
Sherlock Holmes and Doctor Watson:
The Early Adventures
Volumes I, II, and III
With a Foreword by David Marcum

Volume I
A Study in Scarlet (An Excerpt) – by Sir Arthur Conan Doyle
The Adventure of the Persistent Pugilist – Thomas A Burns, Jr.
The Two Bullets – David Marcum
Brother's Keeper – Robert Perret
Bad Blood at Barts – Harry DeMaio
The Inside Men – M.J.H. Simmonds
The Adventure of the Villainous Victim – Chris Chan
The Cable Street Mummy – Paula Hammond
The Piccadilly Poisoner – Roger Riccard
The Adventure of the Modest Inspectors – Derrick Belanger
The Case of the Melancholic Widow – Deanna Baran
Angelique – by Mike Hogan

Volume II
The Adventure of the Substitute Detective – I.A. Watson
The Adventure of the Resident Patient – Sir Arthur Conan Doyle
The Locked-Room Mystery – D.J. Tyrer
The Adventure of the Missing Shadow – Jayantika Ganguly
A Diplomatic Affair – Mark Mower
The Adventure of Stonehenge in London – GC Rosenquist
The Doctor's Tale – David Marcum
The Finding of Geoffrey Hobson – David B. Beckwith
The Adventure of the Last Laugh – Tracy J. Revels
The Penny Murders – Robert Stapleton
The Disappearing Debutante – Stephen Herczeg

Volume III
The Adventure of the Three Fakirs – Annette Siketa
The Mystery of MacLean House – Kevin Thornton
The Adventure of Percival Dubois – Ian Ableson
The Distressing Matter of the Missing Dispatch Box – Will Murray
The Disappearance of the San Sebastiano – S.F. Bennett
The Adventure of the Speckled Band – Sir Arthur Conan Doyle
The Case of the Missing Waistcoat – Emily J. Cohen
The Mystery of the Missing Will – Tim Gambrell
The Adventure of the Persecuted Accountant – Arthur Hall
The Bizarre Challenge of Strange Mr. K – GC Rosenquist
The Broken Watch – M.J.H. Simmonds
The Colchester Experiment – David Marcum

Belanger Books

Lightning Source UK Ltd.
Milton Keynes UK
UKHW021619270622
405019UK00009B/1996